CW00470926

Many Unhappy Returns

Evgeny Gridneff

The greatest secrets are always hidden in the most unlikely places
Roald Dahl

What do we live for, if it is not to make life less difficult for each other?
George Eliot

Copyright © 2021 Evgeny Gridneff   All rights reserved

No part of this book may be reproduced, or stored in a retrieval system, or transmitted in any form or by any means, electronic, mechanical, photocopying, recording, or otherwise, without express written permission of the Author.

ISBN 9798488996502

Cover design by: Genka Krivenko

Chapter Headings

1. A Vacancy on Death Row

To wake up to find herself very rich in the morning, and then to be told some hours later that she didn't have long to live, was a brutal blow for Christina. One of many she had endured in her life.

Some would say she had it coming to her - not the money, but the death sentence. A few would have happily pulled the trigger if she'd been in front of a firing squad, or watched as she sizzled in an electric chair. To say Christina was not liked by certain friends and family would be an understatement.

That very morning 43-year-old Christina Turner was smiling as she closed her front door and gently inhaled the fresh morning air. There was a spring in her step for the first time in ages. It was going to be a new beginning.

She waved to the postman, who was chatting to a neighbour across the road. He wondered if she was about to accost him, which she often did, running and returning junk mail that he'd delivered. Today, because of the letter from the solicitor that had plopped through the letterbox, she felt like crossing the road and giving him a kiss, which probably would have given him a seizure if she had.

For Christina was not the friendliest or most amenable of neighbours.

To see her smiling was a rare sight nowadays. She appeared quite miserable a lot of the time and kept herself to herself. She didn't believe in small talk or spending any time discussing the weather, or if the council were late with the bin collection. The best they might get is a nod of acknowledgement or even a 'Morning... Afternoon...or Evening...' if they were lucky. If then they did try to engage in friendly conversation, Christina would force a gritted smile and say, 'Sorry, must dash...' and disappear into the house. She was never purposefully rude, just simply unapproachable. Nobody knew much about her, even though she'd lived there for several years, which is how she preferred it. The skeletons in her past would have filled many cupboards. She needed to keep those cupboards firmly shut.

Her chirpy, uncharacteristic mood that morning, soon evaporated when she caught sight of a scrawny ginger cat laying on top of her car parked in the drive. 'Shoo!' she hissed and waved her hand as she approached the car. The cat just stared at her indifferently and licked its paw in defiance. Christina was sure it was the same one that had repeatedly pooed on her front mat, or deposited mangled dead birds by the door.

Even when she got within in a few feet of the cat, it continued to lie on the roof, looking somewhat territorial, as if it had a right to be there. Christina, making sure no one was watching, suddenly and forcefully swung her handbag and struck the cat full on, throwing it off the car.

Letting out a distressing howl, the cat leaped out onto the road into the path of an oncoming car, which luckily made an emergency stop, only just missing the cat by inches, as it darted across into a nearby garden.

'Well, I wouldn't have missed it, if it had been me!' Christina mumbled to herself as she climbed into her car.

—

She had no time for cats, dogs or other domestic pets. She spent enough time having to cope with people.

The driver was clearly shaken as he sat frozen in his car, which was now blocking Christina's drive.

She tooted her horn loudly to get the man to move out of her way as she slowly backed down the drive. Still a touch shocked, he then reversed and accidentally squashed the tail of that same cat which had now decided to return to the other side of the road. Christina couldn't help but smile, as she watched the driver in her rear-view mirror get out of his car and look underneath, putting his hands out to the cat, who screeched and clawed his cheek, drawing blood.

'It's turning out to be a fortuitous day' she murmured to herself; mainly thinking of the wealth she'd just inherited.

'Oh, come on!' she shouted out aloud some minutes later, seeing a lycra-clad cyclist ahead, riding almost in the middle of the road and making it difficult for cars to overtake. When she eventually got behind him, she pressed on her horn to try to make him edge nearer the pavement. The cyclist stuck his middle finger up in response. Soon, seeing that the road ahead was clear, she overtook the cyclist, making sure she was as close as possible. This obviously unnerved him and he was forced to mount the pavement and toppled over onto the grass verge. As he started to curse and shake his fist, Christina opened her window and stuck out her middle finger in retort. *'Up yours too, sunshine!'* she silently mouthed.

For once, Christina believed that things were in her favour. Life was going to be different from now on. It was time to get out of the rut she had found herself in. With the newly acquired funds she'd be able to begin to live again. Time to move on and leave a life that was stifling her.

As she drove into the medical centre car park, she noticed a car leaving from the only parking space left. A woman waiting in a large SUV 4x4 was about to drive into the space – when Christina overtook and manoeuvred swiftly into the space.

'Hey, I was here first!' the woman shouted from her window as Christina got out of the car.

'Sorry,' Christina shrugged and smiled, 'I didn't see you...' as she pressed the key fob to lock her car.

'You didn't see me! That's a good one!' the woman sneered in disbelief gesturing at the size of her car, which was almost twice as big as Christina's own little hatchback.

She quietly approached the woman's window. 'Think you've got a right because you drive this ugly monster? Not very eco-friendly is it. You obviously don't care about polluting the environment. Have a nice day...' Christina smiled, turned and made her way to the centre entrance.

'Bitch...' the woman quietly cursed and banged her palms against the steering wheel in frustration.

Christina stood over the receptionist who was typing away at a computer. 'Christina Turner to see Doctor Jervis.'

Without looking up, the receptionist waved a hand 'If you'd like to take a seat...'

'It's eleven o'clock.'

'Yes...?' the receptionist continued looking at the screen.

'My appointment was for eleven o'clock. I'm on time, so I don't see why I should wait'

'You'll be called when the doctor's free. Please take a seat.' The receptionist forced a smile and went back to her screen.

'That's why you make appointments – so you don't have to wait. I was on the phone for twenty minutes trying to make this appointment. *We are very busy. You are held in*

7

a queue. Your call is important to us. ...I'm also very busy and have other important engagements to attend to.' The receptionist ignored her. Christina looked at her watch, sighed and sat down grudgingly.

She looked around her. There were only a few people waiting. An obese mother with a chubby snotty-nosed toddler, who wouldn't stay still; a heavily tattooed middle-aged woman with nose and lip piercings, who was texting on her phone. Christina couldn't understand why people abused their bodies so much with images and metal paraphernalia. She could be quite judgemental and often said what she thought, which naturally upset people. Another time she might have said something to the woman. But not today. Today she felt magnanimous. The tattooed woman would be spared Christina's disapproving looks or snide remarks.

The only other people waiting were a young couple who were holding hands and looking anxious. Christina caught the young man's eye and smiled seductively at him. *'He'd be welcome in my bed any time.'* She mentally undressed him. The man nervously grinned back, until his wife nudged him, glaring back at her with a dirty look.

Christina sighed forlornly, trying to remember when she'd last had a good orgasm with a man. Vibrators were all well and good, but it was never the same as having a man to have sex with.

She had tired of the man who now shared her bed. He no longer provided the excitement she craved. It was another reason she was determined to escape and start her life afresh. The inheritance had provided a way out. The thought cheered her.

The reception door opened, and the angry woman from the car park entered, walking slowly and in discomfort. Christina saw that she was heavily pregnant and just raised her eyebrows dispassionately.

'Ah, Mrs Reader. Please go right through.' The receptionist pointed to one of the doors.

'Thanks. I'm afraid I had to double park...some people are very selfish...' she looked at Christina pointedly, who smiled back, before hobbling into one of the offices.

Christina, feeling a touch guilty, got up and wandered over to the window to look out at the car park. She saw that the pregnant woman had parked her SUV directly in front of her car, blocking her exit. She felt like going out and drawing her nail file across the shiny paintwork of the woman's car. 'What a bloody cow!' she blurted out rather loudly and angrily.

'Sorry...?' the receptionist looked up wondering if the remark had been directed at her. Other eyes turned towards Christina.

'What? Oh, nothing, sorry...thinking aloud about my mother-in-law, when I was newly married. She did make our life hell...' Christina wandered back to her seat, still inwardly livid about her car being blocked.

'Tell me about it!' the mother with the toddler piped up. 'I had a happy marriage until my husband's mother started interfering. I told him it was either her or me. He chose her...'

Christina wanted to say *'I don't blame him, married to a fat lump like you'* but instead added 'Men, you can't rely on them, can you.'

'They're all bastards.' the mother grunted, taking a sausage roll out of her bag and stuffing it in the toddler's mouth to keep him quiet.

Christina nodded sympathetically at the mother, and was glad she no longer had to contend with her own. She realised she had never been the best of mothers. She thought about her son, who she hadn't seen for years. What was he

—

9

like now? Had he forgotten her? Memories about her other life surfaced and made her shiver. She had walked out of their lives and never looked back. She knew they didn't care, and were probably happy to be rid of her, because no efforts had been made to find her when she disappeared.

'Chris Turner…the doctor will see you now in room 2.' The receptionist pointed to one of the other doors.

'It's Christina, and not before time.' She looked at her watch, which said 11.16. As she got up, she saw the pregnant woman come out of another door. She gave her a gentle smile as she passed her. 'Good luck. Hope it goes well. I had a terrible time giving birth to mine. Decided not to have any more after that.' The pregnant woman shook her head incomprehensively, her mind elsewhere, having just been told she was having triplets.

A young doctor was gravely studying a file when Christina breezed in rather forcefully. "It's 11.17! I've been kept waiting for…who are you?'

'Doctor Ives. Take a seat.' He seemed nervous and didn't look her in the eye.

'Where's Doctor Jervis?' Christina gave him the once-over. He looked like he'd just left school, but quite handsome. *Wonder what he's like in bed?'* she speculated.

'I'm afraid he's ill…'

'Ill? Doctors aren't supposed to get ill! Right, I'm running rather late.' She said impatiently still standing above him.

'Now, Chris…Do please sit down.' He took a deep breath. He was dreading this encounter. A first for him.

'The name is Christina. Why does everyone feel they have a right to shorten names.'

The doctor glanced at the file. 'But it says…never mind. I'm sorry…'

'For keeping me waiting, yes.' She reluctantly sat down.

The doctor fiddled about with the file rather awkwardly. He took a deep breath. 'I have the results of your check-up…'

'My annual MOT. I know. That's why I'm here. Keep the alcohol intake down; steer clear of fatty foods and do more exercise. Same as last year. Is that it?' She stood up, preparing to leave.

'I wish it was so straightforward…' His tone became solemn.

'I suppose you want me to give up drinking altogether? A girl needs some pleasure!'

'It's much more serious, I'm afraid…' He looked suddenly pale, and could feel the sweat under his arms spreading. 'Please sit down…'

She sighed as she grudgingly sat down. 'I'm certainly not giving up sex. You'll have to sew it up first!' She loved winding people up, to get them out of their comfort zones. She looked at the doctor whose expression remained grim. 'You're allowed to smile you know. A joke…?'

'Chris…Christina…I'm afraid I've got some very bad news…this is very difficult…. the results of your tests…' He was agonising over his words.

'Please stop pussyfooting. Didn't they teach you anything at medical school? How long have you been a GP anyway? Just qualified, eh?'

'Actually, this is my first job. So, you must understand how difficult it is…'

'Just get on with it. Tell me what you've got to tell me. Is that so difficult? I haven't got all day!' Christina had started to lose patience. She had no time for people who faffed about.

'Alright…' He took a deep breath. '…some tumours have been detected…they're cancerous…'

'What? How? I don't feel ill, in fact I've never felt better. I don't understand?' She tried to take this all in, and was getting confused.

'Not all cancers display initial symptoms…'

'Cancer? So, which one am I supposed to have then?' She humoured him, not taking it seriously.

'Pancreatic. It's difficult to know sometimes what causes it. Have you had any digestive problems lately perhaps? Nausea, vomiting, weight loss, back pain…?'

'I have been sick now and again, usually when I've eaten or drunk too much! I've lost weight recently, and feel better for it. Yes, a bit of back pain, only when I lift something heavy. I've felt fine otherwise. What does this all mean?'

'I'm very sorry…' The doctor suddenly found it difficult to get the words out.

'Meaning? Come on!'

'It's…I mean the cancer is spreading rather rapidly…'

'For god's sake, out with it!' She was now irritated with his awkwardness.

'Meaning – there's not a great deal we can do for you. I could say that there are certain treatments that might help, but in the long term…I'm so very sorry…'

'What are you actually saying? That it's terminal…? Are you sure?' She now felt more confused than ever.

'I'm sorry; I wish I could be more positive and offer some hope. I believe in being totally honest. It's up to you to decide if you want to follow any traditional treatments that might help to extend matters. I can advise what's available.' He had started to regain his confidence now that he'd told her.

'I see…' She suddenly felt confused, unable to grasp what she had just heard.

The doctor said nothing, allowing her to get her thoughts together. It was his first death pronouncement, and sadly knowing it wouldn't be his last. He watched Christina as she sat there silently looking out of the window. Very attractive, very smart. Not a hair out of place and looking in the best of health. Life could certainly be cruel for someone in the prime of life. What really upset him was that he was powerless to do anything to help, apart from offer words of sympathy and comfort. Not that they'd be of any use in that context.

'How long…?'

'For what?' He didn't understand.

'Till I kick the bucket, fall off my perch, give up the ghost, pop my clogs…or in plain English – how long before I die…?'

'Always difficult to predict exactly. But looking at the notes…I'm sorry, it's quite aggressive…three months maybe…six, perhaps longer if you're lucky…but we can never be exact…'

Christina got up and left the room without another word.

The reality of it all suddenly hit her. She was actually going to die? This really was sod's law; on the very morning she'd received the solicitor's letter to inform her of her large inheritance.

Not so much sod's but God's law, if there was one. Retribution for all the bad things she had done in her life, now admitting to herself that she had ruined a few lives. Not least those of family and close friends. She had been a prize bitch. She knew that. Yet what saddened her most was how she had affected her own son's life. That was her main regret.

—

He was never going to forgive or remember her with any affection.

She'd realised only too sadly that perhaps it was too late to be able to make up for it now. She would die alone and nobody would care.

Christina hated the thought of slowly dying a painful and debilitating death in some hospital. It might be better to kill herself now while she was fully in control. What would be the quickest and least painful method? Google would tell her...

2. Send in the Clones

A stretch white limousine drove slowly down the street. Tied to its aerial were half a dozen colourful balloons, a couple which had deflated. In the car, the driver, who was made up and dressed like a circus clown, was scanning both sides of the street.

'Can you see it? Some don't have numbers on the doors. Left or right side of the road?' The driver turned to his companion, who was dressed and made up identically to him. You really couldn't tell them apart.

'Number 35, it's on the left.' The second clown responded casually. 'It's a bit further down. And by the way, as I said before, you do all the talking. I'm your silent partner. Okay?'

'Whatever...hey, this looks like it...' the driver started to slow down.

At number 35, a young face peered out of the window. 'Dad, there's a big white limo coming down the road. It's got balloons...'

'Can't be for us then. Someone either getting married or one of those ridiculous baby showers that seem to be all the rage...' Roger Turner, who was 45 but looked nearer 50, came into the front room tying a black tie over a light blue shirt. Dressed in a sombre grey suit, he looked distinctly uncomfortable.

'Dad... it's stopped right outside our front gate. Looks like there are a couple of clowns inside...'

'Then it's definitely not for us. Probably lost.'

'Dad, what are you doing with that tie!' 17-year-old Tony, dressed casually in bright colours, had turned around.

'What does it look like! I've always hated ties.' Roger redid the knot.

'It's black…Mum left specific instructions that no black was to be worn. She stipulated jolly, bright colours.'

'Your mother had some funny ideas. Anyway, it's a mark of respect.'

'But you didn't.'

'What…' Roger adjusted the tie by loosening the top button of his shirt.

'Respect her. Did you?'

'Not really…But…' He was about to say something derogatory, but decided now wasn't the time.

'Dad, you know today would've been her birthday if she lived.'

'Would it? I'd forgotten. But then again, she didn't remember yours the years she was away. Not even a card – did she?'

'No…Poor Mum. Fancy having a funeral on your birthday.'

'No candles, just a flaming cremation to mark it.' Roger couldn't wait to see her ashes in an urn, proving that Christina was finally out of their lives.

Outside a car horn tooted loudly three times. Tony looked out of the window again and saw one of the clowns standing by the car and waving to him.

'I think that car is for us, you know.'

'You must be joking!' Roger went to the window. The clown waved again, gesturing for him to join them. 'It's got to be some mistake.'

'You think so?' Tony couldn't help but smirk, seeing the flustered look on his father's face. 'We were told a car would pick us up.'

Roger took a deep breath and went out of the front door, closely followed by Tony. 'Can I help you?'

'Mr Turner…?' The clown driver gave a big smile, while the other clown sat in the car grinning.

'Yes…?' Roger did not like the sound of this.

'Brookfield Crematorium. Whenever you're ready.'

'You cannot be serious!' Roger first looked at the clown in the car who smiled and waved back, and then at the balloons.

'I'm afraid a couple of the balloons burst on the way here. We didn't have any spares.' The clown inside the car pulled a sad face.

'This is some sort of cruel joke, isn't it!' Roger turned to Tony who just shrugged.

'Sorry sir. We're just doing our job. Only following instructions.'

Roger looked up at the sky in despair. 'Christina Turner – I'll kill you!'

Tony put a hand on Roger's shoulder. 'Dad…She's already dead. We'd better go. Never been in a limo before. I'm looking forward to this.'

'I'm not…' Roger mumbled as they got in the back of the car. 'There's room for a dozen people in here! Picking anyone else up? Bailiffs, tax inspectors, everyone Christina owed money to before she conveniently disappeared?'

'Just the two of you, sir.' The driver started the engine and slowly drove off. The other clown switched on the CD player, which started to play "The Sun Has Got His Hat On."

'This is going too far!' Roger leant forward. 'Switch that bloody thing off! We're supposed to be going to a funeral not a circus jamboree. Oh Christina, you've always liked to make us suffer. As in life…so in death…'

'Poor Mum…' Tony suddenly felt a touch sad as they travelled in silence, save for the noise of the other balloons bursting along the way.

—

As the limousine drove into the crematorium, the first thing that caught their eye was a large multi-coloured banner draped across the entrance with the words "Happy Deathday, Christina." blazoned across. Helium filled balloons surrounded it.

'I don't believe this! It surely can't get any worse?' Roger addressed the clowns who just looked at each other in silence. He gazed across at the entrance, where one of those one-man-band buskers, covered in instruments, sat dressed like a circus ringmaster. He now started to play "Always Look on the Bright Side of Life" which sounded awful and very out of tune. A moment later a young black girl, clad as a fairy covered in glitter, appeared waving her wand in time to the music. 'Oh God - from the ridiculous to the preposterous…'

Tony couldn't help but grin. 'Dad, this is obviously what Mum wanted.' He quite fancied the fairy. 'She's having a laugh.'

'At our expense. No wonder the solicitor didn't want to divulge what her wishes were for the funeral. If I'd known beforehand…'

'What would you have done, Dad? Not attend your own wife's funeral?'

'Ex-wife, please. It did cross my mind, if I'm going to be honest. She created nothing but misery when she was alive. Even now she's taking the piss…'

'Dad, leave it for today…please…' Tony glanced out of the window to see another white limousine driving slowly in, with all its balloons still intact, stopping by the entrance.

'Who's this?' Two more clowns, again identically dressed and made up like the other two, got out and opened the doors of the limousine to allow a man and a woman to get out. 'It's Uncle Eric! And some woman I don't know. I certainly didn't think he'd come, after…'

'After what your mother did to him, do you mean?'
Roger pointed out.

'I'm just surprised, that's all.'

'Aren't we all?' Roger wasn't looking forward to the
service, and was now wishing it would all be over as quick as
possible. It had taken him a couple of years to try and purge
Christina from his life and move on. Now all that hidden
anger and animosity had resurfaced. 'Bloody woman...' he
mumbled.

Their two clowns were now outside and had opened
the doors to let Roger and Tony out. 'Thank you. I'm sorry
you've had to go to all this trouble. I know you were only
doing what you were told. Hope you got paid extra for
looking like that?' Roger addressed the clowns.

'That's alright, sir. Quite enjoyed it in a funny way.
The lady must have had a bit of a sense of humour.' The
driver clown smiled.

'Which I haven't found funny at all. My dear
departed ex-wife never had much respect for other people's
feelings. Come on Tony, let's get this over with.'

As they walked towards the chapel entrance, Eric
came mournfully across to them. Dressed flamboyantly in a
pale blue three-piece suit and looking like a male model, he
appeared genuinely upset. 'Roger...Tony...' He extended his
arms to give a hug.

'Eric, you know I don't do hugs. I see you've dressed
for the occasion.'

'Roger, I'm so sorry...' Eric gave a tearful look minus
the tears.

'Don't be, I'm not. How are you?'

'Devastated! It was all so unexpected. She just
disappeared one day – and never came back. And now...' He
dramatically raised his hands up to the sky.

'That was three years ago, Eric.'

'There hasn't been a day when I haven't thought about her.' Eric sighed like a lost lover. Although only a year apart, he looked 10 years younger than Roger.

'You're overdoing it, dear brother. I remember you cursed her more than I did when she left. I've often thought how I'd liked to have got my hands on her. Preferably round the throat. Beaten us there, hasn't she.'

'Dad! Please…'

'Tony, I can't change the way I feel. That's how it was. Admit it, she wasn't a good mother either.'

'She was still my mother, whatever…Let's just go in…' Tony led the way to the entrance.

The fairy waving a wand met them. 'Have a nice day…have a nice day…' she chanted happily as she handed them each a funeral programme, blessing them with the wand.

'Don't count on it…' Roger glanced at the front cover, which had a picture of a smiling Christina with the caption 'A New Beginning to an Old End'. He was now dreading what vision of absurdity was waiting for them in the chapel itself. He would put nothing past what Christina might have in store for them.

As he entered with Tony and Eric, he was unexpectedly and pleasantly surprised at how normal everything looked. No flowers, with a plain teak coffin displayed at the front. In the background gentle organ music was playing creating a mellow atmosphere.

There was only one other person already seated in one of the pews. Jennie, the woman who had arrived with Eric, was slightly plump and was wearing a red two-piece suit with a brassy scarf. She was grinning to herself and nodded by way of a greeting to the others as they took their seats.

'Who's she?' Roger whispered to Eric.

'Jennie. Remember, she worked with Christina. They had a business together. Didn't say much more in the car after we picked her up. Just grinned all the way here.'

The four identical clowns now followed them in and stood together at the back. It was impossible to tell them apart.

Eric looked forlornly towards the coffin. 'There she is my sad angel…'

Roger couldn't hold back. 'Devil more likely…hopefully burning in hell…'

'I'd liked to have seen her little face again.' Eric sighed.

'What, to spit on?'

'Dad!' Tony nudged him.

'At least it's not open. Be thankful for small mercies.' Roger felt a bit more relaxed now. 'Well…here we all are! Not a very good turnout is it. I can't say I'm surprised.'

'That's not fair. There might be others coming.' Tony was hopeful.

'It's the truth, son. Your mother was never the most popular of women.'

'To think…' Eric recalled, 'I loved her…once…'

'Did you really?' Roger wasn't convinced. 'But did she honestly appreciate you, Eric.'

Eric paused a moment. 'I don't think so, not really.'

Roger looked at the coffin. 'No…'

'I know she tried to be a good mother to me.' Tony was justifying it more to himself than to the others.

'Tried is the operative word, Tony. Admit it, she was never around when you really needed her.' Roger reminded him.

'She probably had other things on her mind.'

'Why are you defending her now, all of a sudden?'

Tony's eyes quickly filled with tears. 'Because she's dead…that's why…we'll never see her again…'

Suddenly the organ music began to swell. A female priest, dressed in full clerical garb, but wearing badly applied stage makeup, mounted the pulpit.

'Oh God, I hope this isn't going to turn out to be one of those holier-than-thou religious services…Christina was an atheist and hated all forms of religion.' Roger sighed. Tony nudged him again to shut him up.

'Thank you for coming. I welcome you all, as we are gathered here today to celebrate the death of Christina Mary Turner…'

'Surely she means life?' Eric whispered to Roger.

'I'm not so sure…' Roger whispered back.

'Christina was with us for only a short time. The thirty-eight years she spent on this earth were lived to the full…'

'Thirty-eight! She was forty-four! Well, would've been today.' Roger quietly blurted out.

'She told me she was thirty-six?' Eric now added.

Tony had had enough. 'Please! Both of you, shut up! It doesn't matter now.'

'…She will be sadly missed by all of us. I had the personal privilege of knowing her for a few weeks, so I can testify to her generous and loving character. She was a woman who cherished her life and her family…'

Roger couldn't help himself. 'Like hell! Are we at the right funeral? This doesn't sound like the woman I knew.' He voiced rather loudly.

'Please Dad! Let her finish…' Tony gave a week smile to the priest who had paused for a moment without changing her expression.

'The last time Christina came to see me; she had already realised that she could not go on much longer. She was determined to make her peace before embarking on a great new journey…and she was determined to go out with a bang and not a whimper…'

'She's certainly done that…' Roger mumbled.

'…In this coffin lies a life no longer of use. A life that sometimes was wrongly maligned. And as Christina herself admitted to me – she got everything she deserved…'

Tony turned to Roger. 'Isn't that a bit strong?'

'The truth always hurts, son.'

'…Through those curtains is a new horizon. Let us for a quiet moment all send her our loving thoughts, before we convey Christina on her way… Let us remember those good times we had with her….' She bowed her head in contemplation.

In the bedroom Christina and Roger had just finished having sex. He leant back, exhausted but content. She pulled down her nightie, sat up, plumped up the pillow behind her, and picked up a book from the bedside table to read.

'Well…' Roger sighed with a smile.

'Well, what?' Christina continued reading.

'How was it…?'

'How was what?' She turned a page without looking at him.

'Tell me the truth. You know…' He stroked her arm tenderly.

She was now getting annoyed having her reading interrupted. 'What do you want me to say…that the earth moved?'

'I'm just asking you to be honest for once. Did you enjoy it? I certainly did.'

She exhaled. 'I didn't have an orgasm, if that's what you're asking. In fact, it's quite some time since you gave me one.' She turned another page over.

Roger snatched the book from her and threw it across the room. 'Is this more important than us!'

'It's a far better story and keeps me interested if you really want to know the truth.'

'I see, and I don't keep you interested – is that it...?' Her expression now failed to hide the little regard she had for him. 'I suppose your little army of secret lovers DO manage to satisfy you!' He bleated childishly.

Christina turned to him. 'I wish...' She got out of the bed and retrieved her book, leaving Roger exasperated.

Back in the chapel Roger recollected the humiliation. He glanced towards Eric, who was reliving his own memories...

Christina was standing in the doorway holding a shopping list and looking disdainfully down at Eric, in tight t-shirt and boxer shorts, who was exercising with some hand weights.

'.... twenty-three...twenty-four...twenty-five...' He puffed.

'You don't realise how ridiculous you look!'

'A healthy body creates a healthy mind!' He alternated the weights in an up and down movement.

'Is that why MENSA turned you down.' She added quite sarcastically.

'Who...?'

'Never mind. Utilise those biceps when you fill up the supermarket trolley.'

'Oh, not shopping again! You know I hate shopping.' Eric stopped exercising.

'It's that time of the week, big boy. The cupboard is bare. I sincerely hope you don't expect me to do it? That's always been the agreement. You said so yourself that I'm the beauty in the boudoir, not the household whore.' She waved the shopping list at him.

'Just this once, honeybun...' he pleaded.

'I'm not going to argue with you, Eric. There are also some things that need picking up from the cleaners. And while you're out – book the car in for a service, there's a sweetie.' She gave him one of her best false smiles.

He grudgingly put down his weights. 'Sometimes I think you're just using me...'

She tucked the shopping list into his shorts rather suggestively and swanned out before he could complain. He wasn't sure, but he thought he heard her mumble 'You've got it in one, lover boy,' as she left the house.

Eric sadly groaned suddenly realising that Christina had probably used him all along. He smiled across to Tony, whose thoughts went back to when he was eight years old...

In his pyjamas and clutching a well-loved teddy bear, Christina was standing impatiently before him, dressed to go out.

'Where is your father? He should've been here ages ago' She looked at her watch, her irritation growing.

'Don't know, mummy...will you read me a story?'

'Listen, Tony darling, Mummy's got to go out. It's a very important business meeting. Now I want you to be a brave boy and look after the house until Daddy comes home. Do you think you can do that for me?'

'I don't know, mummy...' Tony clasped his teddy tightly to his chest.

'Nothing to worry about, you've got teddy to look after you. There's a good boy. I know Daddy won't be long.' She gave him a quick peck on the cheek. 'Must go…'

Tony was left standing in the hallway as Christina dashed down the stairs and out of the front door.

Tony wiped away a tear as he stared at the coffin. He wondered who the woman in the red suit was, and what she was thinking about. She was no longer grinning; a snarl had suddenly clouded her face as she reminisced…

Christina was in Jennie's office. Bubbly, full of confidence and enthusiasm, she had just finished outlining her business plan to Jennie, whom she had persuaded to invest in.

'You won't regret this, Jennie. I know it can't fail. I've got so many ideas for the business! We're going to be brilliantly successful! Nothing can stop us! I'm so excited that you've agreed to be my partner, and your generous investment will treble in no time. It's a no brainer.'

Sat behind her desk, Jennie was swept along by Christina's passion and commitment. 'Promise they'll be no secrets. This is to be a partnership through and through.'

'You can trust me Jennie, I won't ever let you down…You won't regret it…'

The memory made Jennie bite her lip so hard that she drew blood. She was suddenly tempted to voice her animosity, but managed to restrain herself when she noticed the priest raise her head from contemplation.

'Does anyone want to say a few words before we send Christina on her way?' The priest looked across at the small congregation, who all looked agitated, apart from Tony.

Roger wanted to say *'good riddance'*; Eric, feeling suddenly emotional, nearly blurted out *'why did you leave me?'*; Jennie stopped herself from screaming.

'Bye Mum…' were Tony's farewell words.

The priest seeing the silent, angry expressions, decided not to ask them again. She turned to the coffin. 'Christina…go in peace, and come out the other end smiling…' With organ music now gently playing in the background, the coffin started to move away as the curtains closed around it. 'I think we should all toast that.' The priest gestured towards the back of the chapel, and then slowly undid her cassock to reveal a sparkly evening dress underneath. The fairy then appeared with a tray bearing glasses of champagne, which she started to hand to everyone.

'Now I've seen everything…' Roger despaired.

'Please don't be dismayed, Roger, Christina wanted it this way. Those were her last wishes. You can't deny her that. Let's all drink and bid her a final farewell…' the priest takes a glass of champagne from the fairy. 'And also, to wish her a belated happy birthday.'

Reluctantly Roger, seeing the others had accepted a glass, grudgingly took his. The organ music now reached a crescendo.

'To Christina…' The priest raised her glass from the pulpit.

'Christina!' Came a chorus from the clowns, fairy and busker.

Eric mumbled 'I didn't know it was her birthday…' as he sipped.   Tony held the glass while he wiped away a tear.

Roger pretended to drink but didn't.

Jennie downed the champagne in one go. Now feeling happier, she raised her glass towards where the coffin had been, and whispered, so that no one could hear, 'Burn in hell you bitch!'

3. The Priest in a Glittery Dress

Outside the chapel entrance the two white limousines were parked in a line. Both sets of clowns were waiting by the cars, standing like soldiers in a parade. Since there was not an inch difference in height or size between them, they looked like identical cloned quads.

The priest stood by the door smiling; the multi-coloured sequins of her evening dress glittering in the light. Jennie, who had now regained her composure, shook her hand. 'Splendid service. Most enjoyable. Nice nails by the way.' Jennie noticed the dazzling nail extensions on the priest's hands, bright pink with little red crosses in the middle.

'Thank you. One does ones best. You will join us at a special reception? The cars will take you there.'

'Drink and nibbles...?' Jennie, who was a touch overweight, could never say no to free food and drink. A striking beauty in her youth, she now looked very rough around the edges, personally dreading her coming 50th birthday.

'A celebratory gourmet buffet to tempt the taste buds as a final sending off.'

'How can I resist!' Jennie happily made her way to the first car.

Eric, his mind elsewhere, wandered out oblivious to the priest. 'Mr Turner...Eric...?' she caught up with him. 'Not coming to the reception?'

Eric was still thinking about Christina. 'Reception...?'

'Call it a kind of Wake if you like. Christina wanted everyone to have a good time.'

'A good time? She's dead, for God's sake!' Eric raised his voice, and then regretted it. 'Sorry, didn't mean to blaspheme…I'm finding it very hard to accept that she's…well, she's gone…'

'Quite understandable. Mourning is a natural part of the process, but we must also respect a person's last wishes. And Christina's were that she wanted everyone to celebrate her life. She did love you, you know, in her own special way.'

'Did she?' Eric relaxed. 'I suppose she did…we did have some nice times…'

'So, if you'd like to get in one of the cars, we'll soon be off.' She left Eric just in time to catch Roger and Tony who were standing by the entrance, wondering how they'd get home. 'Mr Turner, Tony… You'll naturally come to the reception.'

'Oh, there's a reception now? Did Christina really plan all this? I've found it all very hard to take, if I'm going to be honest. A bit of a charade to say the least.' Roger pointed to her outfit.

'I'm sorry if it's distressed you. But everything's been done according to her wishes. When she first told me what she had in mind, I have to say I was a touch sceptical and unsure. But Christina managed to persuade me.'

'I'm sure she did. Christina could be very persuasive if she wanted something. But all this just seems, well, out of character.'

The priest smiled. 'When a light is seen, a person can react in so many different ways. Not always what we might expect.'

'Well, this light must have truly blinded her!' Roger sneered.

'Dad! I apologise on his behalf.' Tony felt uncomfortable.

'Not necessary, Tony. You mother warned me that I might receive this kind of reaction.'

'Did she now.' Roger eyed the priest. She had a plain,

wholesome face and looked no older than 35. The makeup and false eyelashes looked odd. 'I have to ask – are you really a priest? Or is it all part of this masquerade?'

'Dad!' Tony was really embarrassed now.

The priest started to laugh. 'Is that what you think?'

'Well, are you? Christina had no time for religion...or for...'

'Priests? Is that what you're trying to say Roger?' She smiled.

'I think you know what I mean.' Roger was still in no way contrite.

'Let me assure you I'm a fully prayed-up and ordained minister. You don't have to call me Reverend...Paula will do. The dress is hired by the way; my personal wardrobe is not so exotic, and I don't usually wear make-up, but it was fun today to look glam for once – or try to anyway. Satisfied?'

'If you say so.' Roger wasn't entirely convinced.

'I do. Right, I believe it's time to go. Please join us.' She made her way to the first car to travel with Jennie.

'Come on, Dad, for my sake if for nobody else's.'

Reluctantly Roger followed Tony to the second car. 'What treats await us, I wonder...?' He grumbled rather cynically as he got into the car with Tony. Eric was sitting quietly in a corner. 'Not going in the car that brought you?'

'I wanted to be with family.' Eric looked mournful.

'Family!' He sneered. 'How long has it been since you last phoned or popped round? About six months? Eh?'

'Been busy. Anyway, you've never bothered to give me a ring in all that time to make sure I was still alive. Works both ways you know.' Eric wagged a finger at his brother.

Roger sighed, and not wanting to get into an argument addressed the clown driver. 'Where are we going, anyway?'

'I'm not at liberty to say, sir.' He started up the engine and then waited until the first car pulled out. The other clown, next to him, put his finger to his lips to mime a secret.

'I hate bloody mystery tours – it's always disappointment at the end. What a farce this all is. At least we weren't subjected to watching the coffin actually being incinerated, accompanied by that terrible busker trying to play 'Chariots of Fire' or something like that. Although I wouldn't have put it past her.'

'Mum wouldn't make us go through that!' Tony protested.

'No? We all went through a kind of fiery hell when she was alive.' Roger turned to Eric. 'Wouldn't you agree?'

'Roger…this has always bothered me. I hope you don't think I stole Christina from you?'

'My dear little brother,' Roger forced a smile, 'I would have given her to you gift-wrapped earlier if I'd known you were that keen.'

'It wasn't like that. At first I tried to discourage her – but you know how persistent she could be if she wanted something.'

'Don't I just. Yet you must've fancied her in the first place.'

'I did, sort of, love her, but nothing really happened. I didn't sleep with her until you were legally divorced.' Eric touched Roger's arm, 'I promise you that.'

'Do you have to discuss this now?' Tony didn't want to hear all this.

'Sorry, Tony, but I want to try and clear the air with Roger, so there's no misunderstanding.'

'I have to hand it to you, brother, you certainly had guts for taking her on in the first place.'

'So why did you send me that white stick soon after she moved in with me, dear brother?'

'I should've sent you a medal if I knew you were going to be that resilient!'

'What for?' Eric was now getting confused.

'For managing to put up with her, for however long it was.'

'It wasn't that bad…I don't think…'

'Wasn't it?' Roger gave Eric a questioning look.

'Well…maybe a bit challenging at times.' Eric stared out of the window. 'Doesn't matter now. She's gone…'

In the other car Paula and Jennie sat silently as they cruised through the suburbs. Paula suddenly snagged one of her nails on the sequined dress as she tried to get comfortable. 'Damn…!' she quietly cursed.

Jennie, looking relaxed and cheerful, turned to her. 'Another nail in the coffin, so to speak?'

'It's a bugger when that happens, isn't it…sorry, I hope my language hasn't shocked you. Priests aren't supposed to swear, are they. But what the fuck!' Paula smiles and looks at Jennie for a reaction.

'I'm not easily shocked. I spent a short time in a convent school. You should've heard the nuns effing and blinding when things went wrong!' Jennie let out a giggle.

'A natural human reaction whoever you are. If you don't mind me saying, you strike me to be a very contented woman.'

'Not always – but today I feel good. Everywhere you go nowadays, people constantly say, have a good day! And you dismiss it as a meaningless phrase. Well, today I am having a good day. A really good day…' Jennie couldn't help but smile.

Paula looked puzzled. 'Why today particularly?'

'A wish has come true…Christina's finally dead…bless the Lord!' Jennie put her hands together in a gesture of prayer. 'Whoops, sorry…have I shocked you now?'

'Not really…Christina told me you might feel this way. She hoped that you would forgive her now.'

'Forgive her? I would've happily danced on her grave if she'd been buried. She doesn't deserve forgiveness, and will never get it from me.' Jennie's expression darkened.

No one spoke further in either car as they travelled a few more miles in convoy, before finally stopping outside a sophisticated looking wine bar.

'Is this it? Are you sure?' Roger looked out at a handsome building in a chic neighbourhood.

'Yes, sir.' The clown turned off the engine.

'What do you mean, Dad?'

'I honestly expected coming to a sleazy joint in some downmarket area. To one of those awful wine bars or pubs your mother was always trying to persuade me to go to. She liked a drink.'

'She didn't go to bars or pubs while she was with me.' Eric was stunned.

'Really. You surprise me.'

'No, she'd bring drink home…' Eric groaned, 'usually supermarket plonk…and we'd get blind drunk on the sofa…'

'I can believe that. Well, let's not be surprised if we're given glasses of cheap house wine with a few crisps and peanuts to celebrate her passing.' Roger rose from his seat to get out as one of the clowns now opened the car door. He noticed a sign on the front door which said 'Closed for private party'.

4. The Sour Grapes of Wrath

The 'Grape Garden' wine bar had a smart, sophisticated interior, decorated in subtle shades of red, green and amber, with snug chairs spaciously arranged around low round tables. It had a relaxing ambiance that welcomed and enticed you in. Roger was almost impressed as he, Eric and Tony entered. It was certainly not what he had expected. Apart from a man in his fifties, who was chatting to two waitresses, the place was empty.

'Ah, the brothers Turner and son, I believe. We've never met, but I feel I know you all so very well.' The man came across holding out his hand.

'How reassuring…' was all Roger could think of in response.

'Duncan Drake.' He shook all of their hands. 'You no doubt know who I am.'

Roger glanced at Eric and Tony who both shrugged. 'No, do please enlighten us, Mr Drake.'

'From Crouch, Wisby and Drake, Solicitors. Mind you, Crouch and Wisby are now dead, but I decided to keep the business name. I now refer to them as my silent partners!' Duncan joked, but saw that they were still puzzled. 'I'm Christina's solicitor. You must remember your divorce, Roger? I may call you Roger, I presume. Do please call me Duncan.'

'How can I forget my divorce, Duncan. But I don't believe we ever met.' Roger was fascinated by Duncan's awful scoop over; thin wisps of greyish hair trying to cover a bald head. How Roger would've loved to have taken a pair of scissors and chopped them all off.

'We've spoken on the phone several times.' Duncan assured him.

'So, it was you who informed me of Christina's death?'

'Always a sad and distressing function of my work sometimes…'

'You didn't come to the service.' Eric didn't warm to Duncan. But then Eric never liked anyone in any form of authority, whose superior use of language could easily bewilder him.

'Sadly, there were other matters to attend to. I believe it was a very jolly affair!'

'Oh, very jolly!' Roger replied sarcastically. 'The 'jolly' details being part of her last wishes?'

'As stipulated in her Will.' Duncan gave a false smile.

'She actually left a Will?' Roger sounded surprised.

Duncan's manner now assumed a more formal note. 'Ah yes, that's to be dealt with later…Oh, here's the Reverend Geddes with Jennie. If you would like to go over there for now, we've arranged some special tables. It's fortunate that we have the whole place to ourselves this afternoon. Now if you would please excuse me…' Duncan went over to welcome Paula and Jennie.

'Actually, before she disappeared, Christina told me she was thinking of making a Will.' Eric added.

'And you believed her?' Roger gave Eric a sad look.

'Why shouldn't I?'

'Oh, come on, Eric, she was often economical with the truth, that's why. You knew that.'

'Dad…Uncle Eric…please. Can't you both just let it rest. She's dead.' Tony slumped down in a chair.

'I'm sorry Tony, but today has been a horrible reminder. I can't forget what she did to us.'

Eric nodded in agreement

'Christina wasn't a very nice person, and being dead does not excuse her faults or her actions when she was alive.' Roger now sat, feeling suddenly tired.

'Uncle Eric, you lived with her. Was she that bad?'

'She never made it easy. To be honest, if she hadn't…Oh, what's the point now…' Eric slid down into his chair.

'If she hadn't what…?' Tony stared at Eric.

'If she hadn't killed herself…' Eric closed his eyes for a moment. 'After she conveniently disappeared, if I'd have bumped into her, I might have been tempted to strangle her…'

Tony was now visibly quite shocked. He didn't know she had committed suicide. Roger leant across and put his hand on Eric's arm in a gesture of comfort. 'I totally understand. I've felt the same many times…'

'Felt what may I ask?' Paula now stood before them.

'Ah, the voice of conscience! Have you got no souls to save, no parishioners to convert?' Roger couldn't resist the jibe.

'It's my half day off. Any saved souls or conversions can wait until tomorrow. I've come to enjoy a glass or two of bubbly. We are allowed you know. You still haven't forgiven Christina, have you?'

'How can you tell…? Why is it when someone dies, and at his or her funeral the eulogies are all about what a great person they were. Nothing bad or negative is ever said about them, even though some did unforgiveable things while alive.' He added sarcastically. 'Am I confined to hell now, since I am finding it hard to forgive her, even though she's dead?' Roger challenged her.

'If you believe in hell, that is. Don't judge her too harshly.' A couple of champagne corks suddenly popped in the background. 'Now, I think we could all do with a drink...' Paula gave them all a conspiratorial smile and wandered off.

'I still find it difficult to accept that she's a priest.' Roger watched her sashaying towards the bar.

'Nice bottom...for a priest...' Eric added wistfully.

Tony sighed, no longer having the energy to argue. He felt his father and uncle were as bad as each other.

'Ah...the three musketeers!' Duncan appeared carrying a bottle of champagne, followed by a waitress carrying a tray with glasses. "Never fear quarrels, but seek hazardous adventures!"

'I'm sorry?' Roger looked confusingly up at Duncan.

'You obviously don't know your Alexander Dumas!' Duncan smiled.

'Who...?' Eric added.

'A famous writer, Uncle, who wrote a book called The Three Musketeers. I'm assuming that's a quote from it.' Tony answered for Eric's benefit, knowing that Eric had hardly ever read a book in his life, never mind a classic.

The waitress handed each a glass whilst Duncan did the pouring. Roger glanced up at the label on the bottle. 'Dom Perignon...?' He was quite taken aback.

'The real thing. And before you wonder, it's not an expensive label that's been put on some cheap sparkling wine.' Duncan smiled.

'Would I think that?' Roger couldn't disguise that it would have been his reaction.

Duncan smiled knowingly. 'Christina wanted you to enjoy the best. To celebrate her birthday as would've been.' He watched them each take a sip, and could see they were impressed. 'She also chose the menu specially.'

'I'm intrigued. Food was never any priority with her. So what are we to expect?' Roger still felt there'd be some kind of catch attached.

'A selection of smoked salmon, caviar and truffles as a starter, followed by lobster thermidor with a side of VEGETABLES, lightly sautéed in a few drizzles of olive oil…'

'Any chips?' Eric added seriously.

'If you want chips, I'm sure we – '

But before Duncan could finish, Roger stopped him. 'But Christina never liked any of those things. She hated what she called 'fancy' food. Her tastes were quite traditional and bland.'

'Meat and two veg followed by a pudding' Eric recalled. 'By the way, what's for pudding?'

'It isn't for Christina. It's for you; she wanted you all to enjoy the best there was. She chose the menu without any prompting from me. For 'pudding' there is chocolate and walnut pavlova with madeira and tangerines.' Duncan smiled as Paula, who had been chatting to Jennie, came over to join them.

'Does that come with custard?' Eric wondered.

'Okay…' Roger held out his empty glass for Duncan to refill it up. 'So, you discussed it while she was still alive?'

'Well…yes, in a way.' Duncan abruptly lost an element of composure.

'You must've known that she was going to commit suicide then?' Both Eric and Tony suddenly became very attentive. Duncan glanced across at Paula with a questioning look. 'Did you know as well, Paula? Now come to think of it, no one actually went into any details about her death. I wasn't allowed to see the body. I took it on trust. I suppose we were all too shocked to demand answers at the time.' Roger studied their faces.

Duncan inhaled. 'I'm afraid that was one of Mrs Turner's – Christina's – requests. That none of her family should see her after…after she had decided to leave us…'

'Who identified the body?' Roger wasn't letting go.

'Er…I did…' Duncan raised his hand.

'Did you know she was going to kill herself. Isn't that somehow illegal?'

'There were extenuating circumstances…'

Eric didn't understand. 'Extenuating? What does that mean?'

'Why did my mother take her own life?' Tony was now curious.

'There were many reasons.' Duncan now felt uncomfortable.

'Name one.' Both Tony and Roger said it at the same time.

'Let me say something.' Paula topped up her glass and took a large swig. 'Just over a week ago, Christina came to see me. She told me exactly what she intended to do.'

'You mean she went to confession?' Roger looked surprised.

'In a manner of speaking…' Paula was doing her best to remain calm and in control, giving Duncan various uncertain looks.

Roger shook his head. 'I'm sorry, but I find that very hard to believe. As I intimated earlier, Christina hated the Church and everyone connected with it. She would sooner confess to a parrot than a priest.'

'I can back that up,' Eric intervened, 'I had a cockatiel once. If Christina had had a bit to drink, she'd often talk to it. Confess like.'

Roger turned to Eric. 'I actually meant that metaphorically.'

Eric didn't understand the word, but thought back. 'Oscar was such a friendly little bird. If Christina hadn't accidentally put bleach in his drinking bowl – he might still be with us now…'

—

40

Roger laughed. 'Are you sure it was an accident, Eric? Christina hated pets and small animals, didn't she Tony?'

Tony didn't know what to say. 'She wouldn't have done that to Oscar!' Eric added.

'Christina was regretful of many things she had done with her life.' Paula spoke quietly.

'So did she tell you about Oscar then?' Eric prompted.

'Not specifically. Just things in general. She told me she felt that some of her actions might have been a little insensitive.'

'That must be the understatement of the year!' Roger roared.

'Please Dad…'

Roger rose from his chair. 'No. I'm sorry, but I'm really getting fed up with all this hypocrisy. The woman was a shrew. Totally selfish and uncompromising. I refuse to be sanctimonious now that she's gone. All this expensive food and drink is not going to pacify me.' He glanced across at Jennie, who was watching and listening silently to the debate. 'And I know I'm not alone in how I feel.' He went across to her. 'It's Mrs Hankin, Jennie, isn't it? Weren't you once Christina's business partner?'

Jennie turned to him. 'That's right…'

'Roger, Christina's ex. You're very quiet. Haven't you got anything to say?'

'What do you want me to say?' Jennie looked up at him curiously, and then across at all the others who had turned towards her and were now listening.

'Well, how do you feel about all this. Didn't your business go bankrupt because of Christina?'

'Yes.'

Roger sat down next to her. 'Surely you must feel a touch bitter?'

'Bitter…?' Jennie calmly emptied her glass and then held it up for the waitress to top it up. 'Because the business went bust soon after she disappeared? Because my house was repossessed? Because my husband deserted me? Do I blame Christina for all that…? What do you think?' She smiled as she took another big swig of her drink.

'You sound awfully calm for someone whose life was subsequently ruined.' Roger was trying to make her out.

'That was three years ago. I've started a new business and a new life. I've moved on…'

'In which case why are you here, if you've moved on?' Roger didn't want to leave it.

Jennie now addressed the whole group. 'I thought seriously about it when I received the invitation. I had to make sure that she was really dead. I wouldn't rest until I'd been to her funeral. You see, since things started to go wrong in my life – which began when I first met Christina – there's been little joy. Today has to be one of the happiest days I've had for a long time…And now – fuck the diet - I can't wait to tuck into that lovely food! I deserve it.' She held up her glass in a silent toast.

Duncan now nodded to Paula, who nodded silently back. 'Right…Before we all settle down to the food – I have been instructed to disclose certain aspects of the Will….'

'I can't wait.' Roger mockingly whispered to Tony.

'I can now declare that you have all been left a special legacy…' This made Roger, Eric and Jennie perk up suddenly. 'If you would all kindly follow me upstairs to another room, where it is more private.'

Roger turned to Eric. 'More empty promises? Perhaps I'll get back that £10,000 Christina took out of my bank account before she disappeared. Pigs might fly first.'

'Yes, and I'll get a new car! She pinched my car when she left, which I never saw again.' Eric admitted.

'You didn't tell me that. You said you'd sold it.'

'I was too ashamed to actually admit it…' Eric pulled a face.

'Lady…Gentlemen, shall we adjourn?' The others now followed Duncan as he went up the stairs.

Paula remained downstairs, and waited until all four clowns entered the wine bar and stood in a line as if waiting for instructions.

5. A Ghost of a Confession

The upstairs room had been arranged like a small viewing room. Perched centrally, on a rectangular table, was a 70-inch flat screen TV, displaying an animated screen saver showing a group of colourful clowns chasing each other round a circus ring. Beside the TV a small DVD player was attached. To the left, on another table, were four parcels wrapped in brightly coloured paper, with a nametag attached to each. A row of chairs was set out in front of the screen.

'Here we are!' Duncan stood by the screen as all the others slowly trooped in.

'Ooh are we going to see a film?' Was Eric's immediate response.

'Not quite.' Duncan gestured for them to sit. 'I must say, I've never had to do anything like this before. Certainly a first!'

'And hopefully a last.' Roger eyed the room suspiciously.

Tony was by the parcel table. 'Dad, our names are on these parcels.'

Eric joined him. 'Presents…how exciting! Can we open them now?'

'They're actually your legacy. A sort of final birthday present from Christina. Please be patient for a moment before we do the honours.' Duncan added.

'Probably all empty…' Roger sneered.

'I assure you they're not.' Duncan grinned like an excited little boy.

Jennie moved across to the table. 'You know what's in them?'

'Oh no,' Duncan shook his head seriously, 'Christina personally packed them, and then gave them to me. If you

---

44

shake them – they'll rattle.'

'So does a snake before it bites.' Roger was not being taken in.

Eric couldn't resist and shook the parcel with his name on. 'It does rattle. Very light. Can't be much in there.' He sounded disappointed.

'If all of you would kindly take a seat, we'll begin.' Duncan picked up a remote from the table. 'Soon all will be clear.' He waited until they'd all sat down before pressing the remote. The screen clowns disappeared, replaced by a large picture of a smiling Christina.

'I don't believe it! What are we being subjected to now? What is all this about?' Roger shifted uneasily in his chair.

'I don't like horror films starring witches.' Jennie murmured.

'Christina felt she wanted to explain matters herself. She recorded this before…before she left us…' Duncan glanced towards the back of the room as Paula now joined them.

Roger promptly got up from his chair. 'I've had enough. This has gone too far! Come on Tony; let's get out of here. I no longer want to be a part of this farce.'

Paula made her way to the front. 'Please don't go before you've heard what Christina has to say. I promise you; it will help clarify a lot of things and give her side of the story.'

'She's determined to see us suffer to the very end…' Roger's bearing suddenly slumped.

'Roger, before you condemn, hear her out first…please.' Paula implored.

'I suppose it's only fair…and I would like to see what's in my parcel.' Eric gestured to the other table.

Jennie looked worried. 'It's all a bit spooky if you

---

want my opinion.'

'Like a ghost coming back to haunt us all. What's she after? Forgiveness? Well, she's not getting it from me, whatever she has to say. I'm not interested. Tony, are you coming?'

'I'm staying, Dad.'

'Please yourself!'

Just as Roger made his way to leave, Duncan pressed the remote. Christina's still frame transposed into a video recording of her talking from the screen: *"Roger, please don't go…"*

Roger stopped in his tracks and turned to look at the screen. Beside her image a photo now appeared. A snapshot of Roger and Christina during happier times. *"You really hated me, didn't you?"* She continued after a pause.

'What is this!' Roger closed his eyes to try to blot out the image.

"Saying sorry won't help to change what you think of me, will it Roger?"

Roger shouted at the screen. 'No, no, no!'

"I didn't think so…if you would just hear me out…" At which point Duncan pressed the remote to freeze frame the picture.

'What's going on? I really can't take any more of this.'

'Spooky, spooky spooky…' Jennie mumbled.

'Roger…Christina told us you'd probably react this way. That's why she said what she did. Rather perceptive of her, don't you think?'

'I always thought she was a witch. Now I know.' Jennie muttered.

'She won't let go, will she…she wants to punish us from the grave.'

Paula moved closer to Roger and placed her hand gently on his shoulder. 'She felt guilty and just wanted

—

46

another chance to explain. She deserves that at least.'

Roger, his energy drained, flopped down onto another chair. 'She deserves nothing. It's too late to turn the clock back now…'

Duncan smiled as he pressed the remote again. *"I know you think it's too late to turn the clock back now…but there's another saying – it's never too late to begin again…"* Sensing another interruption, Duncan stopped it again.

'It is now, as far as I'm concerned.'

'Dad, cool it. I want to hear what mum has to say.'

'I suppose we owe her that at least.' Eric implored.

Jennie added. 'Do we? Surely it's she who owes us.'

'I give up…let's listen to some more lies.' Roger had lost the strength to argue and flopped back into his chair.

Paula nodded to Duncan who pressed the play button again. Throughout the next section of Christina's declaration, a brief montage of family snaps chronicling happier moments in their married life appeared beside Christina's talking head.

"Roger, I know you'll never forgive me. As a wife, lover and friend – I realise I failed you on all counts. You had every reason divorce me. Anyway…I still want to say how very sorry I am for what I might have put you through when we were together. Sorry a thousand times…"

'Pathetic!' was all Roger could muster to mumble.

The side of the screen now displayed another montage showing Christina and Tony together, first as a baby and then as a toddler.

"Darling Tony, my little boy…as a mother I totally neglected you. That's why you had so many different nannies and au pairs, as I was never there when you really needed me. I ignored your childhood and took no notice as you grew up. We can't go back on that. You may as well not have had a mother for all the help and comfort I gave you – or didn't, which was the case. I hope you don't hate me as much as your father. Again, I can only say I'm sorry. Don't think too ill of me…"

—

Tony was visibly moved and wiped away a tear.

Now various photos of Christina and Eric together, some a bit tacky, flooded the side of the screen.

'Oh, that one was taken in Spain!' Eric pointed to the screen.

"Eric…my patient, simple Eric. Even I was surprised how you put up with me as long as you did. I used you. I wiped my feet all over you. I made promises that I had no intention of keeping. I know I drank too much. Even when I was sober, I never gave you the respect that you deserved. You're a kind soul, and I'm so, so sorry…"

Eric, who now looked emotionally worn out, blurted out in anger. 'You scheming bloody bitch!'

'Stop!' Roger turned to Duncan who pressed the pause button. 'Is this really necessary? Haven't we all suffered enough? Switch it off.'

'Wait' Jennie raised her hand, 'I want to hear what she says about me.'

Duncan nodded and continued. Several photos of Christina and Jennie at some business functions came on in the background.

"Jennie…You took me on as a partner in your business in good faith, out of the kindness of your heart. And how did I repay you? I seem to have ended up by ruining you. I didn't do it purposefully. I must've lost the plot somewhere. Then, when everything started collapsing around you, I left you right in it. I'm truly sorry…I know you tried to commit suicide, and I'm thankful you didn't succeed…"

The group stared at Jennie who seemed embarrassed. 'And I'm now thankful that you did…top yourself!' She rose from her seat, grabbed the remote off of Duncan and switched the video off.

'But there's more…' Duncan protested.

'I think we've all had enough. Haven't we?' Jennie looked at the others who nodded in agreement. Even Tony had had enough.

—

Paula came forward now. 'Just a few more minutes perhaps...?'

'So that gorgon on the screen can humiliate us more with her false sentiments!' Jennie turned to Paula and Duncan. 'You should both be ashamed of yourselves, to put us through all this. Christina pay you a lot of money, did she?'

'It's not quite like that.' Paula pleaded.

'Christina requested that certain instructions were carried out… before…before…' Duncan got tongue-tied.

'Before sticking two fingers up in the air as a departing gesture? She always wanted the last word. Come on, the party's over.' Roger made for the door, followed by the others.

Eric then paused and glanced at the table with the parcels. 'What about…?' he pointed.

'Whatever they contain, it's not going to change how we feel. Probably something from the Poundshop. Come on Eric.' Roger took his arm and led him away.

Duncan looked at Paula for help, who just shook her head not knowing what to do in the circumstances. They both sighed and quickly made for the stairs, in a desperate last attempt to stop them leaving.

Downstairs, where all the four clowns were still gathered, Duncan managed to get to the door before them. 'But what about all that wonderful food that's been prepared, and I have to add, at considerable expense.'

'Stuff it! This has turned my stomach.' Roger faced Duncan who was blocking the door.

'I've lost my appetite.' Eric was still thinking about the parcel.

'I couldn't face any food now.' Tony looked visibly pale.

Jennie hesitated. 'It is a shame to waste all that food…perhaps a doggy bag…?' The others looked at her.

'Perhaps not…'

Paula now stood beside Duncan and faced the group. 'You can't just leave now. Have some compassion for Christina's last wishes. Can't you see, she was trying to make amends? She was truly penitent at the way she felt she had treated you all. She deserves some sympathy, surely?'

'Excuse my language – but she deserves fuck all! Now if you'd both kindly move out of the way, we'd like to go…' Roger was prepared to barge through.

'If that's what you wish…The cars will take you back then. They've been hired for the day.' Duncan gestured to the clowns.

'No thank you, we'll get a taxi…Now if you'd please…?' Roger stepped forward. Paula and Duncan both parted and stood silently until they'd all exited.

'It didn't go quite as we expected.' Duncan sighed gloomily.

'No, a bit of a disaster really…' Paula turned to the clowns. 'Sorry…'

One of the clowns, who was looking out of the window, turned back to address everyone. 'Let's not give up yet…All agreed?' The other clowns nodded excitedly, while Paula and Duncan looked at each other as if to say that it was probably a waste of time.

6. The Gifts of Guilt

The taxi pulled up outside Roger's front door. 'I think we could all do with a stiff drink.' Roger got out of the taxi with Tony.

'Or two!' Eric smiled at Jennie who remained seated. 'Are you sure you won't join us, Mrs Hankin?'

'I don't want to intrude…and it's Jennie.'

'Don't be silly, Jennie. Come on, you're looking a bit peaky. A proper drink will do us all good.' He automatically took hold of her arm.

'Well…if you insist…' She shivered slightly. His strong innocent touch had given her goose bumps. It was a long time since she had been touched by a man.

Roger poured out three large glasses of whiskey, and handed one each to Eric and Jennie, then took the third for himself holding it up to make a toast. 'May the vision of Christina never darken our doors again!' Both Eric and Jennie held up their glasses.

'That's a bit harsh, Dad. And anyway, where's mine?'

'Get yourself a beer, there's one in the fridge.'

'I want a whiskey like everyone else.' Tony stood his ground.

'You're too young.'

'Dad, what planet are you from? I'm 17! I bet I've drunk more spirits and tried more drugs than you've had cups of tea.'

'Let him have a glass, Roger, we've all had a trying morning.' Eric took a large swig from his.

'What spirits, what drugs?' Roger stared at Tony.

'Stop being so naïve, Dad. Be thankful I'm not a druggie or an alky. I'm not stupid. Let's leave it at that eh, just don't start interrogating me.'

Roger sat down. 'I give up…help yourself.'

Tony poured himself a small glass, took a sip, and then studied the label on the bottle. 'Cheap supermarket liquor…'

'Connoisseur now are we!' Roger uttered.

Tony took another sip and pulled a face. 'I'm getting a beer from the fridge.' He put his glass down and left the room.

'Waste not, want not…' Eric got up and tipped the remainder of Tony's whiskey into his own glass.

Jennie sat hugging her glass, admiring a picture on the wall. 'Nice house you have, Roger. Very tasteful.'

'Thank you. I had it all redecorated after Christina disappeared. Never liked her colour schemes. So how long was she your business partner? I've forgotten.'

'Two years…felt like twenty sometimes.' Jennie drained her glass.

'We did meet once I believe, didn't we? At some party in a restaurant. I remember, you were with your husband. How is he?' Roger refilled her glass.

'Patrick – he left me soon after.' She took another large gulp.

'Sorry…I never knew much about Christina's work. She never liked discussing it.'

'That's right, she didn't!' Eric interjected, 'I tried to take an interest and ask her about it - not that I'd understand it - but she always told me to shut up and mind my own.'

'That sounds familiar.' Roger topped up his own glass.

'She was a very private person. Never talked about her home life or her family when she was at work. Even when I asked her, she said that she preferred to keep both separate. I'm a bit confused here. Sorry, I don't mean to be nosey, but from what Christina said on that TV, it looked like she lived with you both?'

'Not at the same time may I add. After we divorced…'

'…She came to live with me.' Eric added. 'We never married, although I wanted to...'

'It nice to know that the both of you remained friends in the circumstances.'

'That could be debated.' Roger gave Eric a look. 'Christina was always self-contained, and as far as I knew she never had any close friends. Ones she did have never lasted long, once she had got what she wanted from them. Using people was second nature to her.'

Tony entered the room carrying a beer bottle. 'I'm getting really fed up with you all continually slagging her off! She's dead. She deserves some respect.' He saw that nobody said anything. 'You're all so bloody hard…'

'Because your mother made us so.'

'Well, she didn't make me!' Tony slammed his bottle on a side table and left the room.

'He's really upset, poor boy.' Eric was concerned.

'He'll get over it. We'll all get over it. It's been a trying time for us all, and once more Christina has managed to stir our lives up – even if it was from the grave. But let's look on the bright side, she's gone now – forever!'

'I'll drink to that.' Jennie held up her empty glass.

'Let's all drink to that!' Roger grabbed the whiskey bottle and refilled all their glasses. They all finally started to feel more relaxed.

Outside, one of the white limousines pulled up by Roger's house with two of the clowns inside. They got out of the car, and from the boot they each took out two of the parcels from the wine bar.

As Roger clinked glasses with Eric, he looked out of the window. 'Oh, my God!'

'What is it, what's the matter?' Eric registered Roger's pained expression.

'Look...' Roger pointed out the window. The two clowns, carrying the parcels, were now walking down the path towards the front door in unison. 'When is it going to end? I can't bear it.'

'They've got those presents that were meant for us!' Eric said rather excitedly.

Roger moved away from the window, encouraging Eric to do the same. 'I don't want it, whatever it is.' The doorbell went. 'I'm not going to answer it, and neither are you. Just sit tight, they'll go away. Imagine they're Jehovah's Witnesses.'

The doorbell went again. 'But...?' Eric pleaded.

'No!' Roger now heard footsteps running down the stairs. 'Don't answer it, Tony!'

But it was too late; Tony had already opened the door. 'Oh...'

The two clowns stood before him brandishing the parcels. 'Sorry to trouble you, but Mr Drake thought you should have these, since you forgot them.' The silent clown pulled a sad face.

'Alright. Thanks.' Tony leant forward to take them.

'We were instructed to hand them over personally.' The first clown held on to his.

'I suppose you'd better come in then...' Tony moved aside to let both clowns enter with their packages.

'What's this – a delegation?' Roger directed this at Tony as they all marched into the front room.

'They're only doing their job, Dad. Stop being such a twat.'

'We are really sorry to intrude, Mr Turner…' The first clown said sympathetically.

'I know, just following instructions. So please just put those on the coffee table, and we will wish you both a good day. Happy clowning!'

The first clown coughed. 'Er…we were told to wait until you'd all opened them.'

'What!' Roger let out a loud sigh.

'Dad, just let's get it over with. At least we know there are no bombs or incendiary devices inside, otherwise these two would've been miles away by now.'

The two clowns look questioningly at each other.

'Let's just open them and be done with it.' Eric was keen to unwrap his. 'I'm sure these gentlemen are just as anxious to be rid of us.' He looked at both clowns who smiled and nodded enthusiastically.

Roger put out his hand wearily to be given his. One by one each clown presented the various sized parcels to the four of them, and then stood silently waiting for them to open them.

Eric, still slightly disappointed that his parcel was very small, was the first to tear his open. 'I just love opening presents! It's like Christmas!'

'Don't get too excited, the anti-climax might be too much to bear!' Roger felt his, which was slightly bulkier.

'What's this…?' Eric held a car key on a fob.

'Look.' Jennie pointed to the floor where a folded white piece of paper had fallen. 'Might be a note.'

Eric picked it up, unfolded the note and started reading aloud. *"My dear Eric, I'm sorry I stole your car when I left. When you get home, you will find a brand-new car parked outside your flat. Registration: ET 1976. It's fully taxed, insured and paid for. The paperwork is inside. Love, Christina."* Eric held up the key and beamed. 'This is incredible! I've always wanted a personalised number plate!'

'Do you believe it? What if it's not actually there when you get there?' Roger wasn't yet prepared to trust anything yet.

'You know, I believe it will be.' Eric looked at the clowns who both smiled. 'Go on, open yours!'

'Here goes nothing…' Roger carefully unwrapped his, which turned out to be a rectangular cardboard box. Inside was a thick wad of £50 notes. 'Good God, are they real?' He read the attached note, which was on top. *"Roger, here's the money I borrowed and never paid back. Thought you'd prefer the cash rather than a cheque, which you'd probably say would bounce. No, the notes are not forgeries or from illicit earnings, which I'm sure you will check. I've added interest above the normal bank rate. Love, Christina."* Roger was almost lost for words. 'Well…' He sees the clowns are looking happy.

'See! Mum really did think of us.' Tony now opened his parcel. 'Hey, it's the latest Apple MacBook Pro! Wow!' He showed the laptop to his father, who gave a quizzical look. 'And don't you dare say it's probably a fake replica.'

'Would I?' Roger smirked; his whole manner had changed. 'What's it say in the note?'

Tony opened the note: *"Tony, my little baby. I know you like tech things, and that you've never had much to spend on yourself. Well, I hope this makes up for it. And don't take any notice of your father, who will undoubtedly say the computer's a fake! Love, Mum."* Tony held the laptop as if it was a precious treasure.

—

'Wonders will never cease...' Roger had furtively counted the notes in the wad, to satisfy himself that it was indeed all there plus interest.

'Come on, Jennie; let's see what's in yours! Don't keep us all in suspense!' Eric almost clapped his hands with excitement.

Jennie had been nervously twisting her small parcel around in her hands, whilst the others opened theirs. 'I have no idea whatsoever...it is quite small.'

'As I always say – it's not always the size that counts!' Eric screeched

'Ooh, I don't know about that...' She said rather suggestively, and then embarrassed herself. She quickly tore open the parcel to reveal a set of keys and an envelope. She read from the attached note: *"My poor Jennie. Although I left you in such a mess, I'm glad that you've managed to build up a smaller business from home. But a proper business needs a more appropriate working environment. These keys are for new business premises, which have been fully fitted to cope with your requirements. The enclosed lease is for two years. Build that empire again, Jennie. Love, Christina."* Jennie suddenly burst into tears, and started to shake uncontrollably.

Eric put his arms around to comfort her. 'There, there...'

'I'm sorry,' she blurted out between sobs, 'I never expected...I don't know what to say...after those vile feelings I harboured towards her...' She started to cry again.

The two clowns watched from the side of the room and grinned at each other.

'So, Dad, what have you got to say now about Mum?' Tony challenged him.

'What do you want me to say? That I was wrong about her? I can't just forget what she did to us. All those missing years. I can't excuse that. Okay, she's paid back what she owed, but I can't just dismiss it as if nothing ever happened. I can't instantly change my feelings… it will take time.'

'Well, she's forgiven in my books. Let's no longer speak ill of the dead. What do you think, Jennie?' Eric still had his arm around her.

'I suppose we do need to move on. And in a way…' Jennie jumbled the keys in her hand; '…she has tried to make some sort of amends for what she did.'

Roger still felt uneasy about the whole proceedings. 'You could call it blood money…a fit of conscience before she decided to kill herself.' He blurted out, and immediately sensed antagonism from the other three. 'Okay, okay, I will say no more. I accept her gesture of goodwill, I can't be fairer than that.'

'It hasn't turned out so badly, has it?' Eric jangled his car key.

'I feel worn out.' Jennie took a deep breath. 'And I'm also feeling a touch peckish. What time is it?'

'Just gone two.' Roger was still trying to come to terms with everything.

'Do you think…' Jennie licked her lips, 'that food…at the wine bar…might still be available? It would seem such a waste…'

'Jennie, are you seriously suggesting that we return to that wine bar?' Roger wasn't prepared for this.

'Why not?' Eric added, 'Aren't we allowed to change our minds?'

'Mum wanted us to have a good time, and I could do with something to eat. Come on, Dad, we owe it to her memory. Especially now. Think of it in terms of a birthday party.'

'Well…' Roger turned to the clowns. 'Is it too late

—

58

now?'

'It's never too late, sir! I'll just make a call and we can be off. Room for everyone in the car!' The clown winked at the other clown, took out his mobile and went outside to make the call.

7. Resurrection Farce

Inside the 'Grape Garden' the mood was one of jollity and bonhomie, with everyone in high spirits. The meal had gone well, without any further upsets or arguments. The waitresses had been given instructions to keep topping up glasses. Roger, Eric and Jennie were by now quite drunk, whilst Tony, who hadn't drunk as much, was feeling more melancholic.

Paula and Duncan, who sat at the same table, purposefully didn't drink as much as the others. Throughout the meal they would look at each other and smile, seeing that it was all going so well and to plan.

At another table, the four identical clowns, who enjoyed the same food, were only allowed soft drinks. They had been instructed to keep any noise or chatter down, so as not to distract the other table. One of the clowns had a permanent grin and an expression of satisfaction, watching the main group enjoying themselves so much.

Jennie suddenly gave a loud belch. 'Whoops! Excuse me! I think I've eaten too much…'

Eric, who was next to her, rubbed her back. 'Is that better?'

'You have such a strong touch. You may administer to me any time.' Jennie giggled and then let out another small burp, which made Eric laugh.

Roger turned to Duncan. 'I have to say that was a magnificent meal.'

'I'm so glad you enjoyed it,' Duncan smiled, 'But the credit must go to Christina herself, who organised it all.'

'She referred to it as her Last Supper.' Paula added.

'And what a great supper it was! I shall have to diet for a month…or two.' Jennie patted her stomach.

'Don't you dare!' Eric touched her on the arm, 'You look alright as you are.'

'Why thank you, kind sir. Flattery will get you everywhere.' She squeezed his knee playfully.

'I was hoping you'd say that!' Eric whispered brazenly, which made them both burst out in a fit of giggles.

Roger suddenly declared, without any edge of aggression or sarcasm 'I think we've all been rather selfish.'

'What do you mean, brother?' Eric turned to him.

'We've all pigged ourselves out, and drunk gallons of the most excellent wine, yet…yet, we haven't really spared a kind thought for Christina.'

'I have…' Tony murmured, 'She was my Mummy…and I miss her so…'

'Christina was well aware how you all felt. She wouldn't blame you for thinking as you did.' Paula looked at Duncan who nodded in agreement.

'A lot must have happened during those missing three years.'

'It did, Roger, she went through a great deal.' Duncan confirmed.

Eric became reflective. 'I feel quite ashamed now, having wished her dead a thousand times…'

'Me too…perhaps we've all misjudged her.' Jennie wondered.

'You have.' Tony stood up, and poured some wine into his glass, which he then raised. 'I propose a toast…to the nicest Mum in the world…I miss you…'

Apart from the clowns, who observed with interest, they all stood up and raised their glasses, chanting in unison: 'To Christina!' Then Eric started to sing "Happy Birthday to you…" with the others loudly joining in. After which there was a moment's silence, when they all quietly sat back down.

Roger was still contemplative. 'To have ended this

—

way…'

'The poor soul must have really suffered to have taken her own life…' Eric now reflected.

'Perhaps, from the bottom of our hearts, we should forgive…and let her memory rest in peace…' Jennie suggested. Both Roger and Eric nodded in agreement.

Tony turned to Paula and Duncan. 'I'd still like to know how and why she killed herself.'

'Ah…' Paula looked down.

'It's a long story. I don't think now's a suitable time to go into all that…' Duncan looked at Paula.

'Duncan's right. Not today. Christina wanted you all to enjoy yourselves. To focus on the positive, rather than the negative aspects of the situation.'

'I wish she had come back to us. Before…before, she decided to…' Tony looked pained. 'I mean we might've been able to stop her….'

'Christina had considered that, but she thought you wouldn't listen and turn her away, which would've been worse.' Paula attempted to explain.

'I suppose that's true,' Roger agreed, 'but there are ways and means…'

'We wouldn't have been that heartless, would we Jennie?' Eric turned to her.

'I'm not so sure, if I'm to be honest.' she replied.

'Perhaps we all misunderstood her.' Roger reflected. 'But now…I can't say I honestly feel quite so bitter.'

'And I'm beginning to feel terrible. She could've been given another chance. Whatever it was, I'm sure it wasn't worth dying for.' Eric turned to Paula.

Paula pensively looked at them all. 'Do you sincerely believe a person deserves a second chance – whatever they've done?'

'Of course.' Eric maintained.

Roger nodded. 'None of us is perfect.'

'I'd like to think that people would give me a second chance.' Jennie added.

Tony wasn't letting go. 'You all say that – full of good food and fuelled up with drink and expensive presents to enjoy. But none of you really mean it, since she's now conveniently dead.'

'That's not true!' Roger objected.

'Tony, isn't that a bit harsh?' Eric was surprised.

'I refuse to be hypocritical.' Tony raised his voice in sudden anger.

Duncan held up his hand to quieten them. 'So, let me put this to you all. Metaphorically speaking…if Christina could suddenly materialise – would you hear her out?'

'Without question.' Jennie piped up.

'I'd certainly listen.' Eric countered.

Roger thought about it. 'Well, I suppose she deserves the benefit of the doubt. I'd be interested to hear what she had to say. Is there more of that video we haven't seen?'

'That's very reassuring to hear.' Paula smiled. 'Of course, Tony, you'd be happy to let her explain?'

'I'd be happy simply to see her again…' Tony sighed. 'But what's the point of wondering. It's never going to happen, which makes it all the more tragic…'

Jennie shook an empty bottle of wine. 'Is there any more wine? We need a bit of cheering up again!'

'I'll second and third that!' Eric waved his empty glass in the air.

'Let's see what we can rustle up.' Duncan stood up and motioned to one of the waitresses, who went out the back. 'Do you think it's time for that special bottle, Paula?' He looked across to the clowns, one of whom smiled and nodded.

Paula also looked at the smiling clown. 'Are we sure?' The clown gave a thumbs up. 'Okay…It's your funeral, to quote a phrase...' She gestured to the table where all the clowns were sitting. 'Would you like to do the honours?' One of the clowns who stood up, nodded and smiled.

The clown took a bottle of champagne that the waitress had just brought in, and carefully popped the cork, which hit the ceiling. Jennie and Eric cheered, both holding up their empty glasses. The clown then went round filling all the glasses.

'More champagne…we are being spoilt!' Roger smiled at the clown.

'You deserve it. Thank you all for being so understanding…' The voice of the clown was female, and sounded familiar to Roger.

'What…? Who are you…?'

The clown now removed her wig and false nose and placed them on the table. 'Hello Roger…'

'Mum…?' Tony blinked in disbelief.

'Christina?' Eric blurted out as if he'd seen a ghost.

'I want that second chance you all promised. I really can explain everything.' Christina calmly addressed the sea of bewildered faces, watched on the side lines by Paula and Duncan.

'You're not dead!' Jennie screamed and then promptly fainted.

Eric, the revelation too much for him, put his hand to his mouth and ran out to be sick.

Roger, frozen to the spot, shook himself and then picked up the wig and false nose off the table and walked across to Christina, who stood perfectly still.

To somehow prove to himself that his eyes weren't deceiving him, he replaced the nose and wig on her face and head.

He then gazed at the other three identical clowns who were watching proceedings. 'You were here all the bloody time!' Roger clenched his fist and was about to punch Christina in the face.

'Dad!' Tony shouted, to stop him just in time. 'Mum, you're really not dead!' He gave her a big hug, which she wasn't totally comfortable with. Roger just shook his head and walked out of the wine bar.

'Hasn't everyone rather overreacted? I thought you'd all be pleased – after everything that had been said.' Christina, extricating herself from Tony's grip, now wondered if it was all now going to backfire.

'It's great to have you back! Are you here to stay, Mum?'

'For a short while…I'm concerned about the others though. They rather overreacted.'

'They'll come round in time, I'm sure.'

'Time, which I haven't got…' She glanced down to where Paula was on her knees attending to Jennie. 'There's so much to do …'

'What do you mean? Mum…?'

Christina took a deep breath. 'Oh, my baby. I have to be honest. I really don't have long to live…I won't see another birthday.' She stopped Tony before he could say anything. 'No – I'll explain later. I'm sorry you had to go through all this, but it was my little way to try to get everyone to understand….' She looked at everyone staring at her with looks of disbelief.

'…I'm a different person now. Different from the person who walked out on you three years ago. The old Christina Turner was well and truly buried, or should I say cremated today…You're my only family – and I want to spend my last days with you all…To try and make up for what I did. I've got money, and there's a lot more I want to do for everyone…' She noticed that Jennie had now come to and was looking at her. 'Jennie, my dear friend. Are you feeling better? How do you feel about us being business partners again…?'

Jennie slowly rose from the floor looking completely bewildered and speechless. Impulsively she grabbed a large knife from the table and made a lunge towards Christina, who recoiled in horror and ran to try and hide amongst the other clowns.

In desperation, Jennie, now not able to distinguish the real Christina among them all, started to chase all the clowns, one by one round the wine bar. 'Where are you, you bitch! I'll kill all of you if I have to!' During this outburst, Paula and Duncan tried to stop her, but feared they might get accidentally stabbed, so backed away.

Like a devil possessed Jennie pursued the four clowns, brandishing the knife maniacally. It was lucky for them, that due to the drink and her ample size, she wasn't quick enough to be able catch them. Still, in fear of their lives, the clowns finally all managed to escape through the front door.

A moment later, everyone inside heard a screech of car brakes, a blood-curdling scream, followed by a dull thud outside. Then silence.

Paula, Duncan and Tony ran out to find Roger staring at a body crumpled up on the road in front of a car.

'They all came running out…and then this car turned the corner and drove straight into her. She didn't have a chance…' Roger couldn't take his eyes off the clown, laying there, blood oozing from the head. The other three clowns stood together on the pavement looking shocked.

Paula knelt down and felt the body's pulse. 'Dead…' She immediately began to perform the last rites.

Tony, in tears, stared down at the body. 'Mum….

66

…Mum!' He looked up at Jennie, who was still holding the knife. 'Look what you've done!'

'I didn't kill her! It was an accident…' Jennie dropped the knife.

'You might just as well have…' Tony fell to his knees and held the dead body's hand and stroked it. 'I can't believe she's really dead now…' He then burst into tears.

Paula knelt down to comfort him. 'This wasn't what Christina had planned, poor thing…' She gently took off the wig and clown's nose, but then started closely at the face underneath. 'It's…it's not Christina…'

'No, it isn't me…' One of the other clowns now stepped forward and leant down to comfort Tony. 'It's alright, love. I'm still here…you're not going to get rid of me that easily.' Christina looked up at Jennie, Eric and Roger whose expressions were a combination of horror and incredulity.

8. A Bit of a Fucking Mess

With lights flashing and siren on, the ambulance sped away. By the side of the road the police were talking to the driver of the car who had hit the clown, who looked shaken and upset.

Outside the wine bar was our group of revellers, who silently watched the ambulance depart. The events of the past hour had taken it out of them, sobering them up. Roger, Tony and Eric all looked slightly traumatised. Jennie stood to the side of them, her expression one of bewilderment and loathing. Her fists were clenched in tension. Only Paula and Duncan looked somehow vaguely cheerful and unaffected.

Christina, still in her clown disguise, stood with the other two clowns. It was still almost impossible to tell them all apart.

'Well, since there's no more we can do, shall we all go in and have some coffee?' Duncan announced cheerfully as the ambulance disappeared from sight.

Something suddenly snapped in Jennie, who strode crossly over to the clowns. She furiously tore off a wig from one of them, only to angrily discover it wasn't Christina; and then from the next one, who again wasn't her.

'Are you looking for me, by any chance?' Christina held up her hand.

Jennie grabbed hold of Christina and started to violently shake her. 'You cow! Why did you have to come back? You're supposed to be dead!' She put her hands round Christina's throat. 'You're supposed to be DEAD!!!'

Duncan and Tony quickly ran over, and then struggled, trying to pull Jennie off, who was doing her best to choke Christina.

68

One of the policemen, hearing the commotion, made his way over. It was only when Duncan quickly seized her round the front and squeezed, that Jennie finally let go. 'Get your hands of me you pervert!' she shouted, 'Enjoy a bit of a feel do you! Get off on that, eh?'

'I beg your pardon?' Duncan reddened removing his hands swiftly.

'I could have you for sexual abuse and harassment!' She said very loudly, aware that one of the policemen was now in earshot.

Paula and Tony both helped guide Christina, who was very distraught, back into the wine bar. Roger and Eric, who didn't want to get involved in the argument, joined them inside.

'Jennie…' Duncan, aware of the approaching policeman, went into solicitor mode. 'The fact that you tried to kill Christina, first with a knife, and then set about trying to strangle her, doesn't help you in your defence. Especially as there are quite a few witnesses to corroborate that. Don't make things worse for yourself.'

'Everything alright, Madam…?' The policeman now stood before them.

'No, it bloody isn't!' She turned to Duncan, who gave her a stern, authoritative look. She hesitated before blurting out, 'Go inside and arrest that conniving bitch!'

'And why would I want to do that, Madam?' The policeman gazed at her suspiciously.

'She conned us, pretending to be a clown! We went to her funeral. She was supposed to be dead, but isn't! That car should've knocked her down, not the other clown!' Jennie had started to babble.

'Are you saying, Madam, that I should arrest a female dressed as a clown who should be dead? Is that right?'

The policeman had heard people give many reasons why someone should be arrested, but this looked like a first in his books. Something to regale his colleagues back at the station, he thought.

'She lied... she cheated... and then she disappeared! And then...coming back like that, fully alive! She should be locked up, and...and...' Jennie was now totally tongue-tied.

'And the key thrown away, Madam? Is that what you're trying to say?' The policeman was starting to enjoy this little exchange. It was a break from the norm.

'I can see I'm wasting my time here!' Jennie had lost the will to argue further. 'You wait, you'll be sorry you didn't listen to me. That woman in there is a menace to society, you mark my words!'

'They are fully marked, Madam. Anything else...?

Duncan looked at her with a sarcastic leer. 'Was that it, Jennie? Nothing more to say to this policeman?'

Realising she didn't have a leg to stand on, she just grunted and strode briskly away down the street.

'Poor thing, she's taken it rather badly. I mean seeing that unfortunate man lying in the street after being hit...' Duncan watched her disappear round a corner.

The policeman scrutinized her departure. 'Might she need counselling, sir?'

'Yes, I suppose accidents do affect people in many different ways.'

'Not that kind of counselling, sir. She sounds like a very disturbed woman.'

'I believe the menopause can affect women in many different ways.' Duncan quickly thought of his own wife who often behaved irrationally.

'Ah...yes...' the policeman acknowledged, having had to attend many domestic fights and arguments of middle-aged couples. 'Hormones have got a lot to answer for. Wish we could arrest some of them! Would make our job much easier.' He chuckled before returning to the police car.

In the wine bar, Roger, Eric and Tony sat round a table drinking coffee like a trio of displaced persons. Paula was in another corner wiping some of the makeup off of Christina's face, and doing her best to calm her. Duncan, who had finished paying off the two other clowns, came merrily over to the trio's table. 'Come on now, no reason to look so glum!'

'How can you be so cheerful?' Eric gave him a funny look.

'Especially after what happened to that poor clown.' Tony added.

'You mean Peter?' Duncan smiled. 'It was so lucky he was knocked over by that car.'

'Lucky…?' Roger and the other two looked up in disbelief.

'The Lord works in mysterious ways, his wonders to perform.' Paula now joined them.

'And you…you a priest of all people. You pronounced him dead!' Roger pointed a finger at her.

'I made a mistake, and I'm glad I did. I couldn't find a pulse. The paramedics told me I didn't check in the right place…Silly me…'

Eric was slightly confused. 'But you gave him the last rites?'

'Better to be safe than sorry.' Paula smiled, 'Besides, Peter is going to make a full recovery.'

'No serious injuries or broken bones; just a cut on the head and mild concussion.' Duncan added.

Roger despaired. 'And that's meant to sound

reassuring? If he hadn't been forced to dress up as a ridiculous clown, to satisfy the whim of a crazy woman,' He glanced over at Christina, who was now listening to them. 'He might not have had the accident in the first place!'

She strode over to the group. 'Peter was well paid for his services, as were the others.'

'I hope he has the sense to sue you when he gets out of hospital.' Eric sniffed.

'I didn't knock him down!' Christina objected.

Duncan held up his hand in a gesture of peace. 'It's not Christina's fault. I hired Peter, who happens to be one of my clients. He needed the money.'

'What, to help pay your bills? You're as warped as she is!' Roger pointed to Christina.

'Now hold on a minute!' Christina raised her voice. 'You're missing the whole point!'

'What point is that, Mum?' Tony now felt he needed some clarification.

'Let me explain.' Duncan nodded to Christina, who composed herself. 'A year ago, Peter unfortunately had a similar accident, when he was knocked down by a cyclist on the pavement…'

'Bloody cyclists!' Eric bleated. 'Should be banned from pavements, that's what cycle lanes are for!'

'Anyway…' Duncan continued, 'It caused him to hit his head on the ground, which resulted in him losing his memory. Total amnesia. He didn't recognise anyone; neither his family nor his friends…until today…'

'Are you saying that this accident restored his memory…?' Roger queried.

'Praise the Lord!' Paula whispered.

'When he eventually came to after the paramedics arrived, he suddenly remembered everything.'

Paula smiled. 'A most moving moment which gave

---

me great comfort.'

Christina gave them all a meaningful look. 'Which just goes to prove that you should never reach any conclusions, or make a judgement, until you know the full story.'

Roger wasn't buying it. 'It proves absolutely nothing! I've had enough. Thank you for paying back what was owed, but I'm afraid it's goodbye Christina. I can't say it was nice seeing you again. Come on, Tony.' He got up.

'I'm staying.' Tony remained seated.

'Why? Never forget that it was your mother who abandoned us.'

'Roger, that's not fair.' Christina pleaded.

'Not fair!' He looked aghast. 'So where have you been for the last three years? Not one letter, not one phone call. I tried your mobile, but the number was no longer recognised. I even contacted the Missing Persons Bureau and added your name to their lists. To all accounts you might as well have been dead.'

'Do you really wish I had been then? Would you rather I'd never returned?' Her face crumpled.

'Might have made things easier, instead of this shamble of a charade. Have a nice rest of your life.' Roger turned and spoke to Tony, before walking out of the wine bar. 'I'll hopefully see you later.'

'Uncle Eric...?'

'I'll try and have a word with him. Tony, you know how stubborn he can get, if he feels he's been taken advantage of.'

He now turned to Christina. 'I'm sorry to say this, but you really have been very cruel in the way you treated us. A few expensive presents are not going to make us forget what happened. Three years and no word! I can't deal with this now; I need time to think it through...' He walked out of the wine bar without turning back.

'But there isn't time!' Christina howled, before running tearfully out the back to the toilets.

Paula was all set to follow her, but Duncan held her back. 'Give her a few moments…'

'What an awful fucking mess!' Tony blurted out, and then saw the amused look on Paula's face. 'Sorry. Didn't mean to swear.'

'Of course you did, and don't mind me. The word 'fuck' is often the most appropriate word to use in certain situations. I use it quite often – not during services I must add!'

'Like now?'

'Especially now.' Paula smiled. 'You're right, Tony, it is a bit of a fucking mess. But so is life in general, and we need to try and do our best to sort it out. Why don't you go and see how your mother is. She might listen to you.'

'But what do I say?'

'You'll think of something.'

In the toilet Christina was standing in front of the mirror wiping off remnants of the clown makeup as well as some tears. She stopped to look at her sad reflection with an expression of gloomy resignation. *Happy birthday, Christina! You've only yourself to blame. Who were you trying to kid? You should have known it might not have turned out how you wished…* She closed her eyes for a moment, to try and blot out the reality.

A knock at the door brought her harshly back. 'It's not locked.'

The door opened to reveal Tony, who looked like a little boy who was afraid to ask if he could go out to play. 'And how long have you been in the custom of using ladies' lavatories, young man?' Christina did her best to force a smile.

'Mum, are you alright?'

'I was actually thinking of putting my head down the pan – but you can never tell who's been before you…'

'I'm serious.'

'So am I. Has everyone lost their sense of humour? All this was supposed to be a bit of fun. To lighten the mood. To break the truth in gently.'

'Couldn't you have just come back and simply explained?'

'But would I have been made welcome?' Tony remained silent. 'Precisely, Tony. A no-win situation. Still, at least I tried…and made some financial amends. But that obviously wasn't enough. I hadn't planned to reveal myself today. I just wanted to see you all again, pay back what I owed and go away to die properly, so that you would've been none the wiser.'

'Then why did you?'

'When you all started to think better of me, even saying words of forgiveness, and that I deserved a second chance if it were possible - I couldn't hold back any longer. I now wish I'd stayed silent.'

'I'm glad you didn't.' Tony touched her hand.

'Do you mean that…?' She wasn't convinced.

'Of course I do! Believe me.'

'Difficult to know what to believe. But thank you.' She clasped his hand.

'Mum, what are you going to do now?'

'First, I'm going to get out of this costume, then I going to put on some proper make up. And then…I'm not sure…' Tony just stood there, not knowing what to say. 'Unless you want to watch your mother strip off, I suggest you go back and have another cup of coffee. Unless you want to leave now and join your father?'

'I'll wait. I don't want you to disappear again.' He closed the door and returned to the bar where he poured himself the dregs of the coffee that was left, and sat on his own in the corner checking his phone.

Paula, sitting with Duncan at the other end, both enjoying a glass of wine, looked down at her evening dress. 'You know, I shall be sorry to return this.'

Duncan, who was surreptitiously admiring her cleavage, hummed. 'You do look rather splendid in it.'

'Nice of you to say so. However, I'm not going to miss the high heels, I can feel it in my back, which is starting to ache a bit.'

'The perils of fashion... Paula, is Christina going to be okay? I'm not sure I know what to suggest, since things haven't quite worked to plan. Christina seemed adamant that she would only be an observer.'

'I'm glad she came out, so to speak. How can any of us predict how someone is going to react to any given situation? That's the chance you've got to take. I did, and I'm sure you did too, warn her that it might prove difficult.'

'I did, but you know how determined Christina can be if she wants something. She won't listen if she's already made up her mind.' Duncan was about to say more, when out of the corner of his eye he spotted Christina returning from the toilet. 'Ssh…here she comes.'

Dressed smartly and casually, her hair combed and face made up, she went over to where Tony was sitting, putting on a brave face. 'Bit more like your old mum?'

'You scrub up well.' He made to stand.

'Don't get up. I need to have a word with Paula and Duncan first.' She touched him affectionately on the arm before crossing over to their table. 'I must thank you both for everything you've done.'

'I'm sorry it didn't quite turn out as you hoped.'

Duncan put on his sad news expression. 'But I did – '

'Warn me? Yes, you both did. But you also encouraged me to partake in this charade. Even so, I suppose I have to take full responsibility for my actions.'

'But you know,' Paula smiled, 'I've rather enjoyed today. All the dressing up. It's been fun.'

'Nobody else thought so. More tragedy than comedy...'

'What now?' Duncan studied her.

'I don't know,' Christina sighed, 'Join a circus? I've had some practise.'

'You can't give up now.' Paula leant forward.

'The others will never forgive me now. Whatever I try to do...'

Paula did her best to sound positive. 'They've all had a little shock. It might take a bit of time to sink in.'

'Which you know I don't have...'

'Look, everyone had rather a lot to drink.' Duncan tried to reassure her. 'No one was thinking sensibly. It's been a long day.'

'But a day Peter will always remember!' Paula stressed.

'A bit of good came out of today, at least. I can now die having accomplished something!' The reminder made Christina pause for a moment. 'I'm sorry, I need to get out of this place.'

'Understood. Not quite the birthday bumps that you expected. I'll send you my prayers.'

Christina smirked. 'Send me a man instead. I could do with one right now. Nothing like a good...four letter word...fill in the blanks...sorry.'

Paula emphasised. 'I think I know how you feel. Sometimes I wish...' She stopped herself and gazed heavenwards. 'My turn to say sorry.'

'Don't apologise.'

Paula suddenly felt glum. 'I wish it were that easy…'

'You must never stifle your physical needs. Food, drink, sex. No point in living otherwise…I've had the food and the drink…now I must…go.' Christina started for the front door.

'Where are you going, Mum?' Tony had been quietly listening.

'I need to…think.'

'Can I come with you? Please.'

Christina nodded. 'Duncan, I'll be in touch. Still a few loose ends to tie up.'

'Of course. You know where to find me. By the way the cars and drivers are still at your disposal, to take you wherever…'

'Thank you.' As Christina and Tony got to the door, she turned to Paula. 'I'll pop in to see you later. Remember, Paula, religion should not stop you enjoying yourself. If there is a God, he – or she – doesn't have the right to deny you your true feelings and needs.' At which point they exited.

Paula quoted to herself. 'God is faithful, and he will not let you be tempted beyond your ability, but with the temptation he will also provide the way of escape, that you may be able to endure it… I think I need that escape right now. Duncan, can I tempt you…I noticed you admiring my front?

Duncan looked at her horrified. 'What do you mean?'

'Only teasing! Shall we finish this bottle, shame to waste it…' Paula topped up both their glasses, and now knew exactly how Christina felt.

9. Jumping into the Fast Lane

The two driver clowns were standing by the cars, as Christina and Tony came out of the wine bar. They almost stood to attention when they saw them approaching. 'Mrs Turner...' One of them stepped forward.

'It's Simon, isn't it?' Christina looked closely.

'I'm Jack, that's Simon over there.' He pointed to the other clown who waved.

'Yes, difficult to tell you apart. But then that was the whole point wasn't it! Anyway, thank you for your patience and for entering into the spirit of it all – for which, of course you have been more than adequately rewarded.'

'We've enjoyed it. So, where can I take you now?' He opened one of the car doors.

'You can go home now, Jack. Give me the keys, I'll return the car to the depot later. ...' She called to the other clown, 'Simon, you wait to take Paula and Duncan back.' Christina then held out her hand for the keys to take from the first clown.

'But, Mrs Turner...' The clown looked anxious. He didn't relish trying to get home dressed as he was.

'No buts, Jack. Your responsibility finishes here. You can travel back with Simon if you want to wait. Tomorrow you and he can return the costumes to Duncan. That's quite straightforward, isn't it?'

'Thank you. It's been a pleasure.' He handed her the keys and then went over to join the other clown.

'The pleasure wasn't all mine.' She mumbled as she opened the door to get into the driving seat.

Tony stood indecisively by the car. 'Mum...?'

'Do you want to come with me or not?' She started the engine.

'But you've been drinking.'

'That's where you're wrong. We clowns only had soft drinks. Anyway, I needed to keep sober. That satisfy you?'

'Where are you going?'

'Not sure yet, but I'll know when I get there! So, either get in, or go home.' She uttered impatiently.

The limousine toured slowly around the suburban side streets, well under the speed limit. 'I've always wanted to drive one of these!' She clutched the steering wheel tenderly. 'Purrs like a kitten but with the heart of a tiger…'

A Fiat behind her, which was desperately trying to overtake but couldn't, tooted its horn impatiently. Christina took no notice and purposefully slowed down even more.

'Mum, why are we going so slow?'

'I object being hooted at. He can wait…' She continued at a slow cruise. 'You get a nice perspective this way.'

When she entered a roundabout, the irritated Fiat driver, who continually tooted, now sped in front, cutting her up. As he passed her, he wound down his window and shouted, 'Learn to drive properly, you silly old cow!'

'That's not very nice…I don't mind being called a silly cow…' Christina pressed on the accelerator and started to follow him.

'Mum, to be fair, you were driving at half the speed limit.'

'That's not the point, Tony. As well as cutting me up, which is dangerous, he called me old! I really object to that.' She continued pursuing the Fiat, which now had exceeded the speed limit.

After about another mile, the Fiat took a turning to join a motorway.

——

Christina followed swiftly behind. 'Mum, what are you doing?'

'This is exciting. Just a little detour. Let's see how fast that little prick in front can go in his little tin can!' Christina gripped the steering wheel with a steely grin, and put her foot forcefully on the accelerator.

The Fiat driver, unaware that he was being followed, sped up the fast lane at over 80, tooting and flashing other drivers to get out of the way. 'He is a nasty little man. I don't feel so bad now.' Christina finally got behind him and gave chase, tooting her horn and flashing her lights to get him to move across to the other lane. He seemed determined not to let her overtake, and took the Fiat up to 90. Christina calmly followed his tail, flashing continually.

'Mum, please don't kill us! It's not worth it.'

'Don't worry; I know what I'm doing. I'm fully in control. Before I met your father, I went out with a racing driver. He taught me a few tricks.' She was now almost right behind the Fiat, which was finding it difficult to go over 90. It just didn't have the power. Christina now almost touched the Fiat's bumper, which finally made it give way. Christina waved to the man as she passed him, just as the speedometer reached 100. 'Yes! A ton, I've always wanted to do that!' She screeched excitedly.

'Mum, you've proved your point. Can we slow down now, before the police come chasing after us.'

'Ooh, that was exhilarating! Just what I needed.' She indicated to the nearside lane and gradually slowed down to a gentle 65. She then took the next turning off the motorway and down a dual carriageway at a steady 50 for the next few miles.

'Do you know where you're going?'

'Not really. Just want to try and clear my head before reality clicks in. Let's just enjoy the ride.'

She started to slow down when she noticed a tall crane in the distance, with what looked like a tiny figure standing on top in a sort of cage. 'Look, Tony!' The figure then suddenly leapt off into the air, a rope attached to its feet.

'What was that!' Tony looked back as they passed. He turned round when he saw that she was turning off on to a small road. At the entrance to a field where there were a lot of parked cars, a bright sign advertised *"Today only! Bungee Jumps. £60 a go."* 'Mum, you cannot be serious! I'm not going up there!'

'No, but I am.' Christina drove in and parked.

Christina was at the very top of the crane. She'd been forced to sign an indemnity form to say she had no medical issues, like heart or back problems. After which she was given a quick debriefing about the jumping process and how best to do it. Once she was weighed, a body harness was fitted, followed by the bungee cord, which was attached to her ankles. The view was spectacular. She glanced down to see a small crowd, including Tony, looking up. She didn't in any way feel scared or apprehensive. Quite the opposite, she felt energised and confident. 'Ready to go, Miss?' The crew member was satisfied with his final checks.

'How high are we?'

'160 feet.'

'Killed many customers lately?' She joked.

'Not today, but you could be the first.' He smiled.

'Might be a blessing in disguise. Speed up my departure. How many times have you done it yourself?'

He looked at her with an expression almost of horror. 'You wouldn't get me jumping off here! No thank you…so, are we good to go?'

'Oh yes…!' She took a deep breath, poised herself on

---

the edge and then dived off.

As she plunged down, she gave out an orgasmic scream of total joy. 'Yes! Yes! Yes!' as her face got within a few feet of the ground, and then rebounded up again.

Tony had closed his eyes as she leapt, and now opened them to see her bouncing up and down with a great big smile on her face, until one of the ground crew caught her and gently lowered her down.

'As you young people tend to say – that was wicked, sick and awesome! A real OMG experience. The day is beginning to end on a better note.' Christina and Tony were back in the car driving down suburban streets. She was feeling so invigorated, almost hyper. 'Another one to cross off my bucket list.' She gabbled.

'What list…?' Tony hadn't heard her properly.

'Bucket list, you've surely heard of that? Things to do before you die!'

'Yes, I know what it is; I've seen the film. I thought you said something else.'

'What?' Tony seemed reticent in vocalising it. 'Come on, Tony, what did you think I said?'

'Fuck it list…' He almost whispered.

Christina laughed loudly. 'Much the same thing, I suppose. I know I'm not going to do most things on my imaginary list – so one might as well say fuck it!'

'Mum, are you really going to die? Or is another lie?'

'It's not, and I am. No more lies, Tony, I promise.'

'But you look great. It's hard to believe it.'

'I feel great. I'm not in pain or anything, maybe a bit tired sometimes. I even find it hard to believe.'

'What is it you've got…and how long…?' Tony was finding this difficult.

—

'Cancer…pancreatic. A couple of months, maybe more, maybe less. It'll probably hit me with a vengeance one day and then that'll be it.'

'You're very easy about it.'

'It might sound like that, but I'm really bloody angry! But there's nothing I can do, and because it's terminal the doctors can't help any more. I have to accept it.' Christina's upbeat mood after the bungee jump had now darkened. 'I'd be grateful if we stopped discussing it, and enjoy whatever time we've got left together. Okay?'

'Okay…'

'Ah, here we are. Home sweet home.' The car pulled up by a small block of 1960's flats. 'Not much to look at, but I won't be here long.'

The one bedroomed flat was small and simply furnished, but with an air of despondency surrounding it. Tony studied the mantelpiece, which displayed various framed photos of him, Roger, Eric and Jennie in happier times. He looked around and felt quite sad that his mother had ended up in a place like this.

'My very own hospice. I'm not going to be taken to one, or a hospital when my time comes. I shall die here…'

'You've actually bought this place?'

'Rented it for six months. I know, it's not my style and quite stark but it serves a purpose, and its near everyone who matters to me.'

'But who's going to look after you when…when you can't…?' Tony found it difficult to say the words.

'Look after myself? Don't worry, I wouldn't burden you. I will pay for a Macmillan nurse to see me through. It's all in place. I am quite practical and organised you know. Right, would you like some tea or coffee – or a drink?'

'Coffee please…' Tony watched her as she exited

into the little galley kitchen. He looked once more at the photographs, trying to remember when they were taken.

10. A Flash in the Park

Several miles away at Roger's house, he and Eric sat having coffee; both were in a very pensive, hung-over mood. Suddenly Roger got up and punched the cushion on the armchair with pent up anger. 'Why did she have to come back!'

'Pay her last respects?' Eric looked tired and red-eyed.

'You mean screw us up even more. You know, I reached a point when I'd almost forgotten about her.' He sat down again.

'I could never forget her…'

'And now she crashes back into our lives as if nothing had ever happened.'

'She's dying, Roger…She wanted to spend her last days with her family.'

'And determined to torture us to the very end!'

'She's only asking to be forgiven. Look at the presents she's given us. I can't wait to get home to see my new car.'

'Presents! We're only getting back what she stole or conned from us in the first place.'

Eric slowly took this in. 'That's a point…'

'And where's Tony? He's always been a bit soft about her; despite the way she treated him. I bet she's brainwashing him now. Seducing him…'

Eric looked up shocked. 'Her own son…?'

'I didn't mean that literally. Mind you, nothing that darling Christina does surprises me anymore.'

'Not with Tony, surely!' Eric was outraged.

'You know I don't mean that. Eric, you can be really stupid sometimes.'

Eric shrugged indifferently. 'What you don't know can't harm you.'

Roger gave him a dismayed look, and decided not to pursue this line of conversation. 'I'm going to check that money again…I still can't believe it's all there and real.'

'I expect your father will be wondering where you are.' Christina and Tony were cradling their cups of coffee. 'Probably thinks I'm corrupting you!'

'And are you?' He looked at her.

'I don't want to try and turn you against him – as he, I'm sure, did his best to turn you against me.' She took a sip. 'He did, didn't he?'

Tony let out a sigh. 'He tried.'

'And…?'

'I'm here, aren't I.'?

She emptied her glass. 'You can go whenever you want.'

'I know…what really happened, Mum? Why did you leave us?'

'It seems another lifetime away…' She was about to refill her glass, but thought better of it. 'It wasn't a good period in my life. Your dad and I were divorced, I was living with Eric, the business was having problems…Things got on top of me. I couldn't cope…I just had to go…'

'You didn't even say goodbye!'

'I couldn't! Remember, you locked yourself in your bedroom and then turned on your music full blast.'

Tony was trying to remember. 'Did I?'

'I'd specially come to see you. Your father was at work. It was after you slammed the door in my face, first having called me an interfering cow.'

'I don't remember. Are you sure?'

—

87

'It's not something a mother would forget – considering it was the last time I saw you.'

'But why…?' Tony was completely mystified; he had no recollection of the event.

'Give me your right hand. Don't argue.' He hesitantly held out his hand. She then undid his shirtsleeve to uncover a tattoo of an evil looking skull and crossbones. 'Could you blame any mother seeing her son disfigure himself. You were only fourteen. I might have understood if you had a tattoo of a heart with 'Mum' engraved in the middle…but that monstrosity!'

Tony now remembered the incident and looked embarrassed. 'It was only a tattoo. Dad didn't mind.'

'Your father had other things to worry about at the time.'

Tony unconsciously rubbed his tattoo arm. 'If it's any consolation, I've since regretted doing it. I'm thinking of having it removed.'

'It doesn't matter now.' She got up and took his coffee cup and started for the kitchen.

'Mum, you didn't leave because of me, because of this tattoo? I realise I wasn't the best of sons.'

'No, I didn't. But you were a right little sod at times; you really gave me the run-around. But at the same time, I was a terrible mother. But that's all in the past. It's gone. Let's try and make up for it now. Look, I'm feeling a bit hemmed in. I need some fresh air. Fancy a walk?'

Roger was carefully going through each individual banknote, checking them with a kind of pen.

'What's that? What are you doing?' Eric looked puzzled.

'A counterfeit note detector pen, which can uncover

fakes. I always carry one with me, ever since someone passed on some counterfeit twenty-pound notes, which presented me with a bit of trouble with the bank, when I tried to put them in my account.'

'You've never been very trusting, even when we were kids.'

'It's the world we live in, Eric. You can never be too careful.'

'And if you expect the worst, that's what you will get. An old girlfriend told me that.'

'Philosopher was she…?' Roger had finished checking the money. 'It pains me to say it, but it's all real and all there plus the interest. Eleven thousand pounds.'

'Would you've been happier if they had turned out to be fake?'

'No, of course not, but I find it hard to believe anything Christina says or does.'

'People can change you know. So, do you believe everything that Helen says then?'

Roger stiffened. 'Helen isn't Christina.'

'She's obviously got her claws into you.' Eric knew he had struck a nerve.

Roger went on the defensive. 'She can cook and she's good in bed, and we understand each other. Helen and I have the perfect arrangement. She has her space and I have mine. That's why we don't live together.'

'Well, I'm glad you're happy, big brother.'

'What's that supposed to mean?' Roger was still on the defensive.

'Whatever you want it to. Well, I think I'll be off. It's been a long day, and I'm feeling a bit lumpy after all that delicious food. I feel it when I haven't done my workout at the gym.'

He took out his new car keys and rattled them in

front of Roger. 'I shall drive my new car to the gym later.'

'If it's there.' Roger couldn't resist the jibe.

Eric looked confused. 'Why should the gym have moved?'

'I was talking about…oh never mind. You go and enjoy your new little toy.'

Eric looked doubtful, trying to work out what Roger meant. He accepted that he wasn't as bright as his brother, but still hated it when he couldn't understand some of Roger's ambiguous statements.

Christina and Tony had walked silently to the local park. He sensed she wanted to be alone with her thoughts, so didn't say anything. They eventually went and sat on a bench, and quietly watched the early evening traffic passing by. Walkers with dogs; mothers with toddlers; skateboarders; winos huddled drinking in bushy corners. There was one particular woman in a raincoat, about Christina's age, who wandered up and down the path in her own little world, looking lost and alone.

'I was like her…' Christina pointed to the woman. 'I now realise I was having something like a nervous breakdown when I walked out of all your lives. I remember just stepping out of the front gate, getting into the car and just driving…'

'Where did you end up then?'

'It's a long story, that I don't feel ready to go into now…but I was looked after…' Christina watched the woman wandering aimlessly back and forth. 'That's what that woman needs, poor thing, someone to look after her…'

The woman abruptly stopped moving, and stood in the middle of the path as if in a dream. A man, obviously on his way home from work, came down the path towards her.

Just as he got within a few feet of her – the woman opened her raincoat and flashed him. Clearly shocked, he hurriedly passed her looking down on the ground. The woman laughed and turned, giving another flash. Christina and Tony could now see that she was completely naked beneath her coat.

'You were saying, mum?' Tony smiled having enjoyed the view.

Christina rose from the bench and watched as the woman strode blithely out of the park. 'That could be called naked ambition. Maybe she's found her own way and is perfectly happy…?' She started walking away.

Tony caught her up. 'Mum…?'

'No more questions please. The day has suddenly caught up with me. It's not often one gets a chance to attend one's own funeral. Dying's a tiring business. My final job of the day is to return the car, and then I'll get an unhealthy takeaway, a large drink and settle in for the night. A lot to think about, since the day hasn't quite turned out as I hoped. You going home now?'

Tony didn't really want to go, but he could sense she now wanted to be on her own. 'Can we talk tomorrow?'

'You know where to find me.' She went to hug him, but he moved awkwardly sideways and just let her give him a peck on the cheek. 'Your father never liked hugging…'

'Anyway, thanks for the MacBook.'

'What you've just witnessed with that woman is probably quite tame to what you see on the internet. Watch a lot of porn, do you?'

'Mum…' Tony tried to appear shocked, but wasn't convincing.

'Sometimes what you see is what you don't get. We live in an age of false illusions. Mind you, I can't talk with what I subjected you and the others to today. See you soon.'

Tony stopped her. 'I hope you don't think I behaved like a coward because I didn't want to do the bungee jump?'

Christina smiled, but didn't say anything as she wandered off. As he got out of earshot she couldn't help mumbling *'Like father, like son...'*

Tony walked out of the park and noticed the woman in the raincoat leaning against a railing smoking a cigarette. Although he would be heading in wrong direction, he felt compelled to pass her in the hope that she would give him a generous flash. He strode very slowly and gauchely, giving her a nervous smile as he passed. After taking a puff, she looked up at him. 'Sorry, sonny. I don't flash for juveniles.'

'Bugger!' Tony silently cursed. What made it worse, as he turned back for a final look, was to see her open her raincoat to another man who passed, but who was too busy checking his phone to take any notice of her.

11. Time for an Intimate Workout

After stomping off from the wine bar, Jennie had gone home and thought about drowning her sorrows further, but instead flopped on the bed fully clothed and fell asleep. Waking a couple of hours later, and feeling better, she made herself several cups of strong coffee to sober up.

While rummaging around in her handbag for a tissue, she saw the set of keys and envelope that Christina had given her. She opened the envelope, which contained the papers and the address. The office was only a five-minute car drive away. She had a thought. As it was still late afternoon and would be light for several more hours, she felt a curious compulsion to see these premises – if they did indeed exist. Like the others she didn't fully trust Christina or believe this was genuine.

She unlocked her car and got in. Just as she was about to drive off, she noticed a police car up the road, questioning some kids. It prompted her to stop and reverse back into her drive. Even though she felt capable, she realised she'd had a lot to drink and couldn't afford to lose her license if she got stopped. She reckoned it would only take her twenty minutes to walk to this place. The exercise would do her good and help clear her head.

On a small industrial plot, the seventies office block consisting of two floors looked very presentable from the outside. Jennie found the front entrance and was pleasantly surprised to see her name – JENNIE HANKIN LTD – on a sign on the wall among three others. She took out her set of keys and tried to open the front door of the block.

Of the four keys on the heavy silver key chain, three

didn't fit. 'This is a joke, isn't it! You have to have the last laugh don't you, Christina!' She now fully expected the last key not to fit, but it turned easily in the lock and the door opened.

The building inside was fully carpeted, beautifully decorated with tasteful pictures on the walls. Jennie was still not convinced that it was all real, until she saw her name on one of doors on the first floor. The first key opened it to reveal a fully furnished office suite with a couple of computers, printers, telephones and other equipment. All ready for her to move in and start.

Jennie stood quietly taking it all in. 'Is this real, Christina Turner? There must be a catch somewhere…'

Christina sat in her flat listening to Classical FM and cradling a cup of coffee. She looked tired but absorbed in the music. The piece finished and an announcer came on: "That was Sibelius's Symphony No 1, conducted by Dansak Primero. He will be coming to London for a series of concerts next year. Make sure you reserve your tickets now…"

She got up and switched the radio off. 'Only I won't be here to enjoy it…' She picked up a magazine and angrily threw it on the floor in frustration. Looking upwards she muttered, 'Have I really been so bad to deserve this?' She paused and then straightened herself up. 'Get a grip on yourself, Christina. If there is anyone up there, do you just want me to give up…to die quietly…?' She gazed down at the magazine, which had opened at a page advertising gym equipment. A couple of beefy men with half naked oily bodies posed in the ad. She bent down, picked the magazine up and looked at it. 'You know when to hit someone when they're down…'

She glanced up at the mantelpiece and focused on

the photo of her with Eric. He was flexing his muscles while she looked on derisively. She took a deep breath and gathered herself. 'Well, I'm not going to sit here and rot!'

Not far away a taxi pulled up at a smart block of flats in a leafy suburb. Eric paid the driver and got out. He stood and looked around at the cars parked in front of the building. He was immediately disappointed. The space reserved for his car was empty. Just the familiar residents' cars in their designated bays. He sighed and stamped his foot on the ground in frustration. 'Bloody Christina!' He headed crossly towards the front entrance just as one of his neighbours was coming out.

'Hi Eric, I haven't forgotten about returning that box set you lent me. Just a couple more episodes to see. It's really great!'

'Fine, whenever...' Eric wasn't in the mood to chat.

'You okay?'

'Just one of those days. You know how it is.'

'Your car still being fixed?'

'In the garage for a few more days. On its last legs. See you later.'

'Oh, by the way...' the neighbour turned back just as Eric was about to close the front door. 'Looks like our friend Julia's got one of her rich boyfriends visiting. Another expensive flash car parked out the back. Got a personalised number plate that you would've liked. Anyway, hope the rest of the day gets better.' The neighbour got in his car and drove off.

Eric stood by the open door thinking. Julia lived in the flat above him. He'd briefly had a short fling with her some time ago, but it hadn't worked out.

Mainly because he didn't have the money to take her

out to the kind of fancy restaurants she liked, which he didn't care for anyway. She also hated going out in his car, which she considered inferior, a fact he couldn't argue with. But they managed to remain friends. Since then she'd had a series of relationships with men who obviously had money, judging by the kind of expensive cars that were parked when they came to visit her. Most had personalised number plates.

He hadn't considered going round the back, where there were a couple of parking spaces, reserved mainly for visitors. His curiosity, about what the neighbour had said about the licence plate got the better of him, and he wandered round to the rear of the building. There, standing like a shiny new coin, was a blue Volkswagen Golf Sport. He couldn't see the number plate from where he stood, and was hesitant about getting closer. Might this be the one meant for him, he wondered? He couldn't bear the disappointment if it did turn out to belong to one of Julia's men friends, which was more than likely.

He stood frozen for a moment. Tensely he gripped the car key fob in his pocket. Suddenly the indicator lights flashed on the Golf, and he heard the click of unlocking doors. Eric strode slowly to the car, his excitement building, and glanced down at the number plate – ET 1976. He tried the door and it opened. In the glove compartment he found a folder of papers with his name on it. This was the car Christina had promised him. She hadn't lied. He walked around the car to inspect it for any dents or scratches. It was in perfect condition. He couldn't help but give a whoop of joy. A moment later a bird flew overhead and splattered the bonnet with wet, white droppings. His face darkening, Eric quickly took out a hanky and wiped the mess off, and then buffed up the section with his sleeve until it was perfect.

He looked up to make sure no other birds were nearby. His gaze strayed to his bedroom window on the second floor, where he saw a face staring down and waving at him. He squinted to get a clearer look. It was Christina. What was she doing up there in his flat? How did she get in? But he was mainly annoyed because he was about to take his new car for its first spin. He felt capable to be able to drive and would've taken a chance on not being stopped. He locked the car and glumly made his way into the building.

Christina was sitting on the sofa in the living room when he entered. 'You've had it redecorated. It's not too bad, but the colour of the wallpaper clashes with the sofa.'

'How did you get in here? Learn breaking and entering when you were away?' Eric was none too pleased with this unexpected visit.

Christina held up a set of keys. 'Funny, isn't it? I still had them after all these years.'

'You've no right -!'

'Do you like the new car?' She quickly interjected before he could finish.

'What…? Oh, yes, yes, it's great. Thank you.'

'I chose the colour specially because I know it's your favourite.'

'Look Christina, I appreciate the car, but you shouldn't have let yourself in without telling me. This is my flat and it's private.'

'It used to be our flat, and we never kept any secrets from each other.'

'I never – but you did.' He remembered how secretive she was about aspects of her work or where she went sometimes.

She ignored his comment. 'I haven't been here long. And rest assured I didn't pry into any cupboards or drawers.'

'I should bloody well hope not!' He held out his hand. 'The keys please.'

She threw him the keys, which he caught. 'There's no

need to get angry! I thought you might be pleased. Alright, I made a mistake. I shouldn't have let myself in. I'm sorry…'

He put the keys in his pocket. 'You know, I think that's the first time I've ever heard you say that you're sorry.'

'Isn't there a first time for everything? By the way, I like the new mirror in the bedroom. Maybe a bit tacky, but you can watch yourself sleep.'

'You went into my bedroom…' He looked despairingly.

'I was looking out for you, from the window. You saw me.'

'Christina what are you doing here? What is it you want?'

'Do I have to want anything?'

'You usually do.'

'That's not fair…' Her eyes slowly welled up. 'I was feeling a bit lonely. I was suddenly reminded that I haven't got much time left. I was depressed because today had turned out to be a bit of a disaster. I'd hoped that you might've forgiven me a little, but realised that you all still hated me…' She was doing her best to control the tears.

'I don't hate you as such. I just feel sorry for you.'

'I don't want your pity, Eric. I just want us to part friends, that's all.'

'Why, where are you going?' He was confused.

'Hell, purgatory or just oblivion.'

He looked mystified. 'I don't understand?'

Christina sighed. 'Oh Eric, dear Eric, the years haven't made you wiser. I'm going to die soon and I want us to be on friendly terms before I do…Do you get it now?'

'Ah, yes, of course. I'm really not with it today. The funeral; the lunch; you coming back to life; the new car…But I think it's mainly because I haven't been to the gym today. I'm always ratty if I haven't done my work out.'

——

Christina stood up. 'Look, I'll leave now. You go to the gym, try out your new car. I'm sorry if I've complicated things. Bye Eric, perhaps we can meet up for a coffee soon.' She gave him a peck on the cheek.

'Fancy a coffee now? I can switch the kettle on.' Eric, now feeling a touch guilty, gave her an encouraging look. 'What d'you fancy, Colombian or Costa Rican blend?'

'I honestly don't mind. Your tastes have developed, I'm impressed. You used to be an instant coffee man. How did that conversion happen?

'One of my neighbours across the way, Julia, used to invite me in for a coffee. I got a taste for it.' He exited to the kitchen.

'Get a taste for anything else…?' She smiled and settled back into the sofa.

12. Make Sex Not Love

Roger was in the sitting room reading the paper when he heard the front door slam. 'Tony, is that you?'

'No, it's Helen of Troy!' He shouted as he ran up the stairs and into his bedroom, closing the door.

Roger took a deep, calming breath, as he put down his paper and got up from his chair. As he slowly walked up the stairs, he could hear loud, discordant rap-type music coming from inside Tony's bedroom. Roger walked gently into the room and switched off Tony's sound system.

'I must be going deaf. I didn't hear you knock.' Tony was sprawled out on his bed fiddling about with his new laptop.

'If you listen to that much longer you will go deaf.'

'So, have you come up to discuss musical tastes? What shall we talk about – Art Punk, College Rock, Acid Jazz, Neurofunk with a bit of Grunge?'

Roger sat at the end of Tony's bed. 'You know what we have to talk about.'

'If it's about Mum, I can see her whenever I want to. You can't stop me.'

'It's not, and I don't intend to. That's entirely your business. She's your mother. You're free to be enticed back into her manipulative clutches.'

'You don't let it go, do you, Dad? What is it you want to say?' Tony shifted uncomfortably preparing for another kind of lecture.

'Let me just say one thing.' Roger lowered his voice and spoke softly. 'I can't say I'm happy about your mother coming back into our lives. We did well enough without her. As long as she keeps well away from me and this house, there'll be no argument.'

'That's a bit hard…considering…'

'That's she going to die?'

'Have you no heart, Dad?'

'Your dear mother tore it away from me years ago.' Roger looked tired. The day had caught up with him. 'Now, tell me, what did you say when you came in?'

Tony looked puzzled. 'What do you mean?'

'About Helen of Troy.'

'Just a phrase, Dad. What's the big deal?'

'I know you've never liked Helen. That's your prerogative. But I will not have you making snide comments about her. Is that understood'

'Are you going to marry her? Is she coming to live with us?'

'No, Tony, I am not, and she is not. We've got a good relationship, and that's all there is to it.'

'You mean you go to her place to have sex!' Tony wanted to shock his father.

'That's right.' Roger couldn't help but give a wry smile. 'I certainly wouldn't invite her here for a session. You might catch us at it. Yet, having said that, you might also learn a few things.'

Tony now felt distinctly uncomfortable. 'What's that supposed to mean?'

'Do you really want me to spell it out?'

'Go on, you will anyway.'

'I've been meaning to ask this for some time. Well, you've never brought any girlfriends home.'

'Is that so surprising? It's bad enough when I ask a mate round. You question them like a Nazi.'

'I'm interested in people. What's so wrong with that?'

'The difference between interest and giving them the third degree. One of my friends won't come round if he knows you're here. That answer your question?'

'The question is - do you have any girlfriends? And if you happen to be gay, I won't find that a problem. I'm quite happy for you to bring your boyfriends here.'

Tony angrily got off the bed and stood defiant. 'I am not gay!' He almost shouted. 'How could you even think that?'

'So, do you have a girlfriend?'

Tony's face dropped. 'Does it matter?'

'I'm just asking. Since you commented on my sex life, I have every right to ask you about yours. You're old enough. So, is there someone special you're going out with?'

'Not special…not at the moment.' Tony was embarrassed now.

Roger stood up. 'Perhaps that's your problem.'

'What are you implying?'

Roger crossed over to the door. 'Work it out for yourself. But just think carefully before you make any judgements on other people, whether you like them or not.' Roger went out before Tony could reply. He turned on his music and flopped back on his bed, his confidence and self-esteem having been crushed. He hated to admit, even to himself, that his father was probably right.

Both Eric and Christina were lying in bed, looking up at their reflection on the ceiling mirror. Christina looked relaxed. 'It does give you a different perspective on things. Your bottom moves quite rhythmically. I see you've kept up with the waxing.'

'Back, sack and crack as always.'

'But that tattoo is horrible. What made you have a gorilla etched on your back?'

'Don't you like it? Didn't it turn you on?'

'Not particularly…nearly put me off if I'm honest.'

'Didn't you see it actually come to life? It's a new technique that animates a tattoo when you move.'

'That was the scary bit…' Seeing Eric looking crestfallen, she didn't want to upset him too much, since the sex had been good. 'But you were better than ever. It's just what I needed. Your technique has improved. Been practising?'

'I haven't been celibate since you left. Did you expect me to be?'

'Of course not, silly. But then neither have I.'

'Oh…right…who then?' Eric sounded a touch jealous.

'You mean how many?' Christina unfolded her hands from under the sheets, and started counting on her fingers. 'There was Adam…Bruce…Colin…Demetrius…Eddie…Frank…George…….Hugo… Ivan…Elizabeth…

'Elizabeth?' Eric suddenly sat up.

'I felt like a change.' She continued. 'Kieran…Larry…Matt, and his twin brother Nicholas…'

'Elizabeth…?' Eric repeated, totally confused.

Christina turned and kissed him on the cheek. 'That's not counting all the aliens I was abducted by. Now they had an interesting way with sex. Really big willies.'

'Bigger than mine? What…you were abducted?' Eric now looked really perplexed.

Christina smiled. 'What do you think?'

Eric finally caught on. 'I see…you were joking…?'

'Give the man a coconut!'

'You had me worried for a moment.'

'That someone had a bigger willy than you? What I've always liked about you, Eric, is your gullibility and naivety. It's quite sweet really,'

'I know, more brawn than brains. I know I'm not that clever. I admit it. But you still like my body, don't you? I work hard to keep in shape.'

'That's the best bit.' She sat up, letting the sheet slip. 'So, do you feel you've done your exercises for today? Not feeling so ratty?'

Eric looked at her naked breasts and smiled. 'I still feel a bit irritable…'

'In that case, perhaps you should do another workout…?' She pulled down the sheet completely.

Eric flexed his muscles. 'Perhaps I should. My turn on the bottom, so that I can see yours!' Christina started to giggle as he pulled her on top of him.

Tony was on his laptop surfing some sites, looking disinterested, his hand down the front of his pants, when there was a knock on the door. 'Yes?' He quickly closed his laptop and removed his hand out of his trousers.

'Just popping out for a couple of hours,' Roger said loudly from outside. 'Yes, and before you ask, I'm going to Helen's for sex. I've put a meal in the oven for you. Give it twenty minutes. Don't forget, like last time, when the oven was nearly ruined. Tony?'

'Yes, ok, I won't forget!'

'See you later…' Roger bounded down the stairs and out of the front door.

'Enjoy yourself…' Tony muttered. He opened up his laptop to take another look at the porn site he had clicked on. He stared at it for a few moments and wasn't able to get excited. He closed the laptop and left his bedroom to go downstairs.

***

Helen, an attractive woman in her thirties, completely opposite in looks to Christina, was in her bedroom taking her dress off. She stood in her bra and knickers watching Roger take off his shirt in a preoccupied way. 'The funeral's really affected you.'

'You could say that…' He undid the belt of his trousers.

'Was it an ordeal you poor thing?' She moved across and helped him take his trousers off.

'That doesn't even describe it.' He folded his trousers over a chair.

'Funerals are always such sad affairs. Cremation or burial?'

'Either would've been acceptable. I would have happily have lit the cremator or dug the grave myself. '

'What do you mean?' She pulled down his underpants and revealed a very unexcited member. 'Oh dear, what can I do to soothe your troubled mind?' She knelt down and was about to go down on him, when he stopped her.

'Could you go and kill my ex-wife please…'

'What…?' Helen suddenly rose to her feet in confusion.

It was dark outside. The curtains were drawn, and the bedside lamps switched on in Eric's bedroom. Christina, wearing one of Eric's shirts, was busy rifling through the drawers in his bedside table. She was having a quick rummage amongst papers and odd things, but disappointed that there was nothing of interest. Hearing the sound of clinking cutlery, she quickly got back under the sheets and pretended to be asleep.

Eric entered carrying a tray of food and drinks. Smiling, he put the tray down and kissed Christina gently on the cheek. She opened her eyes slowly as if awakening. 'What time is it…?

'Time to eat, drink and be merry!' He pointed to the tray.

'No smoked salmon and champagne?' She eyed the tray, unable to hide a slight look of distaste.

'You know I don't like smoked salmon. There are a couple of beers, some crisps, salami sticks, a pork pie and a pizza. It's hot, I did it in the microwave.' He said it as if he was producing a menu of tasteful delicacies.

Christina sat up. 'You really know how to push the boat out.' She said somewhat sarcastically.

He looked dejected. 'Sorry, I know it's not up to the standard of the meal you gave us in the wine bar. It's all I had in the fridge.'

She unconsciously popped a crisp into her mouth and pulled a face. 'Ugh, soggy cheese and onion. You do surprise me sometimes.'

'In what way?'

'You take so much trouble and care looking after your body, but you don't seem to care what rubbish you put into it.'

'I feel all right. You know I'm a meat eater at heart.'

'Carnivore.'

'Never tried that. One of those exotic meats? Anyway, when you left so unexpectedly, I wanted to make a new start. I tried eating salads and so-called healthy foods. …'

'What happened?'

'I felt depressed, lost weight and came out in spots. It was awful.'

Christina touched his arm. 'Poor you…I expect you were really pining for me.' She said jokingly.

Eric's countenance suddenly changed. She had hit a nerve. 'Yes, in a way I was. You just didn't care. You've no idea what you did to me.' He became serious and stern.

'What _I_ did to you! Oh, come on!' It was Christina's turn to be serious. 'That's hardly fair.'

Eric smirked. 'Fair doesn't exist in your vocab.. vocablu…'

'Vocabulary?'

'Don't be so clever.' He sulked.

'What's the matter? I thought we were getting on all right? I thought you enjoyed the sex. It was good for me.'

'You're just using me, like you did all those years ago. You came here deliberately to get me into bed, knowing how I felt about you.'

'Excuse me!' Christina was now indignant. 'I only wanted a coffee and to talk. To try and clear the air a bit. You're the one who suggested coffee in the bedroom, because you wanted to show me your collection of fancy boxer shorts.'

'Because I had them specially made for me. It was you who insisted on seeing the ones I was wearing!'

'And you didn't hesitate in pulling your trousers down to show me!' She had him there.

'Whatever. You took advantage of my emotions. You knew I couldn't resist.'

'Didn't I know it, with that huge erection poking out! So, who was using who, eh?' Christina took a piece of pork pie and shoved it in her mouth.

'I really thought you were dead! That bloody funeral took it out of me. You had no right to put us all through that. It completely drained me…'

'One wouldn't have known – from our little workout.'

'Only <u>little</u> was it!' Eric took umbrage.

'God, you're so vain, Eric. I didn't mean that literally.' Christina got out of bed and started to put her clothes back on. 'I'd better go, at the risk of upsetting you even more. Because whatever I say, you seem to take it the wrong way. I'm sorry I came, but I'm not sorry we had sex. It was good, just what I needed, but perhaps that's all we have in common.'

'You were going to marry me...'

'That was before.' Christina wasn't in the mood to go into any details.

'Before what? You're not going until you tell me the truth.' Eric turned the key in the door, and held it in his closed fist.

Christina, now dressed, was about to tackle him for the key, when there was a banging on the bedroom door. 'Eric, it's Sadie! Are you indecent!' Which was followed by a girlish giggle.

'Oh, God...I forgot Sadie was coming.' Eric's face crumpled.

'Someone else breaking into your flat? Or did you have a job lot of keys made?' Christina was beginning to feel put out.

'Is my big boy hiding? Are those delicious muscles ready to punish me... because I've been a very naughty girl...' Sadie rapped on the door.

'Bit of a Sadiest, is she?'

Eric didn't get the inference. 'Just an acquaintance. I didn't know...'

'I'd be here...? Sorry to upset your plans. She your next workout?'

Eric gave her a look that didn't deserve an answer. He unlocked the bedroom door to reveal a statuesque young blonde in her twenties, dressed in a way that left nothing to the imagination. 'Oh…' Sadie was surprised to see Christina.

'Er, Sadie…this is Christina…Umm, I went to her funeral today…but as you can see, she's not really dead…'

'I can see that.' Sadie gave Christina a catty look, noticing the crumpled sheets on the bed.

'Don't worry; I was on my way out. He's all yours.' Christina made for the door.

'Eric didn't tell me his mother was still alive.'

'I bet you he also didn't tell you that he was once arrested for having sex with a minor. I suggest you go home to your mother or you'll land him in trouble. Nice meeting you. Goodbye!' Christina closed the door behind her and left the flat. It wasn't until she was out of the building that she burst into tears.

Silently, Helen put her dress back on whilst Roger, looking wretched, belted up his trousers. 'It's her, isn't it?' She looked tight-lipped.

'No, no…' He lied, 'it's just that I'm not feeling too well. The food at the wine bar was very rich, and I overdid it a bit.' He patted his stomach in a weak gesture.

'Rubbish…you haven't gone off me, have you?'

'How can you say that?'

'You're little – weeny – friend said that for both of us.'

Roger looked down to lace up his shoes. 'I said I was sorry!'

'Maybe I'm losing my touch…' She said somewhat self pityingly.

'I promise. It's nothing to do with you. Okay, it

---

probably is because of Christina. I didn't ask her to come back. I didn't want her back. In some ways I was glad that she was dead…'

'But she isn't – and she has come back.'

'Not for long. Remember, we're divorced. She means nothing to me anymore, can't you believe that? As I've told you, she going to die soon anyway.'

'Are you sure? Not something she's said to get sympathy, so that she can inveigle herself back into your life by any chance?'

Roger thought for a moment. 'I wouldn't put it past her, but I do believe it's the truth. A priest and a solicitor confirmed it. Why should they lie?'

'Why should they indeed,' She replied sarcastically, 'The Church and the Law are not institutions to tell untruths!'

'Helen, please, let's not go down that road. I'm tired, fed up and in no mood to argue any more. I'm sorry I wasn't up to it tonight. I do sincerely believe that Christina has terminal cancer and that she might only have a few months at most. That doesn't mean I want to be with her, quite the opposite. But, because of Tony, she's not going to go away yet.'

'In that case, maybe I should think about killing her. Speed her on her way, so to speak. Then she won't be around to bother us – however long she lives.' Helen added with a smile.

Roger looked at her and realised that she was very serious.

Christina wiped her tears and stood outside the block of flats thinking. She wandered round to the back to where Eric's car was parked. She considered letting the tyres down, but then decided against it. Instead, she took out a set of car keys and thought for a moment. Should she? She had forgotten to give him the spare set of keys. Looking up at Eric's bedroom window and seeing shadows moving behind the curtains, made up her mind for her. She pressed the key fob and the car unlocked. She got in, started the engine and drove away.

The light in Tony's bedroom was on when she pulled up outside Roger's house. She sat in the car wondering about going in, but moments later Roger's car pulled up behind her. In her rear-view mirror, she watched Roger get out and come towards her.

She wound down her window as he poked his head down. 'Hello Roger…' She forced a smile.

'New car, or have you already repossessed it from Eric?'

'Just borrowed it for a bit. Roger…'

'Have you added stalking and spying to your talents! What the hell do you want?'

'Can we talk…please?' Christina pleaded.

'There's been enough talking for today. I don't want to listen to you anymore. Now sod off, I don't want to see you here again.' Roger stomped off up the path and into the house.

Christina sat in the car doing her best to control her rising anger and frustration. She closed her eyes and took some deep breaths until she felt calmer. As she drove off, she could see Roger peeking through the curtains.

13. Arms and the Woman

Jennie was sat in front of the TV demolishing a box of chocolates, watching a reality programme about obese people, when her front door bell went. She opened it to see a sad looking Christina standing before her. 'Please don't close the door. Can I come in?'

Jennie thought for a moment. She felt too tired to argue. 'If you feel you must…'

They went into the sitting room. 'D'you want a drink? Whiskey, was it?' Christina nodded. While Jennie poured a couple of glasses, Christina looked up at a photo of Patrick, Jennie's husband. 'Surprised that I still keep his photo out?'

'No, not really. Thanks.' She took a large swig of whiskey.

Jennie stared at her blankly. 'Have you got a picture of him?'

'No…listen Jennie, I haven't come here to fight.'

'What do you want – another pound of flesh? I've got plenty to spare.'

Christina sat and gestured for Jennie to do the same. 'I know you blame me for everything. The business failing…that little episode with Patrick…'

Jennie, still standing, drained her glass. 'Little! You seduced my husband, after which he left me.'

'It's not as simple as that, Jennie.'

'No…?' Jennie, feeling drained and not having the energy for a full-scale row, slumped down on the settee.

'Jennie, let's be honest. You're not going to believe anything I say, are you?'

'Would you believe you? After you suddenly disappeared, leaving me to sort out the mess?'

'No, you're right. I probably wouldn't.' Christina emptied her glass and stood up. 'Look, I've made a mistake coming here, among many I've made today. Perhaps it's better if I just go. I'm really sorry to have disturbed you.'

'I went to my new office earlier. It's nice…you've gone to a lot of trouble.' Jennie got up and picked up the bottle. 'D'you want another drink?'

'I really don't want to argue with you Jennie.'

Jennie filled Christina's glass. 'So, tell me, what was today about? What were you trying to prove?' She sat back on the settee expressionless.

'That things have changed. That I've changed…' Christina sat down. 'I didn't want to die without making some amends for the obvious pain and suffering I caused.'

'A change of heart perhaps?'

'Something like that…'

'That's interesting since you never had a heart in the first place. You fed on ours. I bet you wished I had killed myself.' Jennie spoke quite calmly without malice.

'Do you really hate me so much?' Christina saw that Jennie wasn't going to answer. 'Look, about the problems concerning the business…'

'Put that aside for now. Tell me about Patrick.'

'We did have a very brief, well I wouldn't even call it an affair.'

'What would you call it – a sympathy fuck?'

'A one-night stand. I didn't start it, Jennie, he chased me for months trying to get me into bed. I wanted to tell you, but I didn't want to upset your marriage.'

'Instead, you broke it up.'

'No, I didn't! Your sainted husband made it quite clear that he wanted a little fling, and did everything in his power to get me to sleep with him. I resisted at first, because I didn't want to ruin our partnership.'

Jennie laughed. 'That's a good one! It's not what he told me when I found out.'

'Of course it isn't! You don't know the half of it.'

'Half of what? More lies and made-up tales? You were always very good, when we were making a sales pitch, to fabricate things as a means to winning over a new client.'

'You never complained when the orders started flooding in. Oh Jennie, whatever I say, you're obviously not going to believe me. I'm wasting my time and I'm too tired to try and justify everything. Thanks for the drink. I hope the business is successful. I'll leave you in peace, and I promise not to bother you again.'

Christina was about to go to the front door, when Jennie opened a drawer and took out a handgun, which she pointed directly at her. 'Finish what you started. I want to hear the other half of it, as you so delicately put it.'

'What are you doing?' Christina stared at the gun.

'Pointing a loaded gun at you, and believe me – it is loaded! Sit down please.' Jennie waved the gun in the direction of a chair, and waited for Christina to sit. 'Patrick got this…from a friend of a friend. Just in case. Just in case we had burglars or intruders – we've been robbed before – …'

'And I'm an intruder?' Christina was keeping calm.

'It was dark. I came downstairs because I thought I heard a noise. Someone had broken in. There was a scuffle and the gun accidentally went off….' Jennie smiled.

'And when you turned the lights on you were horrified to discover the corpse of your old business partner – who should've been dead anyway?'

'Something like that. Clever, eh?'

'And how will you explain the gun?'

'I'll say it was yours. You threatened me with it. Your fingerprints will be on it.'

'You've thought it all out. Don't forget to wipe the fingerprints off my glass.'

'Thanks for reminding me.'

'Jennie, this is ridiculous...' She stood up.

'Sit down!' Christina sat. 'Ridiculous! As ridiculous as what went on at the crematorium?'

'All right, I hold my hands up. It's a fair cop!' Christina put her hands up as if in surrender.

'Put them down! Now tell me what you were going to say about Patrick?'

'You won't believe me anyway, so what's the point?'

'I want to hear.' Jennie continued pointing the gun at her.

'Okay. You remember Meera, that lovely Indian girl we had as a secretary for a few months? Wore those beautiful saris.'

'Yes, the one whose marriage had been arranged, and who hated her husband. Patrick was always joking with her when he came to the office.'

'She looked up to him as a sort of father figure...and he took advantage of that.'

'You're not telling me he had a fling with her too.' Jennie sighed.

'I knew you wouldn't believe me...'

Jennie waved the gun at her. 'Go on...'

'Remember when Meera came in one morning in a terrible state, and with a black eye. It was obvious her husband had hit her. Patrick was there, and insisted on taking her out to lunch to calm her. Remember that?' Jennie nodded. 'That's when it started.'

'How do you know they had sex? It might have been innocent.'

'I suspected something was going on, because it was having an effect on her work. She started to make a lot of mistakes. Remember, we discussed this, and you agreed that I should give her a verbal warning. It was then that she broke down and confessed what had been going on. It was one reason why she left us soon after, because she was ashamed.'

'Why didn't you tell me? Instead of making up that story about her husband forbidding her to work anymore?'

'I was trying to protect your marriage, believe it or not.'

Jennie was thinking. 'I wondered why Patrick tried to persuade me to wear a sari at home. Anyway, was that before or after you lured him to your bed?'

'It was the other way round. I told you, he was very persistent.'

'Yet you didn't think of turning him down. You could've said no.'

'He was very persuasive…we got drunk…I got swept away with it all. I can't say I remember much about it…'

'Yes, he swept me away once. Now he's gone…life's not really worth living…' Jennie suddenly held the gun up to her temple.

Christina got up. 'Jennie…what are you doing?'

'What I should've done originally after you left. Stay where you are! I thought I'd come to terms with things. I even began to see a small light at the end of the tunnel. I was slowly starting to get my life back. Then you decided to come back into our lives and reminded me about everything that had happened. The business…Patrick…I honestly don't think I can cope any more…' She released the catch on the gun and put her finger on the trigger.

'Please, Jennie, don't be silly…' Christina felt her armpits dampen.

'Sillier than holding your own funeral like a circus freak show?'

'Jennie, I beg you. It's not worth it!' She implored, her heart beating fast.

'What do you care? You're not going to be around long anyway. Perhaps we'll join up again in the afterlife, if there is one, and compare notes.'

'Please! Don't!' Christina shouted.

'Here goes nothing...' Jennie holding the gun to her temple, pressed the trigger a couple of times, giving off a succession of harmless clicks. Smiling, she then pointed the gun at Christina and fired imaginary shots at her. 'That got the pulses going, didn't it!' Jennie then threw the gun down on the settee.

Christina couldn't help but look relieved. 'What was that all about? What were you trying to prove?'

'Two can play dead. No different to your little scenario. But this is a real gun, it's just the bullets were missing.'

'What I told you about Patrick was the truth.'

'There are different kinds of truths...I think you'd better go now....'

'Yes, I think I'd better. Thanks for the rollercoaster, it's probably more than I deserved. But then you might have done us both a favour if there had been real bullets...' Christina walked slowly out of the house.

Jennie watched her go with a sense of triumph mingled with sorrow.

14. Hitting a Brick Wall

Christina, tears flowing down her cheeks, drove frenetically along the streets, ignoring the car horns and flashing lights of other drivers, when she carelessly overtook or cut them up. She drove as if she didn't care anymore, whether she lived or died. She felt there was no longer any point to her life, she'd be dead soon anyway. Why prolong the agony and just get it over with? Nobody would care anyway. Nobody would miss her. Tony possibly, but he'd get over it soon enough. As she started to press her foot on the accelerator to go even faster, she realised that her death wish might involve other drivers if she was involved in a crash. Her demise should certainly not include others.

She slowed down and turned off at an industrial estate, and careered around a few streets until she came to a sort of cul-de-sac. About two hundred metres ahead was a large building. There were no other cars or people about. She'd be able to get a good speed up before driving headlong into the wall, which should do the trick.

She turned the engine and lights off and undid her seat belt. She sat thinking for a moment. This was how it was all going to end, not in her bed once the cancer consumed her body, but against a brick wall. It would be a messier end, but she'd know nothing about it. Quick and easy, no one else involved. Oh, how she now wished Jennie had shot her as an intruder. That would've been easier.

She thought back to the time, three years ago, when she was with Jennie in the office going through a number of balance sheets and end of month accounts….

'Jennie, how long have you known about this?' Christina was shocked at the figures she was looking at.

'No – how long have *you* known about it!' Jennie gave her an accusing look.

'I didn't! This could ruin us!'

'Like you ruined my marriage?'

'I'm talking about the business. Are you putting the blame on me?' Christina couldn't understand it.

'There's no one else. I'm getting the auditors in followed by the fraud squad.'

'Jennie, I'm as baffled as you are. We've got to find out how this happened.'

'How you bankrupted us, you mean…'

Christina also remembered coming home to Eric that night and telling him what had gone on….

'It's only some stupid accounts. It'll sort itself out. Anyway, there's something much more important to discuss.'

'What's more important than me possibly going to jail!'

'Christina, stop being so dramatic.' He took her hand. 'I've booked the Registry.'

'Registry…?'

'A month today!' Eric gave a big grin.

'For what?' Christina, her mind elsewhere, couldn't understand what he was going on about.

'Our wedding, silly! It's going to be the best day of our lives.'

'What bloody wedding? We haven't talked about this. I haven't agreed to marry you.'

Eric remained calm. 'Look, you're a bit upset. You've had a bad day at the office. You're always telling me that I should think for myself…'

'True…?'

'Well, I have! But I'm not going to tell you where we're going on honeymoon, until after the ceremony. It's a surprise!'

'Then I'll never know, because I'm not marrying you.'

'Chris, you're being unreasonable.'

'Don't call me Chris, you know I hate it.'

'So, you hate me…' Eric felt dejected.

'No, I'm just not ready to get married again.'

'To me, you mean?'

'To anyone…can we please change the subject, I've got a lot on my plate at the moment.'

'But I've made all the arrangements!'

'Then unmake them. We are not getting married or going on honeymoon. End of conversation!' Christina made for the door.

'Where you going?'

'Out, to get some air. Please don't follow me.'

Christina could still see the lost little-boy look that Eric gave her as she left the flat all those years ago. Would her life have been different if she had stayed and married him? Would it have been different if she'd been on better terms with Tony and Roger? It had been Tony's behaviour towards her that really upset her and made her disappear from all their lives…

Tony had slammed his bedroom door in her face. 'You're an interfering old cow!'

'But Tony, please listen to me.'

Tony turned up his music to full blast. Christina gave up. As she got to the front door, Roger arrived. 'What are you doing here?'

'I came to visit my son. We did agree, remember.'

Roger screwed up his face at the noise. 'What's going

on? What have you said to him? Have you upset him? He always turns up the volume when he's upset.'

'No, actually he upset me with that horrible tattoo on his arm.'

Roger gave her a condescending look. 'Is that all?'

'You don't care, do you? He's only fourteen and you let him run riot.'

'I can handle him. Why don't you concentrate on that little business of yours, and let me worry about my son.'

'Our son! And since you mention the business, there are a few problems regarding that...'

'I see. Can't say I'm surprised.'

'Roger...Would you consider investing a couple of thousand? It would help. You'll get a favourable return.'

'Go to hell! You've got a nerve. Don't you come running to me for any help. Sort out your own mess...'

The memory made Christina shift in her seat. She realised now that coming back from the dead, so to speak, had been a pointless idea. Nobody had really welcomed her back, or wanted her even though her time was short. Tony was the exception, but there was still an awkward distance between them. She looked at the wall ahead. In a matter of seconds, she would be well out of it all. It would be a welcome release for everyone concerned. She switched on the engine. Her only one regret was that Eric would lose his car. She laughed to herself. Dear Eric, it wouldn't be the fact that she killed herself that would really upset him, but that his precious car, which he hadn't even driven, would be written off.

Oh, come on Christina, she thought to herself, get on with it!

She switched on the engine and released the handbrake. Just as she was about to put her foot down on the accelerator, a van from a security firm pulled up beside her, and a security guard, wearing a kind of uniform, got out and tapped on her window. 'Everything all right Miss…' He shone his torch in her face.

She wound down her window. 'It's Ms. Perfectly, thank you. Kind of you to enquire.' She wound her window back up, but he remained standing there.

This time his partner got out of the van. 'Everything okay, Doug?'

'Something's not right…' He tapped on her window again, which she impatiently wound down again. 'Miss…Ms…You're not really safe around here on your own. I suggest you get back on the road.'

'I appreciate your concern, but I'm quite happy here. Why don't you and your friend go and do whatever you're paid to do. Catch those who are up to no good.' She pressed a button to wind the window back up, but the guard placed his torch in between to stop it closing completely.

'I now have to ask you what you are doing here.' His tone became formal.

'If you must know, I'm about to drive this car into that wall. Satisfied?'

'I wouldn't advise that Ms…' He gestured to his partner to go to the passenger door of her car.

'I don't need your advice. It's a free world, which I am about to depart from. I apologise now for the inconvenience, mess and paperwork this will create for you afterwards.' She was about to put her foot back on the accelerator, when the partner speedily opened the door, put the handbrake on, and took the key out of the ignition.

'You can't do that!' She protested.

'Yes, we can. You see, we were hoping for a quiet night without any interruptions while we did our rounds. We can't have you upsetting things by smashing into that wall.

122

That is if you were serious, and not winding us up.'

'Can't someone commit suicide without interference?' Christina folded her arms in annoyance.

'Not on our watch you can't.' The second guard held on to her car key. 'Doug, give the police a ring. They need to take over from here.'

A couple of hours later Christina was sat in an interview room in a police station, having been questioned by a female investigating officer for the last hour. Christina realised that if she told the truth about seriously wanting to end her life, they'd probably send her to a psychiatric hospital to be examined, leading to a lot of complications involving doctors and social workers. Instead, she told the police that she'd had a bad day and was feeling low and needed time to think, and had chosen the industrial estate as somewhere to stop the car. She was sorry to have bothered the security guards, saying she wanted to kill herself. She wasn't serious. She then asked to phone her solicitor who would vouch for her.

Duncan, looking bleary-eyed, with his scoop over not quite in place, arrived soon afterwards to get her out. She was given a caution and released.

'Thank you, Duncan, sorry about all this and getting you out of bed.'

'Did you really mean to end your life?' He enquired.

'Not really,' she lied. 'I was just having a quiet think, away from it all, when these two security guards started questioning me. I couldn't help winding them up.'

'Do you want to press charges? Did they physically touch you?'

'No, no. That's not necessary. By the way I naughtily drove Eric's new car, with the spare set of keys I'd forgotten to give him. I'd better return it before he notices it's gone.'

'Are you still okay to drive?'

'Of course! No problem.' She didn't mention her visit to see Jennie or that she'd had a few drinks. Luckily the police didn't breathalyse her.

'I can follow you to his flat, then I'll drive you home.'

'That would be great, thanks. Sorry about the inconvenience.'

'Don't worry, I'll just add it to your account.' He replied in all seriousness.

Driving back to Eric's flat, Christina again seriously thought about finding another wall somewhere else to end it all. No, she felt that option was no longer tenable. She was still determined to do it – but needed to think of another way, without too much fuss or interference from others.

'I shall find a way to end my life, even if it kills me!'

15. The Grim Reaper's Day Off

When they arrived outside Eric's block of flats, Christina persuaded Duncan to go home. She told him she wanted another word with Eric, who she was sure, would then drive her home. Duncan, who didn't think it was a good idea at this time of night, was too tired to argue, knowing how headstrong she was.

Once he drove off, she looked up to make sure no lights were on in Eric's flat and wondered if that Sadie was in his bed. She was angry with herself for suddenly feeling jealous. Why should she care who Eric slept with? He had his life and she didn't want hers anymore. She got back in his car and drove away.

Again, she thought seriously about either crashing the car against another wall, or finding some river to drive into, but realised neither would have any guarantee of success. Slowly going off those ideas, she eventually came up with a more full-proof way of leaving this world as she pulled up outside her own flat.

Christina checked to see if she had any whiskey and paracetamol in the place. All she found were a blister pack of two paracetamol, and whiskey just enough for a small glass. She cursed, throwing the paracetamol across the room in frustration. 'Why is it so hard to try and kill yourself!'

Despite being one o'clock in the morning, Christina remembered a local convenience store that was open all night, only a five-minute drive away.

She plonked the litre bottle of whiskey on the counter. 'And I'll have four boxes of paracetamol, please. No, make it five.'

The Sikh shopkeeper took the boxes, which were behind him, and put them on the counter. 'You have ID,

---

125

young lady?' He said looking stern.

'ID? Are you serious?' Christina looked askance.

The shopkeeper gave a wide, toothy smile. 'I thought you were under eighteen, so sorry!'

For the first time that day Christina couldn't help but smile herself. It was a momentarily release from the trauma she was going through. 'I bet you say that to all the girls.' She replied.

'Only the pretty ones! That will be twenty-two pounds and fifty-three pee.' He pointed to her purchases. 'You have bad headache or going to a party?' He joked.

'Actually, I going to kill myself. Here's twenty-five pounds. Keep the change.' She put the stuff in a carrier bag.

The shopkeeper gave a hearty laugh as he put the money in the till. 'Thank you. You are a very funny lady! You come back soon!'

'Do you believe in ghosts?'

'There are spirits around us. Sad souls that cannot move on.' He gestured with his hands, waving them about.

'Well, once I've finished this bottle of spirits and taken the tablets, I might come back and haunt you.' She gave him a warm smile before leaving the shop, still able to hear his raucous laughter as she got in the car.

She was passing a church and seeing its impressive bell tower, when another idea suddenly occurred. She stopped the car, remembering this was where Paula was the parish priest. She looked up at the bright full moon and made a decision.

She parked the car nearby, got out with the carrier bag, and made her way to the church entrance. 'Please, please be open…if there is a God…' she whispered to herself.

She closed her eyes and tried the door. It creaked open. 'Thank you,' she whispered again, 'even though I still don't believe in you…'

The church interior was illuminated by the light of the moon filtering through the stained-glass windows, which made it easier to amble through without bumping into the pews. Christina shivered, not from cold, but from the silent, eerie atmosphere. She'd never felt comfortable in churches or with religion in general, from the time her parents made her attend Sunday school when she was eight. Being here now seemed the final irony.

She found the door to the bell tower and was cheered to find it was also open. Climbing a number of stone steps around a narrow winding staircase, making sure she didn't bang her carrier bag against the walls, she reached the top. It was a small enclosure housing a large bronze bell, with a rope attached. Halfway up the walls were a couple of open arched windows. Apart from a small, weatherworn wooden chair it was empty.

Christina sat on the chair and took her purchases out of the carrier bag. Opening the bottle of whiskey, she took a swig. Then she began to open the paracetamol boxes to prize the capsules out of their bubble packs, putting them in a pile on the ground. Finding this a chore and becoming impatient, she suddenly gave up after the second box. 'This is the coward's way out, Christina Turner!' She said aloud to herself. 'Have the courage of your convictions...'

She took another swig of the bottle and stood up. She looked up at the rope hanging down from the bell and took hold of it. If she could manage to tie a noose, she could hang herself, but that would probably set off the bell. No, too complicated. She looked up at one of the open arches. If she could climb up to the ledge, she'd be able to push through and jump out. It was high enough for a fatal fall.

She positioned the chair below the one of the arches and managed after a couple of attempts to get up to the opening. She felt triumphant. 'To think...in a few moments

I'll know if there's an afterlife…and if there is, I'll come back and haunt the bloody lot of them!'

The opening was small, but Christina believed she'd just be able to squeeze through if she took her coat off. She threw the coat to the ground and then thrust her body slowly through. Yet when she got halfway, she found she couldn't move any further. She breathed in to flatten her stomach but wasn't able to squeeze through another inch. 'Oh bollocks!' She cursed, realising she was well and truly stuck in the middle, being halfway out and halfway in. She looked up into the sky and raised her voice, 'Bloody hell! Don't do this to me! Aren't I allowed to end it all with a bit of dignity!'

'Death knows no dignity…' a deep ghostly voice answered.

'What…?' Christina froze.

'You must not deprive death of his job. He will come and fetch you when he's ready…' Thundered the female voice.

'God is a woman! I knew it!' In the confusion, Christina didn't know whether to laugh or cry from fright. She turned to look down to see a cloaked figure below looking up and holding what looked like a scythe. 'Who's that? Is it you Death, have you come to fetch me…please! I'm ready!'

'What are you doing up here, Christina?' The voice now sounded normal.

'Paula…?'

'It's a bit late to be taking the air.' Paula sounded a bit put out. 'What are you doing?'

'As you can see, I'm in a bit of a predicament. Could you give me a hand, I'm starting to get cramp.'

Paula put down the scythe and crossed towards the opening. She stood on the chair and took hold of Christina's arm, which was hanging down. 'Thank you – now push!'

'You surely mean pull?'

'I mean PUSH! I'm not staying, I've made up my mind.'

'You want me to help you kill yourself? Is that what you really want?'

'I've got nothing more to live for. It's going to happen soon anyway. Do me this little kindness. No one will ever know. You can say you found me in the morning...Please...'

'If you're really that passionate about doing it, can you give me a moment to say a prayer to ask for forgiveness?' Christina nodded. Paula closed her eyes and silently mouthed some words. 'Are you sure now?'

'Yes, get on with it!'

Then, taking a deep breath, she took hold of Christina's arm, and with one almighty tug pulled Christina back into the bell tower.

'Ouch! You practically dislocated my shoulder! Can't you tell the difference between pulling and pushing?' Christina cried angrily.

Paula smiled back. 'Maybe that's a reason I was never picked for the school tug-of-war team...'

Twenty minutes later they were both sitting in the vestry. They hadn't said much since the incident. Christina was still quite cross and in a sulky mood. The bag containing the whiskey and painkillers was on a table. Paula sat calmly watching Christina, who silently seemed to be battling with her demons. 'Why did you choose this church?'

'It was on the way and seemed more appropriate than my flat. I imagined someone would find me in the morning, and then call you. You would recognise me and explain the circumstances, and it would all be tied up very neatly.'

'That's very considerate of you.' Paula couldn't hide the slight tone of sarcasm.

'How did you know I was up there?'

'I get insomnia sometimes. I was actually working in here, thinking about Sunday's sermon. I heard someone come into the church, and realised that I had forgotten to lock it. We've been robbed before, so I waited until I heard footsteps going up to the bell tower. That's when I grabbed this old scythe, which has been here for decades.'

'For a moment I really thought you were the grim reaper himself.' Christina forced a weak smile.

'The devil has many disguises. Tell me, why did you feel you had to try and take your own life. Today was difficult, but not that bad surely.'

'It got worse after I left you. I did try and build bridges with the others, but they rejected me quite adamantly. Any form of forgiveness was not on the agenda. I tried and failed. I felt there was no point in prolonging the agony.'

'Tony didn't reject you. Shouldn't you have thought of him, how he would take it?'

Christina furiously stood up. 'It wasn't enough!' She took the whiskey out of the bag and took a long swig. She then offered it to Paula.

'I have to confess – I've never tasted whiskey. Communion wine has been my limit. Until today's wine and champagne, that is. Quite enjoyed that.'

'Try it Paula, you won't be banished to hell.'

'I'm tempted …but as it says in Proverbs 20:1 – "Wine is a mocker; strong drink is raging: and whosoever is deceived thereby is not wise."'

'Oh, stop being so sanctimonious! You church people are all the same. You're always telling others not to do things. Yet how can you really judge what is good and bad, if you've never actually experienced it yourself - and please don't quote the bible again at me. It's only a drink, which some profess to be very medicinal. It's not going to turn you into an alcoholic.'

'It's said that the first drink is always the most dangerous...' Paula teased.

'Stop preaching to me for God's sake! Now you've got me using his or her name in vain.'

'Sorry, a professional habit. Perhaps a little taste will do no harm.' Paula went over to a shelf and took a silver chalice off it. She first blew into it to get rid of any dust and then wiped the inside with a cloth. Satisfied, she held the chalice up to Christina to fill, who poured no more than a teaspoonful. 'My cup doth not overflow...'

'You only wanted a taste. I'm not going to waste it if you don't like it.'

Paula gently raised the chalice to her lips and sipped the whiskey. 'Umm, quite nice...' and then extended the chalice for a refill. 'A bit more this time, thank you.'

'Not so bad after all, eh?' She poured a more generous amount.

'It has a wicked little flavour.' Paula now took a large gulp and felt a satisfied thrill about doing something that was deemed inappropriate in religious circles. She didn't feel guilty. She continually believed that the Church was still too rigid in many ways, and wanted somehow to loosen up people's attitudes towards the clergy, if the Church was to keep and inspire more followers. She constantly felt the need to shake things up, which was one reason she'd agreed to conduct Christina's mock funeral service. She enjoyed the challenge in the belief that what Christina was doing was justified, be it unconventional.

***

An hour later the whiskey bottle was empty. Christina, although not actually drunk, was very relaxed and light-headed. Paula, on the other hand was quite giggly and girlish. She was parading around the vestry in one of the service vestments like a catwalk model. 'This one's my favourite!'

'It has a certain style. Do you wear it with, or without underwear?'

Paula put her hand to her mouth to stifle a giggle. 'Knickers? It depends whose underwear! Sorry, that's a very inappropriate thing to say.'

'I won't tell if you don't. Well, time is marching on, and despite all my efforts to the contrary, I'm still alive, and I don't want to be.' Christina suddenly reminded herself, and emptied the chalice she was now drinking from.

Paula shook the bottle, disappointed to find it was empty. 'Oh…wait a minute!' She had an idea. She went over to a cupboard and took out a bottle of communion wine and waved it excitedly. 'Bingo! It's only 12% but good enough. There's more where that came from!' She unscrewed the top and filled her chalice up. She also poured some into Christina's chalice.

Paula took a large gulp of the wine, and thought seriously for a moment. 'Christina, when you first came to me, you said you wanted to wipe the slate clean. Those were your very words. Tell me, did you really mean it?'

'Of course I did, and in a way still do. But whatever I do seems to backfire and make matters worse.'

'You also need to see it from their point of view.'

'If I saw it from their point of view – I'd never be forgiven!' Christina took a sip of the wine and pulled a face. 'This is enough to make you teetotal!'

'It's an acquired taste, like religion, I suppose. They say you shouldn't mix the grain with the grape, but life is a series of mixtures which we should be open to, rather than condemn or forbid.'

'Which bible quote does that come from?' Christina said condescendingly, while taking another sip from her chalice.

'The gospel according to Paula the priest. Even I have to admit that the bible is slightly out of date in a lot of its pronouncements and directions, and doesn't relate to today.'

'I don't care, really. It's people that matter, and those that matter in my life don't care about me. I just don't want them to think ill of me when I do die.' She took a large gulp of wine. 'You're right, it does rather grow on you.'

'If you kill yourself now, they're not going to suddenly change their opinion, are they?'

'I suppose not…'

'You'd be playing right into their hands. Why should you give them that satisfaction? Fight for the right to be forgiven! Make them feel guilty and really grieve when you are gone!' Paula held her chalice up passionately.

'You're saying I shouldn't give up…?'

'Too bloody right! Make whatever time you've got left meaningful. Make it matter! You have nothing to lose and everything to gain! Fight the good fight! Don't let the buggers get you down! Please don't give up, Christina. I might be a bit pissed, but I know what I'm saying.'

Christina filled her chalice from the bottle. 'Yes…you might be right. Why should I give them that satisfaction?'

'Go for it, Christina! I'll help you. There are ways and means of changing people's attitudes and making them come round. Look upon it as a challenge! Leave this world on a high – and I don't mean jumping off a bridge!' Paula was really fired up now.

Christina had now caught Paula's passion and determination. 'Yes, I'm not going to give up or take the easy way out. I'll drink to that!'

'And I'll make it a double!' She emptied the bottle into her chalice. 'And that also deserves a proper toast from a fresh bottle!' She stumbled over to the cupboard and took out another bottle of communion wine, which she waved in the air. 'You know what? I suddenly feel like a good sing-song!'

'I've forgotten all the hymns I learnt at Sunday school.'

'Forget the hymns – do you know any Hers?' She giggled.

'The only songs I know might not be quite suitable.' Christina smiled.

'You start, and I'll follow…'

Around three o'clock in the morning, raucous laughter could be heard coming from the bell tower. This was interspersed with loud singing, accompanied by the discordant ringing of the church bell. If anyone had stopped and listened carefully to what Paula and Christina were singing, they might have been shocked to hear a selection of dirty rugby songs coming from inside a church.

16. An Arresting Sequence of Events

The clock chimed three times. The façade of the church was illuminated by the headlights of a couple of police cars, their blue lights continually flashing, making dancing shadows over the gravestones, creating an atmosphere of a ghostly fairground. Several houses in the area had their lights on, with faces peering from behind half closed curtains. Some residents, coats over their nightwear, were standing in their front gardens trying to see what was going on.

One policeman was taking notes outside from an elderly woman, who wore a hairnet and stood in furry pink slippers. 'I heard the bell going, you see. Well, it's never been rung at this time of night. Such a jarring racket!'

'What time was this, Mrs Twells?' The policeman noticed the grubby nightdress she wore beneath a fake fur coat. He couldn't work out if it was the coat or the woman that smelt. The smell reminded him of some rundown care homes he'd had to visit during the course of his work.

'Just after two o'clock. I came outside and thought I could hear singing coming from the top. Sounded like a couple of drunks. Anyway, I came a bit closer… and I couldn't believe my ears!' She crossed her arms across her bosom and rocked from side to side to express her distaste.

'What is it you heard then?' He moved a few paces to the left, to try to avoid the odour that emanated from her movement.

'It was absolutely disgusting!' she gurned, having not put her teeth in, which made her look like one the church's gargoyles.

'What was?'

'The filthy words they were using in those sordid songs! And coming from the holy church.'

'What kind of words do you mean?'

'Ooh, I couldn't repeat them. So shocking!' she grimaced.

'Could I ask you to write them down then?' He flipped a blank page in his notebook and offered it to her. She hesitated and looked worried. 'It's important. You phoned us to report the disturbance. We do need a full statement from you.' Giving her a stern look.

'If I must...' Feeling very uneasy, she took his notebook and pen and wrote down some words and handed it back to him as if it was contaminated.

He glanced down at what she had written, and couldn't disguise a small grin. 'Cock...bollocks...fuck...arseholes.... Those were the exact words you heard, Madam?' He said out aloud.

She pulled an embarrassed face. 'There was another word...such sacrilege coming from a house of God...which I can't possibly write down...'

'Would you spell it, and I'll write it?' He had a good idea what it might be.

'C...U...' She couldn't bear to go any further.

'Cunt? Was that the word?' He enjoyed pronouncing it carefully and watching her mortified expression.

She closed her eyes and nodded. 'Is that all? Can I go back in now? I feel quite sick. I hope those hooligans get put away. Using that language in such a sacred place!'

'Thank you, Mrs Twells; we'll need to see you again. Sign a statement for the records.'

'I hope they go to hell...' She mumbled as she made her way back to her lonely, empty house.

The policeman took a welcome breath of the night air; glad she was out of nasal range. As he put his notebook away, he heard a slight commotion coming from inside the church. The door suddenly opened and out ran Paula, giggling and doing a little dance around the graves. One of his colleagues swiftly followed, doing his best to try and restrain her, but she proved too quick for him as she danced away into the cemetery at the back of the church.

Soon another young policeman came out, holding Christina by the arm and trying to lead her towards the car. 'Unless you mean to make an honest woman of me, unhand me young man!' Christina tried to extricate herself from his grip, without much success.

'Please come quietly Miss.'

Christina stopped. 'Ms, I'm old enough to be your mother. Are you arresting me?' She was still drunk, but more in control than Paula.

'Yes, we charged you inside.'

'Don't remember. What for?' She brushed a piece of fluff off his jacket.

'Being drunk and disorderly and causing a public disturbance.' He pushed her hand away. 'By the way, is that your vehicle?' He pointed to Eric's car, which was parked nearby.

'No…I did drive it here. Why?'

'It was reported stolen a few hours ago. You admit taking it?' They were by one of the police cars. He took out his notebook.

'I borrowed it, officer. No big deal.'

'Right. Well, we'll add car theft to your charge. Want to admit anything else while we're at it?'

'Pretending to be dead while very much alive? Holding a funeral under false pretences. Does that count?'

He sighed and put away his notebook. 'Now are you going to handcuff me and show me your truncheon?' She giggled, pursing her lips to give him an invisible kiss. 'Or will you strip search me at the station to see what I've got hidden in my secret places…?' He looked coolly at her before pushing her into the car.

By now Paula was zigzagging in and around the numerous gravestones, waving her arms like a whirling dervish. Finally, the policeman caught up with her and managed to restrain her. 'Have you come to take me away from all this!' She leant over and tried to give him a kiss on the cheek. 'Let me save you…'

He moved his head away, which almost dislodged his helmet. 'Just calm down Miss. It's in your own interest.'

'But this is my parish! My flock look up to me. I cannot abandon them!'

'I'm sure they'll cope. Come along now.' Despite her earlier garbled protestations, about being the priest of this church, none of the policemen believed her. Nobody would have in the state she was in, also the fact that she was effing and blinding while they struggled to restrain her.

'I shall complain to the archbishop!'

'You do that. And you might as well tell the Pope as well. Come along now.'

'The Pope's Catholic, he wouldn't listen to me….'

He guided her towards the car, relieved that she'd finally run out of steam.

Paula stopped and faced him. 'Two bishops in bed together. Which one is the wife?'

'I don't know. Gay, are they?' he humoured her.

'Mrs Bishop of course! Now take me to your leader so that I can bless him!' Paula waved to Christina as they passed the car she was in.

Christina just looked blankly at her and closed her eyes. Paula then got in the other car and immediately passed out in the back.

In the holding cell of the police station, both looking the worst for wear, Christina was laying on the bed whilst Paula was sitting on the stainless-steel toilet doing a very long wee. During the hour that they had been confined, they'd sobered up considerably.

'Ah, that's better!' Paula pulled up her knickers. 'Quite nice in here, almost like a nun's cell.'

'With enough room to swing a rosary…' Christina stared blankly up at the ceiling of the 6 x 8 cell. 'No TV, tea making facilities or trouser press….'

'What do you need a trouser press for?'

'Put my face in and iron out the wrinkles.' She forced a smile.

Paula came and sat on the bed beside her. 'Does that matter now?'

'What, the fact that I haven't got long on this earth? A woman still likes to look good to the very end.' She sat up. 'I'm sorry I got you involved, and that you'll end up with a police record.'

'These things are sent to try us. And I'd be lying if I said I didn't enjoy some of it. Didn't you have a good time?'

'Yes, I did. It helped me to forget what a disaster the day had turned out to be.'

'It wasn't that bad, Christina, it had it's good moments. You knew the kind of reactions you were likely to get, so it wasn't a total surprise. Was it?'

'No…I had hoped…but you can't expect people to change at the drop of a funeral. At least Tony didn't seem to hate me as much as the others.'

139

'There's still time...you said you thought you might have a couple of months. A lot can be achieved in that time. You mustn't give up...' Paula put her arm around Christina.

'The real problem is not so much time, as me as a person. Although I want to win my family around, there is a kind of devil inside that causes me to react in a destructive way. I just can't be nice all the time. Things are said or done that really put my back up, and in effect I behave so nastily. It's a knee-jerk reaction that I find difficult to control. I'm not going to change. Not now...' Christina was on the verge of tears, but stopped herself.

'You can only be you. But I know your heart's in the right place. You've just got to try and exorcise that little devil when he – or she – comes to the surface.'

'If it were only that easy. Could you exorcise it? Get the little bugger out?'

'I'm afraid exorcisms are confined to the Catholic Church. Not in my remit.'

'Why did you become a priest then? You know, you don't strike me as a Holy Mary, dedicating her life to the church. You really let your hair down and came to life tonight. I saw a different you, someone whose repression was suddenly released. You were quite outrageous.'

'That was the drink...'

'No, that was the real essence of you. Look how you loved wearing that evening dress and makeup. How you even encouraged me with the clown and whole service scenario. To pretend I was dead. I was the one who had doubts, but you persuaded me to go along with it. You came up with the whole concept.'

'Sometimes we have to go against the grain to produce the results we're after.'

'That still doesn't answer my question of why you entered the church?'

'It's a long, complex story…' Paula sighed, remembering.

'Most stories are. As long as you don't take two months to tell it, because I'd like to hear the end.' Christina forced a smile.

'I've never told anyone before…' Paula struggled with her thoughts, and appeared upset with the memories that were slowly returning. 'It's not very nice…it has to do with abuse…'

It was Christina's turn to put her arm around Paula. 'You were abused?'

'No…not me…a girl who went to my Sunday school…not actually abuse as such.'

'I don't understand.'

Paula was finding difficulty in vocalising it. 'The Sunday school choir that my father presided over…He was a priest…'

'You're surely not telling me he did the abusing?'

Paula gasped. 'No. No! One of the girls in the choir came to him after school. She was eleven, very pretty and very precocious. She wanted to sing the solo that he had given to another girl. He refused, telling her she wasn't good enough. She then reported him as having inappropriately touched her…'

'What happened then?'

'She was very convincing. Despite his protestations he was thrown out of the church… excommunicated…defrocked.'

'Oh…I'm sorry. How old were you?'

'Thirteen. The other girls at my school ostracised me. My mother and I had to move away to start again.'

'What about your father? How did he cope? What did he do?'

'He committed suicide…I'm sorry I don't want to go into any more details.' Paula looked worn out and tearful.

'Did you become a priest because of what happened to your father? To make some sort of amends?'

'Something like that, I suppose…please, can we change the subject?'

Christina took Paula's hand and squeezed it. 'I spy with my little eye …'

'Something beginning with s..h.. i.. t.? Paula forced a little smile. 'Which is the mess we're both in…? But at least you didn't kill yourself.'

'Not yet, anyway…give it time…' Christina yawned. 'God, the day has finally caught up with me. I'm knackered and just want to sleep.' She stared at the faceless walls surrounding her and closed her eyes.

'I hope that God will forgive me…' Paula, all energy spent, looked up at the ceiling and said a silent prayer.

At the front desk of the police station, three weary looking men were all talking over each other, giving the duty officer a hard time in sorting out matters between them. Duncan was there in his role as solicitor trying to persuade the police to release both Christina and Paula; Eric wanted to claim his car back; Roger was angry because he had been dragged to the station by Duncan, who had been insistent in him attending, because of Christina's unstable mental state.

Eventually Duncan managed to convince the police to discharge Paula and Christina, who were both cautioned and issued with a fine, which Duncan paid. Eric agreed not to press charges against Christina for taking his car, but refused to take Christina home with him, following an argument with Roger, who didn't want to either.

Eric didn't hang around to see them freed, leaving

the station as soon as he was allowed to reclaim his car.

Both the women were quiet when they were released, which surprised Roger and Duncan, who were expecting some sort of verbal fight, particularly from Christina, who just looked numb and faraway. Paula appeared ashamed and embarrassed and simply wanted the earth to swallow her up.

'Christina...Roger has agreed to take you back to his place, if that's alright?' Duncan was ready for an argument and had prepared his reasons, but she just nodded acquiescently without looking either of them in the eye. Roger had hoped she'd object, but now was left with no choice but to take her. 'Paula, I'll take you home.' She simply shrugged as the four of them left the station in silence.

Neither of the women said anything to the men as each was driven to their respective destinations. Roger was relieved not to have any conversation with Christina, who kept on dropping off in the car. Duncan tried some small talk with Paula, but got no response so didn't pursue it. He made sure Paula was safely at her home before returning to his own. It was five o'clock and just starting to get light.

Roger, careful not to make a noise in case it woke Tony, had to help Christina up the stairs to the spare room. She acted almost like a zombie, not saying anything and being submissively led by Roger.

He thought about undressing her, but decided against it, so plonked her on the bed and covered her up with the duvet. She immediately fell asleep. He then crept to his own bedroom and fell asleep himself.

A couple of hours later, Christina woke with a start and wondered where she was. The surroundings looked familiar, but still being half asleep, she just couldn't work it out in her head.

In a kind of sleepwalking daze, she got out of bed and walked out of the bedroom into the hallway. Seeing another door, she entered Roger's bedroom and almost automatically got into bed beside him. He was lightly snoring and didn't stir when she pulled the duvet across to her side. Dropping her head onto the pillow, she quickly drifted off back to sleep.

17. Trouble Beneath the Sheets

Tony was woken by his mobile ringing. The caller ID said 'Unknown' so he didn't bother to answer it, knowing it was probably some robot at a call centre that had randomly picked his number, asking if he'd had an accident or something similar. He looked at the time to see it was gone 9.00, and panicked for a moment, thinking he'd be late for college, then realised it was Sunday. He lay in bed thinking about what happened yesterday with his mother's sham funeral and all that went with it. He wondered if he'd been too harsh in the way he responded to her. It had been a shock and he was still working it all out in his head, trying to come to terms with the whole situation. Yet what most concerned and upset him was his father's aggressive attitude towards Christina. How he wasn't willing to compromise in any way to forgive her, despite knowing that she didn't have long to live. This really bothered him, and he felt that the only way to try and clear the air between them was to talk to his father and see if he could persuade him to be a bit more compassionate towards her if nothing else.

He got out of bed determined to confront his father. If he didn't try and do it now, he might not feel like it later. He knew Roger would be up by now, probably in the kitchen having coffee and reading the Sundays. It would be an ideal time to discuss it while his father was reasonably relaxed.

Both the kitchen and living room were empty when he went downstairs. There were no signs of any breakfast and the kettle was cold. Tony was surprised, since Roger was an early riser and didn't ever lie in. Had he gone out he wondered? The car was still parked out front, and the Sunday papers hadn't been picked up by the front door.

Tony went back upstairs to check his father's

bedroom. He was surprised and primarily annoyed to see two bodies under the duvet, covered up in the bed and obviously asleep. Roger had promised him that Helen would never stay over; they'd conduct their sexual assignations at her place. He never heard her come in. It must've been when he was asleep.

Tony stood at the doorway wondering what to do, whether to disturb them. He was tempted to go and pull the duvet off to wake them. Perhaps Helen would be naked underneath and he'd get a good look. Even though he didn't like her, he had to admit that she was attractive and had a good figure, and many times he had secretly fantasized what she looked like completely naked. It was an appealing thought, and he could always feign ignorance once he'd done it. How was he to know Helen would be underneath? He'd certainly have one over on his father if he did.

He continued to stare at the lumps in the bed not able to make up his mind what to do, when he accidentally sneezed. One of the lumps stirred, and Roger's head popped out of the duvet. 'What's the matter...?' he said wearily looking up at Tony, who continued to stand by the open doorway.

'You tell me.' Tony pointed to the other lump that hadn't moved. 'You said you wouldn't let Helen spend the night here...'

'What...?' Roger was momentarily disorientated, and then realised there was someone else in bed with him. 'She hasn't...she didn't...I don't understand...' He then slowly and carefully peeked beneath the duvet. 'Oh God...'

Tony was starting to get annoyed, mainly because it looked like he wasn't going to get a proper look at Helen in her birthday suit.

He ranted on angrily. 'Your promises mean sod all! You're always telling me I shouldn't do this or that. But you

146

can change the goalposts whenever it suits you! Have a good night, did you…?'

'Yes, thank you…' Christina's head popped up. She gave a big smile.

'Mum…?' Tony didn't know whether to be shocked or pleased.

'Your father was magnificent. Almost like old times. I see your lady friend has taught you a few tricks.' She teased.

'What the hell are you up to Christina? What are you doing here?' Roger sat up and waved his arms around.

'Are you two back together again, is that it?' Tony sounded almost pleased.

'We are definitely not back together! How did you get in here?'

'I don't know. Must've been sleepwalking. Maybe you carried me into bed.' She seemed just as puzzled.

'I did not! I left you in the spare bedroom.'

Tony was really confused now. 'What's going on here? Dad…. Mum…?'

'Did we have sex, Roger, I can't remember…' Christina was half serious, but then glanced at her fully dressed body under the duvet. 'Maybe not…unless you put my clothes back on?'

'We certainly did NOT have sex! I wish I hadn't agreed to bring you here, whatever state you were in.' Roger was getting really incensed.

'Could someone please tell me what's going on!' Tony shouted, which momentarily silenced his parents. 'I've a right to know.'

'It's all my fault, Tony.' Christina sat up with her back to the headboard. 'I pinched Eric's new car, tried to kill myself, then got roaring drunk with Paula at the church. The police came and arrested us and we were put in a cell until Duncan got us out. Your dad I believe, much against his wishes, brought me here, as I wasn't to be trusted to be left alone. That's about it, isn't it, Roger?'

'Is that true?' Tony looked at Roger, not sure if this was another of his mother's stories.

'That about sums it up.' Roger turned back to Christina now. 'I helped you up to the spare room where you crashed out on the bed. I did NOT bring you in here!'

'If you say so…' Christina got off the bed. 'Anyway, whatever…thank you for looking after me. I think I'd better go. Don't worry, I'm not going to do anything silly.'

'Be my guest.' Roger couldn't contain the sarcasm.

'Mum, are you going to be alright?'

'I don't know really. We'll see what the day brings. I need first to clear my head, so I'm going to walk back to my flat.' She smiled at Roger. 'You don't need to give me a lift.'

'I wasn't going to offer.'

'Dad! Mum, do you want me to come with you?'

'That's sweet of you, but no. I need to be alone for a bit. And I'd be grateful if you didn't pay any unexpected visits to the flat. I'll get in touch when I need company. Okay?'

'If that's what you want. You know where I am.' Tony couldn't think of anything else to say.

'Goodbye Roger, and thank you for looking after me. I do mean that. Sorry to have been a pain…'

Roger was about to say '…in the arse.' then decided against it. He remained in bed as Christina left the bedroom and went downstairs.

Tony stood there feeling wrung out again. He thought about saying something to his father, but was no longer in any mood to continue arguing. He shut the door behind him and returned to his bedroom.

***

It took Christina about an hour to walk home to her flat. She still felt a bit hung-over, but the crisp morning air helped her think a bit clearer about the events over the last twenty-four hours.

Without doubt, yesterday had turned out to be an unmitigated disaster. That she had agreed to the whole clown scenario was something she now bitterly regretted. Her original idea had been to have a slightly more formal mock funeral but with a light-hearted feel to it.

She did think initially that she would arise from the coffin in the chapel, like someone coming out of a giant birthday cake, but Paula dissuaded her, saying that it might prove too much of a shock.

They discussed various ways the service could be conducted, and the only condition that Christina insisted upon was that it shouldn't in any way be mournful or depressing, but jolly and amusing.

It was Paula who had come up with the clown idea, and that Christina herself participated as one of the clowns.

She had agreed on condition that she remained in disguise throughout and just be an observer without having to reveal herself. The more they talked about it, the more the prospect excited them both. Duncan's initial response to the whole funeral concept was sceptical. It was too way out of his comfort zone, and he had serious doubts about it coming off. He had suggested that nothing be done until she was actually dead. Then a simple non-religious service, followed by a small reception where the legacies would be handed out. Simple and straightforward.

Both Paula and Christina eventually swayed him round to their way of thinking, after which it was his idea to have the banners, balloons and white limos. It all snowballed from there as the three of them developed and perfected the idea, making the video, finally convincing themselves that it would be a hoot.

Now Christina wished she'd listened to Duncan when he had initially put a damper on the whole idea. She had only herself to blame. She believed having a bogus funeral might soften the blow of her possible return into their lives. After all she'd be dead soon enough. If she'd simply turned up out of the blue, she was sure they'd all turn against her. Well, apart from Tony, that's exactly what had happened, and in her heart, she couldn't honestly blame them. She had after all, without warning, disappeared from their lives for three years.

Unexpectedly hearing hymn singing, she realised she was passing Paula's church and that it was coming from inside. She stopped for a moment, wondering if she should go and visit Paula to see how she was. That is if Paula was actually about and taking the service and even willing to talk to her? No, she didn't feel up to going in. The walk had taken it out of her. Feeling very tired, what she needed now was more sleep. She continued on to her flat, but hadn't dismissed the idea of ending her own life, since she currently felt that there was no point in her living anyway.

Inside the church the small congregation put down their hymnbooks and sat down in the wooden pews to listen to the sermon that their priest was about to deliver. All eyes were on Paula as she stood on the lectern anxiously shuffling the notes she had made.

She'd covered up the dark rings round her eyes with concealer, since she hadn't slept a wink since getting home. 'Today I'd like to talk about temperance and the evil consequences of drink…' She paused to scan all the faces to see if anyone was scowling or even sniggering. There was no obvious reaction that she could detect, which helped to allay some of her fears. She studied Mrs Twells face, the parishioner who had originally called the police, but could only see a devoted deference coming from her. Perhaps it was really true, nobody had actually seen her dancing round the cemetery or being arrested.

After Duncan had driven her home, she dreaded the phone ringing or even a knock at the vicarage door. Would it be a call from the bishop to reprimand or even remove her from the parish? Should she resign and save them the trouble? Not able to sleep she had spent the time composing her sermon, which helped to chastise her own actions. She had thought of cancelling the morning service, saying she was sick, but thought that might only complicate matters. She felt she had to carry on as usual and face whatever was thrown at her. Yet the phone never rang, nor was there any knock on the door from either a church official or even worse, the local press.

What Paula didn't know was that Duncan was a good friend of the police sergeant at the station; both were freemasons who attended the same lodge. Duncan had managed to have a quiet word, and had succeeded in persuading the sergeant to 'lose' any paperwork related to the arrest, and that to tell any local press who came sniffing, to say it was a couple of vagrants who had created the disturbance. The sergeant had no problem with this, since his mother attended Paula's church, and who had nothing but praise for her.

The sermon, which was directed more to herself than the congregation, seemed to go down well. Paula stood at the church entrance thanking everyone who had attended, and waiting apprehensively for someone to make a comment regarding the previous evening's disturbance.

Mrs Twells was the last to exit, making sure the rest were out of earshot before she confronted Paula. 'Nasty business last night. All that noise, and you should've heard the language!'

'Yes…'

'Police everywhere, and I had to make a statement. I was the one to call them, you know.'

'Did you…thank you…' Paula was now ready to be unmasked.

'Did they talk to you? The police I mean.'

'Yes, they certainly did. I was at the station.'

'You poor thing! At that time of night as well. Did you get a look at those hooligans? Youngsters I believe, druggies, with no respect for people or property!' Mrs Twells waved her arms about to register her disgust.

'Hooligans…?' Paula became aware of an unpleasant smell that had wafted over. 'Did you see them?'

'Wasn't near enough. The police had put their plastic tapes round the area. I talked to a couple of neighbours who had come out, but they couldn't see who the police had arrested. They thought they might've been tramps who'd broken into the church. Not a lot of damage I hope?'

'No…a couple of empty bottles.' Paula couldn't believe what she was hearing.

'They didn't graffiti the walls or…or relieve themselves up there?'

'No, we were very lucky.'

'Oh…' Mrs Twells sounded disappointed, because she had no titbit of inside information to regale her cronies with. 'Well, I hope those hooligans are locked up.'

'Don't you feel they might deserve our forgiveness. They're probably lost souls that need our prayers.' Paula was really thinking of herself.

'After the blasphemous and filthy language they came out with! They're not getting my prayers! Anyway, Reverend, that was a very nice service, thank you.'

***

152

'I'm glad you enjoyed it. See you next Sunday?' Paula held out her hand.

'I wouldn't miss it.' Mrs Twells shook it enthusiastically and meandered down the road to her house. Paula sniffed the air and then her hand. She even looked under her shoes to make sure she hadn't trodden in some dog mess.

Back in the vestry Paula said a short prayer, thanking God from saving her from public and professional embarrassment, at least for the time being. She realised there was still a chance that the incident might come back to haunt her, and well aware she wasn't out of the woods yet. Did she now have a criminal record, and would the police contact the church authorities? All she could do was wait and try and deal with whatever emerged, if anything. She still felt quite fragile, overtired and apart from a good night's sleep, needed something to relax her. After a moments battle with her conscience, she put on her coat and headed to a local superstore.

While Christina slept right through the rest of the day, oblivious to everything and everyone, those whose lives she had affected were battling with the aftermath.

Roger and Tony hardly exchanged more than half a dozen words after Christina left. Roger had got dressed and gone over to Helen's flat. He'd agreed to spend the day with Helen on condition that she didn't mention Christina or bring up the subject. He wasn't prepared to discuss it, or what had happened. Helen inwardly felt threatened and jealous by Christina's reappearance, but didn't want to upset him, as he seemed uncharacteristically in such an emotional and delicate state.

Tony stayed at home and masturbated to some porn. He was tempted to go and see how his mother was despite her forbidding him to, but talked himself out of it. He was tired of arguments. He texted a couple of friends, eager to show off his new laptop, but they were too busy to meet up. He went for a walk in the park hoping to see the flasher woman, but the place was deserted apart from a group of winos and some copulating dogs. He returned home, had a microwave dinner, and illegally downloaded the latest film blockbuster to watch on his laptop.

Eric spent the day proudly driving around in his new car with Sadie. They'd spent the previous evening arguing about Christina, until Eric had persuaded her that he'd only slept with Christina because she didn't have long to live. Sadie was almost moved, saying that more people should give 'mercy fucks' to those in need. Whilst they were out, Sadie was keen to christen the car by having sex with him in it. He just wasn't in the mood and was concerned the interior might get scuffed, scratched or messed up with bodily fluids.

Duncan did, over the course of the day, try and ring Christina, but it continually went to voicemail. He thought of driving to her flat, but calculated the possible consequences of doing so.

She might not answer; she could be out; she could've finally found a way to kill herself. Then he might have to break in, find her, call the authorities and that would be his Sunday down the drain. No, he wasn't up to it. If she had done away with herself that was no longer his problem. Christina had already made a more comprehensive Will, so those formalities had been taken care of. Instead, he looked at his numerous boating magazines, dreaming of the day he would retire, buy a boat and sail the seas.

Paula, sprawled out on the sofa in her pyjamas, poured herself a second generous glass of whiskey from the bottle she had bought earlier. She had agonised about buying it, recalling her own sermon about the perils of drink. Was she turning into an alcoholic? Was this the first step down the slippery slope? No, she knew she had the strength to abstain. But right now she desperately needed something to calm her nerves. It would be a once only fall from grace. As she lay there, she experienced the liquid warming her throat and generally relaxing her. She felt much better now and ready to face whatever might be thrown at her in the hours and days to come.

18. Assassins in the Night

Christina woke with a start to see two dark figures standing menacingly over her by the bed. 'Good morning, Christina…sleep well?'

'Roger…?….What are you…' She recognised his voice, but still couldn't see clearly since the thick curtains were not letting in much light.

'We thought we'd surprise you…'

'We…?' She found it hard to focus on the other figure.

'You must like surprises – since you enjoy inflicting them on others.' Spoke the other voice.

'Eric…? How did you get in here?' Christina now recognised the outline of Eric's muscular frame beside Roger's diminutive one. 'I mean, how did you know where I was? Only Tony knew…'

Roger laughed. 'We managed to persuade him to tell us. Getting in was the easy part!'

'You hadn't shut the door properly, so we didn't even have to break in – which we were prepared to do.' Eric added.

Christina remembered entering her flat, but because she was so tired, had probably not banged the front door shut. She'd just gone into her bedroom and crashed out. 'What do you want?'

Roger's voice was soft. 'We've come to make things easier for you.'

Eric bent down towards her and whispered. 'We don't want you to suffer any more.'

'I don't understand…'

'She doesn't understand!' Roger laughed again.

Eric's face was now close to hers. 'You've got this terminal cancer thing. You are going to die, aren't you?'

'Yes...'

'You also planned to kill yourself, didn't you?'

'Yes...' She wanted to sit up, but discovered she couldn't move. Her body felt stiff and frozen, as if she was strapped to the bed. 'What is this about...?'

The curtains were suddenly swished open, letting in bright sunlight. Christina was momentarily blinded, but then saw the form of a third figure standing by the window holding something. The figure now joined the other two. 'Hello Christina, feel a bit more refreshed? Ready to face the day?'

'Jennie...?'

'Nice to see you stunned and confused for a change. Aren't you glad to see us? We did all think of dressing up as clowns to surprise you.'

'I thought appearing like zombies would be much more fun!' Eric raised his arms menacingly and made a guttural noise.

'But in the end, we didn't want to prolong the agony, or put you through any more pain.' Roger smiled.

'We didn't want to be too punishing...like staging a bogus funeral...' Jennie waved the object in her hand, which Christina could now see was a gun. The same gun Jennie had produced at her place earlier. 'You do want to die, don't you?'

'Yes...No...I don't know!' Christina saw three sinister faces staring down at her.

Roger grinned almost sadistically. 'Well, we're here to make up your mind for you. Or should I say - we've made our minds up, so you are spared that decision.'

'Are you...are you going to kill me?' It all suddenly dawned on her.

'Not quite...you're going to do it yourself. Real

bullets loaded this time.' Jennie waved the gun again.

Christina appeared fully awake now. 'What do you mean…?'

'You will take this gun, put it to your temple or into your mouth – and then pull the trigger. Instant oblivion. No pain, no suffering. What could be simpler?' Jennie was enjoying this.

'But the gun is yours…the police will find out.'

'It can't be traced. I told you, Patrick got it illicitly. Christina, my dear,' Jennie addressed her like a little girl. 'You came to my house, remember? You terrorised me.'

'I didn't!'

'CCTV outside my house will prove you visited. I'll tell the police that you had a gun and threatened me with it. It's all been carefully thought out. But what do you care anyway? This is what you've wanted isn't it?'

'Maybe…but not quite like this.'

'So did you think crashing head first into a wall was an easier option?' Roger challenged her.

'And in my new car too! How selfish would that have been!' Eric added indignantly.

'Why should any of you care anyway! You didn't want me back. You seemed pleased when you thought I was dead. You were happy to take money and things off me.'

'Only what we were owed.' Roger reminded her. 'Did you really think that we'd welcome you back with open arms, and that we'd forget what you did to us in the past?'

'How many times do I have to say I'm sorry for what I did?'

Jennie lowered her face close to Christina's. 'A million sorrys would not compensate for how we all feel.'

'There were reasons…if only you'd care to listen.'

Jennie was starting to get impatient. 'We're tired of listening to any more of your lies, your made-up stories. Do the right thing. We'll make sure you get a decent and respectful funeral.'

'Do I have a choice? What if I decide to continue living until I die from my cancer?'

'Of course, there's a choice,' Roger tried to sound sincere. 'Either you pull the trigger or one of us will.'

'I see…. You really have made up your minds. I can't say I'm surprised. I suppose I had it coming to me…and it will be a quick and painless end…'

Eric tried to smile. 'It is for the best you know…'

'In which case I will save you the trouble and do it myself.' Christina held out her hand for the gun.

'Wise choice. Safety catch is off. Bullets in every chamber. All ready to go…' Jennie passed the gun to her.

Christina held the gun feeling its weight. She positioned it first to her temple and then opened her mouth to insert the barrel. She took it out again, uncertain which best to apply. Roger, Eric and Jennie had taken a few steps back, so as not to get splattered with any blood. They looked on intently and unemotionally. 'Of course, we haven't discussed whether it's a burial or cremation…'

'Which ever you prefer.' Roger smiled.

'I wasn't talking about me…' Christina turned to them all. 'I want to know *your* preferences…do you want to be buried or cremated?' They all looked at her in silent bewilderment. 'Sorry, can't wait.' At which juncture she pointed the gun, and in quick succession, shot all three in the head. 'There's always a choice…' She smiled, blowing at the front muzzle of the gun like she'd seen in old cowboy films…

Hearing three bangs in quick succession, Christina opened her eyes. The room was dark and she was still in bed. There was another bang, which she now recognised as that of a car

159

backfiring. She looked at the bedside clock to see it was just after eight o'clock in the morning. Had she really slept right through yesterday and last night? She must've done. The doctor had said that she might experience more tiredness as time progressed. She turned on her phone to check the day, which confirmed it was Monday. There were quite a few missed calls and voicemails from Duncan, which she couldn't be bothered to listen to.

She got out of bed and crept towards the curtains, wondering if there were three dead bodies sprawled out on the floor. The sun flashed into the room as she drew the curtains back. No bodies, no blood. She was almost disappointed. The dream had been too real, and she still remembered that feeling of control and euphoria as she pulled the trigger.

Her throat was dry, so she ambled over to the kitchen and drank two large glasses of water. Her stomach rumbled, and having not eaten for over twenty-four hours, she now felt the hunger pangs. Luckily, she had a loaf and some bacon in the fridge, so made a couple of thick bacon sandwiches, which she scoffed greedily, complemented with a cafetiere of coffee. It helped to revive her and she began to feel more energetic and able to face whatever the day was going to bring.

In the bathroom mirror she studied her eyes and skin to see if there were any signs of the jaundice she had been told would occur as the cancer progressed. It all looked very normal. She was also told to expect some pain in the abdomen and back – but had experienced none so far. Gradual weight loss was another symptom, but if anything, she'd put on weight.

From further googling on the Internet, she'd learnt that in some rare cases the symptoms didn't emerge until the final stages, when rapid deterioration, followed by eventual death, came very quickly. She accepted that this was probably her personal fate. It was one reason why she had refused any treatment, since the prognosis was terminal. Having some quality of life in the last months meant more to her than undergoing countless hospital visits for chemotherapy and feeling shit all the time.

A long soak in the bath made her think more clearly about her present circumstances. The idea of killing herself was increasingly disappearing. One part of her didn't want to give up, the other was determined that she didn't want to make it easier for everyone. Being in a sense fatalistic, her prior attempts to end her life were unsuccessful for an obvious reason. It wasn't meant to be. She had to finish what she had started, which stemmed back to a promise she had made before she returned to London to organise the funeral. She needed to come up with a different strategy to win them back over, so that she could die happily, having balanced the books so to speak.

Having got dressed, it was while enjoying another coffee, that her phone went. 'Good morning, Duncan, I'm still here and haven't done anything silly you'll be pleased to know.'

Duncan's voice registered relief. 'That's good to hear. I was getting worried after you didn't answer any of my calls.'

'And I'm grateful you didn't and come over to check.'

'You needed time to yourself, which is quite understandable. How are you feeling?'

'Pretty good. I had an interesting visit very early this morning. Roger, Eric and Jennie came to pay their respects…well, disrespects would be more appropriate.'

'What…?' Duncan wasn't sure he'd heard correctly.

'They broke into the flat and threatened to kill me.'

'Are you serious?' He didn't like the sound of this. After what had happened following the funeral, he wouldn't have put it past them to seek some sort of revenge.

'Jennie had a gun and she wanted me to kill myself…if I didn't agree, they would shoot me themselves and make it look like suicide. It wasn't a secret that I wanted to kill myself.' Christina was doing her best to sound grave.

He was completely taken in. 'What happened…I mean, they didn't kill you, obviously?'

'No…I killed them instead…each shot in the head…It was a wonderful feeling and a fitting, if messy end! I might need a bit of help here.'

Duncan's mind went into overdrive. The police would have to be called. She couldn't plead self-defence, because she'd already confessed to him. He had it on tape since he recorded all his office calls. She'd go to jail and undoubtedly die there. His quiet little life would be upturned. He was beginning to wish he'd never agreed to represent Christina in this whole charade. 'Are they still there…I mean the bodies?'

'No…they disappeared as soon as I woke up.'

'I don't understand…' He still hadn't got it.

'Oh Duncan…it was a dream – be it a very vivid one.'

'It's not true then?'

'Did you really believe it was?' It was Christina's turn to sound amazed.

'I have witnessed many things in my career. A lot you wouldn't believe yourself, but nonetheless really happened. After what I saw both at the funeral and the restaurant, it wouldn't have been a complete shock if what you described had actually taken place.'

'You surprise me, Duncan.'

'The vagaries of the human condition can never be

predicted. People commit acts that even they didn't think they'd be capable of. Nothing is ever certain, and no one is excluded. Take Paula's actions for instance.'

'That was my fault, I encouraged her to drink. I feel awful about it.'

'She didn't have to. One can always say no. Something in her psyche was attracted to the prospect…'

'What will happen to her now?'

'That's up to her really, but I don't believe they'll be any repercussions.'

'Are you sure about that?'

'Christina, we must remain hopeful… I'm sorry, but I have to go now. An interesting case. A divorce to sort out from a same sex marriage. Although one of the males used to be a woman. Don't understand this transgender stuff. They both want custody of the cats. …Anyway, you know where I am. Keep in touch.'

'I haven't thanked you for sorting out that business at the police station.'

'You have now.'

'I hope you've added, whatever the fine was, to my account.'

'Don't worry, I have. Goodbye for now.' Duncan ended the call.

Christina sat for a moment wondering what to do next. Tony would be at college; both Roger and Eric would be at work; she didn't feel like paying Jennie another visit. She still felt very guilty about what had happened with Paula, and wondered if Paula would even speak to her now.

The morning, which had started bright and optimistically for her, had now turned distinctly grey and despondent. Dark thoughts of a quick end surfaced once more…

19. Feeling the Fear

Whatever was presently going on in Christina's head didn't detract from the fact that she still had to eat. Her cupboard and fridge were practically bare. Starving herself to death wasn't a viable option. If she was going to kill herself it had to be quick. Despite feeling a little despondent, she nevertheless needed to do a shop to stock up on food and essentials. It would give her something to do and at least get her out of the flat.

She drove to the nearest supermarket and started to push her trolley round rather aimlessly, throwing in whatever took her fancy. She used to be an avid label reader, carefully studying the contents for fats, sugars and salts, always buying lots of fruit and vegetables and being quite particular what she put in her body. But now she didn't think it mattered what she ate, so she might as well enjoy all the crap and comfort foods, which tasted great but weren't supposed to be good for you. In went the pork pies, several processed ready meals, pizzas, various cakes and puddings.

When she used to shop, she was always fascinated by what really fat people had in their trolleys, obese customers who were usually huffing and puffing as they pushed their bulky shopping down the aisles. Christina would glance into their trolleys to see all the rubbish they ate, always tempted to say 'No wonder you're so bloody fat!'. Now, ironically, as she headed towards the drinks section, she realised she had the same collection of unhealthy and fattening foods in her own trolley.

From the wine section she chose a couple of bottles of red. As she rounded the corner to the area where the spirits were shelved, she saw Paula who was putting a bottle of whiskey into her basket. 'Paula…?'

'Oh hello…' Paula looked embarrassed. 'How are you?'

'More importantly – how are you?'

'Not too bad. You know how it is…'

'Recommend that particular brand, would you?' Christina pointed to the whiskey bottle in Paula's basket.

'Never tried it before, but it's the cheapest…'

'For yourself, or are you going to treat the winos in the park?'

Paula looked into Christina's trolley. 'Actually, I was going to ask the same of you. Feeding the needy who aren't particular what they eat?'

Christina smiled. 'Touché! Look I'm nearly done. If you are, I can give you a lift back?'

'Thanks. Which mixer would you say goes best – soda, dry ginger or coke?'

'I feel really guilty now.' Christina sat in an armchair in the vicarage drinking coffee.

Paula proffered a plate of biscuits. 'Why, do you think you've made me into an alcoholic because I bought a bottle of whiskey?'

'You said you'd never tried it before…before I practically forced it on you. Now, only a couple of days later, you're stocking up.' Christina took a couple of biscuits.

'And enjoying a small glass in the evening. It's helped me to relax. Things have been quite stressful since our little escapade.'

'And all because of me…'

'You didn't force me. I participated of my own free will.'

'Maybe I'm the Devil incarnate, screwing up the lives of all those I'm in contact with.'

'Don't talk such rubbish, Christina. The Antichrist,

Satan, Beelzebub or whatever people like to call him doesn't exist. The Devil was invented by the Church to frighten people in order to control them.'

'You really surprise me.'

'What's more, as we're on the subject, I don't believe in heaven or hell; the immaculate conception; or that God created the world in six days. Parts of the bible were written by men to create a sense of mysticism, inventing stories to draw in the followers and have power over them.'

'So, what do you believe in?'

'The goodness of the human spirit. That we are all on this earth to learn from each other. If I can create a better understanding between people and help them along the way, then I will have done my job.'

'You don't have to be a priest to do that.'

'No, but I felt a moral obligation to enter the church.'

'Because of your father?'

'Partly…it felt right at the time. To try and compensate what happened to him. Provided a sense of purpose and freedom.'

'Yet quite a drastic one to my mind, because of the demands of the church. You're not really free are you…?'

Paula stopped to think. 'Perhaps not, but I do believe in what I'm doing. Mind you, if word does get out what happened the other night, I might very well be relieved of my duties…'

'Because of me.'

'Stop saying that!

'If I hadn't come to see you in the first place, your reputation would still be intact and you wouldn't be buying bottles of whiskey to drown your sorrows.'

I don't regret anything, Christina. You've helped to bring me out of myself. I've learnt some interesting songs; I I might actually take up dancing and go to classes. You've

---

166

also introduced me to a comforting drink, which I shall imbibe sensibly. And if the worst comes to the worst and I am kicked out of the church, I shall find another way to make this world a better place, or alternatively become a drunken slut offering my body for a good time.'

'And you wouldn't blame me if that happened?'

'The only person to blame would be myself. In the end it always comes down to choices. The ones you personally make.'

'What if you don't have one, and circumstances forcefully push you in a direction you'd rather not go towards?'

'You have to make the best of it.' Paula paused for a moment. 'But that's easier said than done. It can become a journey from which there is no return...'

'And don't I know it! I feel I'm in a tunnel, wedged between a rock and a very hard place, without the benefit of any light at the end of it.'

'We must never give up hope. You must feel the fear and keep going.'

'You're beginning to sound like a priest...' Christina smiled.

'That's the last thing I want to sound like!'.

'You know what you need – what we both need – is a good time, cheering up.'

'I wouldn't disagree with that. As long as we don't get arrested in the process!'

'Tell me, what things really scare you?'

Paula thought for a moment. 'Nothing scares me as such. Not bothered by ghosts. I quite like strolling round the cemetery at night. The peace is quite invigorating.'

'There must be things that give you the shivers.'

'Well.... I don't like gory horror films, fish in tanks, stuffed animals, heights, confined spaces...why?'

Paula sat in the middle of the capsule, her arms folded, looking extremely anxious. 'I don't know why I agreed to this…'

'What's the worst that could happen?' Christina stood by the window enjoying the view as their capsule on the London Eye slowly rose to the top.

'We get stuck for hours, a plane crashes into us, someone pulls out a knife and decides to cut our throats…' She shivered at the thought.

Christina turned to the elderly couple, the only other occupants in the pod, who were taking photographs and pointing out various landmarks. 'Excuse me, you're not planning to cut our throats, are you?'

The woman turned around and smiled. 'Nie mów po angielsku…no English, sorry.'

'There you go,' Christina turned to Paula, 'We're safe, they won't cut our English throats. That just leaves us getting stuck or a plane ploughing into us.'

'Thanks for the assurance. Alright for you. You don't mind dying. I'd like to live a bit longer.' Paula, still glued to the seat, continued to feel uneasy.

Christina took Paula by the arm and dragged her to the window. 'Come on, nothing's going to happen. As you said yourself – feel the fear and keep going! Not only do you face conquering your dislike of heights, but also of confined spaces. Two in one! Say a prayer if it helps, and be thankful for such an amazing view.'

Paula, taking a deep breath while silently mouthing a prayer, held on to one of the window bars, forcing herself to look out at the ever-changing vista. 'London is rather beautiful…' She suddenly felt a sense of calm envelop her.

'Not sorry you came?'

'No…thank you…' Paula squeezed Christina's arm.

'It isn't so bad, is it?'

'It's…it's quite inspiring.' Paula suddenly looked with fresh eyes.

'Good…Proves that most fears are in the head. The day is still young - see that very tall building over there?' Christina pointed to the Shard. Paula nodded. 'Well, that's where we're having lunch – on the 32nd floor. After which we will ascend to the 72nd floor for the best view of London. How do you feel about that?'

For a moment Paula felt a surge of anxiety. 'I'm not sure…I couldn't face going up the Eiffel Tower during a school trip to France. I was the only one of our group who refused. The teacher and the other girls never let me forget it.'

'I'm not going to force you. It has to be your decision. Whatever, I've booked a table and I shall dine alone if I have to. I'll never get the chance again, which I'm sure you'll understand.' Christina spoke very matter-of-factly and gently.

'Can I think about it…?' Their capsule had now reached the very top of the wheel. Paula gazed out and mouthed another prayer to herself.

'Of course, but don't think too hard. We've another little diversion before lunchtime, to hopefully give you an appetite.'

'What's that?'

'You'll see when we get there…Just enjoy the moment…and the sight before you.' Christina, her face almost pressed against the glass, shed a tear as she took in the whole panorama, a vision she was unlikely to ever to behold again.

'I am NOT snorkelling with sharks!' Paula raised her voice,

standing well away from the glass that separated her and the giant stingray that appeared to be staring at her.

'Honestly, It's perfectly safe, really.' Christina was doing her best to convince her, as they slowly wandered round Sea Life at the London Aquarium observing all the exotic fish and sea creatures. 'Coming face to fin with such an iconic beast, how exciting would that be!' Christina had seen that you could book a guided 15-minute snorkel to experience being in close proximity with a number of sharks.

'I am not putting on a wetsuit and diving amongst killer sharks, thank you very much! You go ahead, but don't expect me to stand and watch.' Paula was adamant. 'It's enough seeing these monsters behind glass, even at a distance.'

It had been a bit of a tug-of-war to persuade Paula to even enter the building, a short walk from the London Eye. It was small fish in domestic tanks that she originally meant that unnerved her. The thought of being in close proximity with large amphibians and sea animals would really spook her. Christina pointed out the small, excited children who were all queuing up to see the fish. If they weren't afraid, why should she be?

They strolled across to the next section where a green sea turtle was swimming elegantly inside the tank. 'Such beauty and grace, just like the shark. Are you sure you won't consider?' Christina was persistent.

'Please don't push me, or you'll be having lunch on your own.' Paula really meant it. The brief euphoria she had experienced in the capsule had by now slowly evaporated. She still didn't like observing the fish in the aquarium, but was pleasantly surprised that it wasn't turning out the tough ordeal that she had expected.

'Just testing…' Christina smiled.

'What do you mean?' Paula then pulled a face and

moved quickly away, as they passed a unit with a crocodile, gruesomely lunching on some dead rodents.

'I wasn't serious about swimming with the sharks. You seemed to be coping all right as we went round. I just wanted to see how far you were prepared to go.'

'You do like to push people, don't you! What if I'd agreed to try it – you would've joined me of course?'

'Definitely not! You see, I can't swim and I hate deep water. And if I'm honest, if you had been up for it, I would then have tried to dissuade you. Sorry…'

'And I thought I was complex and perverse!' They both started laughing, and the laughter continued as they reached the Ice Adventure zone where they enjoyed watching the penguins diving, playing and comically strutting about.

Back outside, having completed the aquarium tour, they stood for a moment and watched the throng of tourists on the South Bank, either going towards the London Eye, or to the Houses of Parliament in the other direction. Christina studied the people as they walked past. 'I wonder how many of them are going to die soon…'

'That's a funny thing to say. Well, not funny exactly.'

'For the last few hours, because I was enjoying myself so much, I almost forgot about my condition. Now, looking at all those faces; some happy, some sad, I momentarily felt a little envious. Most will see Christmas, but there would be some like me who won't…' Christina forcefully straightened her back to a more positive stance. 'Sorry, I didn't mean to put a damper on the day. Come on, we haven't finished our little tour of fear-busting attractions…'

'Do you mean lunch in the sky? I'm not sure I'm going to order any fish if it's on the menu!' Paula was starting to feel a little peckish as they slowly walked in the direction of Westminster Bridge.

'Not quite yet. It's still early. There's one more visit.' After a couple of minutes, Christina suddenly stopped outside an entrance.

'You must be joking!' Paula's expression was one of minor terror as she saw a monstrous figure covered in blood standing by the door.

'It's not exactly a horror film as such, which I know you don't like…'

'No…this looks much worse…' Paula was taking deep breaths as she stared at the gory photos of the London Dungeon, and hearing the piercing screams via the sound system, coming from inside.

'Paula, let me bring to mind a Bible phrase which has stayed with me. One I learnt in religious education at school. 'Yea, though I walk through the valley of the shadow of death, I will fear no evil'…this is the perfect opportunity for you to put it into practise.'

'I'll need more than a staff and rod to comfort me!'

'Come on, it's not real. All in your mind. It'll be fun!' Christina was already showing tickets she had pre-booked to a ghoulish attendant.

'You're really determined to put me through it today.'

'It hasn't been so bad so far, has it?'

'It's had its moments, I'll admit. But if I die of shock or have a heart attack – I shall blame you!'

'If you do die, we can exchange notes later, if there is an afterlife. Coming?'

'Ah well, in for a penny, in for a pounding! I've always been a bit of a masochist!' She took Christina's arm as a comfort as they ventured inside.

Ninety minutes later Christina and Paula came out of the London Dungeon almost in hysterics, more from laughter than fright. 'I almost wet myself when that terrible actor who was playing Frankenstein's monster was doing his stuff, strutting like he was incontinent! He couldn't frighten a baby!'

'What about the one who was trying to be Guy Fawkes!' Christina added. 'His performance might have added a bit of sparkle if he'd put the explosive where the sun don't shine!'

They both roared with laughter at the memory. 'Very entertaining and silly. I don't think I've laughed so much in a long time. Christina, I must thank you again for making me see the light – or should I say the dark!'

'It just goes to show that we often deceive ourselves about what we think we are scared of – until we find the courage to face it, and then realise it was just in our heads and not real'

'That's very philosophical, Christina.'

'It's just that recent events have made me think more. About how everything around you changes and nothing is always how it seems, yet people remain essentially the same.'

'Are you afraid of dying?'

'Not really, but I didn't think it would come so soon. Two score and three hasn't the same ring to it as three score and ten…. Anyway, let's put dying and philosophy aside and continue with enjoying the moment. Are you hungry?'

'Ravenous!'

'Top of the world Ma! I thought the views from the London Eye were great – but this is incredible!' Paula seemed mesmerized by the entire landscape that spread before her, as they looked across from the highest viewing point of the Shard.

'Not scared or apprehensive in any way?' Christina could see how relaxed and happy Paula was.

'Quite the opposite. This is absolutely inspiring…I didn't think I'd have the nerve to do this on my own. Thank you for bullying me into agreeing to make that leap of faith. I do believe heights will no longer be an issue with me.'

'That's good. I'm sorry if I did seem to bully you as such, but if you didn't really want to do anything, you wouldn't have.'

'That's true…and thank you for lunch. An inspired choice. I enjoyed it.'

'Pleasure. I enjoyed it too. I think the waiter took quite a shine to you.'

'He was rather fit, but barely out of school. I didn't want to add seducing minors to my drunk and disorderly criminal record.' Paula moved across and gave Christina a warm hug, which she wasn't quite prepared for. 'Today has been very special, you know.'

'I'm glad. I thought so too. We make a great team!' Christina gave her a quick hug back.

Paula now looked thoughtful. 'It's made me revaluate a few things.'

'Like what?'

'Whether I want to continue being a priest…'

20. Sat Nav to Supper and Sex

Returning home after leaving Paula, Christina felt tired and nauseous, with the onset of a bad stomach ache. After being physically very sick, she took to her bed. She believed she'd experienced the first tell-tale signs of her illness - tiredness and abdominal pains. Was it all going to escalate now? Would she die in her sleep?

The next morning, she woke feeling somewhat refreshed and better than she had for a long time. She couldn't understand why and tried to reflect upon it objectively. The tiredness might've been as a result of a very long day with Paula; the stomach pains could've come from the extremely rich meal they'd had, which might have upset her. Yet she'd been warned that she might feel fine one day, and the next very ill. Each case was distinctive, and each individual experienced different symptoms.

Christina sat in her flat speculating on what to do next. She felt she was playing a frustrating waiting game. Waiting for the signs of her cancer to really kick in, so that all decisions would be taken out of her hands. Earlier thoughts of suicide had vanished. Her day with Paula had made her feel more alive, having bonded with someone whom she could confide in, and who wouldn't judge her. She was concerned that Paula was now questioning her own vocation, and wondered if it was because of her damaging influence. Paula had assured her that it was nothing to do with her, but it was a question that was constantly on Paula's mind – whether she was doing the right thing in continuing with the church.

In the taxi home, Christina thought about her aunt and the promise she had made to her before returning to London after the mysterious three years away. A promise she now wished she'd never made. In all her previous conversations with both Duncan and Paula, she had remained evasive about what had really happened during those missing years. It was a secret that she wanted to die with her. She now felt it might be better if she stopped trying to inveigle herself into all their lives. It would be a simple, less stressful way out if she quietly disappeared again. Paula, feeling very positive and energised, had implored her not to give up. She had advised her to lay low for a few days and not contact anyone. Paula was sure they would make the first move and get in touch with her. Christina wasn't so sure, but agreed she needed time on her own.

Over the next couple of days, Christina only left the flat to get a breath of air and some exercise. She'd spoken briefly to Paula who phoned her, thanking her again for treating her to such a wonderful day, confirming she hadn't experienced any ill effects after their meal when Christina enquired. This convinced Christina that her illness was definitely starting to take effect. Yet she continued to feel fine, without any reoccurrence of the symptoms, which frustrated her more than anything. It was as if she was being teased and played with.

Tony texted her several times asking if she was all right, and could he come and see her after college? Christina texted back to say that she was fine and preferred to be on her own for the time being. She promised to get back to him when she was ready for a visit. Duncan had also made another dutiful call to check on her, but didn't have much more to say.

By the fourth day Christina was starting to go stir crazy. She needed some stimulation and to be with other people. She knew she wouldn't be welcome if she contacted

Jennie, Eric or even Roger. They'd made their position perfectly clear. She thought about asking Tony to come round, but wasn't in the mood to talk about the cancer, which he was likely to want to discuss. Paula was away for a few days visiting her mother, so seeing her was out. Having been away for three years, she had no other friends in London, none that she hadn't previously fallen out with anyway.

She was thinking about going into the West End either to see a film or a theatre matinee just for something to do, when her phone rang. It was Eric. She half thought about not answering, but because she was so fed up and a touch lonely, she decided to take the call. 'Hello Eric…I hope you're not ringing to tell me off because I borrowed your car.' She didn't mean to sound so brittle, but that's the way it came out. It had always been one of Christina's failings, in the way she initially responded to people, which often came across as harsh and sarcastic.

'And a very good day to you too!' Eric countered.

'Sorry…'

'So, how are you? I thought you might have got in touch.'

'I didn't think you'd want to hear from me, after what I did.' Doing her best to sound contrite.

'Sure, I was pissed off at the time. But no harm done. It'd been a funny day. The car is great by the way. Thank you. Anyway, how are things?'

'Things are things…nothing's changed. I'm still here – just.'

'Christina, are you mad at me for some reason? I just phoned to see how you were, that's all.'

'I'm sorry…' She thought for a moment, and then made a decision. 'Look, if you're not doing anything, would you like to come round for an early dinner this evening?'

177

'I'm not – and are you sure?'

'Would I ask if I wasn't sure!' Which came out harsher than she intended. 'Eric, I'd like you to come…please. Say about six?'

'Okay-doke! See you then…'

'Eric…' she caught him before he hung up. 'Don't you want to know the address?'

'That's a point. Great, I can use the Satnav in the car!' He seemed more excited at that prospect than actually coming to dinner.

Christina hoped she wasn't making a mistake by inviting him round, but she felt so fed up, that even the prospect of Eric's company was better than nothing. He never had much conversation if it didn't centre on sport, or other male pursuits. He never read books, went to the theatre or art galleries, and the only films he wanted to see were those blockbuster superhero epics which she hated. Christina had felt he was dumbing her down by his lack of interest in anything artistic or creative, which became a serious bone of contention when they were together. Eric wasn't stupid, but neither was he bright. The only thing that had kept them together was the sex.

It had just gone seven, and Eric still hadn't arrived. She was furious. Had he stood her up just to be spiteful? She'd prepared a nice meal, which she'd cooked to be ready at six-thirty, now in danger of being spoilt.

She picked up the phone. 'Eric…where the hell are you! Have you changed your mind about coming?'

'Hi, Christina…I'm on the way – I hope…' Eric sounded preoccupied.

'What do you mean hope for God's sake?' She was starting to lose patience.

'Well...I did leave just before six...it's the Satnav...it's taken me in the wrong direction...I can't understand it...I'm sure I programmed it according to the instructions...'

Christina heard a female voice in the background, sounding like she was issuing instructions. 'Who's that in the car with you? Is it Sadie? I didn't invite her!'

'No, it's the Satnav voice...she's confusing me.'

'But I'm only 15 minutes away from your flat. Where are you now?'

'Not quite sure...Sorry...'

Christina took a deep breath in order to calm herself. 'Eric, might you have an A to Z in the car?'

'Didn't think I needed it, with the Satnav... What was the postcode again...? Hang on, I'll stop the car.'

She spelt it out for him, 'Well, before you end up in Scotland, why don't you just ask someone for directions. Do you think you can do that?' She sounded like a parent talking to her child.

'Just a sec...Ah, right...Put in the wrong postcode! Okay, I know where I am now...should be with you soon.... bye...' He hung up.

'Fuck!' In exasperation Christina threw the phone on the sofa, and went back into the kitchen to try and salvage the meal.

Eric arrived twenty minutes later, looking sheepish as he held out a bunch of roses to give her. 'Sorry...'

'You never change...' Was all she managed to say, so as not to start an argument.

'What d'you mean? I put on a clean shirt and underwear specially!' He said, giving her a school boyish grin. 'Still friends...?'

She couldn't help but smile. 'And don't you dare make any comments about the food. It was ready an hour

179

ago. Don't blame me if tastes awful!'

'I'll blame the Satnav lady with the sexy voice…Turn left here; straight on ahead; right at the roundabout; and at the next junction take off your trousers big boy…'

Christina couldn't help but giggle. Whatever she thought Eric's failings were, he did always make her laugh.

'How many people were in this commune you spent time at when you were away?' Eric was sitting up in bed with his hands behind his head. He had started to ask her questions about where she had been the last three years. Not wanting to tell him the actual truth, a long and complex story, Christina decided to make up a story about living in a commune.

'About fifteen of us…' Christina felt drowsy but happy. She hadn't planned to have sex with him, but one thing led to another after the meal, and she succumbed to his charm, although she had blatantly encouraged him. It was the very release she needed at the time.

'Mainly women…men?'

'Eight men, six women and one whose sex we couldn't determine…Please Eric, I'm not in the mood to go into any specifics.'

'Did you have sex with any of them?'

Christina thought for a moment. 'Only the women to start off with…'

'What…Really…?' Eric was suddenly interested.

'Petra had only one leg, but was quite inventive; Esmeralda was grotesquely ugly, but had the body of Venus; and Tatiana had three breasts which gave you plenty to play with…'

'You don't happen to have a picture of the one with three tits?'

180

'Oh, Eric…' Christina sighed.

'You mean, she didn't have three…? Are you having me on?' He seemed quite disappointed.

'I didn't have sex with anyone! It was a difficult time for me, and I don't want to discuss it further.'

'Don't get shirty. I'm just interested, that's all.'

'Yes, interested in any sordid sexual details! What would Sadie say now if she knew you were in bed with me?'

'I don't think she'd be that bothered to be honest. We have a very open relationship. She's probably in bed with someone else right now.'

'And you don't mind?'

'Not really, as long as she doesn't catch an STD and passes it on to me.'

Christina sat up in bed. 'Oh, thank you very much! I hope you haven't caught anything that you have now kindly passed on to me!'

Eric gave her a little smile. 'Don't worry, I check things downstairs regularly. And anyway, you can talk. From someone who not long ago wanted to kill herself, who's suddenly worried about catching a minor sexual disease when she has a terminal illness.'

'That's a bit strong…'

'Is it? You're the one who's been doing the seducing. I was happy just to have dinner. How do I know you haven't caught something and passed it on to me, 'cause I'm sure you haven't been celibate for the last three years!'

Christina was dumbstruck by Eric's forceful responses. She'd never known him to be so outspoken. She was about to give him a mouthful, since she didn't like being talked to like this, when her front door bell went. 'Who the hell is that? At this time of night!'

'It's only nine o'clock. Might be Sadie. She's been pestering me to have a threesome for ages.'

'What! You're not joking are you…'

'You deserved that. Of course I'm joking. How should I know who it is, it's your flat.' Eric pulled a disgruntled face. The bell went again. 'Aren't you going to answer it?'

Christina grumpily got out of bed and put on a dressing gown. 'Who is it?' She shouted by the door.

'Mum…?'

'Tony…?' She opened the door. 'What's the matter?'

'Nothing, I just wanted to see you…Sorry, have I got you out of bed?'

'Yes, you have.' She was trying hard not to be too severe. 'I thought we agreed that I would contact you when I was ready for visitors.'

'I know…but I was getting worried…can I come in?'

Christina reluctantly moved so that he could enter. As he walked ahead down the small hallway, Eric came out of the bedroom with just a towel wrapped round his middle. 'Hi ya, Tony!'

'Uncle Eric…?' Tony, quite shocked, turned back to his mother. 'You were obviously ready for a visitor, but not for me…'

'Oh, don't be so precious! And please stop looking outraged. Yes, as you've probably gathered, we've been having sex! Want to say anything?'

'I'm…I'm just a bit disappointed…'

'You've no right to be. I'm a free spirit. I'm not married to your father, and you accepted the fact I was living with Eric before I left. Have you become prudish all of a sudden? Isn't your mother allowed to have sex? I'm not dead yet! Would you like it if I arrived unexpectedly and I caught you in bed with one of your girlfriends?'

'You wouldn't…I haven't got a girlfriend… at the moment…' Tony was still feeling embarrassed and uncomfortable, not knowing where to look. Christina's dressing gown had opened slightly, and Eric's towel was on the verge of falling down. 'I think I'd better go…Sorry…' He went towards the door.

'Tony, don't go on my account.' Eric looked at Christina. 'We're done, aren't we?'

'I thought you were going to show me that other position?' Christina, realising her dressing gown was open, quickly closed it up.

'Eh…?' Then Eric realised Christina had said this for Tony's benefit. 'Damn! I forgot to bring the handcuffs. Maybe next time…'

'I'm going…' Tony clutched the door handle.

Christina put her hand on his arm. 'Where's your sense of humour? We were just winding you up. You're very welcome to stay. You're a big boy now, and probably know more about sex than we do.'

Tony didn't think it amusing and was finding it difficult hearing his mother talk like this. 'I'm obviously intruding. Sorry…' He opened the door.

'I get it now. You're still a virgin, aren't you?'

'It's none of your business, and does it matter anyway? You know where I am…Bye…' Tony quickly left, shutting the door behind him.

'What's got into him all of a sudden? I wasn't being unkind, was I?' She went back into the bedroom to where Eric had retreated.

'You hit him where he was most sensitive – in the balls, so to speak.' Eric lay back on the bed.

'What do you mean?'

'The boy is obviously still a virgin, and then knowing his terminally ill mother has just had sex with his

183

uncle did rather upset and confuse him.'

'He should loosen up, and lose his virginity as soon as possible, then he might not be so judgemental or uptight.'

'He's only seventeen. Believe it or not, I didn't lose mine until I was nearly nineteen – and that was with someone older, who certainly put me on the right track, because I didn't know what I was doing.'

Christina smiled. 'She taught you well. Perhaps that's what Tony needs, someone maybe older and more experienced to show him the way.'

'There are ladies of the night who could help.'

'I can't see Tony going to a prostitute. He needs to be seduced by someone who knows what she is doing, without him realising it's been specially set up, if you get my meaning. Do you or your friend Sadie know anyone who might be up for it.'

'That's a very calculated thing to do.' Eric looked at Christina. 'Shouldn't we just let it happen naturally in its own good time?'

'I think it might help Tony with some of his present problems, and help him grow up. I want the best for my boy…'

'Many would disagree…but I can see what you mean. Let me think about it.'

Tony decided to walk home rather than catch the bus. He needed the time to think, to try to calm himself down. He was feeling thoroughly wretched and angry with himself. Angry at the way he'd behaved, angry at his own puritanical attitude towards his mother. She was right, he was a virgin, and he hated the fact that she could see right through him. He wondered if he was that transparent to others? His friends teased him because he was self-conscious around girls, getting tongue-tied in their company. It wasn't because he was short of opportunities. He was good-looking, and his awkwardness made him attractive to a lot of girls. His main problem was, that when he did manage to get the courage to talk to a girl he fancied, although he believed he was being funny, it came out as if he was being sarcastic. His offbeat wit and manner of chat was interpreted in a negative and off-putting way. He lost the girl before he even found her.

The one time, not long ago, when he had the chance of losing his virginity, he completely cocked it up, so to speak. At a party he was getting on swimmingly with a girl he'd had a crush on for some time. She made it quite clear that she wanted to have sex with him, and took him to one of the rooms in the house. The excitement was so intense, as they fumbled and snogged on the bed, that just as she was undoing the belt of his trousers, he ejaculated into his underpants. Feeling ashamed he ran out of the bedroom and left the party. She hadn't spoken to him since, and he'd been too embarrassed to approach her. All this was going round in his head as he walked home. He saw himself as a loser and failure. He felt so depressed, and suddenly understood why his mother might want to kill herself, why people committed suicide. Life wasn't worth living sometimes…

21. A Promise to Put the Past Straight

Jennie was sitting in her office premises, looking round at her new surroundings, deep in thought. Was it all going to work out she wondered?

The original business she had run with Christina concerned the importing, repackaging and the selling of rare, strange and unusual herbs and spices from around the world. It filled a successful niche in the market, until their suppliers took their business elsewhere. It was downhill from then on until they unexpectedly went bust. After Christina disappeared, Jennie started a new company from home, but this time concentrated on selling scented candles and essential oils, which she imported from India, China and Africa. Over the last three years she'd managed to keep afloat, but not enough profit to be able to expand the business or employ any staff. Now that had all changed.

Not one for sitting still, Jennie had spent the last week getting it all set up and working in the way she liked. Although she could cope and run the business on her own, she realised now, in the new office, that if she was to expand to the next level, she needed someone to answer the phone and do the mundane jobs. The problem was that she couldn't afford to pay much. She'd interviewed half a dozen possible office juniors who'd applied. Most were graduates who were prepared to do anything to get a job, and some, Jennie realised, were far cleverer than she was. She discounted the pretty candidates, or those who spoke of high ambitions, who would probably end up telling her how to run things.

Jennie had never gone to college or university and

often felt intellectually inferior to some of the people she dealt with. Yet she had instinctive business acumen and was naturally good with figures, budgeting, and networking. Not one to listen, Jennie was a bit of a control freak, always insisting things were done her way, even if a better way was suggested. She would only work with people who would not argue and did as they were told. As a result, most staff didn't last long in her employ, which became another bone of contention between her and Christina, both of them continually clashing in the way the business should be run.

After seeing twenty people, she eventually offered the job to Kayleigh, a plain-looking, slightly overweight local girl, whose only ambition was to get married and have kids, and who was happy to accept the minimum wage she was being offered. Jennie believed, rather unkindly, that it might be some time before Kayleigh found someone who wanted to marry her, so hopefully would stay in the job for a while. The one who had lasted the longest in the previous business was Meera, whom Christina had declared, during their last confrontation, had had an affair with Patrick, her husband. The very memory now made her shiver, coupled with a distressing phone call she had recently made.

Jennie finished the dregs of her coffee and looked over at her one and only employee, who was spending the morning familiarising herself with the Apple operating system. Kayleigh, with her thick glasses and dull dress sense, concentrated on the screen as she flicked through a manual and tapped away on the keyboard at the same time. 'How are you getting on?'

'Fine, Mrs Hankin, it's quite straightforward really. Be there in no time. I think I've got the hang of doing a mailshot.' Kayleigh responded cheerfully, in a positive manner that had persuaded Jennie to employ her.

Jennie agonised for a second, and then picked up

the phone. She waited impatiently for several moments. 'Come on…pick up…Hello? It's Jennie…look, I'm sorry about the other day…I know…can we meet? What about lunch today? Okay, I know the place…thanks…see you there…' She hung up and sighed, wondering if she was doing the right thing by getting in contact again

'You didn't bring the gun with you by any chance?' Christina smiled as she took a sip of wine after the waiter had left with their order.

'I did rather overreact, didn't I?' Jennie guiltily drained half of her glass in one gulp.

'You could say that. I suppose we were both a bit uptight. It had been a difficult day.'

'Testing would be a better word…Anyway, thank you for agreeing to see me. I didn't think you would after that night. I did behave rather terribly.'

'Yes, you did, but I'm rather glad you didn't shoot me!' Christina tried to make light of it, seeing Jennie's pained expression. 'But I can understand why. It didn't help that I told you about the affair Patrick had with Meera. However, I was telling the truth.'

'I know…' Jennie emptied her glass and filled it up again from the bottle.

'You know?' Christina stared at her.

'One reason I wanted to meet up again. I didn't believe you, but I just couldn't get it out of my head. I managed to get Patrick's number from one of his old friends, and asked him point blank if it was true? I expected him to deny it, which he was always very good at doing. But, without even a pause, he admitted it. He said he was sorry, told me not to contact him again, and then hung up…' Jennie did her best to control the tears.

'I'm sorry. You still miss him, don't you?'

'I suppose I do in a funny way. I accused you of breaking up our marriage, but to be honest things weren't going too well. He always found excuses to go away, and I suspected he was playing away, but was afraid to confront him. In the end, after an argument, I kicked him out and told him not to come back…I thought he would, and I would've taken him back…but he didn't…and the next time I heard was through his solicitor asking for a divorce.'

'Do you know where he is, what he's doing now?'

'No…his friend just gave me his number. Would say no more. I got the impression he was hiding something. Anyway, we've been divorced for two years now…must move on…' Jennie stared out into the distance.

Christina was pleased that she was opening up to her. Perhaps there was a chance that Jennie was coming round to forgiving her. 'Is there anyone else, that you're with I mean?'

'No…I did try a dating agency, but the few dates I had turned out disastrously…the less said the better!' She forced a smile.

'What about the business? Have you settled into the premises?'

'Yes, thank you, they're great. You remember we once talked about expanding into oils and candles?'

'I did. I think I originally suggested it to you?' Christina remembered how she had tried to persuade Jennie to seriously consider it.

'And I poo poo'd it at the time, I know! Well, that's what I've been doing these last few years. I should've listened to you…and maybe…' Jennie paused.

'What…things might not have turned out as they had? We'll never know. How's it going?'

'Slowly. A lot to do. I've engaged an office junior. Hopefully if the business gets going, I'll employ more staff.'

'Good cash flow?'

'Tight…but manageable.'

Christina thought for a moment. 'Would you consider accepting a personal investment in the business to help you along, give you a proper kick start?'

'What kind of investment?' Jennie looked at her suspiciously.

'Say…£20,000?'

'Why?'

'Because I've got the money, and I'd like the business to succeed.'

'How come you've suddenly got this disposable finance? Is it conscience money by any chance?'

Christina laughed. 'The same old suspicious Jennie! You could call it that, but I inherited a tidy sum from an old aunt who recently died. All I ask is that my son, Tony, receives any benefits and profits after my death. There'll be a proper contract to make it all legal and above board. We can discuss the details later. The offer is there. It's up to you. I shall say no more and let you think about it…. Ah, here comes our food. Shall we order another bottle – to celebrate or commiserate?'

Jennie was so dumbstruck, that she grabbed the bottle, emptying the dregs that were left into her glass, which she then swigged down.

After the meal, Christina left Jennie to consider her proposition. She did believe, as she originally had, that there was a healthy, growing market in essential oils and scented candles. She could easily afford the investment and was confident it would yield good dividends, which Tony would eventually benefit from. Christina had no ulterior motive, apart from righting a past wrong, and felt Jennie would be foolish to turn it down.

It was ironic really; she had all this money at her personal disposal, but wasn't going to live long enough to enjoy it. She hadn't lied to Jennie, the money had come from her aunt, which she happened to inherit the same day she was told she had the cancer. Christina recollected the phrase, which summed up the situation for her – the Lord giveth, and the Lord taketh away; also simply called - sod's law.

It was a year ago that her Aunt Beryl had invited Christina to visit her for her 99th birthday. Although physically frail, her mind was as sharp and alert as anyone half her age. They called Beryl the 'Empress' at the exclusive and expensive care home where she lived. Sat in her favourite chair in the communal lounge, she commented on everything that went on around her, and often berated the other residents who she believed had given up on life. She had no time for those who constantly moaned about the weather, their health, the government, and the youth of the day. A forceful character who never suffered fools gladly, quite proud of the fact that people regarded her as a bit of a battle-axe, due to her intimidating manner and the way she casually dismissed those she didn't like. Beryl had been married and divorced three times, but wasn't able to have children, which had been her one regret. She had been a successful businesswoman, and as a result had accumulated a considerable fortune. Christina was her only blood relative whom she had any time for, since in many ways, they were very similar in character.

Christina had always been honest with her aunt, who knew all about her sudden disappearance from the lives of Roger, Eric and Tony. In fact, Beryl was the only one

191

whom Christina had confided in. Beryl didn't totally agree with Christina's actions, but could understand and sympathise why she had been forced to do what she had, since she herself had once done the same. Although Beryl could be quite judgemental, she always had a soft spot for Christina since there were similarities in their lives. Beryl knew about the new life Christina had forged in Aylesbury, and wondered if she was repeating the same mistakes she had made in her previous life in London. Christina had to admit that there was a certain element of history repeating itself.

'I'll come straight to the point. When I die you will inherit what is left of my money. I could've bought this place three times over for the amount it has cost me to live here!'

'I'm sure that won't be for some time yet, Aunty.' Christina patted Beryl's knee, humouring her.

'Sooner than you think. That's why I'm telling you now. I've had enough of living, but I'm determined to get my card from the Queen when I'm 100 next year. Then it will be time to go.'

'I don't know what to say. You're leaving everything to me?'

'Don't be greedy, young lady – not quite everything. I'm giving some to charity; and there are a couple carers who've looked after me for several years, who deserve some help.'

'Whatever you decide to give me…thank you.'

'But you must promise me something.' Beryl sat up in her chair. 'Return to London and make peace with those you left. My money will also help to balance the books, so to speak.'

'That's easier said than done, Aunty.' Christine looked troubled.

'I regret a lot of hurtful things I've done in my life, which are now too late to repair. Like you, I disappeared once and have regretted not returning or making my own peace. Those who I wronged or maligned are all now dead. Please don't make the same mistake.'

'I can't say I don't feel guilty for what I did. But...'

'But is the biggest excuse everyone makes!' She said testily.

'I doubt I'd be forgiven even if I did return.'

'You won't know that unless you do so. Will you at least promise me that you'll give it serious thought? It would mean a lot to me.' Beryl suddenly looked tired and rested her head on the back of the chair, indicating that it was the end of the conversation.

During the following year Christina thought seriously about what Beryl had asked her, but had decided not to return to London. She didn't see the point of unleashing old skeletons to create more stress. She had enough to contend with in the new life she had built for herself in Aylesbury. A life that wasn't quite turning out as she'd hoped.

The next time she saw her aunt was to celebrate her 100th birthday. Beryl hadn't been well and was bedridden when Christina visited her. 'My first wish has been granted...' Beryl shakily pointed to her card from the Queen, in pride of place on her mantelpiece. 'Now for the second and final wish...'

'Which is...?' Christina sat by the bed holding Beryl's thin cold, spindly hand.

'Before that...please...go back to your family and put the record straight...' Beryl then closed her eyes and lay back.

'Aunty...I have thought about what you said...but... Aunty...?' She felt Beryl's hand shudder, after which she gave out a rattling sound and then became still and silent. Christina called one of the staff who confirmed that

Beryl had passed on. She had given up the ghost as she had said she would.

After the funeral Christina kept on thinking about Beryl's last words, but still didn't feel that she could face uprooting herself and returning to London to put that record straight. It wasn't until a month later; after she received official news of her inheritance on the very same day she was told about her cancer, that she decided to respect her aunt's last request. She believed the cancer was a conclusive sign that she should get her house in order. That and the fact that life in Aylesbury had reached an impasse.

Now as she walked home after the meal with Jennie, she wondered if everything that had happened over the last couple of weeks had been worth it. She didn't feel any happier or believed she had made circumstances for herself or the others any better by returning. Her thoughts now centred on the life she had left in Aylesbury. She had disappeared just as suddenly from there without a goodbye or an explanation, as she had from London three years previously.

What a mess she felt everything was. The sooner the cancer took hold and killed her, the better.

22. Virgin on a Discovery

Tony, idly making his way home from college, noticed a young woman leaning awkwardly against the front wall of his house. She looked upset and in some distress. Her bag was on the ground, and one shoe lay next to it with a broken heel. As he got closer, he saw her hair was crumpled and her clothes dishevelled. Her mascara had run, looking as if she'd been crying. Tony looked around but could not see anyone about. 'Are you okay...?' was all he could muster to say, obviously knowing she wasn't.

'No...sorry...I'll be alright...give me a minute...' She fumbled for a hankie in her bag and blew her nose, then started sobbing. 'Sorry...'

Tony, feeling quite helpless, wasn't sure what to do. He looked about, hoping someone might pass to help. The street was empty, apart from some kids on their bikes. Looking closely at her, he could see that part of her blouse was open, revealing the top of her full breasts. He looked away and up at her face. It was a very pretty face, and he could smell her strong, fragrant perfume. 'Is there anyone I can call...?' He took out his phone and waved it self-consciously.

'Take three deep breaths, my mum used to say whenever I got in a panic.' She leant up straight and breathed quickly in and out three times. 'That's better...sorry to be a pain...' She gazed up at him, giving him a gentle smile and touched him softly on the arm, which made him miss a breath. She was so lovely and he was immediately smitten.

'What happened?' He was pleased to notice she had no wedding or engagement ring on her finger.

'This bloke came up behind me and tried to pinch

my bag…but I managed to hold on to it while we had a bit of a to-do…God, I must look a bloody mess…'

You look beautiful and I just want to hold you in my arms… was what he wanted to say, but could only manage 'You look okay…do you want me to call the police…?'

'Naw, too much bother getting the law involved…anyway, he didn't get anything…I kneed him in the balls, breaking my heel in the process…he just ran away after that…scumbag…'

'Nothing I can do then? I'm happy to walk with you wherever you're going. You know, just in case he turns up again…if you know what I mean?'

'Oh, aren't you sweet!' She touched him on the arm again, which made him shiver. 'But I've stopped you on your way somewhere.'

'No, no you haven't…I live here, you see…' He pointed to the house in front of them. 'But I can still accompany you home, or wherever, no problem…'

'You're a real gent. But won't your girlfriend or wife be expecting you inside?' She said this in all seriousness.

'I'm not married…I haven't…it's just me and my dad live here. He doesn't get back from work until later. It's no trouble, honestly.'

'Aw, you are kind…what's your name?'

'Tony…and you are…?'

'My mum calls me Sandra. I've never liked it. My dad calls me a pain the arse!' She started to laugh. Tony would've liked to say, *and I'm sure you have a lovely arse*, but just smiled.

'Well, Tony, it's good of you to offer, but I've a bit of a problem with this broken heel. I'll be hopping up and down like nobody's business. I mean, the shoe's buggered anyway. Have you got anything in the house, you know, like a saw to cut the other one off to make it even - before I
I make my way home?'

'Oh sure, yes, I'll get dad's toolbox from the shed…do you want to come in?'

'You sure it's alright…I don't want to impose…Mind you, I could do with a glass of water, I feel quite dry after all that malarkey with that bloke.'

'You're not imposing. I'm very pleased to help.' Tony opened the front gate to let her go before him.

'Sorry love, could you give me a hand, with this shoe…' She hopped and put her arm around his shoulder and held onto him tightly, as he guided her to the front door. Her soft breasts nuzzling into his side and the scent of her alluring perfume gave him an unwelcome erection.

As they both disappeared behind the front door, a man's head popped up from the inside of a car, parked about a hundred metres from the house. He was looking in the direction of Tony's house. He smiled, crossed his fingers, and mumbled a silent prayer, before driving off.

Helen showed the nice young couple round the empty house. It was the third viewing that day, and the more she wandered from room to boring room, the more she hated this part of the job. She always felt uncomfortable trying to persuade any decent prospective buyer that they were looking around a palace, as opposed to a characterless dump in need of complete modernisation.

Helen had always been someone who often spoke her mind, which sometimes upset or put people off. She wanted to tell this young couple not to bother even considering buying this property. It wasn't worth what was being asked; the neighbourhood was full of undesirable characters; and if they were planning to have a family, the schools were rubbish, crammed with kids who would probably end up in prison.

Yet if she wanted to supplement her income with the sale commission, she had to be creatively descriptive – or in her words, lie with utter conviction. Despite her reluctance to elaborate, she could make a piece of glass sound like a diamond, which made her the estate agent's top seller.

Since she liked the couple, she didn't regard it as a failure when they said they weren't interested. As it happened, when she did return to the office, she learnt that the first two buyers she had shown around had both put in offers. This cheered her up since she hadn't taken to either of them during the viewing, and felt they were very suited to that particular area. In many ways, Helen was also a snob.

On her way home, having the afternoon off, she began to wonder about her relationship with Roger. He had definitely changed during the last few weeks, since Christina had come back into his life. There were small, subtle differences, not obvious to others. He was grumpier, more preoccupied and quicker to anger. Their sex life had definitely changed as a result. Although he performed in bed just as enthusiastically, his heart – or some would say his dick - wasn't completely in it.

Helen was convinced that Christina's presence was having this effect on him, and it made her feel jealous. She hoped that Christina would quickly die, so that she and Roger could get on with their lives as before.

She did love him, and despite his declaration that he wasn't in a hurry to get married again, she nevertheless was determined that they would eventually do so. That was her plan. However, there was still a major obstacle she had to overcome – and that was Tony.

She stopped to buy a few foodstuffs, as she was cooking for them this evening. While she made her way to Roger's house, she hoped that Tony would be going out so that it would be just the two of them. She always cooked enough for three, which Roger insisted on, but whenever she had, Tony made his excuses and didn't eat with them. Hopefully tonight wouldn't be the exception.

From the moment Roger had first introduced her to his son, she sensed his immediate dislike of her. She didn't think it was just a teenage thing, or that he thought she was replacing his mother. It was a simple case, she believed, of hate at first sight. As much as she tried to be as friendly as possible, he just blocked her out completely. He was always civil, but they had never had a one-to-one conversation, which might have helped. Many times she had tried to get Tony on his own, but he would always make some excuse to go out or leave the room.

What made her feel uncomfortable, was that she felt he was always mentally undressing her, in the way he sometimes stared at her, looking her up and down. She hadn't dared mention this to Roger, because she knew he'd undoubtedly confront Tony, which would only make things worse. The only light on the horizon was that Tony was hoping to go to university next year, which would mean leaving home, and then she would have Roger to herself. That's what she clung on to and what kept her going.

Roger had told her not to come before six, which she found odd. He was working from home that afternoon and needed to finish an important project. She looked at her watch. It was just after four. She was sure he wouldn't mind if she came a bit earlier. She wouldn't disturb him, since she had a key and could let herself in. It would give her time to prepare the food and finish the book she was reading. If Tony was about, she might even try and engage him in friendly conversation, but that might have been wishful thinking on her part.

***

Roger was having a bad day at work. As Project Manager for a building company, it was his responsibility for staffing and budgeting. A major project had gone over budget, so he had the difficult job of sorting it out as well as firing a couple of sub-contractors, one of whom happened to be a friend. He usually managed to work from home a couple of afternoons a week, but today he'd had to stay behind after lunch, to attend an important meeting with his bosses to discuss the current problems.

He was grateful that Christina hadn't been in contact since their last embarrassing encounter, when he'd brought her home from the police station, and then Tony had found them in bed together. Roger did feel a touch guilty about not finding out how she was in the week or so since she'd left the house. But work and trying to placate Helen had kept him busy.

Christina's reappearance in his life had unsettled him. He was grateful for the return of the money he was owed, but the whole scenario of the funeral; her rise from the dead, plus the knowledge of her imminent death had really troubled him. It was affecting his relationship with Helen, who was jealous and possessive at the best of times. He hated to admit to himself, but he knew he would feel better once she was dead and out of their lives forever.

'I'm not dead yet, though I bet the others can't wait until I am.' Christina took a sip of wine as she gazed around the restaurant, at the other diners, wondering if any of them had a death sentence awaiting them.

'I'm sure that's not true.' Duncan cut his steak into pieces.

'It's still an uphill struggle to get them to accept me.

I just want to try and simply be friends, before I disappear from their lives for good.'

'I know it's not easy, but I'm sure they'll come round, sooner rather than later.' He forked a piece of steak into his mouth.

'I don't know…I'm still very fond of Roger, but I don't want to get back with him, which is what he might think. Tony is still very confused, but needs to seriously grow up, stop masturbating and experience some real sex. Eric is sweet and great in bed, but not intellectually stimulating. Jennie is mellowing, but I still don't think she trusts me. All in all I still wonder if I'm wasting my time, whatever's left.'

'How have you been feeling?'

'A bit tired, some stomach aches, but nothing else…so far…'

'What does your GP say?' Duncan was having a bit of difficulty chewing on the steak.

'I haven't been back to Aylesbury to see him. Didn't see the point. That was a month ago. So according to his forecast, I have another couple of months if I'm lucky.' She stared at Duncan, who seemed to be having difficulty in masticating his steak. 'Are you alright?'

'The trouble is, that dentures and steak don't always agree with each other. My fault for ordering it, but I've always loved it. Ironically it was a piece of T-bone steak that ruined my teeth in the first place. I bit very hard on a piece of bone, which started the rot…sorry; you didn't need to hear that.' He swallowed hard and put down his fork and knife.

'You want to order anything else?'

'No, I'll finish off the chips. But I will have a dessert. A nice nursery jam roly-poly – with custard!' Duncan licked his lips.

'With a straw to go with it?' She smiled.

Duncan laughed. 'Reminds me of that Shakespeare poem, The Seven Ages of Man: *"second childishness and mere oblivion, sans teeth, sans eyes, sans taste, sans everything"* …I sometimes feel I'm in my seventh age…'

'You're only in your middle years.'

'I've been feeling much older lately.' He sighed.

'Things not happy at home?'

'Quite the contrary. I have a great marriage and I get on with my children. I've never strayed or even been tempted to. Anyway, who'd want a fifty-six-year-old solicitor with bad hair and false teeth? I've been reasonably successful. We're financially secure and the house has been paid for. No complaints or regrets there.' He looked reflective as he stared down at his plate and popped a chip in his mouth.

'But there are regrets somewhere?' She sensed and filled up their wine glasses.

'I suppose it's the job really. The challenge is no longer there…' He took a sip of wine. 'I went into the profession by default. My father was a solicitor, and was keen for me to follow in his footsteps…'

'There must've been something else you wanted to do with your life?'

'I've always loved the sea and thought about doing something nautical. I had notions of joining the Navy, but that was out of the question at the time. It was a case of goodbye sailor, not hello…' He sighed again.

'It's not too late you know.'

'What – to join the Navy?'

'No, silly. To go and do something related to the sea. Buy a boat and go sailing…around the British coast, Europe or even round the world. Have you thought of that?'

'No, no I haven't. What an interesting idea…' His face suddenly lit up with the thought. 'I've been thinking about retiring at sixty…'

———

'If you can afford it, don't wait until you're sixty – do it now! You don't know what's going to happen over the next few years, and then you might find out that it is too late for some reason. I have experience of that...'

'Yes, you're probably right. Something to seriously think about.'

Christina held up her glass. 'Shall we drink to that?' He raised his and they clinked glasses. 'You know, even though I can't swim, I've always wanted my ashes scattered over water. Another of my perverse thoughts! So, if you do decide to sail the seas, I'm happy for you to keep my ashes after I'm cremated, and to take charge of the dispersion. Is that a deal?'

He thought for a moment. 'We'll need to put that in writing.'

'Always the careful solicitor. Come on, Captain, let's order your jam roly poly and then both face the Devil and the deep blue sea!'

Helen noticed the end of a broken heel, from a woman's shoe, by the front gate when she arrived at Roger's house. She kicked it into the gutter, and then carried her shopping to the front door. As she opened the door and entered the hallway, she could smell the scent of a strong fragrance. It wasn't from a cologne or aftershave that Roger used, and she knew Tony didn't use any. As she sniffed the air, she recognised it as being from a popular perfume, one that a female celebrity had her name on. One of the secretaries at the estate agents wore it.

As she looked up at the stairs, she noticed a pair of woman's tights on the steps near the top. As she started to slowly ascend the stairs, she heard moans and groans coming from one of the bedrooms.

She stopped halfway. Her mind went into overdrive. The bastard! Was Roger two-timing her? Was that why he didn't want her to come earlier? Was he fucking that bitch Christina? If it wasn't her, was it someone from his office? No wonder he'd been acting strange lately. Her immediate knee-jerk reaction was to get a large knife from the kitchen and slice his balls off. As she was pondering what to do, she heard a female voice shout: 'That's it…push harder…oh! …that's nice…keep going…you're the best…'

Helen stood frozen to the spot, and then started to scream loudly in frustration. There was a sudden mumbled commotion coming from inside the bedroom. She heard 'It's okay, you stay there, I'll see what's up…' and some moments later a half-naked woman, clutching her clothes, came out and stood at the top of the stairs, looking down at Helen haughtily.

'You alright, love? Sounded like someone was being murdered.'

'Who the hell are you!' Helen looked at the pretty young redhead despairingly. Roger had on a couple of occasions, suggested that she dye her hair red, as he admitted he quite fancied redheads.

'I could ask the same of you, darling. No need to get so uptight. We're finished. You should be proud of him.'

'You bloody slut, get out of here!'

'Excuse me? Who you calling a slut! I was invited in, thank you very much. Ah…you must be Helen. I've heard all about you.' She smiled knowingly.

Helen looked like she was going to explode. Her face went crimson and she clenched her fists. 'Roger, you bastard! Stop hiding in there. Come on out, or are you too bloody scared to face me, you sod!'

The redhead smirked and put her hand to her lips. 'Oops! We seem to have a situation here…'

'What are you mumbling about? Get dressed and get out!' Helen had stayed rooted to the spot at the centre of the stairs, a touch intimidated by the woman who was confidently standing her ground at the top of the stairs. 'Roger, come out!!!' She screamed.

At that very moment the front door opened, and Roger came in. 'What's going on here…?' He glanced up at the stairs to see Helen, who looked like she was about to have a heart attack, and this half naked redhead who had a big smile on her face.

'You must be Roger.' The redhead declared, 'I think you'd better get Helen here a strong drink. I think she's a bit confused.'

Helen looked down at Roger and burst into tears, running downstairs, right passed him into the living room.

'I'm Sadie, by the way…' She accidentally dropped some of the clothes she was holding, giving Roger a quick glimpse of her nakedness, before she retrieved them. 'Whoops! Sorry…Excuse me, I'd better get dressed and leave you all to it…' She then disappeared into the bedroom.

Roger stood there in a fog of confusion. He could hear Helen sobbing in the other room. The vision of Sadie's nakedness settled in his mind like a picture frozen in time, and he found himself partly aroused. Then from the top of the stairs, the smiling face of Tony appeared. 'Hi Dad! You okay…?'

Eric had invited Christina over for a meal. Since she didn't want to be alone, she agreed on condition that she would cook and provide the food. He was useless in the kitchen, only really being able to use the microwave or turn on the oven. Also, his choice of what to eat would consist of packaged and processed curries, Chinese or various forms of pies that you just had to heat up. When she lived with him, she regularly called his culinary capability as Cordon Black, a joke that was beyond him. Fed up with eating the rubbish she had bought herself she had decided to cook something more nutritious.

'That smells nice!' He wandered into the kitchen and stood behind her.

'It's only the onions cooking, I haven't started yet.' Christina was chopping up the garlic and peppers. 'Would you mind not crowding me. Why don't you set the table like a good boy?'

'Aren't we eating on our knees?' He sounded disappointed. 'There's a good programme on the telly.'

'Let's be civilised for once. And use the linen napkins, rather than paper towels. I bet you haven't used them since I left. And you probably don't know where they are, do you?' He shrugged. 'The bottom drawer at the back...'

As he bent down to get them, his phone announced a text message. He looked at it and smiled. 'That's my girl!'

'What's that? Another of your concubines signing in?'

'Concu...what?' He didn't understand. 'It's a message from Sadie. Mission accomplished. You will be pleased.' He punched the air in delight 'Yes!'

'Eric, I hope you haven't invited her round.'

"No, of course not...You remember you said that you thought it was about time that Tony lost his virginity?'

'So...?'

'Well, the deed has been successfully done.'

'What?' She stopped what she was doing. 'You're not telling me that your friend, Sadie, seduced him?'

'That girl certainly knows all the tricks. No man can resist her charms...unless he's gay of course. Even then...

anyway, mission accomplished.'

Christina turned the gas off for a moment. 'This is a joke, isn't it? You're just winding me up.'

'Wait a sec. I'll just text back to congratulate her. I owe her one.' He started to tap message on the phone.

'Eric!' She was now really incensed. 'What have you and that tart done?'

He finished his texting and put his phone down and stood in front of Christina looking her in the eye. 'I'm sorry…who was it that said, and I'll repeat the words… "Tony needs to lose his virginity as soon as possible… to be seduced by someone who knows what she is doing…Do you or your friend Sadie know anyone who might be up for it?" …Sound familiar?'

'I didn't think you'd take me seriously!' Christina was now backtracking, realising that it was exactly what she had originally meant.

'Of course I did. Sadie thought it was a hoot, and was very happy to do it herself. I drove her to the house and secretly waited until she had weaved her magic spell on our Tony.'

Although Christina had calmed down, she was now feeling guilty. Had she done the right thing? It was often a problem with her. She'd say something, or make a request, but never believe it would actually happen. 'Okay, I did say it. But I didn't expect you'd actually do it.'

'Be careful what you ask for!' Eric waved his finger at her.

'I thought you and Sadie were an item? Don't you mind her sleeping with someone else?'

'I've told you before, we have an open agreement to go out with whomever we want to.'

'You mean sleep with?'

'What's the problem? You're not jealous, are you? Getting prim and proper in your old age. You're no angel.'

'But I will be soon! If there's a heaven…' She smiled and they both started to laugh. He went across and gave her a cuddle. They kissed, and just as they were about to take it further – the doorbell went. 'Who's that?'

'How should I know!' He unclasped himself from her and went to the front door. Christina heard him open it and surprisingly exclaim 'Oh…'

'Darlink! I have missed you so much!' A foreign female voice announced rather theatrically, barging her way into the flat, pulling a large suitcase.

Heavily made up, she was dressed like a dominatrix in boots and leather, with dyed curly blonde hair cascading down her back. She took a quick, condescending look at Christina, who was in her apron in the kitchen. 'Ah, I see you have a cook now! I am here now. You can go!' She waved her arm dismissively at Christina, who stood there open mouthed.

Eric, looking sheepish and embarrassed came between them. 'Christina, this is Marta… my wife…'

23. Down, but not Quite Out

Helen had got herself worked up into such a state over what had happened, that she couldn't bear to stay a moment longer in the house. 'I'm sorry, Roger, I'm going home.'

'Shall I come back with you?' Roger was slowly coming to terms with what he'd just witnessed. He could still smell the trace of perfume that Sadie had left.

'Not tonight, I need to be alone. Sorry.'

'What about all the food?' Roger pointed to the carrier bags in the hall.

'Cook it your bloody self!' She made for the front door.

'Wait a minute, why you having a go at me? I've just come in. I didn't know that Tony…well, was entertaining…if you know what I mean.'

'Entertaining!' She mocked. 'I suppose it was your idea to hire a hooker for your little boy.'

'I knew nothing about it!' He protested.

'Then why did you tell me not to come before six then? Working from home, my arse!' She opened the front door.

'I thought I would be, but I had to stay at the office for a meeting. That's the truth.'

'So you say. I'm going. Please don't phone me tonight.' She then left, banging the door.

'Bloody hell!' Roger stamped his foot on the floor in frustration. 'Women!'

'She giving you a hard time, Dad?' Tony, now dressed, a big grin on his face, came confidently down the stairs. 'Probably it's the time of month…' He added as if he was now an expert on women.

'I'll give you time of the bloody month! You've got a

bit of explaining to do.'

Down in the car park outside Eric's block of flats, he was seeing Christina to her car. 'I'm sorry; I didn't know she was going to turn up. In fact, I didn't think that I'd ever see her again…after…well…'

'You and that…that woman, are actually married?' Christina found it hard to believe.

''Afraid so. Six months ago. All legal and all that. A sort of mutual arrangement. The marriage was never…what's the word?….consumed…'

'Consummated, is that what you're trying to say?'

'We haven't had sex. We parted after the registry office. It was a business arrangement. I'd get ten thousand pounds; she'd get British residency. As simple as that…'

'Why didn't you tell me?'

'I haven't told anyone. I needed the money. Small gambling debt that had to be paid off. Anyway, please don't tell Roger, he'll get on his high horse and start lecturing me. I was an idiot, but there you go, these things happen. All sorted now.'

'Except you have a wife who's suddenly appeared out of the blue…You do surprise me, and that's saying something.'

'Look, I don't know why Marta's turned up. Probably just wants to stay a few nights. I'll get rid of her as soon as…'

Suddenly from the bedroom window above, Marta shouted down. 'Eryczek! Vhy are you so long? Pay da cook, tell her to go! Your vife is cook now, I make you delicious Polish food. And after, my darlink, ve vill have our little honeymoon'

'Coming!' He shouted back. 'Oh God, I think she

210

now expects to have sex with me.' He said wearily.

'I'm sure you'll cope, Eric. Ring me when you get divorced…if I'm still here.'

She got in her car. As she drove off, she felt total and utter despair. She had looked forward to enjoying a nice quiet meal, and then the inevitable sex that would follow. Now she was forced once more to spend the evening alone. For a split second she thought of going to Roger's, but realised things were probably problematic there, if what Eric had said about Sadie and Tony was true.

'How much did you have to pay her?' Roger had his arms folded as he watched his son lounging cheerfully in the armchair. Tony's whole bearing was different. More relaxed and less confrontational.

'Not a penny! She didn't ask for any money. If she had, I would've gladly given it. It was worth it. But she didn't.'

'Did she demand anything from you?'

'No! Why are you so suspicious, Dad? Could it be that she might have actually fancied me?'

'She was much older than you. And conveniently by the front gate when you arrived. Don't you think that was a bit of a coincidence?'

'I don't care. I couldn't have wished for anyone better to have sex with – and yes, as you well know, it was my first time; I'm now not ashamed to admit. Yeh!' Tony punched the air with both fists in triumph. 'Result!'

'I hoped you used a condom. If you had any.' Roger sounded like a teacher.

'Actually, I used two; she had some in her bag.

'How very convenient and considerate.'

'She encouraged me to go again, but this time she took charge. It was wicked!' Tony unconsciously put his hand over his genitals.

'What do you mean she took charge?'

'She got on top and rode me. Okay? Or do you want to know what else she did to me with those luscious lips?' Tony could see his father reddening slightly.

'She didn't…didn't take any pictures or video, did she…on her phone, I mean?' The image of her standing naked at the top of the stairs came back to haunt him.

'No…but why would she do that anyway?'

'Put it on YouTube; Facebook; on the Internet…to blackmail or embarrass you.'

'God, Dad, you don't trust anybody. You always think everyone's got an ulterior motive. Can't people just fuck and enjoy the process without wondering if there's some other reason?'

'Are you seeing her again?'

'Probably not. I asked for her number, but she wouldn't give it to me. She just said she knew where I lived.'

'Doesn't that bother you, that she didn't?'

'I'm not going to marry her! Dad, I'm getting bored with this cross-examination. Why don't I ask you some questions? Do you use a condom when you have sex with Helen? Does she get on top or is it always the missionary position? Does she take pictures…?'

'Now listen here, don't be so obscene. And it's none of your business what Helen and I do.'

'Then don't be so nosey about what Sadie and I did. Does it turn you on? Would you liked to have fucked her? Eh?'

'Don't be so ridiculous! And there's no need to be crude.' Roger protested, but that's exactly what he would've liked to do.

There was something about Sadie that captivated him. He was actually a touch jealous that Tony had had that experience with her. Sex with Helen was good, but there were some things she wouldn't do in bed. He felt Sadie wouldn't have such qualms.

'Okay, Dad, are we done? I'm popping out to get some condoms, just in case. Want me to get some for you?' Tony smiled at Roger, who looked distinctly uncomfortable and chastened, as he left the room.

Christina was waiting in traffic by some shops, when she noticed a middle-aged man wandering aimlessly and looking lost. He was dressed rather scruffily in a crumpled suit and in need of a decent haircut. He looked somehow familiar to her, and as the traffic advanced, she felt suddenly impelled to pull into a parking spot nearby.

She watched the man as he shuffled along staring into shop windows, but not really looking. He bent down and picked up a couple of cigarette ends and put them in his pocket. He wasn't exactly a tramp or a down-and-out, because there was something about him that gave the impression he was better than that. Christina wracked her brains because she was so sure she knew this man, but wasn't near enough to get a good look. As he passed closer to the car, she wound down her window to get a clearer view. Then it hit her... 'Patrick...?'

The man stopped and bent down, scrunching his eyes to get a better look at her. 'Who's that? If you're a lady of the night, I'm afraid I haven't got any money. But if you're offering a freebie, I might be interested...'

'No, I'm certainly not!' She said rather indignantly, clearly smelling the alcohol on his breath.

'Patrick, it's Christina, Jennie's business partner... remember?' She got out of the car and stood next to him.

'Christina…yes…the lovely Christina…' He tapped his head as if to wake his brain. 'How could I forget! What are you doing here? You're not in the call girl racket now, are you? If you are, I bet you're popular. Beautiful Christina…'

'Patrick, for God's sake, I am not a prostitute! What's the matter with you, why are you wandering around here, picking up discarded cigarette ends?' She was trying to talk sensibly but began to realise he wasn't in a fit state to be completely coherent. He hadn't shaved for days. He had lost a lot of weight since she last saw him, and his eyes had that faraway, glazed look of a drunk.

'Out for the evening air…' From his pocket he took out a cigarette end and smelt it as if it was the finest cigar. 'Waste not, want not…do you have a light?'

'No I don't. Where do you live?'

'A small residence a few streets away… a cosy little pied-a-terre…'

'Have you eaten today?'

'You know, I don't remember…I must've done…Well, I must be on my way. Wonderful seeing you again. Don't go picking up any strange men now!'

Christina couldn't believe what she was seeing and hearing. The Patrick she remembered was charm itself, an arrogant confidence about him, who never took no for an answer. She didn't recognise this person before her now. Something had happened to make him behave this way. It wasn't just because he was drunk. She couldn't leave him like that. 'Patrick – get in the car. You're in no fit state to be wandering about like that. There's a fish and chips shop near me, and I insist you join me for a meal at my place. No arguments. I'll drive you home after. Understood?'

He made a weak salute, and then held out some loose change from his pocket which he shook in the palm of his hand. 'Not enough for a small bag of potato fingers, I'm afraid…Money's tied up in shares, but nobody is sharing it with me!' He started to laugh.

'It's all on me, don't worry. Now please get in the car.' Christina opened the car door and physically pushed him into the back seat. He didn't resist, but slumped back as if all his energy had drained.

By the time they had eaten and Christina had plied him with strong, black coffee, Patrick had sobered up considerably. He sat at the table looking really remorseful. 'I'm sorry if I embarrassed you…I didn't mean to call you a…'

'Whore?' Christina collected up the plates. 'I've been called worse things lately.'

'It's been a long time…'

'Three years to be precise. What's happened to you Patrick? You look terrible.'

'This and that…not the best of times…have you got anything to drink?' He looked around seeing if he could spot any bottles of alcohol.

'I'll get you a glass of water.'

'I didn't mean…'

'I know what you meant. No, I haven't.' She lied. 'What's been going on? Why are you in such a state? Look at you…you were always particular about your appearance.'

'Appearances can be deceptive. I could be a millionaire who likes to dress down.'

'But you're not, are you?'

'Alas no. How could you tell?' He took a deep breath. 'Sorry, I think I'd better be moving along, leave you in peace.' He stood up half-heartedly, his body language betraying his words.

'I said I'd drive you home, wherever that it is. But only after you've told me what's happened. Why are you in such a state?'

'Why are you so interested? You never bothered before…' He slumped back into the chair.

'Because you were always a pain in the arse, when I worked with Jennie. You never gave up, did you – until you finally managed to get me into bed.'

'We had a pleasant affair…' He was trying to remember.

'Patrick, it was a fumbled one-night stand, and I don't think either of us really enjoyed it. You wanted the conquest and I was curious to see how good you were.'

'And was I…?'

'I don't want to dampen your sexual ego, but because we'd both had a lot to drink, it was a bit of a limp experience. You fell asleep and I was forced to finish myself off.'

'Ah…' He seemed not to care anymore.

'So, are you going to tell me why you were drunk and wandering the streets?'

Patrick leant back in the chair and took a deep breath. 'If you really want to know…. It's not very exciting…'

'I'm listening.'

He sighed. 'You know I had this affair with Meera? Believe it or not, but I actually fell in love with her, and I think she with me. Jennie and I had been drifting apart for some time. I know I played away on the odd occasion. Other one-night stands that I don't remember. I wasn't the only one. Before Meera, I discovered Jennie had had a fling with one of our drivers. Remember Greg?'

'What, that tall ginger boy covered in freckles? He was only twenty! Didn't you get him sacked?'

'When I found out he'd been in the sack with my wife. She denied it at first, but then confessed when I threatened to leave her. Things weren't the same after that.

Then Meera came into my life, which rather drove things along.'

'So it was alright for you to have sex with others, but not Jennie?'

'It wasn't just that. I know it had happened before, before you and she went into business, but I couldn't prove anything. I began to realise that Jennie and I didn't really have a future.'

'But that was at least a couple of years ago.' Christina was still coming to terms with the knowledge that Jennie had had other affairs, which she had never suspected.

'Things went downhill from then on. The business went bankrupt.'

'You know Jennie blamed me for that.'

'Well she would, wouldn't she? Jennie always portrayed herself as the victim. I later discovered that she was fiddling the books, so as not to pay the VAT and taxes that were due. The money went into a private account. The tax people soon caught up with her, and she had to pay everything back, which in effect put her out of business.'

Christine was stunned at this revelation. She had no reason to suppose that Patrick would lie now. 'And I was accused of tampering with the books!'

'Someone had to be seen as the scapegoat. It was just as well you disappeared from the scene when you did. Jennie told them that you were in charge of the accounts and were responsible for doing the tax returns.'

'What!' Christina's expression was one of horror and disbelief.

'But the tax people weren't stupid. I knew you had nothing to do with it, so I managed to find out about this secret account of Jennie's and tipped them the wink, so to speak.'

'And I've just helped to set up her new business in

expensive premises…and all this time I thought it was partly my fault that the original business went bust…'

'Nothing is ever what it seems. There are many sides to a story, not all of them true unfortunately.'

Christina was silent for several moments. 'I've even offered to invest in the business…I had lunch with her recently. She mentioned that she spoke to you, to ask about Meera, and that you told her not to call you again. I couldn't understand it then.'

'But you can now?' Christina nodded. 'Anyway, I'd appreciate you not telling her where I am. I'm done with that woman.'

'I promise I won't. But that's only part of your story. There must be more to have brought you down to this…well…'

'Sorry state? Yes, it is rather pathetic…After I got a divorce from Jennie, I tried to get back in contact with Meera. I found out that she had moved, and eventually succeeded in tracking her down. She was working in a department store. Knowing her marriage was unhappy, I tried to persuade her to leave her husband and come and live with me. She wanted to but was frightened. Her religious and cultural beliefs forbade it. Instead, she agreed to meet me secretly and we enjoyed a few happy months together, until she suddenly disappeared again…'

'Did you manage to find her again?'

'I tried, but without success this time. All I could gather was that she had moved up north to another town, but no one knew where… She was the love of my life…'

'Was? Don't give up trying to find her. Get a professional on to it, I can help you with that. Patrick, life's too short to let go of the happiness that you deserve.'

'And getting shorter…six months ago I saw an item on the TV news. In the Midlands, a young Indian woman had been murdered by her husband. He had killed her because she had brought shame on the family…by giving birth to a mixed-race child…a little girl…'

'Meera?' Christina watched his face crumple.

'Yes…and that child was mine, I know it…' Tears started to cascade down his cheeks.

Christina went across and hugged him. 'Patrick…I'm so sorry…Do you know what happened to the baby?'

'Put in care or fostered. I don't know…I'd always wanted children, but Jennie couldn't. It would be nice to see the baby, if only once. But the thing is, as you may well gather, life's a bit tough at the moment. A year ago I went into business with a friend. That was all fine until I learnt what happened to Meera. You could say I went to pieces, and started drinking. The work suffered and my friend bought me out for a pittance. Not much left. And here I am…' He extricated himself from Christina's embrace, and wiped the tears off his face. 'I think I'm ready to go home now. I would appreciate a lift, if you don't mind.'

'Of course. But you can't go on like this, punishing yourself. You're better than that. I want to help you, and I don't want any argument. I'd like to fund you to be able to find and see your daughter.'

'My daughter…' He repeated.

'Find a private detective, who will be able to make all the relevant enquiries and discover where the baby is…

'Seriously…?' He looked at her.

'It shouldn't be difficult as it's been in the press. Then go and see the baby. What you do after that is your decision. Will you do that? And smarten yourself up and lay off the booze. Patrick…?'

'I will pay you back.' He stood up straight, his whole manner brightened.

'I know you will.' Christina wasn't prepared to go

into the whole scenario about her illness, and the fact that she wouldn't be there for the loan to be paid back.

'I don't know how to thank you…but thank you.'

'I suppose a fuck wouldn't be out of the question, would it?' She added with a grin.

'What…?' Patrick couldn't tell if she was joking.

'That's the whore in me speaking. But in all honesty, you couldn't really afford me!'

Patrick started to laugh, the first time he looked like his old self. 'You always did have an odd sense of humour.'

'Which sometimes has got me into trouble. Come on, lead me to your pied-a-terre…'

Whilst driving Patrick to his rented bedsit, Christina felt like going to Jennie's house and killing her. Patrick's surprising revelations, which she had no reason not to believe, had knocked her for six. He was right; nothing is ever what it seems. Jennie was as much to blame for their marriage breakdown as was Patrick. But it was the knowledge that Jennie had personally deceived her, and then accused her of dishonesty, that really got to her.

Patrick was too ashamed to invite Christina in, when they'd arrived at his street in a run-down area. They sat in the car. 'I hope you don't mind, it's the maid's day off and it's in a bit of a tip…'

'I'm glad you haven't lost your sense of humour. No, I won't insist on coming in. You'll only expect me to tidy up!' She joked. 'I'm really sorry things have been tough for you. Look, here's my phone number. Text me your bank details and I'll transfer some money to help with your search.'

'Are you sure?' Patrick still had his pride, if nothing else.

'I've come into a bit of money, so it's not a problem.

Just promise me one thing.'

'Buy some decent cigarettes and get a haircut?'

'Don't fritter the money away on drink. Use it to find your daughter, because I know you won't settle until you do. And if there's anything else, don't hesitate to phone me. Okay?'

'Why are you being so kind to me, when in the past I was such a pain in the arse, as you so succinctly put it?'

'A lot's happened since. I've changed, you've changed. I feel you've been hard done by, and since I can, I'd like to help, that's all.'

'Thank you…you've given me the resolve to do something positive. Will you tell Jennie?'

'It's none of her business. It's just between you and me. Go and sort your life out. You know where I am.' She started the engine.

He leant over and gave her a kiss on the cheek. 'Thank you. You know I misjudged you.'

'I don't think you're the only one…Goodbye Patrick…'

'Bye…I will repay you.' He opened the door and got out.

She watched him walk over to the large, dilapidated Victorian house where he had a room. A feeling that she'd never see him again came over her. But that was a foregone conclusion in her condition.

As she drove home, she thought of all the ways that she could kill Jennie – from burning her house down with her tied up inside; to getting a gun and shooting her, in the same way Jennie had threatened her. Or she could find and hire someone to carry out the assassination.

But that wouldn't be as much fun. Yet killing Jennie herself wouldn't give her that much satisfaction. Jennie had to suffer, like she herself had to suffer all those years ago.

24. Beaten by the Bartered Bride

Over the following week, Christina heard from nobody, nor was she bothered to contact anyone. She was a bit peeved as she had at least expected to hear from Tony, but realised his priorities had obviously changed since he'd had his first sexual experience with Sadie. He had grown up and obviously didn't need his mother any more. Eric, with the appearance of his new wife, had his own problems, so she didn't expect to hear from him. Roger, she knew, would probably be the last person to communicate. She thought of getting in touch with Paula but then decided she wasn't in the mood to listen to homilies. Duncan was always busy, and she had nothing to say to him. All in all, she simply wasn't in the mood to be sociable.

She did, however, receive a couple of texts from Patrick. First to thank her for the money transfer; and secondly to say he'd found a 'private eye' who was working on the case to find the whereabouts of his baby daughter, and hoped to get some news soon.

Every morning, when Christina awoke, she would gauge how she was feeling, and every morning she felt fine. No symptoms, however small, presented themselves. She had been told that pancreatic cancer tended to be silent and painless in the beginning until it suddenly took hold and affected the whole body with a vengeance. 'Well! What are you waiting for? I'm here, I'm ready – get on with it! But please make it quick and not too painful, that's all I ask.'

She hadn't forgotten about Jennie and what Patrick had told her. She just didn't have the energy to think about it, and began to wonder if it was worth doing anything anyway. Although she knew Jennie had suffered in her own way over the years, Christina felt that this was never as satisfying as personal revenge.

To fill up her time, rather than stay in the flat and live in her head, Christina took full advantage of what London had to offer, and visited art galleries, theatres and cinemas, which helped divert her mind for a few enjoyable hours.

Towards the end of the week, whilst coming out of a theatre one evening, she received a call from Eric. He urgently wanted to see her, and could he come over to her flat? Christina was reticent, since she was in no mood to entertain him or even have sex. As far she was concerned the arrival of his foreign bride had put an end to that. She tried to put him off, but he started to sound desperate, which was uncharacteristic of him. Finally, she relented and said she'd see him at the flat in an hour.

In the shadows a suspicious figure was waiting when she arrived outside her building. She was hesitant to approach, wondering if it was a mugger or rapist lurking in wait. It could be someone wanting to kill her, but this was not how she wanted to die.

'Who is it? What do you want?' She raised her voice, in preparation to scream if necessary. The stooped figure stepped into the light. 'Eric! Don't do that...what the hell has happened to you...?' She saw his face was bruised. Sporting a black eye, his neck looked black and blue as if he'd been strangled.

'Sorry to impose, but I didn't know where else to go...' He looked embarrassed.

'What about your dear brother? Or did he do that to you, after he found out how you pimped his son with that tart?' Christina couldn't resist the barb.

'She's not a tart, and it's nothing to do with her or that. Hopefully Roger still doesn't know – unless you told him of course.'

'I've not even seen or talked to him for over a week.'

'Okay…but he's the last person I'd go to. I'd never hear the end of it. You know how spikey Roger can be?'

'I know what you mean. So…what's this about?' Christina was still not inclined to invite him up, wondering if there was some ulterior motive, despite his bruised appearance.

'Can I come up…I don't want to discuss this out here. Please…' Giving one of his boyish, imploring looks, making it hard for her to refuse.

'Alright, but don't think you're going to get me into bed!'

'You wish! I couldn't perform even if I wanted to…'

'What's that mean?' Christina looked perplexed.

'I'll explain…upstairs…please…'

Christina sighed, got out her front door keys, and they went up one flight to her flat. She took her coat off, sat in the armchair, and folded her arms in anticipation. 'Sit down, Eric, and tell mother what this is all about.'

'That's not funny, Christina, don't take the piss!' He flopped down on the sofa, angrily facing her.

'Alright, alright. I'm sorry, but you have been known to overdramatize a situation.'

'Maybe I have – but this is very serious.'

'Not been gambling again, got into debt and they've given you a taster. Surely you haven't frittered away that ten thousand already? If it's more money you're after, you can forget it!' Christina didn't mean to be so harsh and unforgiving, but something in the way Eric presented situations made her respond in a knee-jerk reaction.

'For God's sake, Christina, stop coming to conclusions before you've heard what I have to say! Always jumping the bloody gun!'

'I stand corrected…sorry. So, who did this to you?'

'Marta…

'Your business bride?' This did surprise her. 'Honeymoon not work out? Sorry, I'm doing it again.'

'For once that's exactly what went wrong – the ensuing honeymoon…I couldn't please her…'

'That I do find hard to believe. Without inflating your already inflated ego, you're a terrific lover, Eric. Lots of foreplay, gentle and tender, and never too rough, but vigorous at the right time. Sorry, that sounds like I'm giving you a reference for an orgy. But I mean it.'

'Thank you. But Marta didn't quite see it that way. Okay, the first night – as man and wife – was fine, but I sensed she didn't enjoy it as much as she made out. It was what followed later that became the problem...'

'In what way?'

'We were getting on quite well until the third night. Before we got ready for bed, she asked if she could tie me up, then blindfold me. I thought nothing of it, even though she trussed me up tightly. She then told me to lie quietly while she got ready, promising me *Great pleasure, darlink*…were her words.'

'Lucky you…' Christina had no idea where this was heading, since Eric liked to exaggerate situations to make them sound more colourful.

'No, not so lucky me! I couldn't move or see what was going on. Then I felt some kind of leather brace being tightened around my neck. I thought I was being strangled! Marta then took off my blindfold…she was now dressed in full leather studded corset and thigh-length leather boots…in her hand she brandished this leather whip…'

'Ah…Were you naked during all this?'

'Completely. She then playfully started to whip me…and with each swish, I could see her getting really excited…and then – '

She stopped him there. 'Eric, I don't want to hear all the gory details. Basically, she was into S & M and you obviously weren't. That about right?'

'It wasn't pleasant, and did nothing for me, or John Thomas, who lay there unwilling to rise to the occasion.'

'Without elaborating please, what happened after?'

'Because it was a complete turn off for me, I couldn't perform in the way that she wanted. She was quite calm, didn't pressurise me further, and put her toys away.'

'What's the real problem? What about the black eye, and those bruises? I don't know if I understand.'

'That happened a couple of nights later. We had been getting on better after that little episode. Nothing was said. She's a great cook by the way! I'm beginning to get quite partial to Polish food.'

'Stick to the story, please!'

'Right…Anyway, while we were getting ready for bed, she begged if she could just tie me up. Nothing else. I didn't think there was any harm in it…'

'You're a glutton for punishment, Eric.'

'I didn't think she was going to go any further! Not by the way she'd behaved beforehand…She's got a nice side to her.'

'I'm sure. So have some serial killers…so…in a nutshell, please.' Christina was on the verge of getting bored.

'Whilst I lay there, she put on this leather catlike mask and placed this neck thing on, pulling it really tight, even though I protested.'

Christina's patience was waning. 'Eric if this is going to get too kinky, I don't want to know. Now get to the bloody point!'

'Okay, okay, I'll spare you painful details. God, it was painful! That woman should be sectioned. Anyway, when I told her to stop and that I wasn't playing this game anymore, Marta did stop. Then out of the blue asked for a divorce and said she would expect to get half of all my assets in a settlement.'

'What did you say?'

'I told her I'd happily divorce her, but as far as any settlement was concerned, she could fuck off.'

'Good for you!'

'That's when she punched me in the eye and squeezed my balls so hard; I thought I was going to pass out. They're still very tender…I might have to get them checked out…' He rubbed his groin with an agonising look.

'Don't you dare show them to me!' Christina waved her finger at him. 'Then what?'

'She got dressed, packed her bag and left. That's before threatening me, unless I agreed to the settlement. It took me over an hour to untie myself.'

'Empty threats. You probably won't hear from her again.'

'That's the problem. A couple of days later I got this solicitor's letter. She was filing for divorce on the grounds that I beat and abused her! I was being threatened with police action and possible jail, unless I give her £15,000 - and the flat.'

'Are you serious? That's blackmail.'

Eric took out the letter and showed it to her. 'It's here in black and white...'

She gazed down at the letter. 'What are you going to do?'

'I don't know…She obviously means business.'

Christina thought for a moment. 'Can I keep this? I

want to show it to Duncan. See what he makes of it, and if he can suggest what to do.'

'Thank you…I knew you'd suggest something practical.'

'That's very big of you. Before, when I lived with you, if I recall, you always seemed to poo-poo any suggestions I made.'

'Did I? Don't remember…' He looked away.

'But now that the poo-poo's hit the fan, you're quite happy to take it.' She meant it in an honest, rather than sarcastic way.

'I wish I'd never married the bitch.'

'But it was the money you married really, wasn't it? For thirty pieces of silver.'

'It was more than that!' Eric didn't understand the reference.

'Look, I'll talk to Duncan. Now, if you don't mind, I'm feeling tired and I think you should go home.' Christina got up from her chair and pointed to the door to make the point. Eric looked disappointed, but nodded meekly. As he rose from the sofa, he grimaced in some discomfort. 'And I suggest you get your bollocks medically checked out as soon as. You don't want to disappoint your friend Sadie.'

'Oh, she's moved on. Got a text message earlier, to let me know she's met a casting director, and is now going to be an actress. That little scene with Tony encouraged her that she could act.'

'Good luck to her. There's a shortage of actresses who can play sluts, whores and prostitutes.'

'Really?' Eric believed her.

'Goodbye, Eric.' She held the front door open. 'I'll let you know what Duncan says.'

After he left, she went and poured herself a stiff drink. Dying didn't seem to be as much a drawback now as dealing with living, trying to cope with other people's problems.

25. It's Murder Up North

'Christina Turner?'

'Yes…?' She was half asleep when she picked up her mobile. She didn't recognise the number

'Detective Chief Inspector John Silbey, West Midlands Police. Sorry to trouble you at this early hour.'

She looked blearily at the clock. It was 6.43. 'Is this a crank call? Because if it is you can go and get stuffed!' She was on the verge of ending the call.

'Do you know Patrick Halkin?'

'Yes…what's he done now?' Christina sighed. Someone else's mess to sort out now. Why were men so useless at managing their lives, she thought?

'We found your number on his phone.'

'Found? What's this about?'

'Would you be available for a chat, say at lunchtime?'

'Can't we do this on the phone, now?' She was slowly waking up.

'We'd rather do this in person. Can we come and see you? You're in West London now, I believe. If you give us your correct address, we don't seem to have it on record.'

Christina was now getting suspicious. How did they know where she was? Was the phone being tracked? Was this some kind of set-up? She'd heard of bogus police phoning up for some kind of scam or robbery. 'Why would you come all the way from the West Midlands to talk to me?'

'We're conducting an investigation into a serious matter.'

She still wasn't convinced this was a genuine call. 'So, what has Patrick done now? Been drinking too much? Found wandering the streets?'

'I'm not at liberty to discuss this on the phone. Please don't make it difficult for us Mrs Turner.'

'It's Ms…Sorry, but can I phone you back? If you'll just give me your number.'

'You have it on your phone already. Please Ms Turner, we need to -'

Christina ended the call before he could finish. She looked at the number of the last call. It was a 0121 code, which she recognised as Birmingham. But that could still be decoy number, which she didn't trust. She decided to phone Patrick's number first. 'Hello Ms Turner, John Silbey here again.' She quickly ended the call without saying anything. It was clear they had his phone, but they could still be bluffing. She next called enquiries to ask for the number of the West Midlands Police. When she phoned, she asked to be put through to a Detective Inspector John Silbey, expecting to hear that there was no one of that name known. 'DCI Silbey?'

'It's…it's Christina Turner…' Recognising his voice she felt a bit foolish.

'Very admirable of you to check up on us. If more people did that, there'd be less crime from those purporting to be the police. Now, if you'll kindly give me your address, unless you'd prefer we talk at your local police station?'

'No…here will be fine.' She gave him the address. The thought of going back to that station after she'd been arrested wasn't a favourable option.

'We will see you about oneish. Is that okay?'

'I'll be here…' The call ended. Christina lay back on the bed in a mood of despair. If it wasn't one thing it was another. First there was Eric with his bartered bride, now it was Patrick. What state was he in now? Had all those texts been simply to keep her happy? Had he used the money she sent, to drink himself stupid? She wouldn't have been that surprised

He was always a charmer with the gift of the gab, yet in many ways weak. She no longer knew what or whom to believe. It had to be something serious if the police were coming all the way from Birmingham to talk to her. Various possible scenarios streamed across her thoughts. Was she going to have to bail Patrick out, because he'd done something silly? Had he found the baby? Had he kidnapped it in a moment of despair? Was the story about Meera and the baby a complete fabrication anyway to elicit sympathy and money? Was she the only one he could rely on to help? He wouldn't go to Jennie, and he didn't appear to have any other friends. Oh, how she wished she'd never stopped that night to talk to Patrick. Even leaving Aylesbury and coming to London had turned out to be a big mistake. She didn't expect that the last days of her life were going to be so complicated.

As soon as Christina had breakfast and got ready, she went out to do a bit of shopping. Whilst out, she received a call from Jennie. Had the police contacted her as well? She thought about ignoring it, but was curious about what Jennie wanted. As she initially suspected, Jennie wanted to accept the investment offer. She felt like telling her where to go, but decided a face-to-face confrontation would be much more satisfying. Christina suggested they meet for a quick coffee locally to discuss it. There would still be time to get back to the flat before the police arrived.

'You don't know how much your generous offer means to me.' Jennie took a sip of coffee as they sat at a corner table in a café.

Christina hadn't said much when they met up, and had managed to disguise her true feelings. They'd exchanged pleasantries, with Christina asking how the business was going; whilst Jennie tentatively enquired about how she was feeling, because she certainly looked good.

'So? What generous offer was this?' Christina acted dumb.

Jennie was thrown for a moment. 'The investment of £20,000 into the business, of course.' She forced a laugh.

'Did I? You know, I don't remember…I think my memory's starting to go. The cancer must be getting to my head…'

'You said you wanted to give the business a kick-start. Those were your words.' Jennie looked at Christina's confused expression.

'I honestly don't recall saying that…'

'I assure you; you did.' Christina just shook her head and shrugged. 'What are you playing at, Christina?' Jennie was beginning to get a touch flustered.

'Playing…? Don't you know the game, Jennie? It's one you should be very familiar with, since you played it a lot yourself.' She smiled.

'What are you talking about? Is this one of your little deceptions, like that funeral nonsense?'

'Not at all, because I know the truth now. How you blamed me for the collapse of the business, when all along you had been syphoning profits into a personal account.'

Jennie couldn't hide the initial guilty shock on her face. 'What are you babbling about?"

'And, may I add, at the same time conducting a string of secret affairs. Greg was one of them, wasn't he? You kept that well-hidden. Not that it was any of my business.'

'What…? Why are you making all this up?'

'I'm not making anything up. Why don't you tell the truth for once?'

'The truth, you call it! When all the time you were trying to cover up all the mistakes you made, putting me out of business.' Jennie had regained her composure.

'No, you made me the patsy, the scapegoat for all your misdemeanours. Please don't try and bluff your way out of it, like you did all those years ago.'

Jennie continued to keep her cool. 'Where has all this suddenly come from?'

'Patrick. He told me what had happened.'

'Patrick…?' Jennie suddenly froze, and went pale. 'When did you talk to Patrick?'

'Week before last. We had a very interesting conversation. He told me what you had done, and how you were finally caught out by the tax people. And that you tried to put the blame on me.'

'He was lying!' Jennie started to raise her voice.

'Why should he? He had nothing to gain or lose by telling me the truth, and I had no reason not to believe him.' Christina watched as Jennie's whole self-control slowly started to crumble.

'He was just getting his own back because I threw him out and divorced him!'

'But you told me he was the one who wanted the divorce. Get your story straight, Jennie, or is everything you tell me made up to elicit my sympathy?'

'What else did Patrick, allegedly, say?'

Christina decided to go for the jugular. 'That you blamed him because you couldn't have children.' To really put the knife in, she had thought about mentioning Meera and the baby, but felt that would be too cruel.

Christina thought Jennie was about to explode. 'I'm not listening to anymore of this drivel!' Her anger rising,

Jennie rose from her seat. 'It's all lies and you know it! It's a very long-winded way of going back on your investment promise – which I'm assuming you're not going to fulfil. Why should I be surprised at anything you say or do anymore? You always were a scheming, lying bitch, and I hope that when you finally die it will be alone and painful!' With that she ran out of the café.

Christina drained her cup of coffee and noticed that the whole café had gone quiet, with all eyes on her and the departing Jennie. 'It's okay. She's just peeved because I didn't give her a 'like' on her Facebook page…'

Detective Chief Inspector John Silbey was a small, thin man in his late forties. He had the tired look of a man who had seen everything, and that nothing surprised him anymore. With him was Detective Sergeant Jim Crouch, who towered over Silbey, whose neck was twice as thick. With his shaved head he looked more like a criminal than a policeman. Christina carefully studied both their IDs at the doorway before letting them in.

'You are very cautious Ms Turner.' Silbey's experienced eyes took in the flat as he entered.

'You police are always telling everyone to check the credentials of anyone coming to the door who you don't know. Unscrupulous people out there happy to rob or dupe us trusting citizens?' She took them into the sitting room.

Silbey gave a wry grin, showing uneven teeth. 'I don't think they'd be able to put one over on you, Ms. Lived here long?'

'A month or so. Please call me Christina. Can I get you a tea or coffee, since you've come all this way?'

'We're okay, thanks. Your last address was in Aylesbury. Is that correct?'

'Yes…Have I done anything wrong? What's this to do with Patrick?'

'Just a few preliminary questions first, if you don't mind. Why did you come to London?'

'Is that relevant?' Christina looked at the two policeman sat before her. Silbey had his fingers entwined, resting on his belly; while Crouch, his partner made notes.

'When we enquired at your Aylesbury address, we were told that you had left unexpectedly and not said where you were going.'

'I did, and I left a note to say – '

Crouch put up his hand to stop her. Looking at his notes, he then repeated in a tiny voice that contradicted his build. 'And I quote: "Going away for a few months to sort some things out. Please don't try to find me. I will get back in touch. Christina…" that correct, Ma'am?'

'Is that regarded as a crime then?' Christina was surprised at what they knew, but was in no way going to make it easy for them.

'No, we're curious to know why you left.' Silbey twiddled his thumbs.

'So, have you told those in Aylesbury where I am then?'

'No. You haven't been reported missing. We assumed it was a domestic matter between you and them. Nothing to concern us with this inquiry. However, we'd still like to know why you are living here in this rented property?'

'I see, you checked that too, after I gave you the address.'

'All routine during the course of our investigations.' Crouch tapped his notebook on his knee.

'So where was I between the hours of ten to twelve today?' Christina studied their faces, as they turned from a look of bewilderment to one of wry amusement.

'Don't you know where you were?' Silbey threw it back at her with a smile.

'Okay, point taken. Just checking, as you seem to know a lot about me.'

'But perhaps you'll still enlighten us about why you came to London.'

'I still don't see what this has to do with Patrick?' Silbey and Crouch just stared at her, waiting for her to reply. 'Alright. I left Aylesbury when I discovered I had terminal cancer, with only a few months to live. I decided to come to London to spend my final days near to the only close family that I have. Does that satisfy you, or do you want a full medical report? Or are you going to tell me you have that already?'

The policemen looked at each other a touch embarrassed. 'We're sorry to hear that...about your condition. We have to ask - how well did you know Patrick Halkin?'

'We weren't close friends. He was the husband of my ex-business partner.'

'Jennie Halkin?' Christina nodded, stopping herself from saying anything derogatory about Jennie, which would only complicate matters. 'When was the last time you saw Patrick?'

'A couple of weeks ago. He was in a sorry state. He was desperate to trace his baby daughter, from an affair he had.'

Crouch checked in his notebook. 'With Meera Banerjee?'

'Yes. But I believe she was killed...Please, can't you tell me what this is all about? I've a right to know after all this questioning.'

Silbey shifted uneasily on the sofa. 'A couple of days ago, Patrick Halkin was found dead in Sparkbrook,

---

237

Birmingham. We believe he was murdered…'

'What…?' Christina lay back in her armchair in a state of shock. 'How…Why?'

'He was shot. We are led to believe that it had something to do with him contacting the Banerjee family, but that's all we can say at the moment. Are we right in believing that you had some money transferred into his account?'

'You've obviously checked already. It was to help him hire a private detective, to find the whereabouts of his daughter. I got a text from him to say that he was hopeful of good news soon… I can't believe he's dead…'

'Do you still have that text?'

Christina got her phone and passed it to him. He scrolled quickly through and then handed it back to her. 'Thank you. That all seems to confirm what we know. We might need to ask you some further questions later. You're not planning on going anywhere?'

'Only to heaven or hell…you might need wings or a devil's trident to find me.'

Both Silbey and Crouch rose from the sofa in silence, not feeling there was an acceptable response to her answer. 'Thank you…Christina…for your time…' Silbey was about to shake her hand, then thought differently.

'I didn't have much choice, did I? I hope you catch whoever did this to Patrick.' She stood up, and momentarily felt unsteady on her legs. She was still reeling from the news.

'We will…'

'By the way, do you know what's happening about any funeral arrangements?'

'Not yet. He doesn't seem to have any family, apart from his ex-wife, whom we'll be talking to shortly. Goodbye…we'll show ourselves out.'

Christina fell back into the chair and broke down in

tears. It wasn't just that Patrick was dead, but because she felt totally responsible. If it wasn't for her, and her money, he might still be alive today. If she hadn't encouraged him to go and find his daughter, all this might not have happened.

She felt as if she had pulled the trigger herself. What had really happened? She knew that although Meera's husband was in prison for her murder; she had two brothers who might have found out about Patrick's visit, and killed him as some sort of cultural revenge to uphold family pride.

She wondered how Jennie would take it, and did consider phoning her later when the news was public. But after what had happened at the café today, she didn't feel that was a good idea in the circumstances. Christina knew that Jennie still loved Patrick, and that the news of his death would hit her very hard. Despite her antagonism towards Jennie, she still couldn't help but feel a little sorry for her.

It was Jennie who rang her the next day, in a complete state of despair, practically hysterical, to tell her about Patrick. The police had been to see her to impart the sad news.

Christina listened to all the details that she knew already, but responded acting shocked, as if she didn't know. From the way she was talking, Jennie hadn't been told about Christina's recent involvement with Patrick, and why she gave him money. Christina didn't feel it was right to enlighten her, which would only add to the blow of his death, she wasn't that mercenary.

Christina, however, refused when Jennie almost begged if they could meet up to discuss what had happened.

Jennie apologised for what she had said at the café and hoped that Christina would forgive her. Christina made appropriate noises and excuses, but wasn't in the mood to placate a tearful Jennie and go over her loss. Patrick's death might have softened her resentment against Jennie, but in

Christina's book, that didn't mean they were going to be friends again. That would never happen. She ended by promising to meet up soon. She also added that she'd be happy to help with any funeral or transport costs if money was tight. Jennie didn't hesitate by accepting the offer, which made Christina smile. People don't change.

26. Getting a Room

Everything went quiet over the next few days. Christina didn't hear back from the police, and there was nothing on the TV news or in national newspapers about Patrick's murder. The only person she heard from was Tony, who asked if he could come and see her. She was very happy to let him, feeling the need for company.

'Mum, you look great! Everything alright?' Tony had brought a bunch of flowers. She couldn't remember him ever buying her flowers, even on her birthday, and wondered what he was after.

'Can't complain. Thank you for these, they're lovely. You're looking pleased with yourself.' Christina could see the change in him. He did look as if he'd suddenly grown up.

'Oh, things are good. Can't complain either!'

'College okay? How's your father?'

'Yeh, doing okay. Dad's the same. Been a bit moody lately.'

'No change then!' Christina joked. 'How's your father's lady friend?' She said with a tinge of sarcasm.

'Helen's Helen, can't say more than that. As you know, there's no love lost between us, but I suppose she keeps Dad happy…so how are things really? You know…'

'My cancer? It's round the corner somewhere, ready to pounce. I wish it would hurry up.'

'You don't mean that.' Tony hated her talking like this.

'I do. It's like waiting for the axe to strike. I'm ready, but it's biding its time. Anyway, shall we change the subject? So, what's new in your life?'

Tony gave a little grin. 'I've got a lady friend…'

'You mean girlfriend?'

'Well, she's a bit older than me…'

'How old? I hope she's not married.'

'Mum! She's a few years older and single. Her name's Rachel, and I'm not marrying her.'

'Only interested, that's all. No need to get precious.' Christina was at least relieved that it wasn't Sadie he was seeing.

'Has your father met her?'

'You're joking! I wouldn't bring her home for him to get on his high horse and pull her to pieces. I suppose he told you about what happened?'

'I haven't spoken to Roger for some time. What did happen then?'

'It's not important. I just brought a girl home. He wasn't too pleased and gave me the third degree.'

Christina thought about saying *and caught you in bed with her*, but she was afraid that she might give away that she already knew, and that would open a can of worms. 'Probably jealous, if I know your father.'

Tony laughed. 'Got it in one! That's why I won't invite Rachel home.'

'So where do you two get together? To be alone, that is. Her place?'

'She shares a flat with two others. It's not easy… Mum, I was just wondering.'

'You want to bring her here, when I'm not about?' Tony looked surprised. 'Isn't that what you wanted to ask me, why you really came to see me?'

'I came to see how you were!' He protested. 'But I was going to ask if I could spend some time with her here. And yes, before you ask, we probably will have sex. Is that a problem for you?

'Not so much a problem…but…'

'But what? You're always going on about how

broadminded we should be. I remember you giving me that little chat after you and Dad divorced and went to live with Uncle Eric.'

'That's absolutely true, Tony. I can't say it doesn't surprise me, but it does. But I can't talk, as you will remind me. You can use the flat, but not in my bed if that's not too much to ask. And don't leave the place in a mess. I'll text you when it suits me, when I'm likely to be out, and for how long. I'll give you a spare key before you go. Now can we talk about something other than my cancer and your sex life?'

'Thanks, Mum, I appreciate it. And just for the record, I do use condoms.' Tony gave a big grin

'I wasn't even going to ask. You're a big boy now. So, tell me what you're doing at college, and your hopes for when you leave….'

Tony left the flat with a spring in his step. He honestly didn't think that Christina would agree to let him use her flat. He had come fully prepared to put forward his request, which in the end wasn't necessary since she had agreed so easily. He realised that might not have been the case, if he'd told his mother more particulars about Rachel. Had he been completely honest, he was certain that Christina would never have agreed.

Rachel was one of his teachers at college. A thirty-year old divorcee, who had taught him the last couple of years. He'd always had a bit of a crush on her, while she playfully flirted with him in class.

It was all very innocent and harmless. She made no inappropriate attempts to take it any further, realising it would've compromised her position as a teacher.

Tony was too shy and inexperienced to make any move, knowing that he'd probably be rejected and be made

---

243

to feel foolish. That all changed after his encounter with Sadie. The whole experience had instilled in him an arrogant confidence, almost as if he'd taken a pill that made you more adventurous and willing to take risks.

At first Rachel, who noticed the change in him, gently rebuffed his attempts to see her after college hours. But his positive and cheerful persistence, and the fact that she found herself strongly attracted to him, made her finally agree to meet him clandestinely. As yet they hadn't had sex, having gone no further than kissing and fumbling in dark corners. Despite her strong desires, Rachel still held back, fully aware that if they were caught, her career would be over. She wasn't prepared to sacrifice that for the sake of a fuck, as she succinctly put it to him. Tony had suggested a hotel, which she discounted on the grounds that there'd be somebody who might recognise them. Tony had begun to feel that if he didn't come up with somewhere safe to go, the relationship, as such, would be over before it really began. He knew he wanted her more than she wanted him.

Now, as he clutched the flat key in his hand, he fantasised about finally being able to sleep with Rachel, and hoped it wouldn't be too long before his mother let him use it. Christina had surprised him. Since coming back into his life, he felt she was a different mother to the one that had disappeared, more approachable and less censorious. This was obviously due, in his belief, to her having to face a death sentence.

His true feelings regarding her imminent demise were conflicting. The little boy in him didn't want to lose his mother; but the emergent adult took it all philosophically. In a way he had already lost her twice; first when she divorced and then went to live with his uncle; the second time when she completely disappeared out of their lives. He had already mourned her a couple of times; the third might not feel so different, albeit more permanent. It was more in a dutiful way that he loved his mother. Her death wasn't really going to upset his world. He knew she had inherited some money, and secretly hoped that whatever was left would go to him when she died. With a decent amount of money to his name, he might not go to university or need to find a job once he left college. So, in a perverse way, he was covertly looking forward to attending her real funeral.

Christina wondered if she'd done the right thing in agreeing to let Tony use the flat for sex. Was this older woman taking advantage of her son's emotions? A predatory female who would abandon him when she got bored? From the way Tony had talked briefly about this Rachel, it obviously wasn't love. He was just a young man out to satisfy his sexual urges; nothing more from what she could sense. She loved her son, but had never felt close to him. He'd been a difficult child, who over the years gave her more grief than pleasure. It was one reason why she never felt very guilty after she divorced Roger and went to live with Eric. Even when she finally had her mini breakdown and disappeared, she felt sadness rather than guilt. In terms of letting him use the flat, she'd decided it might be for a few hours on a Saturday or Sunday, when it suited her.

Patrick's death continued to affect her, as she felt primarily responsible for encouraging him to find the baby. Had he managed to see his daughter, or had he been killed before he had that chance?

There were so many unanswered questions, many of which probably wouldn't be answered. She was tempted to phone Silbey, but realised she'd probably be told nothing since she wasn't next of kin. If anyone would be told anything, that would be Jennie, who was the closest to him as far as family was concerned. Christina was sure Jennie would let her know of any developments, yet was secretly relieved that Jennie hadn't phoned since their last communication. The less contact with her the better.

Since the police had visited her, Christina had completely forgotten about Eric and his marital problem, and that she was going to talk to Duncan. Eric's desperate call, to enquire if there was any news, reminded her. She went and saw Duncan the following day.

'That's what he told me, and Eric's never been one to make up stories. His awful appearance proved that. This woman is obviously out for everything she can get. I began to wonder if the whole thing had been set up from the very beginning to con Eric.'

Duncan carefully read the solicitor's letter that Eric had received. 'And she is claiming he assaulted her…interesting.'

'What do you think?' Christina watched him as he perused the letter again.

'Difficult to make any judgement at this juncture with two opposing accounts. Which, of course, is always the dilemma in law, especially when it concerns divorce.'

'But she's obviously lying! I've never known Eric to be violent. At heart he's quite a gentle, simple soul.'

'That's possibly true, but these allegations from the other party are quite serious. This is from a reputable law firm.' He waved the letter. 'Is that relevant? You're a reputable law firm. Will you represent Eric? I'll foot the bill, of course.' She was starting to get impatient with his slow, non-committal response.

'Naturally I'll need to see Mr Turner and hear the story from his point of view. But first I want to make some preliminary enquiries about his wife…Polish did you say?' Christina nodded. 'Had a Polish girlfriend once. Nearly married her for her cooking! Her pierogi and sour cucumber soup were out of this world!' He licked his lips in remembrance.

'But you will take on his case?'

'Hopefully. I don't want to go into it blind, or waste his time. I need to do some research on the law regarding these types of marriages and see if there is any precedent. I like to feel I am fully prepared before I commit myself – which I'm sure you'll understand.'

'Always the cautious Duncan.' Christina sighed. She remembered how slow and painstaking he was when he dealt with her divorce from Roger; and the persuasion needed when she wanted to organise her mock funeral.

'One cannot be too hasty where the law is concerned. It might be an ass, but it's an ass that has a strong kick. Tell Mr Turner that I'll be in touch as soon as. It might take a week or so. It's advisable, in the meantime, for him to take some photographs of his bruises before they heal.'

'I'll pass that on. Thanks.'

'In the circumstances – all is well…?'

'I'm still here. I don't know what's worse, being told that you're going to die; or the waiting for it to happen.'

'Perhaps it is best we don't know exactly when.'

'I'm not so sure about that. Anyway, thanks for looking into Eric's case. I think you'll find what he told me bears out.'

Duncan smiled but didn't respond. He took nothing on hearsay. He wouldn't make a judgement until he was satisfied that he had all the facts.

Instinctively, from what Christina had told him, it looked like a fraudulent case against Eric. But he wasn't prepared to commit until the whole picture was clearer in his mind, and he had enough information to fight with.

***

Christina left Duncan's office with a sense of frustration. He had always erred on the side of caution, wanting to know every detail, before agreeing to represent her. Yet once he had committed, he would pull out all the stops to get a favourable result. Despite her exasperation at his meticulous approach, Christina trusted him completely.

Eric's response, when she phoned him, was one of anger coupled with petulance seeing he might have to wait until Duncan was happy to talk to him. If that were the case, he'd find another solicitor. Christina, who refused to pander to him, told him to go ahead, it was no skin off her nose. She'd offered to help but it wasn't her problem. He was the one that agreed to marry Marta and got himself into this mess. Eric eventually calmed down, agreeing to wait to hear from Duncan. He'd already had the foresight of taking photographs of the bruises on his face and neck, and had written down everything that had happened. When he offered to take her out to dinner she declined. She wasn't in the mood to spend the evening bolstering his ego or listening to his hard-done-by story, as much as she sympathised with his predicament.

'Fancy a slug?' Paula had made some tea and was holding a small bottle of whiskey, a capful that she had added to her cup.

'No thanks, but isn't it simpler if you pour the tea into the bottle for ease?' Christina was sitting in the vestry of the church, having made a special visit to see Paula.

'You really think I'm on the edge of being an alcoholic?'

'Tea with whiskey in the afternoon? They say that's the first step.'

'I'm assuming you're not going to have one of my hash brownies. They're really out of this world!' Paula picked up the plate of chocolate brownies and offered them to Christina, who eyed them suspiciously. 'One bite and you're in heaven – that's what it said on the M&S packet…'

'In that case…' Christina took one. 'Seriously though. About the drink?'

'Stop being paranoid because you introduced me to it! I bought this bottle ten days ago, and it's not even a quarter empty. I tipple very occasionally, and today is such an occasion. It's nice to see you, Christina. And may I say, you're looking good.'

'That's what worries me. The beauty before the beast strikes. Umm, these are delicious. May I?' She helped herself another brownie and took a bite.

'This is not purely a social visit?'

'As much as it's nice to see you too, No. Paula, would you be willing to conduct a non-religious funeral for a non-believer?'

'Are we talking about your funeral…when the time comes?'

'No, it's for a friend. You remember Jennie, who was at my little do? Well, it's her ex-husband, Patrick. He was murdered.'

'Murdered? Wow! Sorry to hear that. I'm intrigued. Tell me more.'

'It's a long story, which I don't really want to go into now. Anyway, yesterday I got a phone call from Jennie to tell me that the police were releasing the body for funeral. As she's the closest next of kin, the responsibility is hers to make the arrangements. I've agreed to help with the costs. Jennie was quite happy when I suggested that you conducted the funeral – if of course you were happy to do this, without the trimmings of a proper religious ceremony. I know that might be against your beliefs and your position. But I'm asking just the same.'

Paula thought for a moment. 'I'd not be required to wear my service vestments, and an evening dress wouldn't be appropriate?'

'Not in this case. Just a very low-key simple service and send off, followed by cremation. What do you think? Does it compromise your position in the church if they found out you'd done a humanitarian type funeral?'

'Well, the church never seemingly got wind of me getting pissed and locked up, which I find a miracle; so, doing this, which will be in a crematorium chapel anyway, is not likely to bring the archbishop to my door. Besides, I'm still having serious thoughts about leaving the church altogether...'

'How serious...?' Christina showed genuine surprise.

'Pretty serious. I think those odd slugs of whiskey have made me see things more clearly and re-evaluate my position.' Paula laughed as she watched Christina's guilty and horrified expression. 'But plain old tea has had that same effect! The jury's still out on any decision. Until then I'm more than happy to take charge of the funeral.'

'Thank you. I don't think they'll be much of a turnout...'

27. An Arresting Funeral

Not much of a turnout was an understatement. There were only four people waiting outside the crematorium. Christina, Paula, Jennie and Giles, the only friend Patrick had kept in touch with. The hearse carrying Patrick's coffin stood nearby, the black suited funeral staff chatted in a huddle. Nobody said much as they all stood there, waiting for the funeral before them to finish.

Jennie, who hadn't stopped crying, was dressed all in black, sporting dark sunglasses, despite it being a gloomy and overcast day. She kept on glancing back at the hearse, as if expecting the coffin to open and Patrick to climb out. 'He was the love of my life...and now he's gone...' She addressed Giles, who looked distinctly uncomfortable, as she linked arms with him and started to sob, resting her head on his shoulder.

Christina was tempted to blurt out *You two-faced bitch, if you hadn't fucked around, you might have kept him and he'd still be alive today!* She looked across at Paula and shrugged sadly. Paula, in a smart two-piece suit, gave a sad smile, and looked back over the notes she had prepared.

Jennie had been happy for Christina to make and pay for all the arrangements; liaise with the police to have the body collected, and book the funeral directors. A small funeral tea had been arranged at a nearby pub for later.

She was more than pleased to do it, without having to consult with Jennie, giving her something constructive to do. She owed it to Patrick, still feeling guilty that she had been instrumental in starting a chain of unfortunate events that led to his demise. But then again, she wondered, if she hadn't come across him, Patrick might well have drunk himself to death in the end.

The opening of the chapel doors broke the silence, and a stream of around thirty darkly dressed mourners exited. At the same time another hearse; bearing a floral arrangement of 'MUM' on the coffin, trailed by a cortege of cars, arrived in the car park, seemingly the funeral to follow Patrick's. It was looking like a conveyor belt transporting the dead to their final destination.

Jennie glanced up at it and immediately started crying again. Christina thought it ironic. Jennie couldn't have children, and if she'd only known that Patrick had sired a child, she'd really be beside herself. She'd been tempted to tell Jennie the truth, and even wondered if the police had mentioned it during their talks with Jennie. She doubted it; since she was sure Jennie would've said something to that effect. There still wasn't any further news from the police on the murder investigation.

Paula motioned that it was now their turn to enter the chapel for the service. Jennie went in, still holding on to Giles' arm, and while dabbing her eyes with a hankie beneath the dark glasses, whispered something that made him suddenly disengage from her hold. Christina looked around, wondering if there might be any last-minute mourners attending, as she had put a notice in the Times announcing Patrick's death and funeral details. No one else appeared as the doors closed behind her.

The service, as such, took less than fifteen minutes. Paula did a brief eulogy on information she'd gleaned from both Jennie and Christina. There wasn't much to say about Patrick. During this Jennie blubbered loudly, her cries echoing throughout the small chapel, almost drowning Paula's words. Christina felt like telling her to shut up.

She thought it really was a very sad and depressing send off, and wondered if hers would be similar when the time came. She decided there and then not to have a funeral, but to be cremated without a service, and made a mental note to tell Duncan to add it to her Will.

When Patrick's favourite song, Frank Sinatra's 'My Way', gently began to play as the curtains round the coffin started to close, Jennie ran towards it almost screaming in despair. It took both Paula and Giles to restrain her, and guide her back to the pews. Christina just sighed, feeling more disgust than sympathy for this dramatic demonstration of grief and relieved it had come to an end.

As the chapel doors were opened, Christina saw the distant figures of DCI John Silbey and his sidekick DS Jim Crouch standing there expressionless. It wouldn't have been less theatrical if they'd emerged from a cloud of swirling mist. Christina was surprised, yet knew it wasn't unknown for the police to attend the funerals of murdered victims.

They remained standing silently until the four of them had left the confines of the chapel. Christina approached Silbey. 'I'm sorry, but you're a bit late…'

'It's never too late…' Silbey said enigmatically, and then approached Jennie, who was still in a bit of an emotional state. 'Jennifer Halkin, I am arresting you for the murder of Patrick Halkin. You do not have to say anything. But it may harm your defence if you do not mention when questioned something you later rely on in court. Anything you do say may be given in evidence.' Crouch then produced a pair of handcuffs and put them on Jennie.

Jennie took off her sunglasses and gave a manic grin. 'The bastard deserved to die after what he'd done!'

She then turned to Christina. 'And you, you fucking cow, you helped him! I wished I'd finished you off first!' She then spat at Christina, after which Crouch led Jennie away to the waiting police car parked by the entrance.

Paula stood with Giles watching, and mumbled. 'God moves in mysterious ways…'

253

'His wonders to perform…?' Giles added with a slight smirk.

Christina stood frozen to the spot, the spit cascading down her cheek. Silbey quickly scribbled something in his notebook. 'Well, those last few words of wisdom from Mrs Halkin will certainly help our case. You alright…?'

'What do you think?' She wiped the spit off.

'I'm sorry, but I have to inform you that you might be asked to appear as a witness if there's a trial.'

'How long might that be?'

'Depends how long it takes for the defence and prosecution teams to prepare their cases – that is if she pleads not guilty and it goes ahead. Could be months, or even longer.'

'I could be a dead witness if that's the situation.'

Silbey suddenly remembered about her illness and looked embarrassed. 'Sorry…forgot. Would you be prepared to sign a statement, which could be read in court…in the event…'

'Of my demise? Of course. What really happened then?'

'I can't give you any details at this stage. But once things are clearer, I'll let you know if that's okay.'

'You know where I am. Thanks…'

Silbey gave her a brief smile before making his way to the police car, which then drove off with Jennie in the back.

'Well…if anyone had asked me yesterday whether I thought Jennie was capable of murder – I would've said yes, definitely. Today, I am surprised and at the same time, I'm not.' Christina addressed both Paula and Giles, who were both still stunned with what they'd just witnessed. 'Now there are three. You've haven't murdered anyone, Giles, have you?'

'Many I'd like to. Do you know, that woman propositioned me as we came into the chapel? Said funerals made her feel randy.' Giles shivered at the thought.

'You had a lucky escape there. You could've been the one with the handcuffs on! Will you join us for a drink and sandwiches at that pub down the road?'

'I won't, if you don't mind. Best be getting off…' Giles shook both Christina and Paula's hands and disappeared into the car park.

'Then there were two…' Paula tore up her notes and threw them into a nearby bin; full of rotting flowers and scrunched up loving message tags. 'It'll be more like a sleep than a wake!'

'Well, I will toast Patrick farewell. It's the least I can do since I was the one to encourage him…'

'You cannot keep blaming yourself, Christina. You didn't tell Jennie, and you didn't put the gun in her hand. Assuming the police are right and she did do it.'

'Oh, she did it all right! No question in my mind. Anyway, thank you for doing the service. You made what turned out to be a humdrum life, interesting.'

'Everyone deserves a bit of praise and some good words, whatever they've done, even if it's not the realistic truth.'

'Except for Jennie, of course!' They both laughed. 'Come on; let's get at those sandwiches before they start curling up at the edges. I hope you're not in any hurry to dash off afterwards.'

'I have no clocks to punch, no souls to save. Saturdays have always been sacrosanct for non-religious activities.'

'Good, it's just that I've let Tony use the flat for his sexual trysts. I promised I wouldn't be home before six.'

'Sex before six. I wouldn't mind some of that…but

I'll settle for sandwiches before six instead! Lead on!'

It had taken Tony some time to persuade Rachel to come to his mother's flat. She was quite reticent at first, still holding back about having sex with him. Whilst physically she wanted him, her mind was torn about making that commitment. She loved her job as a teacher and nothing was worth having it sacrificed for. Yet the strong carnal pull that Tony had over her rather negated her common-sense arguments.

'Where is your mother's flat?' She was still worried about being seen by someone she knew.

'It's in another borough, miles away from the school. We take your car and drive there. It has underground parking, so no one's going to see us.'

'And your mother knows you'll be bringing me? I find that very odd.'

'My mum's very open-minded. Naturally, she won't be there. She's going to some funeral and will be away all afternoon.'

'Have you told her about me? That I'm your teacher, a divorcee and nearly twice your age?'

'I've said you're a bit older, but nothing else.' Tony was starting to get a bit ratty.

'And she asked no more questions? Doesn't sound like a normal mother to me.' Rachel was still finding it hard to comprehend.

'My mum's not normal. She's going to be dead soon, and she couldn't care a fuck what I do! Look, if you want to forget all about it, that's fine. But I'm fed up going round in circles and fighting with your precious conscience.' Tony knew he might have blown it with her, but was fed up with her persistent cautiousness.

'I'm sorry…I'm always looking at the worst-case scenario in everything I do. My ex-husband went on at me about that. It was one of the reasons we split up…I know that most of what I angst about never comes to pass, so that tells me something.'

'What do you want to do?' Tony responded calmly.

'I do want to be with you…'

'Then let's not waste the moment.' Tony took her arm.

They were in Christina's bedroom, both slowly getting undressed. Tony had decided to disregard his mother's wishes about not using her bed. The sofa was uncomfortable, and he didn't want to have sex on the floor. He felt Rachel deserved better. He'd tidy up the bed later, and she would never know. They had got down to their underwear, when Rachel became almost coy. 'What's the matter…?' Tony watched her stand away from the bed, her hands unconsciously held over the front of her body. 'You've got a beautiful body, don't hide it.' Grabbing his phone, he went across to her, put his arms around her and took a quick selfie photo.

'What are you doing?' She moved away.

'I just wanted to capture this moment. You look so lovely… Come on…' He quickly took off his underpants. 'Someone is pleased to see you!'

Rachel stared at his erect penis for a moment, turned around and started to get dressed. 'Sorry…'

'What's the matter?'

'I really can't do this…' She zipped up her skirt and started doing her blouse up.

'Not big enough for you?' He pointed at his penis. 'Have you been stringing me along all this time?'

'No!' She protested. 'I'm really fond of you…but I just can't go through with it. I hope you understand.' She slipped into her shoes.

'All I understand is that you seemed quite happy to come here. Quite passionate about snogging me just now. What went wrong?'

'I went wrong. I made a mistake. I'm sorry.' Rachel went for the door.

'So…are you going to leave me like this? What about a farewell blowjob, or even a hand job?'

'Don't be so disgusting! I thought you were better than that. Goodbye Tony. Don't try to ring or text me. We are over…' She left the bedroom.

'Over before we've even begun! You fucking prick teaser!' He shouted, but she had already left the flat. He plonked down onto the bed, punching the pillow in a fury that embraced rejection and sexual frustration. 'We are not over…'

28. Resurrection in Aylesbury

'This is it…now it begins…' Christina mumbled to herself as she lay in bed having just come from the bathroom a second time having been violently sick. She felt awful and weak. During the night she had a couple of attacks of diarrhoea, which unnerved her. This was her cancer appearing with a vengeance, as she had anticipated. The stomach pains, nausea, vomiting, diarrhoea…all symptoms that she was told to expect. Once these kicked in, it might be only a matter of weeks before they'd be carrying her out in a body bag to the mortuary.

It was only yesterday that Patrick had his funeral; that Jennie was arrested for murder, and throughout she had felt fine. She had enjoyed her little funeral tea with Paula, and they even managed to stick to actual tea, rather than spirits. She wondered if the cancer had been suddenly and subconsciously activated because of the ordeal of those events? She'd once read that a large proportion of illnesses developed because of what was going on in people's heads. Was her cancer the result of what had happened before she abandoned everyone and disappeared to Aylesbury which had proved traumatic? She certainly had that minor breakdown and had always felt guilty about what she had done. That would be the obvious upshot if one were looking for answers. She had got what was coming to her, so to speak.

Her stomach rumbled with pain, making her run to the bathroom again. She was just in time. As she sat on the toilet, she wondered how long it would be before she actually shits herself?

It looked like it was possibly time for her to get nursing care, which she had prearranged. She didn't want to, but feeling like this and knowing it was going to get worse, didn't leave her with much choice.

She hobbled back to bed and just as she was about to pick up her phone to ring the Macmillan nurses, when it rang. It was Paula. 'Hello…missing me already?'

'Christina…how are you feeling?' Paula's voice sounded strained.

'Shitty, if I'm going to be honest. Looks like the grim reaper has clocked in. You don't sound yourself. You okay?'

'No, I've been up all night being sick and having the runs.'

'So have I…' Christina mulled. 'Do you feel weak, nauseous, have stomach pains?'

'All those…I've never felt so dreadful. That's why I rang, I wondered -?'

'- If I might be feeling the same by any chance?' Christina acknowledged. 'We've obviously both got food poisoning. Must've been those prawn sandwiches in the pub that we scoffed down.'

'That does seem to add up…just a sec, got to run before I disgrace myself…will ring you later.'

Christina put down the phone, as her mind worked out what was happening. So perhaps it wasn't the cancer then, if Paula was experiencing the same symptoms. She already mentally prepared herself for the gradual decline, now possibly being a false alarm. So, when the hell was this cancer going to rear its ugly head? She was fed up with the expectation and the waiting. She had to do something or she'd go batty.

There really was only one course of action, if she was to going to get peace of mind. She needed return to Aylesbury and see the doctor to find out what was really happening to her.

***

It took another couple of days for her to get over the food poisoning, before she felt she was ready to travel. She spoke to Paula, who was also feeling better, but didn't mention what she had planned. She wasn't looking forward to going back; conscious that she might come across those whom she had shared her life with over the last three years. She wasn't ready for any confrontations that would only further complicate her present life, yet fully aware that it was a complication of her own making.

Arriving in Aylesbury, she stopped in a side street near the surgery. Her appointment was not for another ten minutes. She didn't want to have to wait in reception, just in case someone recognised her. She put on a hat and dark glasses, and after a few minutes drove into the surgery car park.

Luckily her doctor was ready to see her as soon as she checked in at reception. Doctor Jervis, her regular GP, sat at his computer tapping away when she entered his room. 'Ah, Christina, what can we do for you today?' He sat back in his chair and faced her.

'I want to know what's going on? When am I going to die?'

Jervis gave her a wry smile. He was used to Christina making odd comments or asking difficult questions whenever she came to see him. 'A question that has been asked from time immemorial. Perhaps it's written in the stars. Who knows…why does that concern you?'

'I'm fed up waiting! I've finally got my head round it, and now I want it to be over as quickly as possible. But apart from a recent dose of food poisoning, I've felt fine. I've looked online about similar cases, and they are all conflicting about how long it takes to die.'

Jervis sighed. He hated when patients started to go on about what they had read on internet sites, either believing they had a particular illness, or asking why they weren't being offered certain treatments or drugs. 'Death comes in many forms with different time limits.' He tried to humour her. 'You've said you've felt fine, so what's the worry?'

'What about the results of my last check up? I was told it would be three months at the most?' She was starting to get irritated by his flippant attitude.

Jervis tapped into his computer to look at her file. 'Results pretty normal. Nothing to worry about. Perhaps drink a bit less and do more exercise. Otherwise, fine. I don't understand what you mean by three months at the most?'

Christina shifted angrily in the chair. 'Normal! You regard terminal cancer as normal? I don't believe this!'

'Christina…what are you talking about?' Jervis was beginning to wonder if there was something psychologically wrong with her. He had known cases of perfectly healthy people suddenly becoming mentally insecure for whatever reason.

'For Christ's sakes, what am I talking about, he says! I was told I had untreatable terminal pancreatic cancer, and three months to live.' Her face reddened.

'Who told you that?'

'Your locum, when I came to find out the results of my check-up. I was told you were ill. It should be on your computer. Ives, I think his name was. Why don't you go and ask him?'

Jervis looked uncomfortable. 'Doctor Ives isn't with us any more…did you say pancreatic cancer?'

'Untreated and terminal he told me.' She emphasised.

'Ah…' He muttered as he started to tap on his computer. 'Oh dear…' He leant back and put his hand to his mouth in contemplation.

'Oh dear what? It would be nice to know what's

going on, or are you going to enlighten me with another enigmatic reply?'

'There's been a bit of a misunderstanding, I'm afraid…' He uncomfortably shuffled his feet.

'Dr Jervis, please. I'm not stupid. Would you just tell me what you are trying to say?'

'You haven't got pancreatic cancer…'

'So what cancer is it then?'

'No cancer. You have nothing wrong with you. There's been an awful mistake.' He looked pale, as if the blood had completely drained from his face.

Christina was stunned. 'I'm all right? I'm not going to die? I don't understand.'

'I'm sorry…it appears Dr Ives was looking at the wrong file when you came in. We have a patient with a similar name, a male called Chris Turner. It was his results that you were given. He had been diagnosed with pancreatic cancer…'

'I'm clearly not a male! How could that mistake have been made?'

'Dr Ives was very inexperienced. He probably just looked at the name, rather than the gender. It's an easy mistake to make sometimes. I'm so sorry…'

'So what happened to this other Chris Turner. Was he given my healthy results, by any chance?'

'No, that didn't occur. But sadly, he died a week ago. I can't imagine what you've been going through. If you believed you were going to…to die.'

'No, you can't. You have no idea.' She gave him a very stern look.

'If you wish to put in a complaint, I would quite understand. I am happy to substantiate everything that I've told you.'

'I'll think about it…well, not much more to say really,

is there? Goodbye Dr Jervis. I won't say, thank you.' She got up and left the room, leaving him in deep thought. He was more worried about a possible Negligence Claim against the surgery, believing Christina the type of person to make it.

Christina walked towards her car as if in a daze. Another car, driven by a young woman, arrived in the car park. She stopped, pulled down her window and shouted out 'Christina!' but Christina didn't hear, having just got into her car. She started the engine and drove out of the car park, totally oblivious to the woman who had been watching her.

The woman reversed back, exited the car park, and started following Christina's car.

29. Following in Her Footsteps

Virtually on automatic, Christina slowly drove back towards London. The news she'd just received put her mind into turmoil. She went from moments of relief and elation to ones of anger and frustration. She realised she'd been living a lie these last months, in the belief that she was going to die. How her current life might have been different if she hadn't been told about the cancer. She might still be in Aylesbury living the life she'd built up over the last few years, albeit a life she was unhappy with. Then again, with the money her aunt had left her, she probably would've escaped. She'd never have gone to London; not gone through that awful mock funeral; not bumped into Patrick, who'd still be alive today.

As all these elements bombarded her thoughts, she was totally unaware that a young woman in another car was closely following her.

'Yes, I'm positive it's Christina. It looks like she might be heading towards London...' the young woman spoke on her hands-free mobile. 'Yes, I will find out where she's going...Dad, don't keep telling me what to do! I'm fully aware of the mess she left us in...Calm down! I'm in complete control of the situation...trust me, I won't lose her...I'm ending this call, Dad. I'll let you know when I've any news...' She sighed irritably. Despite being a control freak, she hated it when anyone tried to dictate to her. With a score to settle, she was going to make sure that Christina was not going to get away from her.

As Christina entered the outskirts of London, she had formulated rough plans as to what she was going to do next.

One of these was that she was never going to return to Aylesbury, to a life that she'd grown weary of, and one she had previously been afraid of leaving. She couldn't face more explanations or continuing living with those she'd just left. Neither was she going to stay in London. There was nothing to keep her. She had, in a way, done what she had promised her aunt she'd do. She had tried her best with Tony, Roger and Eric. They had their own problems, their own lives, which she didn't figure in. There was nothing to keep her there. She would have to start again, in a new life somewhere else.

Perhaps she'd be third time lucky and not fall into the same patterns of relationships and disasters as the other two. Although she wondered about doing another complete vanishing act, she owed it to Tony and the others to at least say a proper goodbye before leaving their lives once more – this time for good.

Her first stop was at Duncan's office. He was always pernickety about asking clients to make appointments, rather than just turn up. Luckily, he was at his desk and not in a meeting when Christina appeared. 'Do you have a moment? I'm sorry I didn't ring beforehand, but matters have taken a turn, and I need to make some changes.'

'Christina, it's always nice to see you. I was going to phone you later, so this is opportune.' Duncan got up and shook her hand as he always did, never being one for a friendly peck on the cheek, however long he'd known people. 'I have made my enquiries, and have news regarding Mr Turner and his marriage problems.' He wasn't giving anything away by his expression.

'Good. You're going to represent him.'

Duncan looked solemn. 'I'm afraid not. This is a much more serious matter, which I am not prepared to undertake.'

Christina' face fell. 'Why? I promised I would cover whatever costs, so what's the problem?'

'There is evidence to support the fact that Mr Turner did indeed assault his wife.'

'But she assaulted him! I saw the bruises! What evidence?' Christina was starting to get worked up.

'It appears she made a recording on her telephone, which documents an argument and the ensuing assault.'

'Which could've been fabricated. And you believe this?'

'Whether I believe it or not is of no real consequence, Christina. I just don't want to get involved in this particular case. I instinctively feel it's not right for me, or that I'd do it justice. Sorry. I'm sure he'll find someone else to represent him.'

Christina thought for a moment. 'Do you really think that Eric might be lying?'

'I can't say. They both accuse each other of assault. Injuries to either party could have been self-inflicted. Divorce cases are notorious for playing dirty. One gets an instinct whether something is going to be more trouble than its worth, and that you'll end up losing anyway.'

'And that's what you feel about Eric's case?' Christina had calmed down, reflecting on Duncan's words, which she took seriously.

'Call it intuition, a gut feeling, which I've learnt to trust over the years.' He glanced at his watch. 'Anyway, I'm sorry to say that I'm seeing another client in ten minutes. You mentioned some adjustments you wanted to make?'

'Yes, I'd like to change my Will, and funeral arrangements.'

'I see. Shall we make another appointment?' He scanned his diary. 'What about same time next week?'

'I won't be here next week. Can we make it tomorrow?'

Duncan looked up sadly. 'Has your illness advanced? You look very well.'

'I am. I'll explain later, but I'm not going to die just yet. It's put a different perspective on everything, so I need to sort things out quickly.'

'That's excellent news! Congratulations! A time for celebration.'

'Don't bring out the champagne yet. A few demanding matters to conclude first. Can you give me some time tomorrow? Please.'

He crossed something out. 'Four o'clock tomorrow?'

'Thank you. You know, the prospect of dying was hard enough; but the prospect of living is beginning to prove much harder…'

Christina left Duncan's office and got into her car and drove off. The young woman, who had been tailing her, finished off the sandwich she had just purchased at a nearby shop, and proceeded to follow Christina. Her phone rang. 'Hello Uncle Gordon…Dad tell you, did he? Yes, it's Christina alright. I'm in London…I'm following her now…No, I'll make contact when I feel it's right…No, I won't lose her! Please, just leave it to me. I told Dad I'd let him know when I had any news…Got to go, bye!' The young woman angrily exclaimed to herself. 'I know what I'm doing!'

Christina decided her next stop would be to call on Eric, curious to find out whether he was telling the truth about the assault. She was glad to notice that his car was parked at the front of the flats when she arrived.

As she approached his door, and about to ring the bell, she could hear shouting from inside, which sounded like an almighty argument was going on. Christina paused and put her ear to the door. It was Eric and a female voice that she heard. 'For Christ's sake, Julia, I'm not going to kill you! Its just a bit of fun.'

'Fun? What's got into you? I refuse to put on that perverted costume and mask! Find someone else to be your bloody whipping girl! I'm going, and don't bother ever knocking on my door again!'

Christina nearly had her ear bashed as the door opened sharply. This woman, in her underwear and carrying her clothes, came tearfully bounding out. She saw Christina standing there. 'You next? Give him a good beating for me!' She ran down the corridor into her own flat.

Eric, only wearing black leather studded boxer shorts, came to the door. 'Julia, please!' He then saw Christina and smiled coyly. 'Oh…Christina…'

'Can I come in? I'm sorry I'm not dressed for the occasion…' She walked into the flat. As she passed the bedroom, she noticed various items that she recognised as fetish and bondage wear, draped over the bed. 'Having a fashion show?' She continued into the living room and sat down.

'It's not what it seems…' Eric made light of it.

'It's everything what it seems. Please, Eric, put some clothes on, I'm not talking to you like that. You look ridiculous.'

'Not turn you on by any chance…?' He thought he would try.

'What do you think?' She gave him a stern look. 'It makes sense now when we were in bed and you asked me if you could tie me up. Lucky I wasn't interested.'

'It was only for a bit of fun…'

269

'I see your little injuries have healed up nicely. Now please put something decent on.'

'It was Julia's idea in the first place…' He returned, having put on a shirt and jeans. 'She rather overreacted.'

'Stop lying. What's going on, Eric? You told me you weren't into S&M. You said it was a reason Marta wanted a divorce.'

'I haven't heard back from Duncan yet. Have you?'

'Please just answer my question, and I don't want any bullshitting.'

'What's the matter, Christina? Very bolshie all of a sudden. Had a bad day? Want to take it out on someone?'

'Yes, you. What really happened between you and Marta?'

'I've told you all that. Why do I have to repeat myself? Don't you believe me?'

'I don't know what to believe, that's why I'm asking. Do you know anything about a video made on a telephone, which supposedly shows you hitting Marta?'

'What…?' Eric went quiet. 'Whose telephone? Where did this come from?'

'Duncan contacted her solicitor and apparently she recorded the row where you hit her.'

'Rubbish! They're bluffing! I'm sure Duncan will prove that.' Eric did his best to sound confident, but the cracks were starting to show.

'Duncan won't be representing you.'

'Why….?' There was tone of panic in his voice.

'He just doesn't want to. It's his prerogative.'

'What's prerogative?'

'Get a bloody dictionary! It's his choice. He doesn't have to. You'll have to find someone else.'

'Who do you suggest then?'

'I'm not suggesting anyone. That's your problem

270

from now on. I don't want anything more to do with it. And I'm afraid you'll have to find the costs elsewhere, as I'm no longer happy to fund you. Sorry.'

'Bloody hell! What's got into you all of a sudden? I thought you were on my side.'

'I'm no longer taking sides, and I'm fed up having to sort out other peoples' problems. It's your mess, which you must clean up yourself. I shall be going away shortly, so this visit is also to say goodbye.'

'Are you about to die then…?'

'No, Eric, I'm not. I've simply had enough.'

'You're not going to help me then?'

'How many times do you have to be told! You're old enough and big enough. Sort it out yourself. I must go…' She rose out of the chair, her patience at an end.

Eric stood there looking like an angry boy who'd lost his favourite toy. 'You're leaving, just like that!' She nodded and made for the door. He stood in front, barring her way.

'Get out of the way, Eric. There's no more to say.'

He suddenly grabbed her by the arms and shook her. 'What is it with you women! You lead us along and then you dump us when it suits you! Well Marta got what she deserved! I should've made a better job of it!'

'And Marta should've made a better job of emasculating you!' Upon which she kneed him heavily in the balls, which made him let go. Freeing herself she ran out of the flat.

Eric lay on the floor in agony, at the same time wondering what emasculating meant.

The young woman looked up from her book, as she saw Christina, looking distressed, run out of the flats and into her car. Christina sat in her car for a good five minutes before driving off. The young woman continued in her quest to follow her, to see where it led her. She still hadn't formulated any specific plan about what she was going to do, or when she would actually confront Christina. She needed to pick the right moment, and was now prepared to remain overnight if it came to it.

30. It's Never Easy Saying Goodbye

Christina found herself confused and in a state of mild shock following Eric's confession. This wasn't the Eric she knew. When they were together all those years ago, he never showed signs of being interested in any fetishes, or was violent in any way. Even when they had sex during the last month, there was no suggestion of S&M, apart from wanting to tie her up once. Something obviously happened with Marta to make him change like this, provoking him into assaulting her. Why did he lie in the first place? It was all too much for Christina to take in. She felt a sense of betrayal and felt she could no longer trust or believe Eric. It was a relief that Duncan wanted nothing more to do with his case. To think that she nearly married him. It was just as well she was leaving. Having jumped from one fire into another was too much to take. Why had her life become so complicated, she wondered? Was it something in her or did unfortunate circumstances follow her around?

She was in no mood to face her next visit, but it had to be done if she wanted to wrap up matters swiftly, and finally disappear from their lives. She pulled in outside Roger's house, hoping that both he and Tony would be in, so that she could say goodbye properly to both of them.

She heard loud and angry noises coming from the front room as she came up the path. What was the matter with everyone today, she wondered? Was there something in the air making people particularly aggressive?

It stopped as soon as she rang the bell, and she saw Roger's gloomy face look out from behind the curtain to see who it was. He gave a look of utter despair, which didn't make her feel any better. She took a deep breath as the door opened.

'It's not a good time, Christina…' Roger held the door half open. He was red in the face, and looked as if he was about to have a fit.

'When would be a good time then?' She wasn't about to move.

'Come back in another three years, perhaps.' He then remembered about her illness. 'Sorry, bit insensitive of me…maybe in a couple of days.'

'I haven't got a couple of days, Roger.'

'Surely…you look fine to me…' He opened the door wider to look her up and down.

'I'm not going to die in the next day or two, if that's what you're thinking. In fact, I'm not going to die. I need to come in.' She'd had enough standing around, and pushed her way in, curious as to what had been going on.

In the front room sat Tony, looking somehow defiant, while standing in the corner, with her arms folded was Helen looking very stern and tight-lipped. An icy atmosphere surrounded the whole room.

'Hi, Mum…welcome to Stalag 13!'

'Would I be mistaken in saying that you've all been playing 'Happy Families'!' quipped Christina as she felt the tenseness.

'Why do you always have to be so bloody sarcastic!' Helen replied.

'Excuse me…?' Christina faced Helen. 'That was meant as a joke.'

'You and your jokes and your clown costumes! Why don't you find a witch's costume, get on your broom and fly off!'

'Helen, please…' Roger interjected.

'I'm fed up always being told not to make waves. Everything was fine until she came back on the scene, and started upsetting everything. And now she comes barging in, even when you've told her not to. What's your problem, Christina? Don't want to let go of something you threw away years ago?'

'Actually, it's the opposite.' Christina remained calm. 'I've come to say goodbye. He's all yours, Helen.'

For a moment Helen was dumbstruck, then replied rather contradictorily. 'Typical, when things become problematical! You need to sort out your son here, before he gets himself locked up. Mind you, that might not be a bad thing.'

'I love you too, Helen.' Tony slumped in his chair

'What's that supposed to mean?' Christina stared at Helen.

'Helen, for God's sake!' Roger put his hand on her shoulder, which she immediately shrugged off.

'Don't patronise me, Roger. I've had enough of Tony's lies. He's not showing any remorse for what he's done, and doesn't seem to care he's ruined someone's life.'

'Hang on! Don't you call me a liar. I'm the bloody victim here!' Tony responded petulantly.

'You really don't have any sense of what you've done, do you?' Helen pointed at him.

'I did my duty to save others going through what I did. No more, no less.'

Helen picked up her bag. 'I'm not listening to anymore of this shit. I'm going.'

Christina felt she'd stepped into some strange play. 'What the hell is going on here? Will someone please explain?'

Helen stopped by the door. 'Ask Tony here.

Whatever he says, I'm sure you'll be the loving mother whose dear son can do no wrong. If you are finally going, hopefully we'll never meet again.' She turned to Roger. 'Sorry, Roger, you know I tried to do my best to help, but to no avail. You need to sort it out between you. I'm not getting involved any more. I feel quite disgusted by the whole affair. I'll phone you.' Upon which she left the house.

Christina stared at Roger and Tony, who were both silent. 'Well…?'

Roger sighed. 'It's a bloody mess. Tony has been having a relationship with one of his teachers.'

'Male or female?'

'Oh thanks, Mum! Her name is Rachel…'

'The same Rachel who you wanted to have sex with at my flat? You didn't tell me she was a teacher.'

'What's this?' Roger looked at Christina.

'If I had, you've wouldn't have given me the keys, would you?'

'Certainly not!'

'I thought so.'

'Can one of you please put me in the picture? I'm the confused one now.' Roger paced around the room.

'First you need to tell me what has been going on. Helen mentioned someone's life being ruined?'

'Mum, Helen likes to exaggerate, making mountains out of molehills.'

Roger stood in front of Tony, looking as if he was about to hit him. 'You've got a bloody nerve to say that after what you've just done.'

'Please, both of you! Stop bickering for once. What's this all about…?'

***

After Rachel had walked out on Tony, following their disastrous liaison at Christina's flat, Tony made every effort, over the next day or so, to try and win her back. Similarly, Rachel did her best to ignore his persistent advances. She was no longer interested, but relieved it had gone no further in the bedroom, which would naturally have complicated matters. As far she was concerned, it was a mild flirtation where nothing had happened apart from the odd kiss, and nothing was going to happen. She had learnt her lesson and was never going to go down that road again. Tony thought otherwise. His teenage pride had been dented, and although his initial infatuation had cooled, he still wasn't prepared to let it end there.

One day, after college had finished, he hung around and waited near Rachel's car for her to come out. She was chatting with another member of staff as she approached her car. 'Please Miss, can I have a word?' He smiled and waited for the other teacher to leave.

'What do you want Tony? I thought I made it perfectly clear that I'm no longer interested. Accept it and move on.'

'You led me on...'

She laughed. 'Don't be ridiculous. I liked you, I enjoyed your company, but I always made it clear that that was as far as it was going to go.'

'That's not the impression I got when you kissed me.'

'A kiss doesn't constitute an affair, or a promise that it would go further.'

'You seemed to enjoy it at the time.' Tony wasn't letting go.

'Okay, it was nice. But going to your mother's flat was a big mistake on my part. I admit that. Now please desist and leave me alone. Or...'

'Or what?'

'I will be forced to report you for harassing me.'

'And then I will be forced to tell them about us.'

'There's nothing to tell. There was no real "us". It'll be your word against mine. I'm going now, Tony. This has to be the end of it. Grow up. Goodbye.' She got in her car, and waited until he got out of the way before she drove off.

'Bitch…' Was all he could weakly muster to mumble. He was fully aware that if she did report him, and he tried to accuse her – they would believe her over him. Rachel was good at arguing her corner, whilst he knew he'd get tongue-tied in such a confrontation. Since they had been careful not to be seen together out of school hours, there was no proof or witnesses to substantiate his story. Despite this, something in him didn't want to let go so easily. He was very much like Christina in this respect. He realised that he couldn't win Rachel back, yet in his head he believed that she had led him on and that she needed to be taught a lesson.

All hell broke loose the next day at school. Tony had gone for broke, by posting on the school's Facebook page, the photo he'd taken on his phone, of him and Rachel in their underwear against a bed in the background. It caused a sensation. Among the college students, Tony's standing went up; while Rachel's repute, with the Head teacher and school Governors couldn't have got worse.

As a consequence, after emergency school meetings, Tony was suspended and Rachel was sacked, since she couldn't really defend herself against such incriminating evidence.

It didn't matter whether they had slept together or not. She had crossed the line from which there was no return. Her career as a teacher had been terminated over a single photograph.

'What got into you to do such a despicable thing?' Christina addressed Tony more in sorrow than in anger, after she heard the whole story from Roger.

'She led me on and then dumped me. She pestered me to ask you about using your flat. I wasn't sure, and didn't think it was a good idea, but she kept on at me. Okay I fancied her. Then, when she got what she wanted, she told me to get lost. She threatened to report me to the school if I said anything, by saying that I tried to assault her…It's the honest truth.' He did his best to sound sincere.

'You actually slept with her?'

'Have sex you mean?' Tony smiled 'She couldn't wait to get into *my* pants!' He boasted.

'Why didn't you just keep your mouth shut and clock it up to experience?' Roger had lost the energy to argue further.

'Because she's a predatory bitch, and the world needed to know about her. I'm sure I'm not the first, or will be the last. I realised I might get suspended, but that was a small price to pay. I don't regret it in any way.' He was defiant again.

'Well you should.' Christina added. 'I don't know, or care who did the seducing. It was only your vanity and ego that was hurt. Not a reason or an excuse to ruin someone's career. I'm really ashamed of you…'

'For once, your mother's right. You went too far. Can't you retract it and say it was all a joke. You'd photoshopped the picture with her head?'

'It's too late for that. Besides, I don't want to. I'm not backing down to please you.' Tony looked at them both with contempt.

'You always were difficult.' Christina sighed as if she'd had enough. 'I really thought you had grown up, but you're still that petulant child who thinks he knows best, refusing to listen to anyone else.'

'I'd agree with all that.' Roger nodded to her.

Tony got up from his chair. 'Well fuck you too! Fuck the both of you!' He then left the room, ran upstairs and banged his bedroom door shut.

Christina and Roger just looked at each other; their feelings bonded for once. 'Believe it or not, I don't blame you, Roger. I'm sure you did the best for him while I was away. I'm sorry I'm going to leave you both again. I know that's not going upset you too much, considering.'

'You said you weren't going to die…?'

'No…I'm in remission, so to speak.'

'Right. Good. So where are you going?'

'I don't know exactly – but I'll know when I get there!'

'Good luck…' Roger leant over and kissed her on the cheek.

'I think you're the one who's going to need the luck.' She gave him a quick hug and left the house.

31. Adopting to Murder

'The world around me seems to be imploding…' Christina sat having tea with Paula in the church's vestry an hour later. 'Is it me, is it all my fault…?'

'Hardly. You didn't shoot Patrick; you didn't assault Eric's foreign wife; and you certainly didn't encourage Tony to either have the affair with his teacher or get her sacked.'

'I still feel somehow responsible. Perhaps if I hadn't come back in the first place, none of this might not have happened.'

'You can't say that, Christina. You told me you weren't happy where you were; you were going through your own personal crisis at the time. You cannot be held responsible for other people's actions – whatever you say or do.'

'But now I'm escaping again, because I don't feel I can cope anymore, especially after today's events. I feel both Eric and Tony have betrayed me. I don't think I could ever trust either of them again.'

'What about the life you built up in Aylesbury? Isn't that worth salvaging?'

Christina shuffled uncomfortably in her chair. 'I can't go back there, it wouldn't work. It wasn't working before I left. Being told I had terminal cancer coupled with the inheritance was the excuse I needed to pack up and leave.'

'I'm so pleased that the cancer turned out a false alarm. Don't you feel you've been given a second chance?'

'To do what? Ruin some more lives? I seem to be cursed to continue to repeat the same patterns over and over...'

'You mustn't look at it like that. You're still young

enough to start again. You have the security of the money you inherited, which means you can pick and choose where you go and what you do.'

'I suppose so. Leaving Roger, Eric and Tony isn't a problem. It'll be easier this time. They won't miss me. Part of me still feels guilty at abandoning those in Aylesbury, but I know I have to make that break if I'm going to move on.'

'It's taking that first step and not looking back is the most difficult.'

'And what about you? Have you thought what you're going to do?'

Paula scrunched her face and looked up at the ceiling. 'I don't know. Funnily enough I've been offered a transfer to a much larger, higher profile church. I sensed that they might be grooming me for a bishopric. That would make my father turn in his grave. He abhorred the idea of even women being priests…'

'Another reason you became one? To defy him?'

'Possibly…I'm not sure I want to become a bishop, and be involved in church politics, even more difficult being a woman. We shall see. I'm a great believer that we are where we're supposed to be, and that I'll be guided to where I should be going.'

'I know where I don't want to be, but I wish I knew where I was going. I sometimes envy people who have their lives mapped out, and know exactly what they're meant to be doing.'

'And then they get a reality check when things don't quite work out as they expected. The only thing we can be sure of is that we can be sure of nothing. Life has a way of pricking our bubbles of certainty. Take your cancer scare and look what happened to Jennie. She could never have predicted her own actions. Maybe that was her destiny.'

'What, to spend the rest of her life in prison?'

'Our destinies are never quite what we might envisage them to be. Prison might even be her salvation.'

'Is that you or the priest speaking?'

'Am I beginning to sound a bit pompous and all-knowing?' Paula pursed her lips.

'A bit…but I won't hold it against you! You know, I can't help feeling sorry for Jennie, but for once she did the right thing.'

'What – murder someone?'

'No, actually admit that she did it. Jennie has spent her life lying, blaming others for her mistakes and misdemeanours. She could have taken a chance and pleaded not guilty. Then there would have been a trial. I would have been called as a witness, which I certainly wasn't relishing.'

'Do you know what actually happened?'

'John Silbey, the policeman in charge, rang me to let me know that Jennie had confessed to the murder, and so there would be no trial. I asked him how and why she did it. He said he wasn't at liberty to divulge the exact details, but gave me a quick overview…'

What upset Jennie the most, after she had been told by Christina in the café that she wouldn't be investing, was the fact that Christina had met up with Patrick, and he had told her the truth about her business deception.

Jennie returned to the office in the blackest of moods. She had been relying on Christina's investment. If Patrick had kept his mouth shut, she could have been banking the cheque that very afternoon. What really wounded her was that she was still a bit in love with him, which made things worse.

Feeling so incensed, she decided to phone him and give him a piece of her mind. If nothing else it would make her feel better. Yet in truth she just wanted to hear his voice. She had half expected for his number to go straight to voicemail, and was prepared to leave a damning message.

'What do you want, Jennie?' He answered coldly.

'I believe you've been telling tales to Christina.'

'Only the truth. I wish I'd spoken up earlier. Is that all you wanted to say?'

'Look, as you well know, I paid for what I did, and now I just want to make a new start.'

'What's that got to do with me? I haven't got any money, if that's why you're ringing.' Although irritated, he did his best to sound calm.

'No…I just wondered if you might consider helping me build up the business? You always were good with ideas. Everything would be above board. I promise…'

'Are you serious, Jennie?'

'Yes…we…we could start again…'

Patrick started to laugh. 'If this isn't a joke, I have to say I'm surprised.'

'Why…?'

'Christina must've told you about my little mission?'

'I don't understand? What mission?'

'That I've come to find my baby daughter, who I'm planning to adopt.'

'Where are you? What are talking about?' Jennie wasn't sure if she'd heard right.

'Ah…you didn't know. Never mind then. I won't rub it in.'

'What baby? I don't understand?' The mere mention of a child made her feel uneasy. 'Patrick, just please explain.'

'It's not worth it, Jennie. This doesn't concern you.' He continued to remain calm, and didn't want to cruelly just end the call. 'For the record, in answer to your question, I don't want to work or be with you. It was over years ago, and

I don't want to hear from or see you ever again.'

This hit her like a sledgehammer. She felt like bursting into tears, but wasn't going to give him the satisfaction. 'You, at least, owe it to me to explain what you meant about adopting *your* daughter?'

'I owe you nothing, Jennie. But since you persist in asking, I shall tell you. You won't like it.'

'I'll be the best judge of that.' She steeled herself.

'Alright…After we divorced, I met up with Meera again and we continued our affair. She became pregnant – with my child. It's a long story, but her husband murdered Meera after the baby was born. I'm here to find my daughter in order to adopt her. My own flesh and blood….'

Jennie found this revelation impossible to cope with, making her heart feel like it was breaking into a million pieces. Why couldn't that child have been hers? Dumbstruck, she just said 'Goodbye Patrick…' before ending the call. She then broke down crying in front of her desk.

'You okay, Mrs Halkin?' Kayleigh could hear the sobs and went over to her.

'Just a bit menopausal…' Jennie composed herself.

'My mum went through all that. We kept clear of her when she was going through one of her turns!' Then Kayleigh realised what she had said. 'Sorry, Mrs Halkin, I didn't quite mean it like that.'

Jennie dried her tears. 'That's alright, Kayleigh. Something for you to look forward to!' She forced a joke, but her mind was elsewhere.

'If I get to live that long! I've done those orders. Anything else you want me to be getting on with?'

Jennie thought for a moment. 'Do you know how you might be able to trace the location of a mobile, say if you lost it somewhere?'

'Nah, but my brother will probably know how. He's

into all that stuff. Got special software. Not strictly legal, but he managed to find a friend's phone when it was stolen. Why?'

'I want to trace an old school friend. I've got the number, but I want it to be a surprise. I'll pay your brother for his trouble.'

'I'm sure he'll be happy to do it. He likes that sort of thing. He wants to be a hacker, the best, when he grows up.'

'Why how old is your brother?' Jennie was intrigued.

'Fourteen. He's a clever little sod. He installed really fast broadband in the house, without us having to pay for it!' Kayleigh proclaimed proudly. 'Shall I ask him to come and see you? It would have to be after school.'

'That's not necessary. We can do it all on the phone, if he could give me a ring…would be good if we could sort it out today.'

'I'm sure that'll be okay. I'll send him a text.'

'Thank you.' Jennie then picked up some paperwork from her desk to indicate the conversation was over.

Kayleigh's brother phoned Jennie a few hours later. He said it was "a piece of piss" when she asked if he could get the location of a phone. She offered him £50, but he wanted £100. She tried to negotiate down, but he stood firm. He asked for it in cash, and for Kayleigh to bring it before he did anything. Finally agreeing, she gave him Patrick's number. He promised to get back to her the following day.

The phone's location was traced to a small hotel on the outskirts of Birmingham. That's where it had remained overnight, which meant that was where Patrick was staying.

Jennie, not wanting to waste time, drove up to Birmingham and parked near the hotel, hoping that she'd catch him arriving or leaving. It was early evening when he finally emerged, probably on his way to get something to eat. Jennie followed him. It was when he had gone down an empty, badly lit street, that she shot him in the back of the head…

'Perhaps it was all meant to happen in the great scheme of things…' Paula reflected.

'Perhaps. We will never know. Anyway, I think it's time I went and had a good think about where I might go or what I might do. I'm seeing Duncan tomorrow to finalise and change some legal specifics in the light of my resurrection. I'd originally left everything to Tony…but now…well, that's changed.'

Paula smiled. 'You could leave it to the church.'

'I could – but I won't! The Church is rich enough. I might decide to spend it all on the good life, and leave nothing.'

'Sounds good to me. You will keep in touch?'

'I make no promises. Thank you for all your help and support. You're a good egg, as my father used to say. Don't let anyone or anything crack you.'

'I have a pretty hard shell.'

Christina got up, feeling quite emotional, went and gave Paula a big hug. 'Say a little prayer that things will work out for me…'

'I will…you're about to enter the beginning of the rest of your life.' Paula hugged her back.

'At least it's now no longer the end…' Christina quickly kissed Paula on the cheek and left.

'May God go with you…'

Outside the church, the young woman was just getting into her car when Christina emerged. She quickly ducked so as not to be seen, but Christina was in her own little world, and took no notice of the other car parked nearby.

As Christina drove off, the young woman switched on her engine, but it didn't engage. She tried several times, but all she got was the whirling sound of grinding. It just wouldn't start. She banged the steering wheel in frustration, which accidentally sounded the car horn. 'Fuck, fuck, fuck!' she shouted, as she realised that not only had she broken down, but that she'd now lost sight of Christina.

She got out of the car and opened the bonnet. As the young woman tried to fiddle about inside, a voice behind her quietly said, 'Is there a problem…?'

Christina, feeling emotional, didn't want to go back to her flat just then. Needing time to think, she drove on in the opposite direction. She switched on the radio to Classic FM and relaxed in her seat as she drove towards Richmond, which had always been one of her favourite haunts. As it was a beautiful evening, she planned to stop by Turner's view on Richmond Hill, and watch the sunset.

Roger, after Christina had left, decided to let Tony stew. He was busy in the kitchen preparing the evening meal. Roger was quite prepared for Tony not to eat with him, so had made some soup, which would keep. Helen had rung him, and apologised for reacting like she did. He understood perfectly since he had felt the same.

He sensed there was no point going over it with Tony, since they'd both said what they had to for the time being. It was something he had to deal with, and all they could do was support him in the best way they could. He invited her over, but she thought it might only inflame matters with Tony, bearing in mind their brittle relationship. Helen did wonder if Tony would ever accept her? If she was going to marry Roger, she had to find a way to call a truce, or kill him.

Roger was relieved the house was quiet, since Tony had not resorted to playing his music at full blast, a sign whenever he was in a foul mood. He went into the hallway and called up. 'Tony, I've made some soup if you're hungry. Anyway, it's there whenever you want it.' He waited for a moment, but there was no response, which didn't surprise him. As he was about to go back into the kitchen, the front doorbell went. For those split seconds before he opened the door, his mind processed who it might be. Someone from the school? The teacher herself? Had Helen changed her mind? Surely it wasn't Christina again?

'Hi Roger, not a bad time is it?' Eric stood there looking a bit sheepish.

'You tell me. Come in.'

'Has Christina been to see you?'

'Earlier today. Declared she was no longer going to die, and announced that she was leaving our lives once again.' They both went and sat in the front room.

'Told me the same. Left in a bit of a strop. But that's Christina, I suppose. Umm, something smells nice.'

'Soup. You're welcome to stay.'

'Heinz, Baxter's or Campbell's?' Eric smelt the air as if he was a connoisseur.

'Turner Broth.' Roger replied sarcastically.

'Don't know that one. Is it new?' He asked innocently.

'Homemade, Eric. Will that confuse your culinary palette?'

Eric looked momentarily puzzled, not wanting to admit he didn't know what culinary meant. 'Sounds nice…'

'Hello Uncle Eric.' Tony stood at the door. Roger stopped himself from making any comments.

'Tony. How's tricks? Met any nice girls lately?' Eric would have loved to have told him that he was behind Sadie's seduction of him, but sensed now was not the right time.

Tony glared at Roger, who indicated that he hadn't said anything to Eric about what had been going on. 'Depends on what you mean by nice?'

Eric laughed. 'True, sometimes it's the not-so-nice-ones that prove the more interesting in my experience.'

'Well, I'm ready to eat if no one else is.' Roger exited into the kitchen, in no mood to get involved in the conversation.

Ten minutes later they were all sat at the table hungrily devouring the soup, with bread and cheese. 'Do you think we'll ever see Mum again?' Tony looked at Roger.

'I very much doubt it…as things were left.'

'I'd be surprised if we saw her again.' Eric added, 'Do you think all that stuff about her having cancer, with only a short time to live, was put on?'

'I don't know. Christina has always been one for dressing up things in order to get what she wanted.'

'Dad, do you seriously think she made it all up about dying?'

'I honestly wouldn't put it past her. But I can't see why. She could have just come back because she was feeling guilty about what she had done. Paid us back what she owed us, and then disappeared again. I suppose the only reason, if she did make it up, was to gain our sympathy. So that we wouldn't tell her to go to hell.'

'But we did tell her to go to hell.' Eric remembered.

'She talked to me about getting nursing care at her flat nearer the time, because she didn't want to die in hospital.' Tony added.

'When I asked if she was going to die, she said no, she'd had enough, which I didn't understand.' Eric didn't mention that she kicked him in the balls, which still felt painful.

Roger sighed. 'Maybe we'll never know, if she has gone for good this time.'

'Perhaps it's for the best…' Eric helped himself to more soup. 'This is really good, Roger. You must give me the recipe.'

'I'd stick to opening tins, Eric. You don't want to upset Messrs Heinz, Baxter or Campbell, do you?'

While they all laughed, relaxing for the first time, the front door bell went. Tony got up. 'I'll check who it is first, in case it's one of those Mormon Witnesses, or tea towel sellers. Tony went and peeked behind the curtains. He saw two policemen standing there, their patrol car parked by the gate. Tony went into a sweat. Had they come for him? Had Rachel made a complaint, perhaps accusing him of rape? He didn't know if he could cope with all that.

'Dad…it's the police…' Tony gave him a look as if to say 'please help'.

'The police…?' It was Eric's turn to sweat. Had they come for him, because of what he'd done to Marta?

The doorbell went again. Roger got up, suddenly feeling weary, and very apprehensive about what to expect. He opened the door. 'Mr Turner…?'

'Yes…?'

'Can we please come in.' Both policemen looked grave as they entered.

Eric and Tony stood in the front room both looking guilty and terrified, wondering if they were about to be arrested and taken away.

'Christina Turner is your ex-wife, we believe?'

'Yes…' Roger took a deep breath. 'What has she done now?'

'We're afraid to say that she been involved in a

serious car accident.'

'Is she…is she dead?' Tony asked.

'She's in intensive care in hospital now. We've been told it is touch and go, whether she survives the night…'

32. Black Holes and Death Wishes

Christina never made it to her destination. After leaving Paula, she went the pretty way, hoping to drive through Richmond Park, where she and Roger used to take Tony when he was young. She was humming happily away to a piece of music on the radio, and thinking about possibly going abroad to settle down somewhere warm. Perhaps Spain or Italy, to start her new life. She imagined herself sitting by a small pool attached to a brightly painted, villa, surrounded by greenery, overlooking a lake or the sea.

She was doing about 40mph in a 30mph zone, when she noticed some road works ahead, with a temporary traffic light that had just turned red. She started to brake – but the brakes didn't appear to respond, however much she desperately tried to press them. She just couldn't stop, and frenziedly watched her car rapidly career towards the traffic light.

It all happened so quickly. There was no time to think. As if in slow motion, she saw the car crash through the traffic light and barriers, and descend into a large crater-like hole. Then everything went completely black…

The hospital was teeming with frantic activity when Roger, Eric and Tony arrived at the A & E entrance. The reception area was busy, with numerous friends and family queuing to try to find out what was going on with their loved ones.

The two receptionists were doing their best to answer queries, but were getting slightly stressed with the sudden bombardment and volume of agitated enquiries. It appeared there had been several car accidents, and three females had been brought in, which added to the confusion.

When Roger finally got to the front of the queue to ask about Christina, the young receptionist couldn't tell where she actually was, since there had been some mix up with names, all three women having been brought in virtually at the same time. Roger eventually found someone senior and insisted on knowing what was going on. As there was still confusion over names, it was difficult for them to say what was happening to whom. Apparently, one taken to intensive care had since died; the other was having major surgery; and the third was still in intensive care. There was general anxiety amongst the doctors in trying to identify the three women.

Roger, Eric and Tony, among other anxious relatives, were told to wait for a consultant to come and talk to them. 'D'you think Mum's dead?'

'I don't know!' Roger replied irritably. 'We all thought she was dead when we had to go to that stupid funeral. Then we thought she was going to die soon due to the cancer. Nothing with Christina is ever straightforward.'

'Do you think the crash was an accident, or did Christina finally want to end it all like she tried before?' Eric wondered.

'We might never know…if she is dead.' Roger saw a doctor approach him.

'Mr Turner?' The consultant looked distinctly uncomfortable.

'What news on Christina?'

'That's the problem I'm afraid…there's been some muddle about who is actually who?'

'You mean there's been a major cock-up!' Tony volunteered.

'You could say that.' The doctor sighed. 'Since all

three cases were roughly the same age, arriving at the same time, and were emergencies, the actual paperwork got mixed up. Unforgiveable, but it's happened.'

'So where are we with Christina…Is she the one that's dead?' Roger wasn't in the mood for pussyfooting, and wanted straight answers.

'That's the difficult part. The lady who died needs to be identified…'

'Are you asking me see if the corpse is my ex-wife?'

'I'm afraid it's not a pretty sight, since the injuries were quite severe. However, before we have to go that far, there were certain identifiable marks on the body. Did your ex-wife have a tattoo of a panther on her back, which weaved down to the buttocks…?'

'She didn't, when I last saw her…undressed. But that was nearly five years ago. She might have got it done since. Wouldn't put it past her.'

'That's not Christina, she had no tattoos.' Eric piped up.

'How do you know? You hadn't seen her for three years.' Roger turned to Eric.

'We've spent a bit of time together, recently.'

'You mean you've been sleeping with Christina after she came back?' This somewhat surprised Roger.

'So? No law against that! She's a free agent. Don't get so precious about it!'

'You didn't waste any time did you!' Roger gave him a dirty look.

The doctor felt he had to interrupt. 'Well, at least we've established that the deceased is not Christina….' He looked up to see another doctor beckoning him over. 'Excuse me a moment.' He went across the room to listen to what the other doctor had to say.

While they were conferring, Roger, Eric and Tony

---

were silent. The doctor returned, looking even more concerned. 'Another bit of distressing news, I'm afraid…'

'Someone else die…?' Roger had read the doctor's face.

'Sadly. The other woman didn't survive surgery. I'm afraid to say there are no identifying marks this time…'

'So, are you asking us to go and identify this other woman?'

'That might not be necessary. There is still the woman in Intensive Care. If she is not Christina, we must then assume the second fatality is her – and will then need to be formally identified.'

'This woman in Intensive Care. How is she?' Tony asked.

'It's still very much touch and go, I'm afraid. She might not pull through. We've done all we can. It's now a matter of waiting…if you would like to follow me…'

The woman in the bed, with wires, drips and tubes attached everywhere, was sleeping. Her neck was in a medical brace, and her face had a few bruises and cuts, but there was no mistake that this was Christina. 'It's Mum, she's alive!' Tony was relieved.

'For the moment…' Roger meant it realistically.

Eric scrunched up his face at all the paraphernalia surrounding Christina. He hated hospitals. 'She looks like the bride of Frankenstein with all that gear!'

'It's what's keeping her alive. She's been very lucky so far.' The doctor moved towards the door. 'You can have a few more minutes. Then I think it would best to leave her.'

'What do you think her chances are?' Roger asked.

'To be honest, very slim. The next 24 hours are critical, that is if she survives the night. We've done all we can at this stage. It's in nature's hands…'

He then left them standing round the bed. His job now was to break it to the other families that the two casualties hadn't survived. Although he was always sympathetic to their loss, he'd lost any emotional response years ago. It was just another life that they couldn't save. Another statistic to be filed away.

'I think we'd better leave her.' Eric couldn't wait to get out.

Roger nodded. 'She does look a sorry sight. Poor Christina...' He wondered if this would be the last image he'd see of her.

Tony bent down and took hold of her hand. 'Bye, Mum...hopefully see you tomorrow.'

Just as they were about to leave the room, a small faraway voice uttered. 'Thank you for coming...' They all turned to see Christina with her eyes half open. 'I think I looked better as a clown than the bride of Frankenstein...'

'I didn't mean...' Eric realised she had obviously heard him.

'Of course you did, Eric.' Her voice was tiny and sounded drowsy. 'But I won't hold it against you...even if I have to pass on to the next life, if there is one...'

'You'll pull through, Mum.' Tony said it without any warmth.

'I heard what the doctor said...after all the false alarms, ironically this could be it...Roger, if it does happen, will you promise me something...?'

'What's that?' Roger was hesitant, wondering what she wanted.

'Don't worry...I'm not going to ask you to do anything that will be against your precious sensibilities.'

'Go on...' Roger still felt uncomfortable.

'Should I die...I've already made arrangements to be cremated, and my ashes to be scattered by Duncan...will you all have a meal on me, and only remember the nice things in all our lives…I know it will be hard, but that's all I ask…'

'Of course…' Roger accepted it would be difficult not to resort to bitchiness under normal circumstances.

A nurse came in. 'I think it's time you all left. She needs her rest.'

Christine forced a brief smile. 'Yes…I need my rest in peace…I could be asleep a long time…'

'Come on now, none of that sort of talk.' The nurse checked the monitors and adjusted Christina's bedcover. She then turned back to Roger, Eric and Tony who watched her. 'Off you go now.' She waved her hand dismissing them.

Different thoughts went through all their minds as they silently left the hospital.

Roger felt no emotion or distress. If she died, she died. It would certainly simplify matters, and he could get on with his life with Helen. Christina's survival would be a burden, as his conscience wouldn't let him abandon her completely, if she was in any way incapacitated. They had been married for over ten years. But it was a marriage that had been built upon a lie, which still haunted him.

Eric liked, but didn't love Christina. She had been a good lover, cook and housekeeper when they were together. He had hoped that her money might help getting him out of the mess he was in with Marta. He had seriously thought of killing Marta just to get her off his back. She had literally wanted to skin him alive in more ways than one.

It wasn't her fetish preferences that made him suddenly turn violent. Some of it, like the dressing up, did turn him on. It was when she demanded the flat and all his money as well as a divorce, that he lost his temper. Yet what finally pulled him over the edge was that she admitted their marriage had been a total scam in order to wipe him out. That's when he lost control and beat her up. Now he hoped that Christina would pull through, to give him another chance to get her to help him with sorting out his legal dilemma.

Tony did love his mother, but in a dutiful way. They had never been really close. Her divorce and the time when she went to live with Eric wasn't as traumatic as he made out it to be. Even when she disappeared for three years, it didn't really affect him. During that time whenever he got stroppy or didn't get his way, he would make out it was because his mother had abandoned him. It was the best card he could play, and managed to elicit some sympathy for his moods and actions. He still didn't regret what he had done to Rachel and he didn't care that he was suspended from college. He couldn't help but be a touch annoyed when Christina had revealed that she was not dying of cancer any more. He believed, and it had been intimated, that he might be the sole heir to all her money. Now he couldn't help but secretly hope that his mother didn't pull through. Since her fortune might soon be his, he could leave home, college and really enjoy life.

Helen was the one who was most upset when she heard the news about Christina. Not because she'd had an accident and was in a critical condition, but that she was still alive.

Following Christina's departure, prior to the accident, Roger had rung to tell Helen that Christina was finally out of their lives, and it would be the last time they'd probably ever see her.

Helen wasn't so convinced, believing that Christina was like a bad penny who'd always somehow return and upset their lives. The fact that she no longer had cancer was another reason she didn't believe it. Roger had tried to reassure her, that as far as he was concerned, Christina meant nothing to him, and hadn't for years. He was just as keen to finally see the back of her.

Helen fantasised about creeping into the hospital, detaching and unplugging everything that was keeping Christina alive. Other than that, she could simply put a pillow over her face for a breathless and final send off. She also visualised Tony being prosecuted and jailed for what he'd done to the teacher. With those two finally out of the way, she'd have Roger to herself, and despite everything, she really did love him.

After the others had left, Christina had been given a sedative to make her rest. Lying in the hospital bed, she felt imprisoned, unable to move a muscle, having cloth restraints in place so as not to disengage the numerous wires and tubes that were attached. She drifted in and out of sleep, not able to distinguish what was real and what wasn't…

The faces of Roger, Tony and Eric concertinaed in and out of vision, all talking in different languages and pointing their fingers at her in remonstration…and as they faded into the background Jennie appeared, her head shaven and covered in boils, shaking prison bars and gnashing bloodied teeth…

This horrific image was suddenly superimposed with the figure of Patrick happily cuddling a baby, which then vanished from his arms, as a gun appeared to blow his head apart… Christina now saw herself running down an endless road, being chased by a group of faces from her life in Aylesbury, all brandishing oversized machetes…they started to gain on her, and finally caught up with her…she lay on the ground seeing all the machetes poised, about to cut her to pieces…

'Christina…?' She felt a gentle arm on her as she

opened her eyes. As she slowly focused, she could see the compassionate face of Paula looking down at her. Was she still dreaming? Would Paula turn into the Devil and throw her into the fires of hell?

'Paula…are you real…?' Christina mumbled through dry lips.

'I sometimes wonder myself. How are you?' Paula smiled.

'As you can see…all trussed up and ready to party…'

'Glad you haven't lost your sense of humour.'

'Have you come to read me the last rites? I'm still not a believer, you know.'

'I hope that won't be necessary…Roger rang me. Do you remember what happened?'

'Car brakes failed…and I fell into this black hole…' Christina closed her eyes for a moment. 'I still feel I'm falling into this bottomless pit…' When she opened her eyes again, she thought she saw a shadow move in the corner of the room. 'Is there anyone else here…?' She couldn't look up because of the neck brace.

'Ah…I've got a nice surprise for you.' Paula said it with some excitement. 'Jane has come to visit you. You remember Jane…from Aylesbury…'

'Hello Christina…' As Jane appeared from the shadows, Christina's face suddenly contorted and her body went into spasms. Paula ran out and called for a nurse, who immediately alerted an emergency team.

The nurse told both Paula and Jane to leave the room while doctors and nurses frantically attended to Christina who was now in the middle of a major fit.

'I wonder what happened?' Paula innocently turned to Jane.

Jane gave a wicked smile. 'Probably the excitement of seeing her step daughter again…'

From inside the room they heard the doctor shout. 'Come on, come on…we're losing her…'

33. Unhappy Returns of the Day

Christina looked down at the doctors and nurses desperately trying to resuscitate a body that she recognised as her own, but felt no emotional attachment to the figure that lay convulsing below her. It was just another shell that had served its purpose, which she had no regrets to leave. So this was what death was like, she wondered, as she floated above the hospital room, not really taking much notice of all the frantic activity going on beneath. She was drawn to the window, and found herself slowly drifting through it into the open air…

Everything looked brighter and more defined. The clouds somehow sparkled with energy, and the sky was the most luminescent blue she had ever seen. A feeling of love and peace engulfed her. She'd happily float like this for all eternity…when suddenly she found herself being quickly drawn into the centre of a kind of swirling kaleidoscope, which took her back through the years up to the pivotal point when she first left London…

It was her fortieth birthday. Having felt restless and unsettled over the previous months, she regarded reaching forty as a significant milestone, which depressed more than excited her. Nothing seemed to be going right in her life. It looked like the heavens were conspiring against her. Her financial situation was dire. She felt stifled and imprisoned in an existence that showed no signs of improving. All those close to her appeared to be doing their best to undermine and treat her disrespectfully. Her confidence and self-esteem had reached its lowest point.

The previous day at work had proved traumatic, when Jennie had declared that the business was heading for bankruptcy, and it was all as a result of Christina's incompetency and bad management. Christina couldn't understand it, yet Jennie was able to skilfully convince her that she was at fault, which made Christina doubt her own capabilities and whether she really had slipped up.

What made it worse on that particular day was that no one had actually remembered her birthday…

Over the last week she had made various subtle hints about it being her birthday, so she had woken with a sense of anticipation. Eric was doing his daily 100 push-ups by the bottom of the bed. 'Good morning…' she said, trying to sound jolly.

'Hi…when you get up, could you do me a fry up…two eggs, three slices of bacon and some mushrooms…' Eric uttered between push-ups.

'Anything else, lord and master…?' Christina replied sarcastically.

'Perhaps a couple of sausages…make sure they're well cooked.'

'Shouldn't you be making me breakfast? Or is it a surprise?'

'What? You usually do your own breakfast…' He continued with his exercise, taking no more notice of her as she grumpily got out of bed.

There were no cards, flowers or presents secretly waiting for her on the kitchen table. She felt like screaming in despair. It was only last week that she had finally agreed to marry him, after he'd pestered her for months to make it legal.

They'd been living together for nearly a year, and had got along quite well. She loved him in her own particular way and hoped that getting married might change things for the better. She would do her best to educate him in some of the fineries of life, and rid him of his peasant and common ways.

She now realised she was living her own lie, and that nothing would actually change, however much she tried. He just wanted a permanent housekeeper, someone to help pay the bills, and all that was in it for her was good sex – but that now was no longer enough to keep her happy. Primarily she needed mental stimulation, which Eric would never be able to provide. He had no interest in the Arts or anything intellectually thought provoking. He was a man whose lips silently moved every time he read something. She was living with a man who was really just a body without much of a brain. This conclusion helped to make up her mind that morning.

Had Eric remembered her birthday that day, made her breakfast in bed, her life might well have taken a different course to the one she finally took...

After he left to walk to the gym where he worked, she packed up all her belongings and left in his car. She had decided to drive over to Roger's house, to ask if she could stay a few days until she found somewhere else to live. Since their divorce, they had remained on reasonable terms, mainly for Tony's sake.

Now, as she rang the bell, she secretly hoped that they might have remembered her birthday. She realised that had been too much to expect, when she saw Roger's unwelcoming face as he opened the door. He was about to leave for work and grudgingly let her in. He showed no concern or sympathy when she told him that she had left Eric, and needed somewhere to stay until she had sorted things out.

'Sorry, Christina, that's not a good idea.'

'Not just for a couple of days? I'd be happy to sleep on the settee.'

'It won't work. Can't you find a small hotel or B&B?'

'I haven't got much money…that was another thing I wanted to ask. Could you lend me a couple of thousand until I can get straight?'

Roger looked at her as if she was asking for the shirt off his back. 'Are you serious? I thought you were in business with this Jennie woman. Can't you ask her?'

'We've got a few business problems to sort out, and the cash flow is a bit dry.'

'Sorry, I really can't help you there.'

'What about that ten thousand I gave you a few years ago? While we were still married.'

'What about it?' Roger didn't like where this was going. 'It was for a new roof and towards a car that was necessary – for both of us.'

'The roof that you still live under, and a car that you kept when we divorced. I never personally got that money back.'

'You never said you wanted it back at the time. I was, and still am paying the mortgage on this house.'

'We were able to buy this house because my parents gave us the deposit. I have a right to get some of that money back.'

'You have no rights, Christina. That was made clear during our divorce. You were the one to leave the marriage, not me. Don't forget that…Now I really have to go, and I'd be grateful if you weren't here when I return.'

'Can't you be any clearer?' She responded sarcastically.

'I'm in no mood to argue. Shut the door behind you when you leave.'

'Is Tony at school?'

'No, your lazy son's still in bed. Said there were no classes today. Goodbye Christina, sorry I can't help you out

---

306

of your dilemma.'

'Won't, you mean…' But Roger had already gone out of the room and had left the house. 'And a happy birthday to you too, Christina…' She mumbled as a sad afterthought. She didn't so much mind that he refused to let her stay, she half expected that, but had counted on Roger giving her some money, which theoretically had been hers. She hadn't expected him to be so cold and unsympathetic in the circumstances. He had made it quite clear that she was no longer welcome.

She sat down for a moment to try to work out what she was going to do next. Roger had been correct when he said that she had relinquished any rights after their divorce. She had been the one to walk away from the marriage, and had made no demands on either the house or possessions. Duncan, who represented her, had advised her to claim half the property rights, but she had refused as she felt she was at fault because she left. It was nothing to do with either she or Roger seeing anyone else at the time. The marriage had simply died, not that it had ever been that much alive during their eleven years together. Roger had become distant and uncommunicative, and as much as she tried to inject some passion and interest, Roger continued to remain somewhat withdrawn, making no effort to improve their relationship. It had come to a point when she could no longer continue living under the same roof, as she might as well have been invisible.

At first, she had worried about the effect it might have on Tony, who was only eleven. But he was going through a difficult, uncompromising phase and treated her with utter contempt.

Despite feeling guilty about divorcing Roger and leaving Tony, there was no other alternative that she could see.

Soon after Eric started to play a major part in her life. She was lonely. He would always listen and make her laugh. A series of sleepovers resulted in her agreeing to live with him. What surprised her was that Roger never objected or made any judgements about her relationship with Eric. They still all saw each other, even having family dinners together over the next couple of years. It wasn't so much a happy, but a more relaxed existence which she found easy to cope with.

Now that was all disintegrating and Christina felt she had to finally break all ties. She couldn't go back to working with Jennie; she no longer wanted to live with Eric; and Roger wanted nothing more to do with her. There was only Tony, now fourteen, who was the final link, and whom she needed to talk to before she made any final decision about what to do or where to go.

'Hi, Mum…what you doing here?' Tony was standing at the door in his shorts and t-shirt that he wore in bed.

'Why aren't you at school?'

'Oh, don't you start! I've already had Dad going on at me. Lessons were cancelled today. Teacher's ill…Alright?'

'What, all the teachers?'

'I'm not going in…and you can't make me.' He said defiantly, waving his hands about.

Christina then noticed something on one of his arms. 'What's that on your arm?'

Tony proudly moved closer to reveal a skull and crossbones tattooed on his forearm. 'Cool, isn't it!'

'No, it isn't cool. It's hideous! When did you have that done?'

'Last month. Dad didn't mind…'

'Typical of your father. Well I do mind!'

'Tough. You don't live here anymore, and it's none of your business.'

'Don't you dare talk to me like that! You're my son, and I have every right to say what I feel.'

'Your rights stopped when you left us.' He said rather pointedly. 'Chill out, Mum. Life's moved on.'

'It's in your best interests. Have some respect at least.' Christina despaired; she didn't want to have to leave on bad terms.

'Oh, why don't you fuck off!' Tony shouted before leaving and running up the stairs, slamming his bedroom door shut.

Christina's expression showed hopelessness. She felt there was no point in pursuing any further conversation. Tony switching on his music to full blast only strengthened her resolve to 'fuck off' and get out of all their lives and start again somewhere else. Before she left the house an idea crossed her mind, as her eyes glanced at the old bureau that stood in the corner of the room. That's where they used to keep bills, statements and papers in one of the drawers.

She opened a drawer and quickly looked over a recent bank statement of Roger's. He certainly wasn't short of funds, in fact there was quite a lot in the account. He was obviously doing very well. She saw his chequebook underneath and made a decision. She would only take what she was owed, £10,000, and it would still leave him with a lot. She tore out a blank cheque and put it in her bag. It wouldn't be a problem, as she knew how to forge his signature. She would put it in her account straightaway, and by the time he noticed she would be far away.

She sat in Eric's car, having deposited the cheque at the bank, wondering whether to drive it back to the flat. She needed to get out of London as soon as she could.

First she made a phone call to an old school friend who lived in Aylesbury, and asked if she could pay a visit. She was pleased that her friend agreed, who also said she was welcome to stay over.

It was now a matter of returning the car to the flat; getting a taxi to take her to the station, to catch a train to Aylesbury. She had two large suitcases and a couple of bags containing all her worldly possessions. A lot of stuff she had left at the flat, which she couldn't be bothered to take. The very thought of lugging all that onto a train, and then a taxi at the other end, filled her with dismay. The events of the day, so far, had drained all her energy. Sod it, she thought, she'd helped Eric when he bought the car, and felt it was as much hers than his. She would drive to Aylesbury and decide what to do with it later, which made her feel better.

Leaving the outskirts of the London suburbs filled her with relief and a sense of complete freedom. This escape was her birthday present to herself. She decided she was going to take things a day at a time, and see where it led her. For once she really felt that this was the beginning of the rest of her life….

…Like the kaleidoscope in reverse, Christina now saw herself being pulled swiftly away from the car, up into the sky, and then almost like a speeding bullet, back through the hospital window and down onto the bed….

'Christina…can you hear me…?' She slowly opened her eyes to see half a dozen faces staring down at her.

'She's back!' One of the nurses exclaimed. Everyone started to clap.

Christina remembered where she was now. 'Oh bugger….' Was all she could summon up to say.

34. Scenes of Murder, Beatings and Abduction

'What do you think her chances are now?' Paula was talking to the doctor in the corridor outside. It had been an hour since they had resuscitated her.

'Still too early to say, I'm afraid. The seizure didn't help matters. We need to make sure nothing excites or upsets her. It's best she has no more visitors for the time being.'

'I understand. Thank you.' After the doctor had left, Paula turned to Jane. 'Well, your visit certainly created a stir.'

'I don't see how…' Jane replied in all innocence. She was standing by the door, looking through the glass panel at Christina, who lay sleeping. 'Probably the guilt of being found out.'

'What's that supposed to mean?' Paula looked Jane in the eye. She couldn't work out if Jane was being flippant or that there was some deeper meaning.

'It's not for me to say really. That's Christina's problem.' Jane replied enigmatically. In her mid 20's, she had the look of a perfectly styled window mannequin. Smartly dressed and made up like a beauty consultant, there was nothing warm about her. Her whole manner was steely and humourless.

'You said you were her stepdaughter. Why didn't you tell me first of all?'

'I didn't think it was important at the time…'

Paula thought back to earlier that day, when she first

encountered Jane in the church car park after Christina had left. Jane's car had broken down, and she had come out to see if she could help. The young woman she talked to then, was different to the one before her now. She was profusely apologetic about breaking down in the car park, saying that she'd try and sort it herself, before calling a breakdown service. Paula invited her in for a tea or coffee if she wanted, and left her peering under the open bonnet.

It was only ten minutes later that Jane, having fixed her car problem, accepted Paula's invitation. Jane explained that she had been driving nearby, and thought she had recognised Christina, who was driving into the church car park. She had followed her in, yet didn't want to disturb her if she had gone into the church for prayer or silent contemplation. Having decided to wait outside, she unfortunately just missed Christina when she left.

Jane explained that she knew Christina from Aylesbury, but had lost touch. Paula had no reason not to believe her, since Jane seemed very sincere and friendly. She asked Paula a lot of questions about Christina, without revealing much about herself or Christina's life in Aylesbury.

They had chatted for a couple of hours, when Paula got the call from Roger to tell her that Christina had been involved in an accident and was now critical in hospital. She relayed this to Jane, who became very tearful, and asked Paula if she could come with her to the hospital…

'You're now saying that you are actually related to Christina? I don't understand?'

'It's quite simple really. She married my father. Why's that difficult to understand?' Jane replied coldly.

'Christina is married…?' Paula couldn't quite get to grips with this revelation. Christina had never mentioned it.

In fact, now that she came to think of it, Christina never elaborated on her life in Aylesbury.

'Look, I'm sorry, but I haven't got time to regale you with the family history. I really must go. But before I do, I'd like to wish Christina a speedy recovery.' Jane opened the door to Christina's room.

'The doctor said we shouldn't disturb her.'

'I'm only going to quickly wish her well.' And before Paula could say anything else, Jane was in the room and had leant down to quietly whisper in Christina's ear, out of earshot of Paula. 'Die, you bitch…and may you go to hell…'

The following evening, Roger was having supper with Helen, and recounting yesterday's visit to the hospital.

'She was in a pretty bad way….'

'What was her face like? Disfigured in any way?' Helen couldn't hide her animosity, knowing that Christina seemed back in their lives for the time being.

'Only a few superficial cuts and bruises on the face.'

'She's got the luck of the Devil…' *Probably one of Satan's brides*, Helen wanted to add, finding it difficult to disguise her disappointment. She had visualised Christina being completely unrecognisable. And if she survived, having to endure years of plastic surgery, and who would still, hopefully, end up looking like something out of a horror film.

'I wonder what happened? Luckily no one else was involved. Christina did tend to drive rather fast when we were married. It's a miracle she never got any speeding fines.'

Helen suddenly sighed. 'Do you mind if we change the subject?'

'We can't ignore what's happened.' Roger reminded her.

'You might not, but I can. Roger, you know how I feel. You have to agree, and you've said it yourself, she's cast a shadow over our lives during last couple of months.'

'I know, I know…' Roger was in no mood to go over this perpetual argument again. Helen would get worked up and end up leaving in a bad mood. He was glad at least that Tony wasn't in the house, which would have fuelled any discord. 'But I can't simply forget that she's in hospital fighting for her life. We were married for eleven years. You must understand that?'

'Only too well. You're a good man, Roger, and I know you want to do the best you can. But you've also got to consider the effect it's having on us. It's like an invisible wedge that is wrenching us apart…'

'I won't let it.'

'You haven't been yourself since she reappeared, and to see you like that hurts me. I just don't know what to do.'

'I understand, and Tony doesn't help. It worries me that you two have never got along…' Roger suddenly looked completely forlorn.

'And we probably never will, if we're honest.'

'He's got his own demons to sort out, and I seem to have no control over him anymore. This teacher business is still hovering over us. He's not showing any remorse and the school won't have him back. It's all a bloody mess…'

Helen got out of her chair and hugged him tightly. 'I know…we just have to be strong and make sure nothing drives us apart. I do love you…'

He gave her a kiss. 'I know…' But then the doorbell rang ruining the moment. 'Now what!' He reluctantly extricated himself from her embrace to go and answer the door.

'These things are sent to try us.' She forced a smile, which soon disappeared as Roger re-entered followed by two men.

'It's the police...' Roger said reluctantly, as he gestured to the plain-clothes detectives to take a seat.

'Sorry to disturb you. We're conducting some general enquiries.' The first detective addressed Roger, while the second nodded to Helen. 'Mr Turner, do you know of anyone who might've had a grudge against your ex-wife?'

'Christina?' He was puzzled.

'I assume you only have one ex-wife?' The first detective gave a wry smile, glancing at Helen at the same time.

'Yes, sorry. What is this about?' Roger composed himself.

'Look, I think I'll leave you all to it.' Helen suddenly looked uncomfortable, and made for the door.

'No need to leave on our behalf, Miss.' the second detective said, giving her a stern look to imply that she should stay. She returned to her chair looking quite awkward.

'Has anything happened to Christina?' Roger wondered if they had come to tell him that she was dead. 'She was stable the last time I phoned the hospital.'

'Her condition is still critical. So, do you know of any enemies she might have, or had?'

'I don't understand. Why?' Roger looked confused.

'We believe that someone tried to kill her.' Both detectives watched Roger and Helen carefully.

'Kill her? In what way?'

'The crash she had in her car was no accident. Her brakes had been tampered with. We believe it was deliberate.'

'What...' This really unsettled Roger. 'Why would anyone want to do that?'

'That's our very question, Mr Turner. Who would

want to try and kill her?'

'She naturally had disagreements with people, but no one I know who'd go so far as actually want to kill her. Not to my knowledge, anyway.'

'What about you Miss?' The policeman turned to Helen who looked distinctly mortified.

'I…I don't really know Christina…We've only met a couple of times…'

'What would your first impression of her be then?' He asked pointedly.

Helen wanted to say that she thought Christina was a scheming bitch, who was doing her best to drive Roger away from her, and that she hated the very sight of her. 'Very determined…won't suffer fools gladly…can't say more than that really.' She responded, glancing at Roger who gave her a harsh look.

'You wouldn't call her popular then? No family arguments recently?' He directed this at both Helen and Roger.

'Are you implying that I might have something to do with Christina's accident?' Roger angrily replied.

'We're simply trying to find out who would want to do this and why. Because if she does die, it will turn into a murder case.' At that moment his phone went. 'Yes? When? We're at Roger Turner's house now…Ok…I will. Thanks…' He put his phone back in his pocket. 'Got some more bad news, I'm afraid.'

Roger looked at him. 'Christina…?'

'Is she dead…?' Helen finished the sentence, her heart beating heavily.

The policeman gauged both their reactions before adding. 'It's your son, Tony. He's been badly beaten up and is on his way to hospital. It's quite serious. I've no more details I'm afraid.'

316

'Tony...?' Roger was shocked. 'We must get to the hospital...' He stood up.

'We'll give you a lift if you like.'

'It's okay, thanks. I'll take the car. Helen, will you come with me?'

'Of course...' She put her hand on his arm, but her thoughts were racing ahead. If Christina died...and then what if Tony died...Roger would be completely hers. It was too much to wish for.

During the first part of the journey to the hospital, Helen said nothing, sensing Roger wanted to be alone with his thoughts. Then, out of the blue, he suddenly asked her. 'Didn't you, some time ago, take a course in vehicle maintenance and repairs?'

'Yes...' She looked surprised. 'Why?'

'I remember you were able to get my car started last summer. I just wondered why you took such a course?'

'I was fed up being ripped off by garages just because I was a woman. Apart from being able to sort out small problems myself, I wanted to understand the mechanics if the car had to be fixed in a garage.'

'I see...' He replied enigmatically.

'Roger...are you implying that I had something to do with Christina's accident?' Her voice sounded unsteady.

'I'm implying nothing...just curious...'

'Roger, I don't believe you could even think that...' But the uneasy way she responded made Roger decide to say no more, and she remained silent for the rest of the journey.

Tony knowing that Helen was coming to the house that evening, decided to go out, so that he didn't have to be around her. She would only make snide remarks about what he'd done to Rachel, which would inevitably end up in a row. Even if she said nothing, her silent, accusing looks would be enough to aggravate and create a bad atmosphere. He wished he could somehow do something similar to Helen as he'd done to Rachel. Perhaps Helen had some secret that she didn't want publicised? It was worth exploring, he thought, as he made his way to a pub where he was going to meet up with some college friends. His Facebook post gave him a kind of celebrity standing, and he'd become one of the 'lads', even gaining a few new friends.

As he wandered through the tree-lined park, unaware that he was being followed, he still felt no remorse about what he'd done. He could fully justify his actions to himself. She had dumped him after stringing him along. She deserved everything she got. The price he had paid by being suspended was well worth it. His only regret was that he didn't get to have sex with her.

'Hey, it's Tony, isn't it?' A couple of men in their mid 20's suddenly came up behind him in a remote area of the park. They were smiling and appeared very friendly.

'Yes.' Tony smiled back. Although he didn't know them, he wondered if his fame had spread.

'You're the fella who put that picture of you and that teacher online, aren't you?'

'That's me!' Tony smiled proudly.

'You shouldn't have done it, you know.' The first man smiled.

'That was a big mistake, Tony.' The other man looked sadly.

'It was just a bit of a laugh.' Tony dismissed it.

'Not very funny, may I say…we think you need to be taught a lesson out of school…' Before Tony could reply, the first man, swiftly applying a knuckle-duster to his hand, smashed Tony in the nose, breaking it. A moment later the other man punched Tony in the stomach, making him collapse to the ground in agony. From then on, both men started kicking him on all parts of his body until he was unconscious. Having finished the beating, they emptied his pockets; got his phone, and made a call for an ambulance before smashing it. As an afterthought they took a photo of him sprawled on the ground, his face a blood-splattered mess. 'Now there's a pretty picture our little sister, Rachel, will be pleased to see...' They smiled at each other before running off.

'Who could've done this, and why?' Roger stood before Tony's bed in the hospital. He looked a sorry mess. His face and chest were bandaged up, and one arm was in plaster, looking like a trussed-up Mummy.

Helen daren't say that Tony had probably got what was coming to him. But even she was shocked at the state of his injuries. 'Poor boy...' Was all she could utter.

'He's still in a coma.' Answered a doctor who entered the room. 'We've patched him up as best as we can. It's just a matter of time now...'

'Until what?' Roger asked.

'Until we can gauge if there's any brain damage, if he regains consciousness. He took quite a beating. A broken nose, arm and some cracked ribs...and of course a kick to the head.' The doctor outlined the injuries, as if it was a boring shopping list.

'You mean he might be brain dead?' Roger looked down at Tony.

'There is the possibility of a permanent vegetative state...Depends on how, and if he responds in the next day or two. Sorry to be so blunt, but you might as well know the worst-case scenario.'

'Oh God...' Helen blurted out. She wasn't so much thinking about whether Tony would regain all faculties, but that if he were mentally impaired, with Roger forced to look after him, it would be another reason she and Roger might be driven apart.

'Time will tell...if you'd excuse me...' The doctor left the room.

'What a bloody disaster. First Christina...now Tony...What is happening to this family?' Roger crossed his arms and turned to Helen. She just shrugged, although she would have liked to say *What they both deserve?*

It's said that ill fortune comes in threes. It was now the turn of Eric to have his life turned upside down.

He hadn't done anything further regarding the business with Marta. After the first solicitor's letter it had gone quiet. No other letters had popped through the door. He was slightly in denial, hoping that it might all go away, but realistically knowing it wouldn't. Marta was a very determined woman out for all she could get. Was he the first, or were there others who had fallen for the scam? He now realised he'd been a fool, and out of pure greed had married her without having thought of any possible consequences.

On his way to the gym, Eric fantasised about ways to get rid of Marta. He was an avid fan of crime thrillers, and began to think how he would do it. He imagined strangling her, then getting her body into the boot of his car and driving to a remote forest spot where he would dig a large hole and dump her in it...

But to make perfectly sure, before covering it up, he'd pour acid, quicklime or whatever was necessary to disguise identification. That would probably be the ideal solution, and even though it was too late now, he doubted that he'd have the nerve to actually go through with it. Still, the very thought cheered him somewhat.

So the last person he expected to see as he neared the gym was Marta herself, standing on a corner, dressed like a hooker canvassing for trade. 'Eryczek!' She waved as soon as she spotted him. She was smiling and gave the impression that she was really pleased to see him.

Eric might have been a fool, but he wasn't that foolish to be taken in by her friendly enthusiasm. This was no chance meeting. She had been waiting for him. 'What do you want, Marta?' He said sternly.

'Darlink, do not look so cross! You are not happy to see me?' She was behaving as if nothing had happened.

'What do you think?' He looked at her.

'I forgive you, darlink. No bad feeling.'

'What are you talking about?'

She pointed to the odd bruise on her face, most of which had been concealed by makeup. 'Maybe I deserve. Maybe I ask for too much…you vere angry, I understand.'

Eric relaxed a bit. 'I'm sorry about hitting you, but you did rather provoke me with your demands.'

'I know, darlink. I'm Polish, ve get excited…ve must settle this in a nice vay, so ve part like friends, yes?'

'Your solicitor's letter was rather threatening.'

'I try to tell him not to be so hard, but he insist. Vot did your lawyer tink? Ve have no reply.' Marta studied his face.

'I'm…I'm still making my mind up about that. Is there any way we could settle this without having to go through solicitors?'

Marta smiled. 'Is possible…if ve can agree…Vot do you tink is fair?'

'I'm happy to agree to the divorce, and having considered things, give you some money to tide you over so to speak. Look, shall we discuss this in the café at the gym?'

Marta's pursed her lips. 'No, ve talk here. Vot kind of money?'

'Say £5000…?' Eric felt he was being more than generous.

'£5000!' Marta laughed. 'Is joke, yes?'

'It's all I've got…'

'You have flat…'

'That's out of the question! I'm not giving you that!' Eric took a deep breath to steady himself.

Marta remained calm. 'Okay. Maybe you sell flat. Ve split price. Zat is fair.'

'That's not bloody fair! Where am I going to live? Sorry, I'm not going to agree to that.'

Marta paused for a moment. 'You hit me. I have video. You not agree, you vill go to jail…'

Eric had had enough. 'Don't you threaten me, you bitch. You're getting nothing. Sue me, get the bloody police involved. I'll prove you conned me from the start – and you'll be the one to end in prison!' He knew he was chancing his arm, but she had left him with no choice.

Marta pulled a sad face. 'Is your final vord…?'

'My final word is – fuck off!' He started to walk away.

Marta sighed and then signalled to a van that was parked nearby. The van moved off towards Eric, who was strolling angrily along. The van stopped a few metres ahead. Two men then got out, and within seconds had grabbed Eric, knocked him out, and bundled him into the back of the van, which then drove off at speed.

Marta gave the semblance of a smile, as she looked about her, knowing that no one had been witness to this little scene. 'You are very silly boy, Eryczek…dis vill cost you more…'

35. Recycled Love on the Rebound

'I'm sorry, I can't cope anymore. I think we should give ourselves a bit of space.' Helen felt she couldn't hold back any longer.

'What's that supposed to mean?' Roger was driving home from the hospital.

'You've got enough on your plate, first with Christina and now with Tony. They're your priorities. I'm only going to get in the way and complicate matters.'

'How can you say that? That's not fair.'

'What is fair in the circumstances? I sympathise with what's happened and what you're going through, but I don't feel the same.'

'You mean you don't care?'

'To be brutally honest, you could put it that way. I'm sorry.'

Roger sighed, feeling it was all becoming too much. 'You want to walk away, just like that?'

'Only until things are clearer. I don't want to keep fighting with you, Roger. You know how I feel about both Christina and Tony. That's not going to change. I can't help how I feel. I know it makes me sound like a hard-hearted bitch, but it's the truth.'

'You can't leave me now. I need you.' Roger had pulled up outside his house.

'You need to concentrate on your son and ex-wife until you know how things stand.' Helen opened the car door about to get out. 'I'll walk home from here.'

'Please don't go yet…' He pleaded. 'At least give me the chance to tell you something that I've never shared with anyone before. It's about Christina…I've meant to tell you before, but I was afraid Tony would somehow get to know about it.'

Helen closed the car door and sat back. 'What's that?'

'Let's go inside. I need a drink. I think you could do with one too.' Roger got out of the car and Helen followed. Whatever it was that he was about to impart she could tell by his expression that it was serious.

Christina opened her eyes to see a bald-headed middle-aged man, whom she didn't immediately recognise, staring down at her and smiling. 'Hello Christina…' Sporting nearly a week's growth of beard, Duncan was awkwardly holding a small bunch of grapes.

'The grapes of wrath by any chance?' Christina forced a smile.

'Glad to hear the accident hasn't affected your sarcasm.' He plonked the grapes down on a side table. 'I didn't bring flowers because they are not as nourishing.'

'Is it really you Duncan, or am I having another of my weird dreams? I've been having a lot lately.'

'I can assure you this is not a dream, unless I'm the one who's dreaming of course. How are you?'

'I keep thinking I'm at death's door, but thankfully it hasn't opened yet.'

Christina, still in pain, managed to sit up in the bed. 'You know, the beard suits you, and I'm glad you got rid of that awful scoop-over…and you're not even wearing a tie! What's happened to you, Duncan?'

'I'm taking advantage of my mid-life crisis.'

'Getting a sports car and a nubile young blonde to go with it?' Christina couldn't believe the change in Duncan. It wasn't so much his physical appearance as his whole demeanour, which was different. If anything, he looked and sounded younger.

'I'm not changing my old Skoda or trading in my wife for a younger model – but I am going to buy a boat.' He said this with a sense of excitement.

'Good for you. Sail those high seas.'

'More likely the low seas, probably around the South coast. I'm selling the practice and we're going to relocate and retire to Dorset, where my wife was born.'

'What made you decide?' Christina adjusted her position to feel more comfortable; careful not to show the pain she was experiencing in doing so.

'Well, you did really. I thought about what you had said about not waiting to retire, and to do what I really wanted to, before it was too late. Thank you...' Duncan uncharacteristically touched her arm in appreciation.

'Well, at least I seem to have said something right for a change. Usually all I ever seem to have done is upset people...and they're undoubtedly upset even more that I'm still alive...'

'I talked to the police, who told me someone had purposefully tampered with the brakes of your car. They asked me if I knew of anyone who might have reason to have done it.'

'One of the nurses mentioned the police come to see me, but thankfully were told I wasn't in a fit state to answer questions. What did you say?'

'I said I didn't know of anyone. Would you have any idea?'

'A few persons come to mind who might want to be rid of me. I've offended a few in my time – but maybe not enough for them to want to kill me, perhaps. But you never know!'

'Well, I'm glad they didn't succeed. You were

lucky....'

'I wonder about that...Can't say there's a lot to live for as things stand...'

'That's a silly thing to say, Christina. Feeling a touch self-piteous?' Duncan gave her an austere look. 'You haven't got cancer. You've everything to live for.'

'I wish I knew what that everything was...but I suppose you're right. I am feeling a bit sorry for myself. Not sure how long they're going to keep me in here, but we do need to talk. I want to make some adjustments to my Will.'

'Of course. Let's get you up and about first...'

What Duncan didn't mention, before he left, was that her son Tony was in a nearby ward still in a coma. Christina knew nothing about his predicament, since the doctors felt she still wasn't well enough to be given this news, concerned that it might cause another seizure, which could be fatal this time. Christina had thought about why he hadn't been to visit, but then dismissed it. As her feelings toward him had changed, she assumed he didn't care anymore. She also wondered why Eric hadn't come to see her. Was he still annoyed that she wasn't going support or pay for his dispute with Marta? Apart from Paula and Duncan, the only other person who came was Roger. Even then, they had nothing much to say to each other. She felt he'd come out of duty. It certainly wasn't out of love....

'It's the truth...I was never in love with Christina.' Roger took a large gulp of whiskey.

Helen, having refused a drink, sat watching him stony-faced. 'Yet you were married for over ten years...'

'I know, I know...it was only later that I realised we shouldn't have got married in the first place.' Roger was finding this difficult.

———

'But she was in love with you?'

'Yes…well, I doubt so much towards the end.'

'What are you trying to tell me. I still don't understand.'

Roger took another sip and paced across the room. 'I married Christina on the rebound…'

'From whom?' Helen was suddenly interested.

'From someone I was engaged to at the time. Her name was Sophie. We'd been going out for three years, and I naturally assumed that we'd get married…but it wasn't to be. She suddenly met someone else, dumped me and married this other man, all within a space of a month.'

'Did you love this Sophie?'

'Yes.' Roger poured himself another drink.

'More than you say you love me?'

'Please Helen, not now…I'm trying to explain.'

'Where does Christina come into this?'

'She came to work in the same office as me. This was after Sophie left me. Christina knew nothing about her, and I never mentioned it. She never hid the fact that she fancied me from the start, and although I found her attractive, I wasn't initially interested.'

'But you got together, nevertheless?' Helen was trying to take it all in.

'It didn't happen immediately. We got together during an office party. It was Christina who did the chasing, and because we seemed to get on, things developed from there really.'

'You fell in love with her.' Helen watched Roger's reaction.

'No…it was never love on my part. I know she loved me and I seriously thought it was enough for us to get by on. She was the one who proposed and I went along with it. I thought why not? We married six months later…'

'And still stayed married for ten years.' Helen added somewhat sarcastically.

'I realised I'd made a mistake during the first year…'

'So why did you stay with her if you felt that way?'

'She fell pregnant with Tony. I didn't have the heart to leave her then. We muddled on after that…'

Helen sighed. 'Just like we're muddling on now?'

'It's not the same.' Roger raised his voice slightly.

'How is it not the same? You tell me that!' Helen's frustration was coming out.

Roger put down his glass and sat next to her on the sofa. 'Because I was never in love with Christina, but I'm in love with you.'

'As much as Sophie…?' She regretted it as soon as she said it. 'Sorry…I can't help but feel insecure.'

'I love you, and that's all that matters now.' He put his arm around her shoulder. Yet at the back of his mind, he still wondered if Helen had anything to do with Christina's accident.

'I love you too, but what really matters is what is going to happen specifically to Tony, and I hate to say it, to Christina. That's going to have a strong bearing on our future…if there's going to be one.'

'Yes…you're right. Why does life always have to be so bloody complicated? I don't want to lose you.' He thought for a moment. 'Will you marry me?'

'What…?'

Roger got down on one knee. 'Helen, will you marry me?'

'Do you mean that…?' She looked shocked.

'No, of course I don't bloody mean it, you silly cow!' He joked, giving her a kiss on the mouth. 'Well? Do I get an answer or are you going to play hard to get?'

'First things first, before I decide.'

'Which is…?'

'I want you to take me up to your bedroom and undress me…'

'And then what?' he said innocently.

'Prove how much you love me. In your very own bed, which we've never shared.'

'And then will you agree to marry me?'

'Depends on how you rise to the occasion…' She smiled.

35. Life in a Parallel Universe

As Christina lay in bed thinking about her life, and about everything that had brought her to this point, she realised how unpredictable it all was. With hindsight she would have made different choices. But even those choices had no guarantees that things would work out, or that life would be better. The main thought going through her head now was what to do next if she did fully recover and leave hospital?

One of her main concerns were the people she had left in Aylesbury. She had managed to disappear from their lives, and had hoped her death from the cancer would make them none the wiser. That seemed more difficult, now that Jane knew where she was.

Jane was one of the key reasons she had decided to leave Aylesbury after she had been told about her terminal condition. Jane, who had literally become the stepdaughter from hell. How she wished now she had never married Alister in the first place; and even more so how she wished she'd never gone to Aylesbury for a start.

Various people had had a significant effect on her life, to bring her to where she was, yet what didn't occur to her was the effect she had had on other people's lives. Her very presence had led them to make certain decisions, or be plunged into particular situations to alter the course of their own existences. It was a two-way street where all their lives were intertwined and connected.

Whether the element of fate exists or that everything is random is a never-ending lifelong question. The future is undetermined. There are many possibilities and knock-on effects….

...A chance meeting; going a different way; a particular relationship; following a hunch; how we respond to something - all have the effect of taking our lives in numerous directions.

Now, as Christina lay in hospital, she was oblivious to what was going on outside. What could be the fates of those closest to her? What would their destinies be? There were many alternatives and possibilities.

Take Tony for a start. What if he did not recover or come out of his coma? After a time, Roger would be persuaded by the doctors to turn off the life support machine and let Tony die peacefully. This would have a detrimental effect on Roger's relationship with Helen, because of the guilt he would feel. They would call off their proposed wedding and part. Roger would take to drink and eventually die alone. Helen would have a series of disastrous relationships with younger men, followed by marrying an older man for his money, finally ending her days in prison for his murder. Her cellmate would be Jennie, who would make Helen her bitch.

After Marta's associates kidnapped Eric, his life could take a different course. Refusing to accede to her demands, he would be beaten, drugged and smuggled onto a boat and dumped in a remote part of Turkey. Due to a head injury inflicted during the voyage, he would suffer from amnesia, and be unable to remember anything; who he was and where he was from. After his arbitrary wanderings, eventually crossing the border into Iran, he would attach himself to a group of rogue mercenaries and become a fighter, only to be killed later by a landmine. Marta would illegally take possession of his flat and assets and settle down to becoming a much sought-after dominatrix to influential members of the establishment and be awarded an OBE in later years.

If Duncan suddenly had second thoughts about selling his business, retiring and buying his dream boat, his life would steer itself in a different direction. He would continue as a solicitor into his mid-sixties, but due to regret and frustration at not having taken that chance, would die of cancer before he was seventy.

Since Paula was at a mental crossroads over her religious calling, her life could go in one of many ways. By staying in the church, she would eventually rise to the position of Bishop. It would be an achievement that wouldn't make her happy. A scandal of her own making would see her socially ostracised by both the church and the public, and she would commit suicide. If she left the church, she would either become a councillor, helping young people; or lead a hedonistic existence that would make her infamous at a price, yet able to live to an old age.

And what about Christina herself? What would her fate be? If she did recover from hospital, and then if she decided to go her own way abandoning everyone, she would become the fatal victim of a hit and run accident. The car or the person would never be found, but it would be believed by the police that it was deliberate. There could be other outcomes for her, which would depend on the fates of those closest to her, and which direction they had decided to take. It was still all a moveable feast…

But the above is all in the future, to possibly materialise in a parallel universe. In this world the various outcomes were actually quite different…

The nurse was attending to Tony, checking the vital sign

monitors and life support machine, which was helping him breathe and stay alive. There had been no change over the last few days, and she believed there wasn't likely to be any. She had seen this so many times, often ending with the machine being switched off. It was such a waste of a young life, she thought as she left the room

Roger had come every day, sitting with Tony and doing his best to talk to him. He found it difficult trying to communicate in this way, when there was no response. He never stayed more than an hour, which was all he could cope with. He'd had numerous conversations with the consultant, but was told that there had been no change, and that Roger must prepare himself for the fact that Tony might never come out of the coma or recover. He also had to accept the possibility of the ventilator being switched off if there was no improvement, which Roger found difficult to even contemplate.

He had tried to contact Eric to let him know about Tony, but Eric's phone was not responding. When he rang the gym where Eric worked, he was told that Eric hadn't been in for some time, and they thought he might have gone away on holiday. This was typical of Eric, many times over the years he'd just gone away without telling anyone. So, in effect, no one took much notice of his disappearance, particularly Roger.

He had dutifully looked in on Christina, and they'd had brief chats of no consequence, mainly because of the drugs that made her sleepy. She still didn't know about Tony, and when she asked Roger why he or Eric hadn't visited, he said that Tony was suffering from a bout of flu at home, and until he'd fully recovered it was best he didn't come to the hospital.

Eric, he believed was away on holiday and was not contactable. Christina accepted this without further question. Roger was glad to leave the hospital, always coming away feeling depressed and hopeless.

Although his relationship with Helen had got closer since the marriage proposal, she refused to completely commit herself or discuss their future until the fates of Tony and Christina were much clearer. She secretly imagined creeping into the hospital at night, disguised as a doctor, first turning off Tony's machine, and then smothering Christina with a pillow. That would certainly clear the way for her to marry Roger. She even believed that she might actually get away with it.

The night nurse was doing one of her regular nocturnal checks. She tucked in Tony's bed blanket at the sides, even though it hadn't been disturbed. 'There, nice and cosy!' She checked the tracheostomy tube attached to his windpipe, making sure the airways were clear. 'May God be with you, dear boy...' She had heard from the other nurses that it was likely that the ventilator might be switched off in the next day or two, since there had been no visible improvement in Tony's condition. It was now simply a matter of getting final consent from his father. 'May the angels look after you...' She mumbled more to herself as she walked towards the door.

'Jesus loves you...' Came a strange voice from inside the room.

The nurse turned towards the bed and noticed that Tony's eyes were open. 'Did you say something?' She asked, not believing there would be a response.

'Jesus will save you. Give your life to Jesus...' Tony's lips murmured, in a voice that sounded distant and guttural.

She moved to get a closer look, and saw that his eyes followed her. 'Tony? Tony, can you hear me...?' She bent down close to his face, detecting a faint smile.

'I am the resurrection and the life. Whoever believes in me, though he die, yet shall he live, and everyone who lives and believes in me shall never die…' The voice coming from Tony's mouth rasped suddenly, the very effort of speaking having taken its toll. He then closed his eyes, but the smile still remained.

'Good Lord…' The nurse whispered, believing she had just witnessed a minor miracle. She then ran to the nursing station to alert the duty doctor.

37. Martial Artist Saves the Day

Almost at the very moment that Tony came out of his coma, Eric, about twenty miles away, was having his own resurrection.

After being kidnapped, Eric had come to in the back of the van, finding that his mouth, hands and feet had been tightly bound by gaffer tape. He'd been put into a sleeping bag that had been zipped up, with only his head uncovered. It was dark apart from a bit of light coming from a chink in the van doors. He tried to wriggle, but discovered his body had been encased in a kind of wooden box, very much like a coffin, which restricted any movement. He could feel the van beneath him as it sped along the road and heard two men arguing in what he recognised as Polish. He came to the conclusion that this had something to do with Marta. They slowed down and the van pulled in somewhere and stopped. The engine was switched off. Eric then heard what sounded like the shutting of metal doors.

It was some time before the back doors of the van were opened. He felt the box being lifted, carried out, and then laid on the ground. Gazing up it looked like the interior of a large garage, but then he heard the rumble of a train passing overhead, and realised he was in a space beneath some railway arches.

Two faces stared down at him. In their mid-twenties, they looked a couple of college graduates pretending to be thugs. They mumbled something in Polish to each other, which sounded like they didn't know what to do next. Eric reckoned, from their expressions and body language that they'd never done this before. One of them got out a phone and garbled some monosyllabic words and then listened to the person on the other end giving instructions.

The two figures then disappeared from view, and the next thing Eric saw was a white cloth being placed over his nose. He smelt chloroform, and then everything went black...

Eric had no idea how long he'd been unconscious. As he opened his eyes, he found himself sat on a wooden chair with his legs and hands bound. His lips felt dry and he realised there was no tape covering his mouth.

'You must be thirsty, Eryczek...' Marta sat some metres away, with her two associates standing next to her, like obedient servants. She motioned to one, who unscrewed a small bottle of water and inelegantly shoved it in Eric's mouth. More water spilled over his front than into his mouth. 'I am sorry ve haf to do dis...'

'No you're not...' Eric forced out the words, still able to smell the traces of the chloroform. 'What do you want...as if I didn't know...You won't get away with this...'

'All you haf to do, darlink, is sign a few papers. Very easy. No vorries.' She took out a large manila envelope from out of a bag and waved it.

'And then what? Conveniently kill me...?'

'Eryczek, you vatch too many gangsta film.' Marta knew she wouldn't resort to actually killing him. She did have in mind, knowing a friend who had a boat, that if he didn't co-operate, she'd get her friend to dump Eric covertly somewhere remote in another country. Turkey was a possibility.

'I'm not signing anything...' Eric suddenly felt defiant, in no way feeling afraid. He could sense these men were amateurs, who didn't, in any way, look threatening. 'You can shove that idea...wherever...'

Marta sighed. 'You are being very silly boy.' She raised her voice, and shifted angrily in her chair. Eric glared at her provokingly. The two men looked at her for guidance.

They weren't used to do doing these kind of jobs, and felt way out of their league. One of them mumbled something in her ear, making her smile. 'You know vot he vants to do to you…if you do not agree?'

'Give me a kiss and then call me a taxi?'

'It is no time to joke!' She screeched frustratingly. 'Dis is very serious. He tinks ve should cut off your fingers vun by vun until you sign. Vot you tink of dat?'

'I see…but how will I be able to sign without any fingers?' Eric gently threw it back at them.

He watched as they huddled together in hasty conference, muttering in a language that sounded more severe than their actual expressions. By now, having fully regained his senses, Eric surveyed the situation he was in. More concerned than afraid, he was trying to work out how best he could free himself from this predicament. He was sure that they wouldn't go as far as killing him. But as for inflicting any sort of physical punishment, he wasn't so certain. From the response he had given, he hoped his fingers wouldn't be cut off now. What else might they try to get his co-operation? Were these men even up to the task of doing something of that nature anyway? They just didn't look or act the type. All these questions bombarded his brain as he observed the three of them arguing and gesticulating amongst themselves.

Then, when it looked like they had made a decision and were in agreement, one of the men went over to a makeshift table scattered with odd, rusting tools and picked up a pair of black pliers. They felt stiff, so he squirted some oil from a small can.

After several attempts he managed to loosen them, opening and closing the pliers like the snapping mouth of a crocodile, as he walked cockily towards Eric.

'Eryczek…didn't I say vot beautiful teet you haf? It vood be pity to ruin your smile…' Marta smirked, feeling confident that they had come up with a sure-fire solution. When she had lived with him that short time, she noticed how fastidious he was about the care of his teeth.

Eric's face crumbled. 'You don't mean…you don't seriously mean you would actually pull my teeth out?'

'Ov course not! You sign and beautiful teet stay shiny.'

'I told you, I'm not signing anything.' He bravely called their bluff.

Marta's expression hardened. 'You haf vun more chance. Now sign!' She waved the manila envelope.

Eric took a deep breath. 'No…'

Marta turned to the man with the pliers and nodded. He looked uncertainly back at her. Did she actually mean it? Marta let out a stream of what sounded like Polish profanities, gesturing wildly for him to get on with it. He stood there hesitantly, holding the pliers. He just couldn't go through with it. The other man suddenly grabbed the pliers off of his friend and went over to Eric and forced Eric's mouth open. Just as he was about to connect pliers with teeth, Eric let out a piercing scream. 'No, please…not my teeth! I will sign! I will sign!'

Marta motioned for the man to stop and move away. 'Goot boy…you see, it vos not so hard.'

'You didn't give me much choice!' Eric spluttered, now looking weak and helpless.

'You haf choice. Sign or no teet.'

'And then what are you going to do with me? After I've signed? Are you going to kill me…?' Eric had visibly changed, and now was acting like a jittering wreck

'I am fair. You vill be free to go.' She said with total conviction, even though she didn't mean it. It was too

339

dangerous to let him go. Eric needed to conveniently disappear. She would get her friend with the boat to help her. 'So… you sign.' She took the papers out of the envelope and held them out.

'And how do you expect me to do that?' He bleated.

'Vot...?' She then realised that his hands were bound and laughed. 'I am silly girl!' She ordered one of the men to get a knife and cut Eric's bindings.

'I'm…I'm doing this under protest…I hope you understand that…' He was almost in tears.

'I understand, darlink. Ve haf mutual understanding.' She took the papers, and extracting a pen from her bag, laid them all on a clean surface of the makeshift table. She had expected a bit of resistance from Eric, but hadn't anticipated him reacting in such a weak and pathetic manner.

Having the binding of both his feet and hands cut, Eric slowly rose from the chair, but then immediately collapsed on the floor, his legs seemingly giving way. He looked small and pathetic lying there. 'My legs…' he spluttered.

Marta ordered both men, who had started laughing, to go lift him up and help him to the table.

None of them quite expected what was to happen next.

It only took thirty seconds for Eric to overcome and knock out the two men, and get Marta onto her knees in an arm lock. 'You know…I've waited nearly twenty years for a moment like this. All those lessons I had in judo, karate and kendo have finally paid off. Impressed with my little bit of acting? By the way, I'm sorry, but I've changed my mind about signing anything.'

'Darlink…you are hurting me…maybe we talk dis over…' Marta stared at her two associates who lay immobile on the ground.

'Nothing to discuss 'darlink'. You made your position absolutely clear, now I'm going to make mine even clearer.' He picked her up and dragged her to the table. With one hand he clutched her hands behind her back, with the other got hold of the pliers. 'You wouldn't look so pretty without your teeth...' He put them down and picked up a rusty knife. 'And even less attractive with a few well positioned scars...' He waved the knife in front of her face.

'Please, Eryczek, I vil do anytink...' It was now her turn to panic and plead.

'Of course you will. A few questions first. Our two Polish friends there, can I assume that they are here illegally by any chance?'

'My cousins...dey are goot boys...'

'And their mother loves them, yes. But they didn't enter this country by normal means – is that right?' He tightened his grip on her. Marta nodded. 'They are naughty boys then. Deserved to be whipped, wouldn't you say? You're quite good at that...'

'Vot do you vant?'

He loosened his grip, and with the knife still in his hand, guided her back to where her bag was by the chair. He extracted her phone and handed it to her.

'First of all, you are going to phone your solicitor. You will tell him that you want to go ahead with the divorce, but that you have changed your mind about either pursuing criminal charges or demanding anything from me. You expect nothing but a straightforward divorce on the grounds of your adultery.'

'Vot adultery...?' Marta looked confused.

Eric pointed at the two men on the ground. 'Don't tell me you didn't have sex with them. You did, didn't you?' He placed the tip of the rusty knife lightly on her nose. She nodded. 'You will also tell him that you will pay all costs, and

I will give him details of my solicitor when I have engaged one. Understand?'

'I haf not much money to pay costs!' She begged.

'I'm sure you'll be able to find it. Now make that call. He will naturally try to dissuade you, but you will insist that is what you want. If you try and be clever you will be very sorry…and I'm not acting now.' Yet there was a part of him that wasn't sure what he would actually do should she try and call for help.

'You are bastard! I vish I never marry you!' She exclaimed dramatically.

'My wish too, *darlink*. Now please make that call.'

Marta sighed and then pressed the number. She said exactly what he had asked her. The solicitor did try to argue on the other end, but she managed to stay firm and in control which did impress Eric. He realised how hard and determined she was. Whatever happened afterwards, he was quite sure she'd get back on her feet and con some other fool. He was also relieved that he wouldn't be forced to harm her. He wasn't sure if he'd be able to anyway.

'Vot you do vid me now?' She asked after she finished her call.

'You are going to write a little letter.'

'Letter? Vot letter?'

'Just a bit of insurance for me, just in case you decide to do something silly after I let you go free.' On a piece of blank paper, which was among the documents she had brought, he dictated what he wanted her to write. It was in the form of a confessional. About how she tricked him into marriage, and how she wanted to strip him of all his assets; how she wanted to blackmail him through her solicitor; how she then organised him to be kidnapped and had threatened him with bodily injury if he didn't comply to her demands. She continued to protest, but ended up writing what he wanted.

'Vot about my cousins?' She asked after she signed the letter.

'I'll deal with them, but I promise they won't come to any real harm. You just worry about your own skin. Now…as they say…piss off, and never let me see you again.'

Marta was about to say something, but thought better of it. She didn't really care about the fate of the two men, who certainly weren't her cousins. She was more concerned about her own survival. She picked up her bag and promptly left without another word.

Eric then set about tying up the men, who remained unconscious, to two chairs. He emptied their pockets and took their wallets and phones. He then went outside to find out exactly where he was. Using one of the phones, he called the police and anonymously told them about a couple of illegal Polish immigrants who could be found at that address.

He was quite pleased with himself and his performance as he drove their van away from the arches to where he would finally dump it and then get transport back to his flat. He began to have serious thoughts of maybe training to be an actor, who could do his own stunts. He quite liked that idea. It appealed to his growing ego

38. Antony is Reborn

Tony's sudden recovery was the talk of the hospital. Many regarded it as a miracle. The medical staff firmly believed that he was a lost cause and would never come out of the coma. How wrong they all were, and even the consultant who had been pressing for life support to be turned off, was incredulous at this sudden turn of events which he couldn't give any medical reason for.

What was most surprising, and in a way slightly unnerving, were Tony's whole manner and the way in which he greeted and talked to everyone who came to see him. This Tony was virtually the complete opposite of the Tony before the assault. Those who were religious believed God had touched him, whilst the cynics looked upon him as some pious fanatic who had literally gone nuts.

'Father, so nice of you to come and visit me. How is dear Helen?'

'What's happened, Tony…?' Roger couldn't take in this cheery person who was now all sweetness and light.

'Don't look so worried! All will be well; Jesus will save you.'

'I don't want to be saved, thank you. I'm glad you've recovered, but I don't quite get what you're on about?'

'I have been shown the error of my ways, father, and I want to pass on the message of God's love for everyone.'

'What happened to 'Dad'? Or are you taking the piss?' Roger didn't trust Tony, and wondered if he was playing some sort of game.

'I am your son, and I love you.' Tony gave a look of compassion.

Roger ignored this. 'Do you remember what happened, and how you came to be in this state?'

'I had sinned and I was rightly punished. The angels brought me to Jesus, who forgave me. I have been truly born again, and I am back to help spread the word and save you all.'

'Save us from what, Tony?'

'From yourselves. You christened me Antony, which is how I would now like to be called.'

Roger sighed. 'I don't believe this! You are winding us all up, aren't you?'

'You sound very disturbed, father. I will pray for you. Pray that you will be given understanding, and that you will be able to see the light.'

'Jesus! I think I'm the one who needs his head examined.'

'Jesus has heard you, and will calm your troubled spirit.' Tony smiled. 'Now if you don't mind, I must pray for guidance. You may go…' He closed his eyes and put his hands together in prayer like a little boy.

Roger felt any further response would be futile. Things were going from the sublime to the ridiculous. As much as Roger disliked his son sometimes, he much preferred the old version to the one that was now emerging. He felt the assault had really messed with Tony's head, and there was no telling where this would go. At this moment, as much as he hated himself for even thinking it, he wondered if turning off the life support might have been more of a blessing.

'What do you mean he's got religion?' Christina, now able to sit up in bed, watched as Roger paced about the room. 'And why didn't you tell me Tony was at death's door, barely a stone's throw from here?' She added angrily.

'We didn't want to upset you…in the condition you were in.'

'How very thoughtful of you. My son had almost been killed, was in a coma, unlikely to recover, and you couldn't be bothered to let me know.' Christina was trying not to agitate herself too much.

'Don't blame me! It was the doctors who thought it best not to inform you.'

'So, would you have let me know before or after – if his life support was turned off? Tell me that.'

'I don't know…please Christina; I'm doing my best to explain. Tony, or Antony as he wants to be called now, has literally come back from the dead which we should be grateful for.'

'But you say he's a different person, that he's found 'God' or 'Jesus' and wants to save us all?'

'That's the gist of it. I don't know what to think…' Roger looked worn out.

'Is he playing silly buggers, trying to make us feel guilty? I wouldn't put it past him.'

'That's what I thought of at first…but he really isn't the Tony we know. That crack on the head has certainly changed his personality, and I honestly don't think he's faking it.'

Christina sighed. 'Ah well, I suppose we should be grateful that he's alive.'

'Who's alive? What's been going on? Christina, how are you?' Eric appeared at the door.

'And where the hell have you been?' Roger faced his brother.

'I've been a bit tied up…but it's a long story - for another time…You wouldn't believe me anyway.' Eric smiled and went across to Christina and gave her a peck on the cheek. 'Glad to see you're better.'

'Are you really?' She said coldly, 'Beaten up any other women lately?'

Eric sighed wearily. 'That's not fair. There was a reason.'

'What are you both talking about?' Roger queried. He knew nothing about Eric's secret marriage to Marta, or what had happened.

'Not important...' Eric replied, 'Just something from the past...it's all been sorted.'

'Really?' Christina looked at him. 'Murdered Marta, have you?'

'Who's Marta?' Roger was lost.

Eric looked hurt. 'You really believe I would go that far?'

Christina regretted her comment. 'No...you say it's been sorted?'

Eric nodded. 'We've come to a mutual agreement, so to speak. And before you say anymore, I do have regrets and feel guilty about what happened.'

'Can someone please put me in the picture?' Roger was getting increasingly frustrated and confused.

Ignoring Roger, Christina pointed at Eric. 'If you feel so guilty, Eric, I think you'd better go and see your nephew Tony, or should I say Antony. Perhaps he will purge you of all your sins and bestow a blessing on you.'

'Eh? I don't understand.' Eric had yet no knowledge of Tony's predicament.

'You don't understand!' Roger turned to Eric, who was now looking puzzled. He raised his voice. 'What is going on here? Will one of you please tell me what you're talking about!'

Suddenly a horrified look came across Christina as her eyes turned towards the door.

Both Roger and Eric also turned to see two men, similar in age and build, who could be brothers, standing by the doorway. 'Hello Christina…we were very worried about you…' One of the men stepped into the room, the other stood behind.

'And who the hell are you?' Roger demanded.

'I could ask the same of you.' The man replied.

'I am Christina's ex-husband if it's anything to you.'

'Really? And you are…?' The man now addressed Eric.

'Eric…Christina's…well, ex-partner…I mean, I'm his brother…' Eric wondered if this was the police.

'You never cease to surprise me, Christina…' Jane smiled as she came into the room.

Roger turned back to Christina, who looked like a petrified rabbit caught in the headlights. Frozen and unable to speak, the colour had completely drained from her face. He turned back to them. 'I've had enough of this! Either you explain why you're all here, or I will call hospital security to remove you.'

'Yes…' Eric added puffing himself up, 'Explain yourselves…or leave...'

'We've come to see my wife…. Christina.' The first man quietly declared.

'She's my step mother.' Jane added.

The second man moved beside them. 'We're family. She's my sister-in-law and we're going to bring her back home. To where she belongs.'

As an incredulous Roger and Eric turned from the men to Christina, as she let out a piercing and desperate scream.

39. The Aylesbury Embrace

Before she passed out from the sheer force of her agonising scream, a number of scenes flashed across Christina's mind. It was her fortieth birthday, the day she left London to start a new life elsewhere....

Christina felt she could breathe more easily as she left the outskirts of the capital. A sense of true adventure enveloped her, as urban gave way to suburban merging into pure countryside. She had no feelings of guilt leaving Roger, Tony and Eric behind, and couldn't get far enough away from Jennie and the business. She didn't think they'd be desperate to try to find her since there was not a lot of love lost between them. The £10,000 she took from Roger would give her a cushion until she could get back on her feet, and she didn't think there would be a problem disposing of Eric's car when the time came.

Arriving in Aylesbury, her school friend, Kath, welcomed her with open arms. Kath had just come through a messy divorce and was also trying to rebuild her life. Christina had envisaged spending a day or two in Aylesbury before moving on further afield. She fancied the idea of finding somewhere in the Lake District to finally settle, where she had enjoyed many family holidays when she was little.

Kath, who didn't have any children, persuaded Christina to stay a bit longer. She was grateful for the companionship, and since they got on so well, Christina wasn't in any hurry to leave. It would give her time to think.

The days turned into weeks, which quickly developed into months. Christina had never felt so free and alive. She and Kath enjoyed meals out, the cinema, and days away.

They'd been close friends at school, and it felt as if they'd never been apart.

They were the sisters neither had. Often, when they went to pubs in the evening for a drink or to listen to local bands and singers, men would try to chat them up. Despite being flattered, neither at that time was interested in getting involved with anyone.

They were simply content with each other's company and to enjoy the moment.

Although she shared the house with Kath with her own room, she knew she'd ultimately want her own space and also to find herself a job, since her money wouldn't last forever. After about four months, Christina seriously felt that perhaps she should start thinking about leaving Aylesbury, since she couldn't see herself settling permanently there. She quite liked the town, but started to yearn for the open green spaces of the Lake District.

Kath had told her that she could stay as long as she liked, but Christina felt she should leave while things were still good between them. She knew Kath would eventually meet someone, which undoubtedly would complicate matters. She herself wasn't in any hurry to have a relationship, although she was aware it wouldn't be too long before she would want male company and sex.

Little was she aware how circumstances would dictate her next move.

She had been out for a walk in a park, thinking about her possible journey northwards, when she was cornered in a secluded area, by a couple of youths. They demanded her bag, rings, watch and phone, and anything else in her pockets.

When Christina told them to get lost, one of them pulled out a flick knife and threatened to cut her face up if she didn't comply. She tried to run away, but they were far quicker and stronger. One had grabbed her, while the other desperately tried to pull her bag off, which she held on to tightly, determined not to let go without a struggle.

It was then her knight in shining armour appeared, in the guise of a sweaty jogger. In his late 30's, Gordon Fodd, who had been in the army, was a keep-fit fanatic. He not only swiftly and effortlessly overcame the two youths, but also proceeded to divest them of the knife, their phones and anything else in their possession.

Skilfully pinning them both to the ground, he took their photo from his phone, and then told them to take off their jeans. Once they'd done this, he told them to fuck off, stop mugging people, or he would send the photo to the police.

The image of two trouser-less youths running for dear life, despite the shock, made Christina laugh. Gordon explained that he wouldn't actually contact the police. He didn't want to waste time giving a statement. The youths had hopefully learnt their lesson. Christina had agreed, since she, for her own personal reasons, didn't want to get involved with the police.

It was the start of a close friendship, which resulted in Christina staying in Aylesbury, but moving out of Kath's house into Gordon's small flat.

She didn't fall in love with Gordon. He was a nice man and the sex was great, but he didn't stimulate her intellectually, since he had no interest in anything artistic or creative. She couldn't help but compare him, in a way, to Eric. They were quite similar, and she wondered why she was attracted to that kind of man, then realising that it was for the sex, which had more priority at that time.

It was during their brief relationship, that she was introduced to Gordon's brother, Alister. He was a widower who had lost his wife to cancer a few years previously.

Christina and he immediately hit it off. Alister, a University Professor, was an intellectual who loved all the arts, having a wide knowledge of most things.

His only failing was being a racist and against immigration, especially against black people. He kept that mainly to himself and was careful never to make a public issue of it. Although the brothers were similar in looks, they couldn't have been more different. Among friends they were regarded as the brawn and the brains.

Alister, on various pretexts, often visited or phoned them. He would invite both to various functions and exhibitions, knowing that Gordon wouldn't be interested, but that Christina would be. It was his way of getting her on her own, as he slowly became besotted with her.

She was attracted to Alister and liked his company, but kept her distance as far as any intimacy was concerned. She didn't want to be in the middle of a ménage a trois, even though she suspected that Gordon wouldn't mind.

Theirs had become a relationship of convenience, which she soon found herself getting bored with. Gordon stimulated her sexually, but after a time it was not enough. She found herself doing most of the cooking and laundry. An unpaid housekeeper who kept his bed warm.

She still had ideas of moving to the Lake District, but her main worry was that she was running out of funds.

It was Alister who introduced Christina to Daphne, who had her own business, buying and supplying herbs and spices to shops and supermarkets.

When Christina admitted that she knew quite a bit about the retail side of that particular business, when she worked with Jennie, Daphne offered her a job, which Christina happily accepted. Thoughts of the Lake District once more drifted into the background.

Eventually, after a few months, when she amicably split with Gordon and temporarily moved back in with Kath, Alister started to pursue her relentlessly. At first, despite becoming very fond of him, she held back because she didn't want to get involved again so quickly. However, one of the main reasons she didn't encourage him or let herself get serious, was because of his daughter.

Jane, in her early 20's, was very protective of her father. She took an immediate dislike to Christina, making out she was a gold digger after Alister's money. Although he couldn't be called exceptionally rich, he'd inherited a substantial amount from his father who'd been a successful antiques dealer. As much as Christina tried to win Jane over, it became a constant struggle. Alister believed Jane could do no wrong, and placed her on a pedestal as a role model to young women. Although he loved his daughter, he was not prepared to be bullied or dictated by her.

Jane, after her mother died, had been the one to encourage him meet other women. Now that he was getting close to Christina, Jane seemed to take exception. She just didn't like Christina. It was as simple as that. There was an inbuilt hatred that even she couldn't rationalise. For no knowable reason Christina brought out the worst in her. But whatever the reason, Jane remained cold and aggressive, despite Christina's numerous attempts to make friends.

Christina believed that everyone deserved a second chance, whatever had happened in the past.

She knew something about Jane that Alister didn't, which made her a bit more sympathetic towards her, helping her to try to understand the person Jane had become.

It was something Gordon had told her in confidence, which in turn Alister's wife had told him before she died. Christina was sworn to secrecy, because Alister would be devastated if he ever found out.

When Jane found herself pregnant at 14, it was only Jane's mother who knew. Her mother persuaded Alister, on a pretext of broadening Jane's education, for the two of them to go abroad for a few months together during the summer holidays. Alister readily agreed, oblivious to the true reason – which was to get her an abortion. It wasn't just because Jane had got herself pregnant. The prime reason being that the baby would have been mixed race from Jane's brief relationship with a black boy at her school. Her mother, knowing Alister's feelings about black people, knew this was the only solution. Jane herself agreed to it. She was not ready to be a mother, and because the last thing she wanted to do was upset her father.

It all happened without Alister or anyone else knowing, and life resumed fairly normally after they returned. But as result of some complications after the abortion, she was told it was unlikely she'd be able to have children.

It was during the time that Jane had gone to Italy to work, that Christina and Alister became much closer. She was enjoying her work with Daphne and generally starting to build a life in Aylesbury. She didn't make or have any contact with those she left in London. There was no point since she now felt settled in her new life.

She kept her past life a secret, and made-up various stories about her previous existence. No one knew she had been married and had a son. She kept Alister ignorant of that fact, even when he finally proposed to her and she happily accepted. Her only condition was to keep her name and not adopt his, which he grudgingly agreed to.

During this period, Christina had genuinely fallen in love with Alister. The fact that Jane was out of the equation made things much easier for her. They had a simple Registry Office wedding with Kath and Gordon as witnesses.

It wasn't until they returned from honeymoon in the Maldives, that Alister let Jane know he had married Christina. He knew that if he'd told her beforehand, she would've created a scene and done everything in her power to stop it, even if she was a thousand miles away. As it was, distance helped to soften the flare-up of Jane's response when she was finally told the news.

The year that followed was one of the happiest Christina had ever had. She felt she had finally exorcised her other life in London. The only person who knew about her past was her aunt, Beryl. Without telling Alister, Christina paid regular visits to Beryl in her care home in Oxford. She was the only one she felt she could confide in, offload the truth, and who wouldn't be judgemental.

It was during the second year of her marriage that things started to go wrong. Alister, who had been invited to give numerous lectures at other universities in the country, appeared to become preoccupied and distant. Although he was away no more than two or three days at a time, she felt him gradually cooling towards her.

The passion, albeit never that intense between them, seemed to have diminished in slow stages. He was no longer the romantic person who had chased her persistently. She wondered if he was having an affair, but there was nothing in his behaviour, or anything that she could sense that pointed to this. Perhaps he was going through some sort of mid-life crisis and needed time on his own. Christina decided not to challenge him and to wait to see how things progressed.

Their relationship didn't improve. If anything, it got progressively worse.

Alister became moody and didn't want to discuss anything in detail. His excuse always being that he had problems at work, which needed to be resolved. Although they started to bicker, Christina, still very much in love with him, continued to give him the benefit of the doubt and hope that things would eventually settle.

The next component to create problems was the return of Jane from Italy. Alister refused to listen to Christina's objections of her coming to live with them in the house, even temporarily. In the months to come, although there were no major upsets or arguments, Christina still felt a bit rejected. Jane and her father had become itsy-bitsy together and silently excluded her from their world. Christina remained patient, and hoped this was only a phase and that once Jane got another job and moved out, things would get back to normal.

What kept Christina reasonably sane and occupied during this period was her work. That at least was the saving grace at the time.

The business appeared to be doing well, a lot of it due to her input. Daphne seemed pleased, although Christina sensed there was trouble in Daphne's marriage. Her husband was a bit of a philanderer, and had once even casually suggested, in a pub get-together, that he and Christina should have a fling. She politely rejected the idea, but didn't have the heart to mention it to Daphne, which in retrospect she felt she should've done.

Then one day Daphne called Christina into her office and blatantly accused her of fiddling the books. The accounts didn't add up, and they were short by nearly £50,000. There wasn't enough to pay the tax and VAT that was due. Christina was confused and couldn't understand it.

She knew she hadn't done anything wrong, but Daphne was so skilled in defining the facts and arguing the case, that Christina started to have doubts about whether she had actually messed up.

Daphne intimated that it could bankrupt them, and since she believed it was Christina's fault – despite having no firm proof – suggested that Christina ask Alister for the money to tide them over. When Christina told her that she wasn't prepared to do this, Daphne threatened her with criminal proceedings. Again, she felt history was perversely repeating itself, with what had happened with Jennie. Was it her? Had she done something subconsciously?

All this erupted a few days before Christina learnt that she had inherited Beryl's fortune, and news that she had terminal cancer. She did consider lending Daphne, if it was indeed her fault, the money that she could now easily afford. However, the sudden shock, following the visit to the doctor, made her change her mind.

With her marriage in the state it was; the thought that Jane would never move out; the threat from Daphne; her promise to Beryl; suddenly becoming rich and then discovering she didn't have long to live – all contributed to Christina deciding to escape once again and disappear from their lives…

The hospital room was cleared of visitors while a doctor attended to Christina, who had worked herself up into such a state, that she had to be sedated. Roger, Eric, Alister and Gordon were all told that there would be no more visiting that day.

The four men, left practically speechless by this turn of events, eyed each other suspiciously, as they sat round a table over coffee in the hospital cafeteria.

'Christina never told us that she had remarried.' Roger addressed Alister.

'She never told us she'd been married before - and had a son.' Alister responded.

'When we were together, she always changed the subject, whenever I asked where she had been for the last three years.' Eric added.

'You and her were also an item?' Gordon was puzzled. 'I don't understand. She didn't mention she'd been involved…told me nothing about her past…' He then lost his own thread of thought.

Alister took a deep breath. 'It seems Christina deceived us all.'

'Yes…' Roger was stumped for words.

'Two separate halves of a puzzle that need to be solved; wouldn't you agree?' Alister adopted his lecturing stance. 'Perhaps if we shared our stories, in order for us to try and understand what has been going on?'

'I agree. Look, it's lunchtime. Can I suggest we go to a restaurant or pub to do so?' Roger was just as keen to resolve this.

'What about Nando's?' Eric suggested.

'I think not.' Alister pulled a face.

'I like Nando's. Their Peri-Peri chicken is great.' Gordon licked his lips.

'My favourite too!' Eric agreed with Gordon.

Roger glanced at Alister who raised his eyebrows in sympathy with him. 'Yes, well it's a bit noisy in there. Let's go to a pub I know near here, where it's quieter. I believe they do southern fried chicken on their extensive menu. Would that suit?' Roger turned to Eric.

'Okay with me. I like southern fried chicken.' Eric nodded.

'Hope they do it with chips.' Gordon added.

Alister sighed. 'But I think it's more important that we try and piece together this rather unfortunate turn of events regarding Christina.' He looked at Roger.

'Yes, she has a bit of explaining to do…'

358

40. Starting Again with a Bump

When Christina eventually came to from her sedation, she instructed the hospital staff that she didn't want any more visitors until further notice. She realised what a god-awful mess she was in, and didn't want to compound it by trying to explain her motives to a group of angry people. She understood why they must be angry, but she was too tired to face anyone, much less justify her actions. It had become all too much for her. She needed time alone to think.

A few days later, when she was able to move around, she paid a visit to Tony who was still confined to bed. He gave her a silly smile as he looked up from a bible that he was reading. 'Hello dearest mother, have you come to be saved?'

'Yes, saved from my family...or should I say families...' She replied sarcastically.

"Believe in the Lord Jesus, and you shall be saved, you and your household ...but whoever does not believe shall be condemned." He quoted.

'My place in hell is already waiting, Tony. It's too late to save me. How are you?' She looked at her son, but could see it wasn't the Tony she knew.

'Antony has seen the light and been saved. Praise the Lord!'

'You were always something of an actor, a bit of a drama queen when things didn't go your way. Is this cod bible bashing a way of detracting from your own guilt? Is it?' She decided to challenge him.

He turned to some marked pages in his bible. *"If we confess our sins, he is faithful and just to forgive us our sins and to cleanse us from all unrighteousness..."*

'If you say so...' She realised it was pointless having

a normal conversation with him. 'I hope you get better soon.' She kissed him and went towards the door.

'I shall pray for you.'

'You do that. Perhaps you could ask your friend up there, to whisk me away from here, from all those who just want to humiliate and destroy me...'

"For he will command his angels concerning you to guard you in all your ways." He spouted, as she walked out of the room despairingly.

During the following week, despite numerous requests from her two families, and even Paula, to visit her, Christina refused categorically to see anyone. She even declined to accept phone calls or answer text messages.

She had been thinking about her future, trying to decide what to do once she was discharged from hospital, which could be any day now. Should she stay in London and try and start again; or go back to Aylesbury, face whatever music, and try and rebuild her life there? People didn't change – well, apart from Tony – so life would continue along the same old patterns. Neither was the ideal solution, or one that appealed. She knew she would feel trapped whichever choice she made.

She wondered if her life had been dictated by her own parents' actions. Was it something in her genes? When she was seven, her father left them, and disappeared to New Zealand to start a new life. At sixteen, it was her mother's turn to leave her job and family and move to Ireland where she remarried. Christina, not wanting to find her father in New Zealand, nor desiring to move to Ireland, went and stayed with her aunt, Beryl, until she was old enough to stand on her own two feet.

There was only one satisfying solution to her present

predicament – that was to start again from scratch. This time she would definitely head for the Lake District. She realised that the only way to accomplish this, without anyone knowing, would be to secretly leave the hospital and disappear. Having done it twice before, she had no qualms or thoughts that she couldn't succeed again.

The day soon came when the consultant declared her fit to be discharged. Even he was surprised how Christina had recovered so quickly, when he had doubted, at one point, she would actually make it. He told her to take care and not to overdo it. She thanked him and the nurses who had looked after her, and decided to pay Tony a final visit before leaving the hospital.

He was busy turning over the pages of his bible and marking certain passages with a pen. 'Hello Tony…' She smiled. He didn't look up. 'Antony…?'

'Mother!' He sounded excited. 'I've just read this marvellous passage. 2 Corinthians: 5:17 – *"Therefore if any man be in Christ, he is a new creature: old things are passed away; behold, all things are become new…"* It means it's never too late to see the light and start again.'

'How very apt. I'll certainly take note of that…I've come to say goodbye.'

'Where are you going?' Not all that interested, he was still flicking through the pages,

'Not exactly sure, but I'll know it when I get there.'

'May God go with you and lead you.' He said without looking up.

'Thank you…I'll need a bit of guidance…Well, I hope it all works out for you…'

'I have no fear, Christ is with me now…goodbye, mother…I do love you…'

With a tear in her eye, she went and kissed him on

---

the forehead. 'I love you too…' He smiled and then disappeared into his bible. Christina took one final look and then left the room. She suddenly felt no guilt or remorse at leaving him. He didn't need her. He had his faith, which would undoubtedly see him through.

As she walked down the hospital corridors, she worked out what her next move would be. She'd get a taxi to a national car rental place; hire a car, which she could then drop off at another branch in another town. There she would buy a new car and head northwards. She would then take things as they came. There was no point in being too precise. It was the start of a new adventure. The money that she had inherited would give her the freedom to be able to do what she wanted, and not have to worry. She felt energetic and ready to face the world.

However, what she wasn't ready to face, were the actual faces of Roger and Alister waiting at the hospital entrance. She suddenly wanted to run back into the hospital and escape through another entrance – but it was too late. They'd seen her and were advancing towards her. Both appeared relaxed, but Christina could detect coldness in their eyes.

'Hello Christina, so pleased you're better.' Alister forced a smile.

'We were very worried.' Roger added.

'Were you now? I see you've got acquainted. Welcoming party, is it?' She tried to guess what might be coming next. 'How did you know I'd be released today?'

'I spoke to the consultant yesterday, who said you'd be discharged this morning.' Roger sensed she was not pleased.

'We didn't like the thought of you coming out alone.' Alister did his best to sound sympathetic.

'It's 'we' now, is it? How very cosy. Well, thank you

very much for the thought, but I'm quite happy on my own. So, if you don't mind, I'll be getting on my way. Lots to do.' She made to pass between them, but they both closed in together to stop her.

'We feel we require some sort of explanation regarding your actions over the last few years. You owe it to us.' Alister said it as if he was admonishing a pupil.

'I owe you nothing. Now please let me get on with my life.'

Roger pleaded, 'Come on. You can't just dismiss what's happened…'

Alister continued. 'There are other people's lives to consider, you know.'

'What do you want of me?' She was already losing whatever energy she had.

'Just some answers to a few questions, that's all.' Alister stooped down trying to remain calm, but starting to get irritated.

'Okay…' She sighed. 'Fire away…'

'Not here.' Roger gestured towards the car park. 'We'll go back to the house, where we'll all be more comfortable.'

'You mean you'll be comfortable. Alright, I suppose I do owe you both some sort of explanation. But I warn you, you might not like what you hear.'

'Let us be the judge of that.' Alister almost grunted.

'We're all adults here. I'm sure we can take it.' Roger tried to lighten the mood.

'Then let's get it over with.' Christina started to march towards the car park. Roger looked at Alister who just shook his shoulders in acceptance, as they followed on behind.

***

'You didn't say there'd be a jury ready to pass sentence!' Christina exclaimed sarcastically, as she came into the sitting room, where a sea of faces stared unwelcoming at her. Before her, Eric, Gordon and Jane were seated looking solemn. 'There's someone missing isn't there? To make up the accusers?'

'Who do you mean?' Roger wasn't quite sure. 'I didn't think it appropriate for Helen to be included.'

'I didn't mean her.' She addressed Alister. 'I'm talking about Daphne, who I thought might have quite a few questions.'

Alister and Jane looked at each other ominously. Alister cleared his throat. 'Yes, well that's another story for another time. It doesn't concern us here…'

'Oh, come on, Alister! Don't give me that rubbish. You want me to answer some questions, but I also have a right to ask some. You always used to go on about how everyone should be allowed to have his or her say. What's this with Daphne?'

'Daphne's in prison…'

'Really? So she was misappropriating company funds, and then tried to put the blame on me. The bitch! She made me almost believe it was my entire fault. She deserves to be put away.' Christina felt relieved that she wouldn't be put to task on that.

'It's nothing to do with the business…although they found out she had been fiddling the books.' Alister paused a moment. 'No… Daphne murdered her husband…'

'What…?' Christina felt she was having a déjà vu experience, remembering what had happened with Jennie. This again was history repeating itself.

'She caught her husband with a younger woman. She bludgeoned him to death with a hammer, and then cut his balls of with a knife.' Jane added with some relish. Both Eric and Gordon shifted uneasily in their seats.

'Jane!' Alister raised his voice. 'The details aren't necessary.'

'But they are.' She responded. 'It's the details that make you understand it more. Details that we all want to hear from little miss vanishing act here.'

'Are you referring to me, by any chance?' Christina suddenly dismissed thoughts of Daphne and turned to Jane.

'Who else has managed to deceive and screw up the lives of two families!' Jane answered venomously.

'Come on, Jane, we need to discuss this fairly and calmly.' Alister interjected.

'Fairly! What's fair about it? You'll just pussyfoot around it all, and let her make you believe that we're all at fault rather than her.'

'Never has a truer word been spoken.' Christina took a deep breath. She no longer felt intimidated; because it suddenly dawned on her that she had been the victim all along, not the perpetrator. They had, individually, undermined her confidence and made her out to be the cause, when they were, in reality, the guilty ones. How blind and trusting she had been all these years. 'You are all responsible for the reason I did what I did. And if I'm going to be completely honest, it's all of you who have screwed up my life. Yes, I do blame you. And I am more than happy to give you my reasons.'

'See! I told you she would try and turn it around to her advantage.' Jane sneered. 'She's a lying bitch, and nothing's going to change that.'

'And you're so transparent, Jane.' Christina wasn't going to let her get off so easily. 'There are no secrets in your past, are there. Nothing that you are ashamed of? Nothing that you've done to deceive others? Tell me that.'

Jane's expression changed. 'What are you talking

about?'

'Now come on, you two, let's not get too personal. This concerns us all.' Alister tried to act as referee.

'Not get too personal! That's a joke, Alister.' Christina's confidence started to grow. She knew she was right to start challenging them. 'Bringing me here in front of everyone is not personal?'

Roger tried to calm the situation. 'We just want some simple answers. That's not much to ask, is it?'

'And you believe we'll get the truth anyway?' Jane was not letting go. 'She'll spin us a tale to make her look good, and us bad. That's the sum of it. It's a waste of time if you want my opinion.'

Christina paused for a moment and scanned at all the eyes that were scrutinising her. She felt she had no option now but to fight back. 'So, Jane, you who can do no wrong in your father's eyes – does he know the truth of why you went abroad with your mother when you were 14?'

Jane visibly paled. 'I don't know what you're talking about. See, she's turning it back on us, to divert away from her.' She turned to the others to gain support.

'Christina, what do you mean?' Alister saw that Jane was uncomfortable.

'Come on, Christina, this is nothing to do with Jane. Stop changing the subject.' Gordon interjected, realising what might be coming.

'Let's bring this one into the open first, before you all decide to condemn me.' Christina faced Jane. 'Would you rather tell your father, or shall I do the honours?'

'What's there to tell? Mum and I went for a tour of Europe when I was 14. He knows all about that!' She was starting to mumble.

'But does he know the real reason?'

'Don't Christina, please…' Gordon was now looking

mortified.

'Sorry, Gordon, I know I promised not to, but in the circumstances, I'm left with no choice.'

Alister had lost patience. 'What is going on here? Someone enlighten me please.'

'With pleasure.' Christina no longer felt she could hold back. 'Gordon here will confirm this. That trip to Europe, Alister, was for the sole reason for Jane to have an abortion because she had become pregnant. Ah, but that's not all! If she'd had the baby, it would've been b –...' But Christina wasn't allowed to finish.

Jane had swiftly grabbed hold of a brass ornament on the mantelpiece and struck Christina on the head, who immediately dropped to the ground. 'There, you fucking bitch! Take that! I should have done a better job on the brakes of your car!'

'Jane!' Alister shouted. He looked down at Christina, seeing a pool of blood starting to seep around her head. 'What have you done...?'

'Sorry, dad...she deserved it...' Jane showed no remorse.

Eric knelt down to the body and tried to feel a pulse. 'I think she's dead...'

'Good. May she burn in hell....' Were Jane's last words.

41. Hell Isn't So Bad

Hell was hotter than Christina imagined.

The heat, so intense, beat down on her like a scalding breeze of fire. She felt her skin burning and sizzling. This is what it felt like being burnt at the stake. She was afraid to open her eyes, knowing she'd be blinded by the brightness. How long would it be before the flames consumed her? Before this inferno seared her very spirit? Or was this how it was going to be for the rest of eternity...no end to the fire that could never be extinguished?

Had she been so bad to be condemned to such a fate? Christina felt the hot fluid dripping down her face, her arms, and her legs. Either she was going to be burnt to a crisp, or drown in the scalding pool of her own sweat. This was a never-ending nightmare that would haunt her forever. She felt her dry mouth open to let out a silent, pitying scream...

Immediately she felt a cool touch on her arm. 'Christina, it's alright...you're safe now...' came a soft, gentle voice.

Christina opened her eyes a fraction. Although the brightness was quite blinding, she could just make out a misty figure in a white gown leaning over her, a bright golden light, like a halo, shone around the head. 'Are you an angel...am I in heaven...?'

'This is a kind of heaven I suppose.' The voice replied amusingly.

'Well, it feels like hell...are you trying to offer me a false sense of security...because you're really the Devil in disguise?' Christina, still half asleep, couldn't focus on the figure before her.

The figure laughed. 'A lot of people think I have

368

gone over to the other side, that the Devil has tempted me. Maybe he secretly has…but I have no regrets.'

'What do you want of me…?' Christina felt momentarily dizzy. 'My head…'

'Christina, I warned you not to fall asleep in the sun. And I bet you didn't apply any more sun cream. Look at you! Sweating like a pig and starting to look like a boiled lobster. Come on, we're going in the shade before you get sunstroke.'

'Where are we…?' Christina blinked and gazed around her. A lush of greenery, surrounded by palm trees, which were silhouetted against the bright blue sky. She was lying on a sun lounger by a swimming pool in a large area covered in grass, beautiful flowers and exotic bushes. She could see others sun bathing, reading or swimming. 'I remember now…sorry, I was momentarily confused. I must've been dreaming.' She wiped her face with a towel, as she returned to a sense of reality.

'You certainly were! You had me worried for a sec. I thought that bash on the head had started to affect you.'

Christina touched her head. The side that had been stitched still felt a little tender. 'What, like Tony? Turn religious and try to convert people? Well, you'd be able to guide me there, Paula.'

'Not any more. That part of my life is truly behind me now. I'm much preferring to become hedonistic rather than evangelistic.' Paula watched a bronzed and well-toned male running and diving into the water. 'There are many pleasures out there that religion can't compete with.'

'I feel it's my fault that you hung up your dog collar.'

'No, it was always there. You just made me come to terms with my true feelings. So thank you for helping me to see the light, or should I say bright sunshine.'

'That probably means we'll both go to hell!' She smiled, wiping the rest of her body with the towel.

'Probably the only person going to hell is Jane. Attempted murder on two counts.'

'I actually feel sorry for her. I don't think prison will suit her. That will be hell.'

'And as far as heaven or paradise is concerned, we're lucky to be in it now. I do so love Italy. Don't forget, we've got a massage in half an hour, followed by a facial and manicure.'

'Hopefully then followed by champagne, and then a good seeing to by that yoga teacher who's been giving me the eye.' Christina smiled. 'I shall do my Downward Facing Dog pose or Full Straddle Forward Fold. They should, with any luck, awaken his Cobra!'

'You're terrible!' Paula laughed. 'You're legally still a married woman.'

'It's not long before my divorce to Alister comes through. In the meantime, I'm certainly not going to wait until it's official. We are, after all, here to be pampered.'

'Yes…' Paula breathed in her surroundings. 'I do in a strange way feel born again…'

'I suppose I could say the same. Three times I believed I was going to die. So hopefully, like a cat – I've still got six more lives left!'

About The Author

Evgeny was born in London and lived with his parents and grandparents in a council flat on the White City Estate in Shepherds Bush. His mother and father were both Russian variety artistes and circus performers. His early years were spent touring with them in numerous circuses and variety theatres in England, living in caravans and theatrical digs, and being educated in a different school each week. He must have gone to well over 100 schools. Between the ages of 8 and 9 He shared a large bus with six chimpanzees when his parents toured around Europe with a chimpanzee act. The chimps became his surrogate brothers and sisters. He had no formal schooling during this period, and most of his reading matter came from 'The Dandy', 'The Beano' and 'The Beezer' which his grandmother sent him from England.

After a more formal education, He trained at the Central School of Speech and Drama and then spent 8 years in the theatre as a Stage Manager /Actor working for both the Royal Shakespeare Company and the National Theatre.

After which he worked for many years at the BBC as a Script Editor and Producer on series including **"TENKO" "TO SERVE THEM ALL MY DAYS" "BLOTT ON THE LANDSCAPE" "STAR COPS"** and **"THE HOUSE OF ELIOTT"** where he co-created the storylines and wrote 3 episodes.

Books By This Author

A Stink in the Tale

England has never had a Prime Minister who made people laugh so much. His jokes have the nation in stitches. Parliament has become like a music hall stage on which he entertains the House with his unique brand of humour – humour that is often coarse and vulgar, and majors on flatulence in all its nauseous guises. But ironically it is the much-maligned fart that may ultimately bring about the Prime Minister's scandalous downfall …

Following in the long tradition of scatological British humour previously practised by authors such as Tom Sharpe and Spike Milligan, A Stink in the Tale is a rip-roaring comedy-thriller replete with intrigue, adventure and unexpected twists and turns.

ComeBack

What would prompt a happily married woman to murder her husband? Could the tragic events of over a century ago provide the answer? Julia believes she has lived before...

It is intriguing mystery on many levels, connecting a set of characters in two contrasting time periods. Is reincarnation a provable fact or simply a fitting fantasy? Yet the real truth, in any time, can be ambiguous.